Praise for
Heart of Brass

"Fabulously entertaining—a great romance in an inventive, believable steampunk world!"
— Stephanie Laurens, *New York Times* bestselling author of *The Capture of the Earl of Glencrae*

"*Heart of Brass* is riveting! I couldn't put it down. I can't wait for the next book. Kate Cross is fabulous!"
— Victoria Alexander, #1 *New York Times* bestselling author of *My Wicked Little Lies*

OUT OF THE VAPORS

Five paused in the stairwell of his lodgings and pressed the heel of one palm to his forehead. It felt as though there was something worrying at his brain—like a cat pawing at a closed door.

Luke.

He clung to the rail with one hand, trying to keep himself from falling down the narrow stairs as *her* voice rang in his head. He hadn't been able to get it out. Every time he thought of her, pain followed.

Luke. It was what she had said to him in her bedroom. She had said it like he should recognize it, and just now it had sounded almost plaintive—regretful.

She knew him, and though he knew everything about her he didn't know the connection. She had the upper hand—had him at a disadvantage. That she made him feel that way was simply one more reason to kill her. And he would. . . .

HEART
of BRASS

A NOVEL OF THE CLOCKWORK AGENTS

KATE CROSS

A SIGNET ECLIPSE BOOK

SIGNET ECLIPSE
Published by New American Library, a division of
Penguin Group (USA) Inc., 375 Hudson Street,
New York, New York 10014, USA
Penguin Group (Canada), 90 Eglinton Avenue East, Suite 700, Toronto,
Ontario M4P 2Y3, Canada (a division of Pearson Penguin Canada Inc.)
Penguin Books Ltd., 80 Strand, London WC2R 0RL, England
Penguin Ireland, 25 St. Stephen's Green, Dublin 2,
Ireland (a division of Penguin Books Ltd.)
Penguin Group (Australia), 250 Camberwell Road, Camberwell, Victoria 3124,
Australia (a division of Pearson Australia Group Pty. Ltd.)
Penguin Books India Pvt. Ltd., 11 Community Centre, Panchsheel Park,
New Delhi - 110 017, India
Penguin Group (NZ), 67 Apollo Drive, Rosedale, Auckland 0632,
New Zealand (a division of Pearson New Zealand Ltd.)
Penguin Books (South Africa) (Pty.) Ltd., 24 Sturdee Avenue,
Rosebank, Johannesburg 2196, South Africa

Penguin Books Ltd., Registered Offices:
80 Strand, London WC2R 0RL, England

First published by Signet Eclipse, an imprint of New American Library,
a division of Penguin Group (USA) Inc.

First Printing, May 2012
10 9 8 7 6 5 4 3 2 1

ALWAYS LEARNING   PEARSON

This book is for Joey and Allison, who started out as steampunk acquaintances and quickly became two of my favorite people. I'm so glad my research led me to you!

It is also for my husband, Steve, who will gladly put on a top hat and frock coat and venture to a convention with me. Sweetie, you're the best.

Chapter 1

London, the Age of Steam

"You shouldn't go in there, ma'am. 'Tis no place for a lady."

Arden Grey, known in polite circles as Lady Huntley, and in less polite as "that poor woman," carried a small carpetbag in her gloved hand as she approached the factory door, pewter-colored skirts swishing around her matching pumps. Overhead the lights of a police dirigible swept across the scene, illuminating the night in a wash of glaring silver.

The veil attached to her tiny black top hat did nothing to shield her eyes, and Arden squinted against the intrusive brightness. "You will soon learn, sir, that I am not the usual sort of lady." She'd been born and bred to be one, even married an earl to maintain the illusion, but during her unusual life she'd seen and heard—*and done*—too many dark things to own such a gentle, ignorant title.

The Scotland Yard man tugged the brim of his hat at

her in reply, and stepped back so she might pass. It was obvious from the tight set of his lips that he opposed her presence most vehemently, but knew his place well enough not to voice his disapproval again. In this thoroughly modern world there were still those who believed a woman ought to keep to home, rather than engage in any manner of business.

Tell that to Queen Victoria.

Sagging floorboards creaked under her boots as she entered B. E. Hammond & Sons, the varnish long since worn off this particular section of wood. The foyer was well lit and unassuming, and smelled vaguely of oil and metal. It was quiet now, but during the day this entire building would hum and vibrate with the sounds of working machines. The air would be humid and thick, tasting of steam and the sharp tang of industry.

She fancied she could smell blood, but it was most likely copper. When people used to oppose her father's support of the Automatization Movement, he would reply that it could not be a coincidence that the very life in a man's veins smelled like the same metal used to construct early automatons. He died in the middle of building what would have been his finest work, a piece that now sat hunched, gears gummed up, in the corner of his W.O.R. laboratory. Four years it had sat there, and despite all the brilliant minds the Wardens of the Realm—the mysterious government agency to which Arden herself belonged—set to work in that room, the project had yet to be completed. Arden had even provided them with the schematics of the machine, but to no avail. The automaton remained elusive, an example of her father's genius that would never come to fruition, though the Wardens would continue to try.

Then again, she was a fine one to throw stones, she who clung to a hopeless dream.

Another Scotland Yard man came through a set of double doors and paused there, holding one of them open. "This way, Lady Huntley—if you please."

No, she didn't please, but she walked past the man and through the doorway all the same. She'd rather be at home with a glass—or several—of fine Scotch whiskey, but she'd been summoned here instead. Granted, it had been a welcome rescue from insipid conversation and weak sherry with a group of females who would inevitably take her aside one by one and ask her if she might construct one of her "special devices" for them.

Few people knew the extent of her talents. To most of the world she was simply Lady Huntley, a woman who refused to accept that her husband was most likely dead. She wasn't the mechanical genius that her father was, but she had made a bit of a reputation amongst her sex for an invention she stumbled upon quite by accident. A device very similar—but far superior—to one sold by B. E. Hammond & Sons. It could have been quite scandalous, but since one of the Princesses Royal privately declared it a "miracle of modern medical science" in the field of feminine health, scandal became discreet acclaim. A treatment for "hysteria" that did not require the indiscretion of a trip to a sanitorium, but could be used in the privacy of a lady's boudoir.

The delicate silver chains that hung from the piercing on the side of Arden's nose across her cheek to her right ear quivered under the ceiling fans as she entered the large open room of the factory's assembly department. Recently she'd increased the number of chains from six to seven. One for every year her husband had been missing.

Missing. Not dead.

Two more Scotland Yard men—peelers as they were often called—stood with another man she assumed to be the senior Mr. Hammond, based on the distressed look on his face.

The policemen removed their hats when they spotted her. One of them was Inspector Grant, with whom she'd worked on several prior cases. Mr. Hammond held his fine, but worn, beaver top hat in his shaking hands. His graying hair stuck up in tufts around his head, as though he'd had his hands tugging at it. He had the countenance of a man who had seen—or done—something he should dearly like to forget.

As she approached, Arden withdrew what looked like a small lady's compact from her bag. She pointed the device in the direction of the factory owner and watched the tiny hand beneath the glass swing around like the needle of a compass, finally coming to land on the word REMORSE. The sentimentometer was one of her favorites of all her father's work, even though he'd developed it when she was but a child to determine whether or not she had done something naughty.

She snapped the lid shut and slipped the brass mechanism back into her bag. "Gentlemen."

"Lady Huntley." Inspector Grant greeted her with a curt nod—his only deference to her station. "Thank you for leaving your evening's entertainments to aid us in this grim affair."

"No thanks required, Inspector," Arden replied in her usual crisp tones that often sounded far too severe for her liking. Lucas used to tell her she had the voice of a governess. "What has happened?"

The inspector pointed his pencil at the pale gentleman to his left. "Mr. Hammond was working late this evening in his office above stairs. When he came down to check everything was as it should be for the night, he found the body of a young woman." He gestured for her to follow him and she did. The factory owner stayed behind, working the brim of his hat until it threatened to lose all shape.

"Did you take a reading of Hammond?" Grant asked quietly as they maneuvered through the jammed workspace of wooden tables littered with tools, automaton parts and gears. "Says he was listening to phonographic discs as he worked and didn't hear a peep from down here."

She shook her head, gaze wandering distractedly over the tabletops. "I detected no guilt or malevolence from him. But he does feel remorse. Could be a guilty conscious, or perhaps he is simply mortified that a crime was committed on his property with him being none the wiser." She stopped and picked up a rubber tube that was shaped like . . . a penis. She held it up with her forefinger and thumb, dangling it in all its flaccid splendor in front of the inspector's face. "I didn't know that the Hammonds had begun to incorporate rubber in their designs."

Grant flushed a deep red—the color of a cooked beet. He couldn't quite meet her gaze. "Er . . . yes. You may be aware that Hammond started this factory to make medical instruments to aid in the treatment of hysteria. He was one of the first manufacturers of automatons in England." He cleared his throat, as though he wanted to say more but didn't quite know how to word it, or how to justify it.

He didn't have to. Arden knew all about Hammond and his inventions. A contemporary of her father's, some of his earlier designs were rather ingenious, but it was his work in the field of mechanized human "marital enhancements" that had made him one of the wealthiest businessmen in the kingdom. Any man who dedicated his life's work to the carnal pleasure and emotional well-being of women couldn't be all that bad, could he?

But a murder certainly wouldn't be good for business.

A few steps on she spied a female automaton lying on one of the tables, its realistic limbs splayed, revealing a degree of anatomical correctness that would have made a bawd blush. Arden's lips tucked to one side in a caustic smile. Mr. Hammond obviously had decided to tackle the treatment of gentlemanly vigor as well.

Inspector Grant threw a tarp over the machine, but whether he did so to protect Arden's delicate sensibilities or his own was a mystery that she hadn't the inclination to pursue. Though it did not take even an ounce of emotional sensitivity to ascertain that the inspector was deeply mortified.

When they neared the end of the aisle, Arden detected a familiar, unpleasant odor, one she associated with murder: a mix of what she could only describe as fear, blood, and chamber pot.

Two more peelers and Inspector Grant stood between her and the source of that smell. Well, most of it.

The leg in the torn stocking and expensive silk pump looked like that of a burlesque automaton at first, so white and still was it. Were it not for the blood staining that stocking she might have been able to tell herself that it *was* merely a machine.

"I beg your pardon, Lady Huntley," Grant said in that faint northern accent of his. "But this isn't a pretty sight. You may turn back if you like."

She gave him what she hoped was a grateful smile and not a grim twisting of her lips. She'd often been told her smile could sometimes look a little ... demented. "Your concern does you credit, Inspector. I assure you I shall endure whatever it is you wish me to see." She could do without seeing a dead body, particularly a bloody one, but if these men could look at it dispassionately then damn it, so could she. It wasn't as though it was her first corpse.

Inspector Grant's face was a resigned shade of pale beneath his muttonchops and heavy mustache. He nodded in acquiescence. "Pull back the sheet please, Mr. Fence."

An ashen-faced youth swallowed hard and bent down to do as he was instructed. Arden's confidence in being able to escape the viewing with the contents of her stomach intact diminished slightly.

The sheet—stained and wet with so much blood it was almost black in spots—pulled back with the resistance of the rind of an orange reluctant to leave the flesh beneath, to reveal the head of a pretty young woman wearing pearl earrings. Her neck was long, decorated with a matching pearl necklace, but beyond that . . . a pile of raw meat. Arden stared for a moment, her eyes not quite able to make her brain see reality. Finally, after a few moments—and a rather inspired bout of gagging from young Mr. Fence—she saw the scene for what it was.

Someone, or something, had torn this precious little girl apart. Her pale blue eyes were wide open, as was her Cupid's bow mouth. Her flawless skin, the pale robin's-egg waxy color of death, was dotted with freckles of blood. She was not a factory worker—a pair of fine silk gloves lay not far from her body. Nor was she a member of the demimonde, for she was far too fresh and sweet looking, and not nearly as fashionable. Her demure, ruined gown cost more than what the retching Mr. Fence probably made in a month.

She was a member of the upper classes, quite possibly of noble birth.

Dear God.

Mindful of her skirts, she lifted them as she moved around the clotted puddle to stand at the girl's head. She squatted down, tugging off her right glove so her fingers could touch the porcelain coolness of a stiff, delicate wrist. The girl had been dead for several hours—long enough for her body to lose all warmth and become fairly rigid.

A thin bruise spread like a stain beneath Arden's fingers. She glanced up at Inspector Grant. The older man was the only one of the three who didn't look ill. He was too experienced, too little shocked by humanity's capacity for violence to be sickened by it anymore. Instead, he looked resigned. And worried. A murdered debutante meant trouble on so many levels for a man in his position.

"She was bound?" she inquired, swallowing against the rolling of her own stomach.

Grant nodded, his shrewd gaze resting on the ravaged girl. "Most likely the bugger—pardon my French, my lady—brought the poor gel here by force."

It was possible, she supposed, but this bruise was purple and slightly yellow, not the usual raw red that one would expect if she had been recently restrained. This bruising was older and could have many causes.

The inspector jerked his head toward the entrance. "Fence, Brown, make use of yourself elsewhere." He watched as the two relieved young men walked away before navigating around the corpse to squat beside her. "Do you think you might . . . be able to use your apparatus on her?"

That was often why she was brought to such scenes. And dear Grant was always so considerate to never take her compliance as a certainty. It was her father who had come up with the general principles of the mechanism prior to his death, and Arden who completed the device. If he hadn't left so many unfinished projects, who knew what might have become of her? Mourning him and missing Huntley, she might have done something rash, especially without her mother to turn to, but instead she turned to cogs and gears and the reassuring hum of steam engines. Loss had given her more purpose than she'd ever wanted before.

"I will try," she told him, as she had every other time he asked. She rested the bottom of her carpetbag on her bent knees and pulled the mouth of it wide open. She didn't have to rummage through a muddle of automata and tools as her father always had, because she had outfitted the case with internal straps and pockets to hold each and every item. She barely had to look in at all to find what she wanted—two pairs of specially augmented goggles, connected by coils of wires.

"Inspector, if you would be so kind?"

Grant's gaze jerked up from the mechanism. "Of course." He took the bag from her lap and placed it to his left, as far from the carnage as his reach allowed. "Explain to me again how these Aetheric Reminiscent Oscillation Goggles work."

Despite the smell and horrific visage before her, Arden smiled slightly as she placed the more ornate pair of goggles over the girl's open eyes. She had begun using the device two years ago and the inspector had yet to refer to it by the correct name. "Aetheric Remnant Oscillatory Transmutative Spectacles," she corrected. "You could use the acronym A.R.O.T.S. if you prefer."

He shook his head. "I'd rather not use the term 'rot' in any capacity given the circumstances, my lady—with all due respect."

Arden glanced at the girl's decimated torso and the decay that had already begun, as she carefully placed the small metal prongs of the headgear on the appropriate spots on the poor thing's skull. "Indeed. You are familiar, of course, with Aether?"

"Of course," he sounded vaguely affronted that she had to ask. "It's the Breath of God."

As a woman whose religion was more science than spirituality, it took considerable restraint for Arden not to argue with the inspector. However, she was not one to besmirch another's beliefs, no matter how ill-informed she believed them to be. "The energy of every living creature, yes," she said. "Some believe it to be the soul, while science argues that it is the result of an electro-chemical process in living tissue that lingers even after we shuck our mortal coil."

Grant sniffed. "Sounds a bit far-fetched to me."

But the "Breath of God" did not? A god who took her husband away from her? Who killed her father and made her mother . . . what she was? If it was the breath of such a creature that gave the engine of her heart fire then she would rather suffocate on a cold hearth. For every religious zealot there was another who decreed the Aether as the playground of the Devil himself.

"Regardless," she continued through a clenched jaw, "there is no dispute that sometimes this energy lingers— around a body, or in a place where the person met their end. These goggles allow me to see the last things this young lady saw by utilizing that very energy." The dark lenses over the sightless eyes of the girl would prevent any light or new images from penetrating once the prongs stimulated the appropriate areas of her brain, es-sentially restoring them to life for a short period. Once engaged, the optical response would parlay those images to Arden's own goggles, where she would view the expe-rience as though it were her own.

"Bloody amazing," Grant allowed. Then, with fresh pink suffusing his cheeks, "Beg your pardon, my lady."

Arden waved his concern away with a flick of her wrist. Then, something caught her eye. She frowned. "In-spector, did Hammond or your men rearrange her cloth-ing?"

"No, ma'am. She's exactly as she was found."

Frowning, she leaned closer, and using the ear wire of the goggles in her hand, lifted the edge of torn gown. A small, bare breast, smeared with crimson, lay beneath. Elsewhere the fabric molded to the gore-soaked area, but not here.

"He took care to cover her," she murmured.

The inspector nodded, seemingly unimpressed by her keen detection. "I reckon the monster knew her."

Arden settled back on her heels. Her knees were beginning to ache from squatting so long. "Let's see if she knew him as well, shall we?" She wiped the ear wire with her handkerchief before placing the second pair of goggles on her own face. With them on she was practically blind, and would remain so until the image transfer began.

Then she would see things she would later regret seeing.

She wound the key protruding from the side of the small control box attached by even more wires to both sets of eye gear. The simple engine inside, attuned as it was to Aetheric energy—a vast resource Arden believed could rival steam and even the new wonder of electricity— whirred to life, sending a charge to the dead girl's mind.

Fuzzy images began to swirl before her eyes, dim and out of focus. She adjusted dials on either side of her goggles, making the images a little clearer. Sometimes, depending on how long the subject had been dead, she had to use all the lenses and settings she had to work with, and even then sometimes she only got a grainy, half-formed image.

She was not to be so fortunate that evening. She had barely slipped the secondary lenses into place when everything came together in razor-sharp clarity.

The girl was running through the aisles of this very factory, the world jostled around her as a man in evening clothes chased her. She saw only his shoulder and part of his side, not his face, but she didn't appear to be running for her life, but with the lazy gait of a girl wishing to be caught. And catch her he did, turning her in his arms. A man's torso came into view—neither too broad nor too thin. His cravat was perfectly tied, decorated with an onyx pin in the shape of a horseshoe.

Arden's heart quickened, as it often did in these macabre situations. Everything was so keen, and sharp. If she could find a way to determine the emotional state and auditory memory as well, it truly would be an immersive experience.

The girl's arms reached for the man, whose face remained maddeningly out of sight. Slowly, her gaze lifted, past the cravat pin, to the throat and jaw of the man wearing it, then the mouth.

"Just a little further," Arden whispered as her heart pounded hard against her ribs. "Come on, dearest. Just a little more."

The world seemed to jump in front of her eyes. Her gaze dropped from the man to the space between their bodies.

Arden cried out.

Her chest was ripped open.

"Lady Huntley!" It was Grant. She could feel his warm hand on her arm. "My lady, are you all right?"

She shook her head, afraid that she would indeed vomit if she opened her mouth. Her hands clutched at the spectacles, and she wanted nothing more than to rip them off her face, but she held on until the images before her faded to blackness, signaling the girl's death. Only when she was certain there was nothing more to see did she remove the apparatus from her own head.

"My dear lady," Grant began, staring at her with wide eyes. "You look . . ."

"Like hell," Arden supplied, smiling at his surprise. Just as quickly her mirth vanished. "He ripped her open while she was alive. She felt it. Saw it."

The inspector turned his gaze toward the dead girl just as Arden did. He reached out and stroked the girl's hair, as a father might. "Poor thing."

"Indeed," Arden muttered, attempting to pull herself together. She raised the back of her hand to her nose and took a deep, calming breath. The bergamot she'd dabbed on her glove lessened the scent of death, reminded her of happier things.

"I didn't see his face, unfortunately. All I can tell you is that he wore expensive clothes and had an onyx cravat pin in the shape of a horseshoe." She sighed. "She knew him. They were lovers. If those marks on her wrists were made by him, they were done so with her consent, and before this rendezvous."

Inspector Grant went pale beneath the dark of his whiskers. "Knew him, you say?"

Arden met his gaze evenly, her typical tight rein over her emotions returning. "Yes. You are not wrong to be alarmed, Inspector. I'm fairly certain your madman is an aristocrat as well."

The inspector swore beneath his breath, and this time he did not apologize for his language. Arden didn't blame him. She'd curse as well, for the inspector's chances of catching this monster just dropped considerably, never mind the odds of actually bringing him to justice.

"If she'd only looked at him I might be able to identify him," she mused ruefully.

Grant shook his head and patted her shoulder one last time before he remembered his station and removed his hand. "Do not fault yourself, my lady. You have been of enormous assistance already."

As Arden removed the spectacles from the girl and

used her palm to close her eyes, she didn't feel as though she'd been of much use at all. She quickly ran through the images in her mind once more. "He was older. Not elderly, but not a boy—perhaps in his late twenties or thirties."

The inspector wrote this down in his little leather-bound notebook.

"And, Inspector Grant?" When he looked up from his writing she said softly, "You should request Dr. Stone examine the body."

A soft flush flooded the lawman's face. The poor thing really had no idea how to handle such situations. He had more modesty than a fourteen-year-old girl. "I see."

Dr. Evelyn Stone was generally employed by Scotland Yard when a female victim had been molested in some way, but her talents were more extensively employed by the Wardens. The brilliant young woman had machines and formulas for making identifications and finding insights into crimes that baffled and impressed the agency to no end.

"She may find something that will aid in our investigation."

Inspector Grant's head snapped up. "*Our* investigation, my lady?"

Arden's lips twisted into a grim smile. "You're going to require my ongoing assistance with this one, sir. I travel in the same circles as our killer, and can therefore go where you cannot."

"Lady Huntley, I cannot allow you to put yourself in harm's way." He was clearly flustered. "To include you so thoroughly in a Yard investigation would be grossly unfair, not to mention ungentlemanly of me."

Not to mention it was terribly gauche of her—a lady—to engage in such horrid pursuits. No doubt that had much to do with her desire to do it.

"*You*, my dear friend, cannot prevent it," she informed him with a touch of warmth to her determined tone. She rose easily to her feet. "Now, do be a good boy and accept that you are powerless in this instance, and escort me back to my carriage."

Being the considerate gentleman he was, Inspector Grant could not refuse a lady's request—especially not the request of such a high-ranking lady as a countess. He also stood and offered her his arm, which she took with a faint smile on her lips.

Arden was all too happy to leave the awful vision of that poor girl behind, but she knew the memory of the sight, as well as what the girl had seen, would linger for at least a fortnight until she managed to put them away with all the other awful things she'd ever seen and buried. Or drowned.

Each peeler she passed tipped his hat and bid her a good evening. The transport team was there to collect the body, and the "cleaners" had arrived to ensure all evidence was collected and every trace of the crime erased. It was standard protocol when the details of a crime were to be kept undisclosed, and since the young woman obviously was of good birth, they had been brought in to save the family from being dragged through more unpleasant scandal than necessary.

Such precautions also kept the jackals of the press from plastering the tragedy all over the pages of the papers and sending the country into a paranoid tizzy that another Jack the Ripper was on the loose. They'd learned their lesson with that particular nasty piece of work.

"You have my gratitude for coming here tonight, my lady," Inspector Grant spoke, as he opened the door of her carriage. Two metal steps flipped down.

Arden turned to him, one foot on the bottom step. "That's very lovely of you to say, Inspector. Thank you."

It wasn't as though she had a choice—it was her duty. Even though she did not answer to Scotland Yard, she reported to the Wardens—an organization higher up the clandestine ladder—and they would expect her to do all she could to aid in the apprehension of this monster.

Grant nodded, and closed the door once she was inside the vehicle. The driver started up the steam engine, and within moments the carriage jerked into motion, the comforting chug filling the interior.

Arden leaned back against the cushioned seat, a wave of weariness washing over her. She was just about to close her eyes when the dirigible made another pass overhead, illuminating the factory yard. Something—someone—on the roof of the factory made her sit bolt upright.

The factory was only two floors, so the distance to the roof wasn't that far, but when she looked up she swore her eyes were wrong, that they were deceiving her.

The man on the roof was dressed in black, so she couldn't tell if he had blood on him or not, and he dove out of sight when the bright light washed over him. However, his clothing wasn't what caught her attention, but his face. A face she knew as well as her own. A face she had once traced every inch of with her fingers, kissed with her lips.

It was the face of her husband.

Chapter 2

His target had escaped him.

The man called Five ran along the roof, keeping to the shadows to avoid the damned dirigible and its glaring light. Below him the carriage carrying his prey rolled through the damp cobblestone street. He kept pace with it as he ran, approaching the edge of the factory roof with an easy speed.

When he reached the edge he jumped and hit the ground in a crouch, the impact reverberating through the heavy soles of his boots as his coat flared out around him. The cobblestones seemed to groan under the impact.

Nimbly, he lunged into his former pace, keeping almost abreast of the vehicle as it traveled through the semideserted street. Not a lot of traffic in this industrial part of the city at this time of night—only the factory workers on the night shift, and they were too busy slaving away or sneaking out for a smoke or a suck of gin to notice an abnormally fast man race by.

Moisture hung in the air, the by-product of so many

steam engines—as though London wasn't damp enough. It permeated his skin and clothes, causing the long leather coat to cling to him uncomfortably. Still, he ran.

An old-fashioned carriage hauled by polished brass automaton horses rolled down the street toward him, metal hooves clomping sharply on the stones, steam billowing from the exhaustion vents disguised as nostrils. It was a hearse, probably on its way to the factory where he had tracked his prey.

"Is it done?"

He was accustomed to the voice in his head now, the intrusive demands familiar instead of distressing. It made the sharing of information particularly simple.

"Not yet," he replied in a low tone.

"What's the delay?"

He turned a corner, following the carriage down another street. "Peelers."

"Avoid apprehension at all costs. Take extra care if you must, but do not *fail."*

"Failure is not an option." Onward he ran, not the least bit winded. He was rarely ever out of breath anymore—it was the way they'd made him.

He didn't remember what he had been before the Company found him. He was told he had been a criminal of some kind, that he was being offered a new beginning—a chance to repay his debt to society. Now, he was extraordinary, a weapon against evil.

Though the lady in that carriage didn't look evil to him. In fact he'd been rather startled by her face. It wasn't that it was a particularly beautiful face—he'd seen prettier women—but there was something about her auburn hair, peaches-and-cream complexion and shapely mouth that gave him pause.

Nothing gave him pause. Not ever.

He followed the carriage all the way to the exclusive

Mayfair part of London. Despite having no memory of ever being there before, it had seemed strangely familiar when he first happened upon it earlier that evening. When he spied on his target from outside a ballroom window he thought he saw people he knew, but for the life of him he could not remember their names or how he might have come to make their acquaintance.

The only explanation was that he had been so well and efficiently briefed on this Arden Chillingham Grey—Lady Huntley—that she and all her friends seemed recognizable to him. That had to be the reason he felt as though he could find his way through her sandstone mansion with his eyes shut.

The carriage pulled up to the front of the house. A footman readily appeared to assist his mistress from the vehicle as Five watched from his perch atop the high wall that surrounded the house and grounds. When the lady was inside and the carriage on its way round back to the stables, he jumped off the wall and ran across the damp, perfectly manicured grass to the back of the house.

A patrol automaton—man-sized and armed with pistols for hands—came up from a hole that had opened in the ground. Five leaped back into the shadows to avoid detection. The metal had no face save for a pair of irisless eyes that served as scanners, searching for unfamiliar life forms. Slowly, it stepped off its platform onto the grass, the hole grinding closed behind it. It would likely patrol the grounds until dawn and then return to its grave. Fortunately, it strode off in the opposite direction of where Five remained hidden. By the time it made a full rotation, he would be gone.

Then he heard the sound of another hole—rusting metal screeching in his ears—opening behind him.

Bloody hell.

Five slipped around the corner as fast as a blink. Gaslights flickered along a gravel path that led to a lush garden, casting a warm glow that he tried to avoid as he crept closer to a trellis against the side of the house. Private security automatons were sensitive to sound as well as movement. A sneeze or wrong step might very well bring one or both of them down upon him. He could probably destroy each with relative ease, but the noise was bound to raise the alarm inside.

An assassin's best weapon was stealth. Right now he had to be fast as well.

He took a running leap and jumped, pushing himself up with a brief foothold on a ground-floor window casing to grab the edge of the balcony above. He pulled his body up enough so that he could wrap one hand around the balustrade. From there it was easy to maneuver up and over.

The balcony was dark, but the room beyond illuminated with a single lamp. Five peered between the parted gauzy drapes to gauge his location.

It was a bedroom—large and clearly feminine. Could he be so fortunate as to have climbed to the lady's chamber to discover nothing but a layer of fragile glass between them?

Sure enough, she was there, sitting at her dressing table as a young woman removed the pins from her mass of hair glinting with copper in the lamplight. The sight of long, silky locks falling down her back caused a peculiar pinch in his chest. He watched, almost mesmerized as the maid, having removed all pins, ran a silver-backed brush through the thick waves.

The lady looked up, holding her own cinnamon gaze within the mirror. A fraction to the right and she would have seen him, but she was too preoccupied with her thoughts to notice him. She looked sad and shaken as she removed the small gem-set gold studs that secured the chains in her nose and ear. Why did she wear them? he wondered as she placed the jewelry in a carved wooden box. And the ring she removed from her left hand—was it a wedding ring? If so, where was the fortunate groom? Surely he wouldn't allow such an intriguing woman to sleep alone?

Five knew it was wrong, and he didn't care. He stayed where he was, a Peeping Tom as the lady stood and allowed the maid to assist her in undressing. The shimmery gray gown slid down her arms, revealing a fine lawn chemise beneath a corset better suited for a courtesan than a lady: silver satin embroidered with turquoise, magenta and green butterflies. It pushed her breasts together and up as though offering them on a platter. His mouth turned arid as a desert at the sight of them.

He hadn't been with a woman in more than a month, but even if he'd gotten shagged five minutes ago, he would still appreciate this woman's body. Her waist was nipped, her hips flared. He watched brazenly as the maid loosened the lacings on that work of art enough to easily unhook the front, releasing her mistress from its confines.

The chemise was so thin he could see the shadows and blushes of her body beneath. She wasn't yet naked, and he could feel a familiar tightening below his waist—and then she stood there in nothing but her stockings and shoes.

Christ Jesus.

He tore himself away from the door, flattening himself against the side of the house. What the hell was he doing? He was there to kill her, not pant after her like a randy mutt. He had to get control of himself. He had to focus, because it had only taken the sight of her tits for him to think it was a shame she had to die.

His lungs filled with cool night air, exhaled and filled

again. Each cleansing breath eased the arousal inside him, returned his mind to its former cool detachment. When he returned to the door, she was no longer in the room, but in the mirror he could see the adjoining bathing chamber where she soaked in a tub of steaming water, her hair spilling over the side.

She drank from a squat crystal glass as she soaked. Whiskey it looked like. Good, that would make her more relaxed, less likely to fight back.

Five stayed there, outside her door, his breath occasionally fogging the glass, for a long time. Eventually, she pulled the stopper from the tub and let the water drain. She'd consumed another two glasses of whiskey during the bath, and when she wrapped herself in a thin, red silk kimono she swayed on her feet.

No, she would not fight him. She might even welcome him, he thought with his other brain—the one located between his legs. Scowling, he pushed that thought aside.

She extinguished the lamp as she walked past, but his eyesight was keen and the moon bright enough that he could still see her. She dropped the robe across the foot of the sleigh-shaped bed and slipped between the sheets naked, skin glowing from the bath.

He waited a little while longer, until he was certain the whiskey had lulled her into a deeply relaxed state, if not into actual slumber. Then, he turned the door handle. The door was unlocked—people rarely locked outside doors this far from the ground—fortunately for him.

Silent as a cat, Five slipped into the darkened bedroom. The scents of warm water and bergamot welcomed him, closing around him like a favorite robe. He made not a sound as he crept toward the bed where she slept. Even his coat was silent, the butter-soft leather so well-worn and conditioned.

Her breathing was the steady and shallow in and out

of one firmly in the grasp of Hypnos. He eased himself down onto the mattress to sit beside her. She didn't stir.

It was a mistake, but he allowed himself the luxury of studying her now that he was this close. Did he think that a more intimate vantage would allow him to see what it was that made her so unusual to him? Why she was so strangely intriguing? He felt drawn to her, pulled by an invisible force he couldn't identify. He couldn't seem to stop himself from lifting his hand and reaching out to brush her hair back from her temple. She slept on her back, face turned slightly to the left.

Long, thick lashes brushed against her cheeks, several shades darker than the brows arched so strongly over both eyes. Her nose had the barest tilt to it, and her mouth was a perfect bow—lush and bold.

But it wasn't her mouth or her long neck, or even her hair that was her best feature. No, that had to be her skin—perfect unblemished skin the color of fresh cream poured over a bowl of peaches.

Five touched his fingertips against the smooth, pale flesh of her cheek. Such skin looked as though it would feel like cool porcelain, but she was warm to the touch.

He should do it now. All he had to do was snuff her out—like the fragile flame of a candle. It was easy—fingers around her throat and a few minutes of breath-stealing pressure.

It *should* have been easy, but as he withdrew his hand, her eyelids fluttered and opened before he could make his escape.

Perhaps it was a sign of weakness, but he didn't relish the thought of having to look into her eyes as he killed her. Normally there was a sort of honor to meeting his prey's gaze, but not this time.

His hands moved to her throat as she looked up at him. He clenched his jaw, a sour taste in his mouth. His fingers had begun to curl around the warm flesh when her gaze widened and she gasped.

"Luke?"

Five froze at the sound of her voice. His heart—normally calm and steady—jumped against his ribs like a caged animal fighting to get out.

She sat up, blankets falling around her hips. His useless hands fell away, palms skimming down her soft arms. He wanted to pull her close and kiss her. He knew she'd taste of whiskey and cloves. She always used clove tooth powder before bed.

How the hell did he know that?

He stared at her, gaze searching her pale, startled face. She had gained a little weight. It looked good on her, softened her. How could he know that either?

"It's me," she said, as though he should know exactly who "me" was. "Arden."

As if she knew who he was.

He met her gaze, frowning. *Arden.*

A terrible pain lanced through his brain—sharp enough that he cried out, pressing the heel of his hand against his forehead to keep it from cracking and letting his brain ooze out.

"Luke!" Hands touched his shoulders. He could only feel her—the pain blinded him.

"Retreat," a voice in his head commanded, cutting through the pain. Any more of this and his head would explode.

He pushed her away and staggered to his feet, and as soon as he put that small amount of distance between them the pressure in his skull eased. His vision began to clear in time to see his intended victim tossing back the bedclothes. He had to escape. If she caught him he would die. He knew it.

Five tore through the glass doors. Shards exploded

around him, spraying both out and into the room under the force of his body. He grabbed the balcony railing and threw himself over it as though it was no more than a low wall. He landed on his feet on the grass and took off running toward the street. One of the patrol automatons spotted him and fired a shot that whistled past his ear. He didn't slow down—the pain in his head had eased, but a bullet would change that for the worse if it managed to permeate his reinforced skull.

He ran all the way to the hotel where he had lodgings for his time in London. He didn't stop until he was in his room, the door locked behind him. He didn't know what had just happened, other than that he had failed to complete his mission. His superiors would be pissed, but that couldn't be helped.

Did she know him, or had she confused him with someone else? And did he know her once upon a time, or was he confused as well? These were questions he could not answer.

One thing he knew for certain—the woman he was supposed to kill had seen his face, and whether he once knew her or not, there was no way in hell he could let her live.

"Perhaps you only *dreamed* that it was Huntley," Hannah Merritt suggested as she fixed two cups of fragrant tea. Humid jasmine filled the air.

Seated in the delicate rose-hued parlor of Hannah's town house, Arden fixed her friend with a rather sardonic gaze despite the watering of her mouth. Hannah's tea was a particular favorite, as were her cook's biscuits, of which there was a plateful. Arden had already indulged, and what she had eaten sat with a pleasant weight in her belly. Up until now she'd ingested nothing but coffee, one slice of toast and a measure of bourbon. The first had been to clear her confused mind, and the second had been to prepare her stomach for the third once she could think straight.

"Fancy it was a dream that shattered my balcony doors as well?"

"Of course not," Hannah retorted with a *tsk* of her tongue, setting the china pot on a special holder of thin coiled copper tubing that circulated steam. Tea never went cold in this house. "Obviously you had an intruder. Are you certain you won't reconsider my offer of having you come to live here? I have plenty of room since Mama's passing." She offered a cup and saucer with three biscuits arranged on the edge.

"You are a dear friend, and I'd prefer you to remain so." Arden took a sip of hot, fragrant—delicious!—tea. "Why ever would I want to leave my house now that Huntley has returned?" She deliberately mentioned him once more since her friend so pointedly did not believe her.

She did not miss the sympathetic glance Hannah shot her way, nor did she acknowledge it. She bit into a biscuit instead, savoring how the sharp ginger flavor mixed with the more subtle tea. Hannah worried that she didn't know her own mind, but if there was *anything* she, Arden Emmerson Chillingham Grey, knew, it was her own mind.

At least for now.

"I haven't gone mad, Hannah," she announced, dunking what was left of her biscuit into her tea before popping the sodden morsel into her mouth.

Her friend had the grace to look affronted—though it could just as easily have been horror at Arden's manners. "I would never think you had. Not for an instant. Why, you are the most unemotional, dispassionate woman I know." She grimaced when her mind caught up to her tongue. "I mean that you think more than you feel." Another wince.

Arden arched a brow, suppressing the smile that threatened. "Stop it, I beg of you. Such incessant compliments will swell my head." She'd known the other woman too long to truly be offended. They'd been friends since school. Hannah hadn't cared that Arden's father had a lesser title and not much of a fortune—or that he actually *worked*. In turn, Arden hadn't cared that Hannah sometimes spoke before she had a chance to think.

Flushed and flustered, Hannah fluttered a hand in Arden's direction. "You know what I mean. You are not the sort of woman to allow herself to be carried away. You place practicality above passion."

"You're really not making me feel better." She made sure to inject a degree of humor in her tone to soften the bite of the truthful statement. Hannah meant it as a compliment, but Arden hadn't always been emotionless. At one time she'd been quite happy to let passion and feeling rule.

But the source of that passion had disappeared almost seven years ago while on assignment, and ever since she'd found herself at a loss.

Until last night when she'd opened her eyes, certain she was dreaming, and seen her husband's face staring down at her. She had just started to think maybe she would never see his crystalline blue eyes again. Had started to forget just how sharp his nose was, how jet-black his hair. He was older but it *was* him.

He acted like he didn't know her—a vicious insult added to the injury his long absence had already wrought.

One of her hands was seized in Hannah's surprisingly robust grip. "What did Lord Henry say when you told him?"

Arden rolled her eyes at the mention of her brother-in-law. "I haven't told him, and I do not plan to until I know for certain."

"A wise course." Her friend looked so relieved, as though she believed there was a chance Arden would give up the silly notion that her husband still lived. After all, she was the only person in all of England who believed it. Even Luke's own brother had given up hope a long time ago.

Her husband's family hadn't offered much in the way of support after Luke disappeared. His mother had never really liked her, and Arden hadn't known his father. Fortunately, she'd had her own father to lean on for a brief time. And her mother, for an even briefer moment.

Her mother-in-law's coldness hadn't surprised her, but Henry's had. He was always so keen to please Luke, Arden had thought he might actually declare himself her personal protector. That hadn't happened. He'd become more and more distant, and then he began his plans to take over the title. Arden had successfully foiled him for years, but soon the seventh anniversary would roll round and then she would be powerless to stop him. Then she might very well need to take Hannah's offer of a room until she found her own house.

"I must confess I hope Lord Huntley returns just so I don't have to see you in half mourning anymore, or those morbid chains."

Arden raised her fingers to the fine strands of silver. "Queen Victoria herself commended me for my obvious devotion."

Hannah snorted. "Of course she did, but she's an old woman and you, my dear, are not. You still have plenty of life left."

A sharp remark about Hannah's own life rose to Arden's lips, but she bit it back. There was no need to be cruel, especially not when she knew how badly her friend wished her situation was different. Hannah was two years younger than Arden's eight and twenty and had given up almost all hope of ever finding a husband or having children. It wasn't that she was unattractive, and she was certainly rich enough. She simply hadn't found a man she "liked well enough to spend the rest of my life looking at him."

Arden had once suggested she take matters into her control and have a child—she could always go abroad and come back with a child and a conveniently dead husband's name. The suggestion had *not* been well received.

"You are right," she conceded with no little amount of enthusiasm. "It is time I gave up my mourning." No need for it now that Luke had returned. How she wished she could be happier about it, but he hadn't recognized her at all. Hadn't known her. Could he have forgotten her? Or were there darker forces at work?

"Fancy a trip to the dressmaker's?" she inquired, coming to the determined conclusion that she needed to find out what was going on rather than speculate with maudlin thoughts.

"Now?" Hannah's face brightened so vibrantly Arden felt a pinch of guilt beneath her breastbone. The particular dressmaker she had in mind was Madame Cherie, who was also a Warden. She inclined her head toward the parlor door with a curve of her lips. "Fetch your coat."

Hannah leaped to her feet and rushed off to do just that, leaving Arden alone to give in to the chuckle she could no longer contain.

A short time later, footmen handed both of them, and Arden's maid, Annie, into the shiny black steam touring carriage she'd purchased just before the Season began.

Unlike the high, old-fashioned contraptions many of her peers—and Arden herself when occasion called—were often driven about town in, this was lower, with an open top. It looked nothing like a horse-drawn carriage—or even the horseless sort—and she scandalously drove it herself.

Hannah's normally smooth brow furrowed with trepidation as she settled in on the leather bench seat. "Are you quite certain this is at all safe, Arden?"

Arden adjusted a pair of driving goggles over her eyes, positioning them so the leather cups fitted comfortably against her face. "Of course it is! You don't mean to suggest I would ever put you in danger?" She softened her words with a smile.

Her friend didn't look convinced, or very contrite. "Not knowingly, of course not." She peered nervously over the side as she lowered the veil of her hat over her face.

Grinning, Arden glanced over her shoulder at Annie, who was perched on the small seat in the back of the carriage, bonnet tied securely under her pointed chin. "You snug and secure back there, dear?"

"I am, ma'am," the maid replied eagerly. How fortunate Arden was to have an employee with such a spirit of adventure.

"Excellent. We're off!" She released the break, adjusted the accelerator lever and wrapped gloved fingers around the steering wheel. The carriage jerked into motion, eliciting a small squeak from Hannah and a burst of laughter from Arden.

In the country, or late at night when city streets weren't so terribly congested, she would drive fast—the carriage could reach speeds in the vicinity of 35–40 miles per hour. That wasn't possible now, not with the streets thick with carriages and horses. Once they left Mayfair it would be even worse, with omnibuses, bicycles and pedestrians added to the throng.

The new elevated train system would help with congestion and with the unfortunate mess that was the subterranean train system. Who would want to chug through the foul-smelling darkness of belowground when you could zip about above it all? It would be like riding a low-flying dirigible through the city.

Personal flyers—that's what the people of England needed. That would truly be exhilarating. Imagine buzzing around town on an ornothopter! Perhaps she would work on a design for such a contraption.

On the way to Madame Cherie's Oxford Street location, they passed support structures for the elevated rail system. Arden turned her head to glance at Hannah. "Extraordinary, aren't they?" The base was big enough for two carriages to drive through side by side, and at least four stories high. There would be hundreds of these bases all over the city, each supporting a large section of track.

"Yes," her friend agreed, not looking. Her knuckles were white on her bonnet ribbons and the side of the vehicle, hanging on to both as though her life depended upon it. "A tad fast for my liking, however."

Arden smiled and turned her attention back to the street, turning the wheel to avoid a dog that ran toward them barking like mad, tail wagging. Hannah gasped beside her.

By the time they reached the pretty little storefront of Madame Cherie's *Maison de Couture*, Hannah was positively stiff and Arden was having difficulty hiding her annoyance behind amusement. Honestly, did her friend have to be so distrusting as to think she would allow her to come to any harm?

But Hannah had been raised in a sheltered environment, much different from Arden's own upbringing in a house ruled by a man dedicated to creating the impossible and a woman determined to make certain her child was fearless. Hannah had been raised to be a proper lady—afraid of most of the world and its wonders—while Arden had been tossed into that world with all the hope and excitement of a penny dropped into a wishing well. It was no wonder they gravitated toward each other in school—each so fascinating to the other despite their difference in class. Of course, once Arden married Luke, class ceased to matter.

"Come inside, dear," she cajoled, taking one of Hannah's stiff hands in her own. "A little shopping will soothe your nerves."

Hannah obeyed, and by the time they entered the pleasantly warm interior of the shop with its swaths of beautiful fabric and air that smelled faintly of perfume, some of the color had started to return to the dark-haired woman's cheeks.

They were greeted by Madame herself. "Darlings!" she cried, opening her tattooed arms.

Madame Cherie was a little shorter than Arden, putting her somewhere in the vicinity of about five and a half feet. She had thick black hair streaked with white that she wore piled haphazardly on top of her head, dark eyes thickly lined with black kohl and bright red lips. Her skin was the color of cream with just a touch of coffee, and decorated with so many colored pictures Arden often made a game of trying to sort them all out. Today Madame Cherie showed a shocking amount of skin by wearing the latest fashion amongst the artistic crowd—a short violet leather vest that left her midriff bare and a long, gauzy skirt in black and silver.

"Bonjour, Madame," Arden replied. *"Comment ça va?"*

"Tres bien, mon amie." The woman, who was no more

French than Arden was, but far more convincing, fixed her with a direct look. "I had hoped to see you soon, Arden."

"The *countess* is in need of a new wardrobe," Hannah interjected coolly, having found her voice.

Madame—whose given name was Zoe Harper—arched a brow as black as a crow's wing, calling attention to the tiny crosses tattooed along her temple. "*Mais oui.*"

Arden didn't really fancy being caught in the middle of a female equivalent of a pissing contest, so she patted her friend on the shoulder. "There's no need to stand on ceremony here, Hannah dearest. Madame and I have known each other too long to be concerned with titles. Why don't you pick out some fabrics while we discuss designs? Whatever colors you think I should have."

There wasn't a woman in the fashionable world who would turn down the chance to dress a friend however she wanted. Hannah's green eyes brightened considerably before she scurried off to begin hauling bolts of brightly colored silk off the walls.

Both of Zoe's brows jumped at one particularly garish shade of puce. "I believe you might regret that, my friend." There was no hiding the amusement in her voice—not that she would have tried.

Arden smiled. "I still reserve the right to veto any choices. Might we step into the back, dearest? I have something I wish to discuss with you."

The darker woman linked her arm around Arden's. "And I, you."

They left the main room of the shop and passed through a curtained doorway into the sewing room where both humans and automatons—or *androïdes* as the French called them—worked on stitching and constructing gowns for the shop's many clients. The automatons worked much faster and more precisely than the humans, but there were simply some things metal could not do better than human hands.

Zoe's office was located just off this room, so they could sit in relative privacy, their conversation muffled by the sounds of the workroom. Zoe closed the door all the same.

"I believe my husband has returned," Arden said, wasting no time in getting to the point of her visit. She stripped off her gloves with perfunctory tugs on each finger. "He snuck into my room and was hovering over me when I awoke. Do you know anything?" Zoe knew almost everything that happened in London, having contacts in all levels of society. She was one of W.O.R.'s best intelligence gatherers, though there were some that sought to brand her as a spy-whore—selling secrets to the highest bidder.

Arden knew better. Her friend's moral code might be a tad ambiguous, but once she gave her loyalty to a person she never wavered. Arden was equally loyal to her in return.

"Your . . . husband."

"Yes, only he doesn't seem to know me. It's as though he has some kind of amnesia." Frowning, Arden finished with her gloves and looked up as she slapped them into one palm. Zoe was watching her with an expression that could only be described as a mixture of trepidation and horror. "Good lord, Zoe, what is it?"

Her friend took a bottle of whiskey from a cupboard behind her desk, removed the top and took a deep swallow. Then she passed the bottle to Arden. "It all makes sense now."

Without being given or demanding an explanation, Arden took the bottle and drank, shuddering as the potent liquor hit her stomach in a most comforting manner. If Zoe hadn't bothered with glasses it had to be bad.

She took another drink, then gave the whiskey back. "All right, tell me."

Her friend also tipped the bottle as she leaned against the edge of the desk. Her handsome face wore a ravaged expression, and her dark eyes were bright and rueful.

"Word has it that the Company has sent a ghost after you."

Arden's stomach rolled, threatening to send the whiskey back up. "Ghosts" were Company assassins, called such because they were often able to achieve their bloody goal without being seen or heard. She pressed a shaking hand to her abdomen, but the sick feeling remained. She didn't know how or why, but she knew who the assassin was. "Luke."

Chapter 3

Five paused in the stairwell of his lodgings and pressed the heel of one palm to his forehead. It felt as though there was something worrying at his brain—like a cat pawing at a closed door.

Luke.

He clung to the rail with one hand, trying to keep himself from falling down the narrow stairs as *her* voice rang in his head. He hadn't been able to get it out. Every time he thought of her, pain followed.

Luke. It was what she had said to him in her bedroom. She had said it as if he should recognize it, and it had sounded almost plaintive—regretful.

She knew him, and though he knew everything about her he didn't know the connection. She had the upper hand—had him at a disadvantage.

He despised vulnerability. That she made him feel that way was simply one more reason to kill her. And he would. She had done something that marked her for death—made her deserve it—and as her personal grim reaper it was his duty to deliver her judgment.

He would not fail next time.

The Company knew he hadn't completed the mission and had ordered him to report to an address in Whitechapel this afternoon.

The hem of his leather greatcoat swished against his legs as he continued down the stairs, the pain in his head lessening. As he stepped outside, Five slipped on a pair of tinted spectacles that eased some of the ache in his skull. He swung his leg over the seat of a heavy black-and-copper-colored velocycle parked near the door and slipped on soft, worn leather gloves before starting the machine's engine. It chugged and roared to life, eager to tear through the damp, cobblestone streets.

It didn't feel right to him to stay in this particular part of town. There was somewhere else he should be, but he had no idea where. He had no idea who he was, but his accent was English, so it made sense that he came from London or perhaps nearby. It was a posh accent too, which didn't make sense with what he had been told about his background. It made him think of other things that didn't make sense in his life. But those thoughts hurt too, so he tried not to think them.

He steered the heavy machine into traffic, its ridged wheels gripping the cobblestone street. As he maneuvered the steering bars to guide him around a slow-moving omnibus, an image flashed in his mind—of him, driving a cycle of much higher quality than this one down a dusty country lane. A woman's arms were wrapped around his middle, and her laughter rang with wild delight in his ears.

So clear and sudden was the vision that he almost lost control of the cycle. Swearing, he managed to keep from taking a spill into a rather nasty-looking gutter.

He shook his head as he righted himself. A memory. Could it be that he was regaining his past? The thought plagued him all the way to Whitechapel, where he stopped in front of a nondescript building off Dorset Street, near Miller Court.

He knocked on the door and waited. Within a few moments he heard footsteps approach, and then the heavy portal opened to reveal a tall, thin man he'd seen perhaps two or three times in the past.

"Ah, Number Five. Right on time, I see. Promptness is a virtue, you know. Well, inside with you. I'll take you to the Doctor. He's been waiting for you."

The Doctor. A slight coil of unease wound low around Five's spine as he tucked his spectacles into his coat pocket. He couldn't remember the man ever doing anything awful to him, but wariness filled him regardless. He followed the thinner male down a narrow hall to the last door.

"Here you are. Go right in, lad."

Five thanked him and settled his gloved hand on the latch. It clicked under the pressure of his thumb and the door opened, creaking wide to reveal a small sitting room.

The man he knew as the Doctor stood just inside, on a worn but quality rug of bright crimson and dark blue with traces of gold. He was dressed in crisp trousers, snowy shirt and cravat and a dark brown waistcoat embroidered with hunter-green. His dark hair was heavily pomaded back from his high forehead, revealing the craggy countenance of his face. His moustache had traces of gray in it, but he didn't seem old, yet neither was he young. He was short and lean, but he was the kind of man that made others shift uncomfortably from the coldness of his gaze.

"Five," he said by way of greeting, not looking up from the tray of implements on the table beside him. "Come in."

Five did as he was told. He always did as he was told. Odd, but he suddenly realized he hated being told what to do. He was accustomed to giving the orders. How would this man react if Five told him to go straight to hell and walked out? "What is this place?" he asked.

"Just a building the Company owns," the man replied. "We acquired it after an associate of ours did some work here back in 'eighty-eight. He was one of our best."

"What happened to him?"

"He was killed by the Wardens."

The Wardens. In the business of spying, the rivalry between the Wardens and the Company was the longest and the most volatile. To say that the two were on opposite sides would be an oversimplification. Sometimes they were on the same side, and even then they fought one another. No, it went beyond right and wrong. Their dissension was based on something more complex than morality. They were enemies hell-bent on destroying each other, but wouldn't know what to do without the other there to fight against. The only relationship he could compare it to would be a marriage between two people who despised each other but refused to separate.

Or like that of England and France. "Is that a bloodstain on the wall?"

The man didn't glance at the mark. "Yes. A woman named Mary Kelly was killed in this room."

"Was that the 'work' your 'best' man was up to?" He wasn't certain what made him ask, or what put the sardonic twist in his voice, but he knew he didn't need to hear the other man's answer — the stiffening of his shoulders was enough.

"I hear you've been having some difficulty carrying out your present task." The Doctor finally deigned to look at him — barely a passing glance. "I'm going to remedy that. Have a seat."

The chair was like a barber's chair, only with shackles on the arm and leg rests. Five eyed it warily, not quite ready to give himself over just yet. "Since arriving in London I've been . . . remembering things."

The smaller man tilted his head thoughtfully, his gaze focused elsewhere. "Is that so? What sort of things?"

Five shrugged. "Little things—driving in the country, how to get to certain places. I think I might have been someone important, and married."

The Doctor smiled, but there was little humor in it. "We all like to think of ourselves as someone important."

"I'm not imagining things," Five retorted somewhat defensively.

Now the smaller man met his gaze—directly and unflinching. "I didn't say you were, but in a case such as yours, it is perhaps best to do a little investigative work before we tell ourselves you are regaining your memories. Now, in the chair, please."

This time Five did as he was instructed. He sat down in the chair and tried not to drive his knuckles into the doctor's scarred face as the man closed one, then the other shackle. He was now totally at the mercy of another. The realization brought a thin layer of sweat to the back of his neck.

"Any other concerns I should know about? Any idea why you were unable to achieve your objective last evening?"

He leaned his head back against the padded rest. "I had my hands around her throat and she woke up. She said . . ." He frowned, not wanting to give the name away. "She spoke as though she knew me. I felt as though I might have known her too."

"But that is impossible," the Doctor argued, piercing the skin of Five's arm with a needle. Five watched as the plunger was depressed, releasing God-only-knew what into his blood. "She is a countess, and there is no way a man such as you would have ever known a woman of her social stature."

That was true, but it didn't change that she had known him. "It threw me off-kilter. I was told to retreat, and so I did." He looked down at his shackled wrists as he spoke, unable to look the other man in the eye as he lied. He had run because she scared the hell out of him, not because he had been told to.

The world tilted slightly. Five blinked as the floor seemed to sway beneath him. Christ, what was in that syringe? He opened his mouth to ask, but his tongue refused to work.

"She won't be able to discombobulate you so easily next time. Close your eyes please. You might feel a slight discomfort—"

The rest of what the Doctor said was lost as white-hot pain lanced through Five's mind. It was as though someone had literally set lightning loose in his head, so bright was the flash. His body arched, limbs straining against the restraints as his brain burned. His own cries echoed in his ears, reverberating throughout the room.

Writhing, Five fought as the pain intensified. It felt like needles of ice piercing his brain, as though his mind was a collection of butterflies being pinned for exhibition.

Again and again the needles stabbed until he couldn't take anymore. The pain and the drug finally took their toll and he faded into sweet, welcoming darkness.

When he woke, the Doctor was sitting on a stool by the table not far away, watching him and sipping a cup of tea.

"How long was I asleep?" he asked.

"Not long."

He tested the shackles. He could snap them if he wanted. "May I leave now?" He didn't like the Doctor. He didn't know why, but the man made his flesh creep.

"In a moment." The Doctor set his cup on a saucer and rose to his feet. "I want to ask you a few questions first, just to make certain you are feeling better."

"Better?" He scowled. "Was I sick?"

"A little," the small man replied, clasping his hands behind his back. "What is your name?"

"Number Five," he replied with a scoff. Did the man really think he wouldn't remember who he was?

"Have you ever been to London before?"

"No."

"Has anything you've seen here seemed familiar to you?"

"No." He'd only been in town for . . . a day? Or was it two? And seeing the sights hadn't been high on his agenda. "Are we finished?"

The Doctor made no move to unlock the shackles. "Almost. What is your mission while here in London?"

"To hunt down the woman who murdered Victor Erlich three years ago."

"Arden Grey, Lady Huntley." The smaller man's eyes narrowed, as though looking for some kind of reaction, and then widened again. "What are your orders when you find her?"

Five looked up, a slow smile of anticipation curving his lips. "To kill her."

The murdered girl was identified as the daughter of Baron Lynbourne. Her name was Angeline, and she had been eighteen years of age. Her parents had held hope of her finding a husband that Season. She was reported to be a spirited girl with a pleasant personality, liked by all who knew her.

The only thing that could have made the tale more tragic would have been if she were an only child. However, Lynbourne and his wife had other children to help them through their terrible grief. Their lives would never be the same, regardless. That was why it was called "loss," after all.

Arden wasn't acquainted with the baron and baroness, at least not closely. Of course they had been introduced once upon a time, and often were invited to the same events, but that was the extent of their familiarity. Still, she ordered an arrangement of white calla lilies to be sent round to them, along with a card expressing her condolences.

That was all she could do. Her loyalty to the Crown prohibited her from approaching them on a more intimate level, but even if it did not, she would hardly open a dialogue with the grieving parents. What would she tell them, that she had seen their daughter's mutilated corpse? That she had seen the moments of her death? These were not the details that comforted the distraught, and they would serve no purpose but to cause them more pain.

But she sent flowers because she was no stranger to loss, or to grief.

Three days had passed since she'd awoken to find Luke in her bedroom, and she was beginning to wonder if he had indeed been a dream, or some grand figment of her imagination.

There was no way she could have imagined his touch—or the ruination of the French doors. No, he was very real.

Was it true what Zoe surmised? Had he been sent by the Company to assassinate her? It seemed too fantastical to believe, but it was just probable enough to tighten her chest. It explained why she'd woken to his hands around her neck, and why he had run. It also explained why he didn't know her.

What in the name of God had those villainous bastards done to her husband?

Tears burned the backs of her eyes, clutched at her throat, but she held them at bay. She would not cry. Tears were the refuge of the hopeless and the helpless, and she was neither.

It was odd that she turned to friends within the Wardens for strength and assistance, when it had been Luke who brought her into that world. Of course, growing up as she had and aiding her father in his work, she had seen some of it, but it wasn't until her marriage that she slowly began to insert herself into that life of intrigue and danger. Becoming a full agent after his disappearance had been just another way to hold on to him—look for him. Who would have thought that it would become such a large, defining part of her? She had purpose. More important, she had a distraction.

Arden knew Luke would be back for her—felt it in her bones. She had neglected to tell Zoe that, however. No doubt her friend suspected it as well. She probably wondered if Luke was a traitor not only to his wife but to his country. Arden had to admit the terrible thought had crossed her mind.

It was time to get out of the house and stop dwelling. This sitting about feeling sorry for herself would not do any more good than feeling helpless would.

Three of the garments she had ordered from Zoe had been delivered the day before—God bless automaton sewing skills! Arden went to her room and summoned Annie to help her dress in a suitable costume for going out.

Opening the armoire, she made her selection of clothing, placed the hanger in the slender compartment to the left, then closed the door and pushed the button on the side of the wardrobe. The heavy oak trembled slightly as the small engine within chugged to life. Soon, she heard the familiar sound of boiling water whooshing through pipes and the gentle hiss of steam—the remnants of which drifted from the copper pipe on top. The entire process lasted perhaps a minute before shutting down. Arden waited another minute before she opened the door once more.

The ensemble she had chosen was a wine-colored gown with a jaggedly ruffled skirt, short sleeves and a bodice made of snug-fitting leather in a matching shade. The front had tightly cinched buckle closures that eliminated the need for a corset beneath. The built-in steam chamber in the armoire had released any wrinkles that might have marred the fabric. She was dressing when Annie arrived to do her hair, which was quickly twisted into a thick knot on the back of her head.

She finished the ensemble with black velvet boots that hugged her calves and a tailored black pelisse which ensured she would be warm in the damp outdoors.

Annie went to call for the carriage with the Huntley crest on it to be brought round. As much as Arden loved to drive her smaller vehicle, in case of threat she was safer inside an enclosed carriage with a driver.

And if that threat happened to be her husband, perhaps he'd see the familiar coat of arms and remember who he was. She sincerely doubted it would happen that way. In fact, she rather hoped that if the sight of her didn't make him remember, then nothing would. It was a selfish hope, but she held it nevertheless.

She pinned a small velvet top hat onto her hair, positioning it with a jaunty tilt toward her left eye. Satisfied that she looked suitable to her social position, she gathered up her gloves and bag and left her room.

Downstairs Arden smelled the clean, lemony scent of a scrubber cleaning the marble floor. The machine stood waist-high, and looked very much like a large, tall cooking pot. A boiler beneath kept the water hot and provided power as the machine propelled itself around the hall, cleaning the floor with long, armlike limbs that had scrub pads instead of hands.

"I'm so sorry about that, my lady," Mrs. Bird, the housekeeper, gushed as she bustled seemingly from out of nowhere to push the little automaton on its way as though it were an errant child. "I meant to have the floor cleaned before you came down."

Arden smiled. "Don't fret so, Mrs. Bird. I shan't expire from seeing housework being tended to. Although you may want to have Ronald look at the scrubber when it's done. It sounds as though it might be having difficulties."

The housekeeper nodded. "Of course, my lady."

She didn't miss the faint blush that filled the widow's smooth cheeks. "You might also want to take one of your apple tarts. I know for a fact that Ronald's very fond of apples."

The woman's eyes widened a fraction. "Is he now? That's very good to know, ma'am."

Still smiling, Arden pulled on her gloves and bid the housekeeper a good morning. Then she ventured out into the gray, drizzly day where her carriage sat waiting. It was a fairly large, impressive vehicle, with puffs of steam drifting from the gleaming brass pipe on the back. Burgundy and black lacquer, it had large black wheels and a padded bench for the driver up front. It was a formal carriage, and could be secured to a team of horses should the occasion—such as a royal invitation—arise. Queen Victoria respected modern advancement, but expected it to respect *her* more. Court fashion was always a decade or two behind the times, no matter if it was for hair or horses.

She glanced up at the driver. "Downing Street, Gibbs."

The burly man tipped his well-worn hat. "As you wish, my lady."

One of her footmen opened the carriage door for her, and the small steps automatically flipped down for her to climb. A large drop of rain landed on her cheek, and she turned to the footman to ask him to run into the house and fetch her umbrella, but Mrs. Bird was already there, object in hand.

"Thought you might be wanting this, my lady."

Gratitude curved Arden's lips. "What would I ever do without you, Mrs. Bird?"

The older woman flushed, but she met Arden's gaze—something servants rarely did. "God willing neither of us will ever have to find out, ma'am."

Arden's throat tightened and she swallowed against it. "Indeed." She climbed into the carriage, not daring to wonder at what might happen should Henry succeed in having Luke declared dead, despite her certainty to the contrary. She certainly had enough money and options to live out the rest of her life as she wished, but for nine years this house had been her home and the people in it her friends, family and employees. Many of them had been with the Grey family their entire careers. She couldn't expect any of them to give up working for an earl to come work for her.

The footman closed the door. Arden tapped her umbrella on the roof to let Gibbs know she was ready to depart. The carriage eased into motion, the familiar sound of the engine a soothing rhythm. It had an almost mesmerizing effect, lulling her into a state of tranquility despite the emotions threatening to rage inside her. It felt very much like when Luke first disappeared. She'd been lost and numb and yet so very, very angry. Yet she'd been unable to give into that rage—not as she wanted anyway. Grief always ruined it, and now she feared if she let it out it simply would never stop.

So she pushed it down, as she did most strong emotions, and forced herself into a state of dispassionate disinterestedness so she could think clearly. However, she wasn't too keen on thinking at the moment either.

The carriage swayed a little as it traveled over cobblestones worn smooth by decades upon decades of carriage wheels, horse hooves and human feet. Arden leaned her weary head against the soft cushions and closed her eyes.

She jerked awake when the carriage stopped, bolting upright and immediately checking her cheek for drool. Thankfully there wasn't any. Weariness clung to her as she blinked and straightened her hat and hair, brushed her hands over her coat and skirt to smooth them.

She peeked around the closed blind. They had reached her destination.

When the door had been opened and the steps lowered, Arden stepped out into the light but steady rain, glad for her umbrella, which she opened and held over herself for shelter.

"Go find yourself someplace warm and dry to wait, Gibbs," she instructed. "In the carriage if you like. I will be ready to depart for home in thirty minutes." He was dressed in the appropriate outerwear for such a day, but she would feel guilty if he came down with a cold.

When he walked away she turned to the row of buildings before her.

Number 13 Downing Street did not technically exist, having been remodeled and partially absorbed by one or two of the other buildings close to the redbrick dwelling that was the official address of the Prime Minister. Of course, Lord Salisbury didn't actually live in the house — he had a much grander estate befitting a man of his rank on Arlington Street in St. James's.

But for her purpose there was still a number 13. It simply wasn't visible on the surface.

Number 13 housed the Wardens of the Realm's London Office. They had smaller locations scattered throughout the Empire, but this was the largest, and home to the Director, who ran the organization. The Wardens were spies, for lack of a better term, dedicated to the protection of Britain and all Her interests. There seemed to be no shortage of intrigue in Europe and the world, much of it involving England, directly or indirectly. Sometimes the job was about keeping someone alive, or making sure someone else disappeared without a trace. And sometimes, it was so political Arden's eyes crossed at the subtleties, backstabbing and dual nature of it all. When those moments got to be too much, she reminded herself that both her father and husband had dedicated themselves to the agency — and to their country. She could do no less.

There was a black door on the building right in front of her to which she had a key. Past that door was a small foyer that housed nothing but an elegant oak and iron-grated lift. The matching gate in front of the lift was locked, but she had a key for it as well and easily walked through to the lift itself. She slid the polished door open, stepped over the slight gap between box and floor, and then shut herself inside, latching the door securely.

She took a punch card from the lining of her bag — the same place where she kept the keys to this mysterious place — and slipped it into the slot provided. There were no buttons to push or levers to pull, for the analytical engine of the machine read the information on her punch card and took her to her desired location. Normally she used another card that did require a floor selection, but today she was going to see the Director, which required a special card that only a handful of people were privileged enough to own.

The lift moved slowly at first, grinding and hissing as the steam engine that powered it came to life. Many people would be afraid to be in such a seemingly decrepit piece of machinery, but Arden wasn't concerned. There were safety precautions in place in case of emergency, and her father had built the lift, so if there was an issue she could probably fix it herself—if she survived.

The cage jerked into motion—she placed a palm briefly against the wall to steady herself. A soft hiss whispered around her as the floor beneath her feet began its descent.

Down one floor the lift crawled; then it hesitated and she felt something like a giant hand close around either side—jostling the cage as it clamped hold. Chains and cables jangled as they were released. There was a slight drop, followed by a jar that never ceased to make her curse like a sailor. Then the lift moved backward, burrowing into the building rather than beneath it. Instead of relying on cables and pulleys, it now sat upon a track that ran parallel to the street above. It spent several minutes on this route before it stopped and the door—this time the one at the back of the box—was cranked open by an unseen mechanism that sounded as though several of its parts required lubrication.

Arden remembered to take her punch card before exiting the lift. The heels of her boots tapped sharply on the glossy polish of the white and black-veined marble floor as she strode briskly toward her destination.

Both sides of the large hall were lined with sconces holding brightly burning lamps, filling the subterranean hall with blue-tinged light. She'd wager ten pounds that it wasn't gas in those lamps. Another ten said she'd have better luck sprouting wings than finding out just what the blue substance was.

There was only one door other than that to the lift behind her. It was actually a double door made of carved oak—tall and wide enough for a pair of giants to walk through. A guard stood on either side, dressed in livery of black and gold, the brass buttons on their jackets embossed with the image of a gryphon wearing a crown of roses. It was the symbol of the Wardens—the gryphon symbolizing England and the mythical creature that protected the kingdom, and the roses symbolizing virtue and superior merit.

Spine straight, Arden stood before the guards, fixing them both with a level stare. "Lady Arden Grey, Countess Huntley to see the director."

Neither of the guards' countenances changed, but the smaller of the two—the female—moved to turn the knob on the door nearest her and opened it, bowing as Arden wordlessly swept past.

She stepped over the threshold into what could have been a drawing room or salon in any aristocratic lady's household. The walls were covered in cream-colored, delicately hand-painted paper from the Orient depicting birds in flight. The carpet was pale as well, and just as exquisite in its subtle pattern. All of the furniture was made from dark wood, and upholstered in the darkest crimson velvet.

A young man sat at a desk near the back of the room, not far from yet another door—the entrance to the Director's office. He glanced up, his spectacles glinting in the light. "Good day, Lady Huntley."

"Hello, Mr. Chiler. Is she in?"

"Of course. Allow me to inquire if she is able to accept visitors." The young man rose to his feet and moved to the door. The hand he lifted to knock was almost skeletal-looking—but bones didn't have rivets and bolts. Mr. Chiler's fingers could crush a normal man's hand with very little effort. Arden knew this because she had seen it happen.

A voice called out for him to enter, and he slipped into the office, closing the door softly behind him. All Arden could do was wait for his return. The Director would either have time for her or she wouldn't. There was never any hidden agenda, not here.

Seconds ticked past on the large clocks on the wall. One was set to London time, another to New York, another to Berlin, and one to St. Petersburg. There were others, but before Arden could glance at them, the door to the director's office opened and Mr. Chiler reappeared.

"You may go on in, Lady Huntley," he said in his soothing baritone.

"Thank you." Arden brushed past him to cross the threshold into the inner sanctum.

The room was large, decorated in muted shades of violet, burnt orange, gold and rich fuchsia. Plush sofas and chairs were topped with thick, colorful cushions. Swaths of silk draped the walls, brightened by the light of the lamps. Paintings of India adorned the walls, their bold colors contrasting with the monochromatic photographs of London that hung alongside them.

A large desk sat at the back of the room—a thick slab of ebony atop the backs of four hand-carved elephants, each different in appearance, painted to look as though they should be carrying a rajah through the streets of town.

The woman standing in front of the desk was by far the most exotic part of the room. A little taller than Arden's own above-average height, she was built like an hourglass in black trousers tucked in knee-high black boots, and a fitted dark-purple waistcoat that was boned and laced like a corset. Her thick black hair was coiled into a large, heavy bun at the base of her skull, and large, piercing amber eyes stared out of a face that was just a little too dark and exotic to be wholly English.

Dhanya Withering was rumored to be the illegitimate granddaughter of Queen Victoria, though no one had ever seen any evidence to prove this theory. Her mother was from India and ran a successful bakery in the West End where Arden often went when she had a craving for something delicious and sweet. She had developed quite a taste for cardamom thanks to Dhanya's mama.

"I hear you had some excitement at your home a few nights ago," Dhanya said in lieu of greeting. Her faintly accented English sounded lyrical and exotic to Arden's ears.

"I did," she replied. "Zoe seems to think the Company wants to see me eliminated."

One already incredibly arched brow quirked as the darker woman gestured for her to sit. "I had heard a similar rumor, yes. The price of having the satisfaction of dispatching Victor Erlich to his just reward, no doubt."

Arden wouldn't describe having to kill a man to save herself as satisfying in any degree, but she didn't voice that. It was the only time she'd ever harmed another person. Her talents normally kept her out of harm's way, inventing gadgets and weapons for W.O.R. agents. With God's grace it would be the last time she ever had to take a life. She still dreamed of Erlich on occasion—his wine-soaked breath and grasping fingers.

The director didn't seem to notice her suddenly reflective state—or she chose to ignore it. "I also heard that you believe the man who snuck into your home was none other than your errant husband."

Was she surprised Dhanya had already heard this? No.

"Indeed I do." Arden seated herself in a violet wing-back chair, watching her friend and superior W.O.R. member as she poured them each a cup of chai tea and placed several sweets on a plate. Arden didn't know the names of them all, but there were small golden logs topped with cream, swirls of bright orange batter that had been fried and dipped in sweet syrup, and different-colored squares topped with silver leaf. The sight of them set her mouth to watering.

Dhanya joined her, offering her first tea, then a sweet. "You know that if your husband is working for the Company, the rest of the Wardens will call for an inquiry into your own loyalties."

Arden nodded as she took a bite of a sticky swirl. Bliss! "To be honest, Dhanya, if my husband is truly alive, I don't care if the Wardens want my blood."

The darker woman watched her closely. "Is he a traitor or a victim, then?"

"Victim," she replied immediately. "He looked at me as though I were a stranger."

Licking a drop of syrup from her thumb, the director leaned back in her chair. "You believe his mind has been tampered with."

"I do. When Luke left seven years ago he was determined to bring the Company to an end once and for all. I am convinced they caught him and have somehow altered his mind."

A frown furrowed Dhanya's usually smooth brow. "I have heard of such things happening, but I've never witnessed it for myself. I've always thought it to be the agency equivalent of a monster in the cupboard—something to keep operatives on their toes."

Arden found her tone dubious at best. Why did everyone doubt her judgment? "I *know* my husband. It was Luke."

The director raised her honey-colored gaze. It was like staring into the eyes of a lioness. "Arden ... my friend. You do realize what will happen to this man, especially if he is your husband?"

Arden's heart staggered against her ribs. "He is one of *us*, Dhanya."

Not a flicker of emotion crossed the other woman's face. "Which is precisely why if you see him again you have to try to reach him. It is because of who he might be and what he might know that we cannot allow him to continue to be used by the Company. If you cannot turn him, or find some way that he might serve our cause, I will have no choice but to give orders that he is to be terminated."

If fear could have fingers, it would have her very soul in those icy digits. "You cannot kill my husband."

The cool façade dropped for a second, and she saw real sympathy—pain even—in her superior's gaze. "If he has been programmed to murder you and is willing to carry out those orders, I will put a bullet in his brain myself."

Arden swallowed hard against the bile churning in her stomach, threatening to rise in her throat. She set her cup and saucer on the desk, unable to countenance the thought of eating or drinking. "I understand."

"I do not think you do." Dhanya leaned forward. "I'm giving you the chance to find him first. I pray to God I don't regret it, but I have faith in your abilities. Find him and fix him and I will rejoice in his return with you, but if you cannot ..."

There was no need for her to say it again. Arden understood perfectly. "I will find him," she vowed—as much to herself as to Dhanya. Then she rose to her feet—ashamed to find her knees trembling. "I have taken up enough of your time. I will leave you now."

The darker woman also stood, and came around the desk to give her a hug. "You may not believe this, but I very much hope that you succeed."

Arden nodded, not daring to speak for fear she might burst into tears. She had only just found Luke again and now was faced with the very real possibility that she might lose him again—for good this time.

Just as she turned the doorknob to make her exit, Dhanya called after her, "It's good to see you in some color, Lady Huntley."

She managed a smile while inside wishing she'd worn the protection of her blacks and drabs. She wouldn't have felt quite so vulnerable in them.

She said good-day to Mr. Chiler and made her way back to the surface, as far away from the oppressive secrecy of the W.O.R. offices as she could get. The din and dirt of the city was a welcome balm to her troubled soul.

All she had to do was find Luke. He could be anywhere in London, making her task much like attempting to find a hairpin in a pile of automaton scrap. But if that was what she had to do to save his life, to have him return to her, then she would do it, even if it meant putting herself in danger.

The pavement was wet, but the rain had stopped, so she didn't open her umbrella on the way to her carriage. Gibbs stood by the gleaming vehicle, smoking a cigarette. He threw the rolled tobacco to the ground when he spotted her, crushing it beneath his heel.

Normally she would inquire as to how he spent his time, or thank him for being there when she returned, but she couldn't summon the energy to put on a smile and be the good lady.

Gibbs opened the carriage door for her. "Is everything all right, ma'am? If you'll excuse my impertinence, you look a little pale."

Arden smiled wearily as she stepped up. God love the man for being such a pet. "Just tired, Gibbs. Do not fret. 'Tis nothing a strong cup of tea and a nap cannot cure." If only it was truly that simple.

"I'll get you home straightaway, my lady. You just sit back and get some rest." He closed the door as soon as she was inside, and hopped up onto the bench.

Arden was just about to take his advice when she noticed something on the seat across from her. Frowning, she leaned forward to investigate and gasped at what she saw.

Lying on the cushions was a freshly cut, almost bloodred poppy—her favorite flower.

Someone had been in her carriage. Someone had known exactly where to find her and had left this flower so she would know she was being watched. Followed.

And only one person had ever given her poppies before. It was why she had carried a bouquet of them the day she married him. It seemed she might not have to search out her husband after all.

He was going to come to her.

Chapter 4

She was so beautiful it was a shame to have to kill her.

Five watched from the shadows outside the mansion as his prey stood inside, drinking her third glass of champagne served by gleaming automatons that were little more than silver trays on top of moving dustbins. She was surrounded by a small crowd made up of what he assumed were old friends and new admirers, listening intently to what she had to say.

And what man in his proper mind wouldn't admire her? She wasn't a conventional beauty—her features were too strong for that—but she was the kind of woman a body didn't forget, who drew men to her like moths to a lamp. She gave off a wounded air, which attracted the predator within him, but he had been at this intrigue long enough to recognize danger when he saw it. She was no more weak or helpless than he was.

She had gotten his gift, but unlike most women who would have been frightened by such an invasion of privacy, she flaunted it, wearing the bright flower in the upswept mass of her russet hair. It was a bold accessory, made all

the more so by her lack of jewelry save for small gold earrings, and pale gold gown. His instinct had been correct—
poppies suited her.

"Do you have her?"

For the first time in a long while he was annoyed by
the intrusive voice in his head, coming through the tiny
mechanism implanted in his ear. "I'm watching her now."

"What is the delay?"

"I can't very well walk into the ballroom and strangle
her."

A very pregnant pause followed, and for a moment he
thought his employer was gone. *"You will do it tonight."*

His sigh sounded like a growl even in his own ears.
"That is my intention."

"Do not make me regret choosing you for this mission."

Five gritted his teeth. How tempting it was to tell the
man to go bugger himself. Instead, he said nothing and
went back to watching the lady whose life he was expected to take. Pity, that.

"Five?"

"I'll do it." He clenched his jaw to keep from adding
"piss off" to the promise.

Silence followed. Then, a soft click. His superior had
severed the connection.

Shifting on the balls of his feet, Five adjusted his
perch in the tree outside one of the ballroom windows to
one of more comfort. Being idle drove him mad, despite
such alluring visuals.

He wore a set of spectacles that brought everything
closer, allowing him to take in even more detail. His
lovely lady lost some of her glow when a new gentleman
approached her. She seized another glass of champagne
from an automated footman that resembled a strange
combination of man and crane—a human torso held
aloft by long, spindly legs, with even longer arms that

could extend a tray up to six feet into or above a crowd. Its lack of a head made it strangely off-putting. Lady Huntley didn't seem to mind.

This dandy looked to be a gentleman in his mid- to late twenties. He wore impeccable evening dress of black and white, and his dark sideburns were long and neatly trimmed—not quite muttonchops. He looked vaguely familiar. . . .

Five started, frowned and adjusted a knob on the side of the goggles to see if he could bring the man into closer view, sharper focus.

The man looked like *him*. Very much so. How was this possible? Who was he? Was this the mysterious Luke? Had his intended prey mistaken him for someone else in the dark?

For reasons he couldn't fathom, he wanted to kill this man. A sense of deep betrayal had wormed its way up from his gut to twine around his heart. At the moment that feeling didn't matter so much as the fact that the lady did not seem pleased to see the man at all. In fact, they seemed to be having a rather displeasing conversation. So much so that she walked away from him while he was still talking.

Curious. And relieving. If she'd given any hint of intimacy between them he would have snapped the bastard's neck.

Christ, but the resemblance was uncanny. Was it possible that they were related? It was highly possible that Five could be the by-blow of some wealthy nob. That would provide some explanation for his accent and familiarity with Mayfair.

Gliding through the trees, Five watched Arden Grey as she walked almost the entire length of the ballroom. Then she made an abrupt turn toward the French doors that led to the balcony.

She would not be content to stand on that smooth

stone and lean on the balustrade, that much he knew. She was the kind of woman who had to walk off her frustration, release that swirling energy with physical exertion and perhaps a curse or several. No, she would descend the curving stone steps to the gardens below, and perhaps head for the maze.

He would follow her and complete his mission; then he would be free of her and could leave London. Though the image of the man who looked like him would haunt him for some time. *She* would haunt him.

He crouched and waited for her to enter the garden before slipping soundlessly from the tree. The grass didn't even rustle as he stepped upon it. Then, he began to stalk her.

Five moved as he had been trained to—as quietly and gracefully as a cat. He removed the spectacles and secured them in his jacket pocket. Without them he could still see very clearly, and the torches along the path ensured that he was able to keep his eye on her with ease. Her gown caught the moonlight, shining like a beacon to guide his way.

Unaware of being followed, the lady moved at a moderate pace. From where he followed, he could hear her swearing, but she said nothing that gave him any insight as to who the man was or why he upset her so.

In the middle of the maze—which his lady found with surprising ease—she stopped near the pond. A statue of Venus stood in the center of the water like a modest maiden caught bathing in the nude. Smooth stones lined the rim of the pool for a pleasing aesthetic—no doubt there were brightly colored exotic fish in there as well. These wealthy sods had the most ridiculous trophies of their importance.

"Do you often attend parties to which you were not invited and follow unsuspecting ladies into dark places?"

Five's head jerked up. His prey was watching him as though she had known he was there all along, which was, of course, impossible.

Wasn't it?

"I would hardly call you unsuspecting," he replied softly. "In fact, I'd wager you're incredibly suspicious of people in general."

Her eyes narrowed. Even in the darkness he could see the odd expression on her face. "It is a flaw, I know, but it has served me well in the past. But then, this isn't the first time you've followed me."

"Surely you knew I'd come for you again."

She inclined her head and regarded him without an ounce of fear. He respected that, despite being irked by it. "The last time I saw you was almost a week ago. I thought perhaps you'd forgotten about me."

Was she actually flirting? He shrugged. He had lost track of the days as he sometimes did when on assignment. Still, it bothered him that he was missing time. "And now I have you."

She smiled at that—an expression he couldn't quite decipher. "You've had me before, sir. Or do you not remember?"

Again that tickle in the back of his brain. An itch he couldn't scratch. "I'm fairly certain you are a woman any man would loathe to forget."

Her smile saddened. "You don't remember."

"Should I?"

"No, I suppose not. Though I have many memories of you."

He walked toward her, slowly—as he might approach a feral cat. Unease tied a knot deep in his belly. "Then you have me at a disadvantage."

"I sincerely doubt that." She sighed. "You obviously followed me for a reason. What is it?"

Now that he was face-to-face with her, he found his readiness to end her life had waned considerably. There were many things he wanted to do to her, but killing her was not one of them. Still, he had no choice.

"You murdered a man who was very important to my employer." There was no need to lie to her—better she know why her life was about to be terminated.

"I'm afraid you're going to have to be more specific than that."

His eyebrow jumped. Was she sincere or mocking him? "You have that much blood on your hands?"

She crossed her arms over her lovely bosom. "I have no trouble sleeping at night."

"It doesn't bother you that Victor Erlich's widow mourns him still?"

She smirked at him. "Erlich wasn't married. Is he what all this fuss is about?"

"You killed him." He wanted to hear her confess to her crime. Surely she knew there would be retribution?

"And now you're here to avenge him, are you?"

Five gave a curt nod. "I'm here to make certain justice is served." So why hadn't he done it already? Why was he standing here waiting for her to tell him what he already knew to be true?

"Hmm. What was he to you?"

"I beg your pardon?"

"Erlich." She took a step toward him. Inexplicably he wanted to take a step backward. "Was he a friend of yours?"

"I didn't really know him." Now who stalked whom?

She came another step closer, but no more, keeping just out of reach. "You did—a long time ago. You once tried to kill him yourself."

Erlich had been part of the Company just as he was. There was no way he could have tried to kill the man. He might not remember his past, but he knew in his heart that he hadn't been without a sense of right and wrong.

"You're fighting for the wrong side, Luke," she told him. "You think you're doing the right thing, but the Company is using you. You're nothing but a weapon to them."

Five's temper flared. The way she spoke—with that sneer in her cultured tones—made him feel like an idiot, but worse, she made him question the only thing he knew and believed in.

No one else had ever inspired doubt in him like this woman did.

He closed the distance between them in the blink of an eye, startling her. "Forgive me," he said.

She fought him. He wouldn't have respected her quite so much if she hadn't. She struck at his face and chest, not with her nails or open palms, but with her fists. The woman knew how to throw a punch.

He wrapped his arms around her, preventing her from hitting him again as the taste of blood filled his mouth. Then she began kicking at his shins, throwing him off balance.

They fell to the damp grass with her on top. He rolled so their positions were reversed. Her legs tangled in her skirts and he held them with his own. He pinned one of her arms above her head with one hand, leaving him only his right to finish the job. Her other arm was pinned between them. Still she writhed and struggled beneath him. There was nothing seductive about her movements, but Five's body reacted as though she lay beneath him willingly.

He was there to kill her and his cock was hard. Christ Almighty, she drove him to depravity. When this was over he'd no doubt feel the shame of it.

"Stop fighting," he commanded. "This will go much easier for both of us if you just give in."

She stilled, and gazed up at him with eyes that were full of disappointment rather than fear. "You're going to kill me."

"I have to," he explained. He shouldn't have to explain; she knew what she had done. "I'm sorry, but you brought this upon yourself."

Her expression hardened. "I never asked Erlich to try to rape me. I never invited him to put a knife to my throat."

Five went very still. There was so much sincerity in her words that for a moment, he almost believed her. "You'd say anything to save your own life."

"I don't have to say anything at all," she retorted through clenched teeth.

Five wrapped his fingers around her throat and squeezed hard. Releasing her wrist, he came up on his knees and straddled her. It would be quicker—more merciful—if he used both hands. Her breath caught and she gasped for air, struggling against him.

Sudden pain bowed his spine. He gasped as his limbs spasmed, snapping his teeth together as his fingers unclenched. His vision blurred. Blood spread its salty copper on his tongue.

What the hell had she done to him? It felt as though he had lightning in his veins. He twitched, eyes rolling back into his head. She'd better kill him, because if he came back from this he was going to come for her again, and next time he would not be so kind as to simply strangle her.

Then lightning struck him again, and he collapsed on top of her as everything went black.

Chapter 5

Had she killed him?

Arden squirmed out from underneath Luke's incredibly—*incredibly*—heavy form. Once, she'd loved the weight of his body on hers, but not like this—not after sending enough electrical current through his body to bring down an elephant. She'd used the same device to kill Victor Erlich. Of course, she'd used considerably less power on her husband.

He hadn't expected her to simply lie there and allow him to kill her, had he? If so, the Company had truly wiped his memory, because he of all people should know that she was nothing if not resourceful.

Now that she had him, what should she do with him? He was extremely heavy—more than he ought to be, so there was no possible way she could haul him to her carriage, or anywhere else for that matter. Even if she could, it was bound to cause a sensation if they were seen.

What if Henry stumbled upon them? The cretin had already spoken to the family solicitors about having Lucas declared dead in absentia. If he saw his brother as he was now, he'd have him declared insane and hauled off to a private asylum, where they would drug Luke enough to quite possibly contain him, and that was if he were lucky. More than likely they'd declare him a traitor and execute him.

It was foolhardy of her, but she paused for a moment as she knelt over her husband's prone body. He wouldn't be unconscious for long, and she should use this time to physically restrain him, but it had been so long since she had had the pleasure of simply looking at his face.

In the misty light his skin had a gothic novel pallor, his hair an inky black. The lines fanning out from his eyes were more numerous than she remembered, but softened in slumber. Below his long nose his wide mouth was bracketed by faint half-moons so sharp and thin they seemed to have been cut by a wicked blade.

Her well-manicured nails dug into her palms as she curled her hands into fists. Which of the Company's butchers was responsible for this? Who dared abuse Luke's mind so thoroughly that they had obliterated all traces of her and their life together?

She'd make something special to torture them with in case their paths ever crossed.

Rising to her feet, she made her way to the fountain on legs that shook more than she would ever admit. He'd frightened her, her husband. The man who had never once lifted a hand to her, who would never dream of harming her, had come so very close to ending her in a most brutal fashion, and didn't seem the least bit concerned about it.

All right, perhaps he'd worn a touch of remorse in his expression, but not much.

To her shame, scalding tears welled in her eyes as she sat down on the rough stone. How could he have forgotten her? Regardless of what the Company did to him, how could he not look at her and know her? She would never have forgotten him, no matter what they did. Was it because of how they'd parted just before he disappeared?

Her shoulders slumped. Forgetting her was the only excuse for not coming home, and the only way she could redeem him in her own eyes and those of the W.O.R. office. The total obliteration of his past would be the only thing to save him from certain death.

Her fingers trembled as she reached inside the low bodice of her gown and pulled a small device from between her breasts. It resembled a tiny, delicate tuning fork, but was so much more. She tapped the prongs against the side of the fountain and lifted the instrument to her mouth as it vibrated in her hand.

"Alastair, I'm in the maze, by the fountain. I need you. Quickly." Then she wrapped her fingers around the prongs, forcing it to go still. Dear Alastair always came when she called. Tonight he was wearing one of the earpieces that went with this particular invention. The auditory amplification fork vibrated at a particular frequency matched by the earpieces, easily carrying the words of the person holding the fork to the person, or persons, with the proper receptors in their ear.

Arden tucked the device into her bodice once more. Then, something made her go completely still—an extra sense, perhaps, or a disturbance in the Aether. Regardless, she raised her head determined not to reveal that her heart now beat furiously in her throat. Lucas was no longer prone on the ground, but standing a few feet away. He wasn't terribly steady on his feet, but the fact that he was up brought a string of curses falling silent from her lips. *Hurry, Alastair*.

She met her husband's glittering gaze and rose slowly to her feet. Did he want to kill her or kiss her? And why did he just stand there? He had been sent to kill her and could have had the job done twice by now, especially since she hadn't been aware of his return to consciousness. He shouldn't have recovered so quickly. Death was far less disturbing than that damn smile on his face. And people said her smile could look mad.

She arched a brow at him as she folded her arms across her chest. "If you're trying to intimidate me, sir, it won't work."

"No," he replied, the word taking the smirk from his lips but not his eyes—nor his tone—"You don't seem the least bit frightened to find me awake and standing here."

"I'm not." This was why her father made the sentimentometer, because she could lie as naturally as breathing.

"You should be." He took a step closer, shearing the distance between them by more than a full foot. Arden stiffened, but didn't flinch. She refused to retreat from him and held her ground even as some small part inside her shrank back. It was the part of her that realized Luke was no longer the man she knew, but a man who had every intention of killing her.

Still, she would not give up hope. After seven years of having nothing but, she would not forsake it now.

Suddenly, his head whipped to the side, eyes narrowing before turning his attention to her once again. "Did you call in reinforcements, my lady?"

Alastair. She could hear his approach as well, God love him.

"Yes," she replied, amazed at just how firm her voice sounded. "Did you believe I'd simply wait for you to wake up and allow you to take another crack at killing me? You had better have your head examined by your physician as soon as possible if so."

He chuckled. "You sound just like a governess I once had." Then he frowned and blinked.

A memory! Arden's heart leaped in joy, despite the comparison that once annoyed her to no end. "Do I?" Rustling leaves heralded Alastair's imminent arrival. Just a few more moments and then they'd have Luke in custody and could set to work fixing what the Company had done to him.

"Yes," he said, closing the distance between them. "You do."

Before she could speak, or even breathe, Arden was hauled against him by a rough hand on her back. He was solid and warm, more muscled than she remembered. Her heart leaped into her throat, but she refused to let fear or any other emotion get the better of her.

His kiss was exactly as she remembered. All doubt vanished as his lips moved against hers in a manner she could only — gleefully — describe as possessive. She would have wrapped her arms around him and returned the kiss with all the longing she'd locked up inside these long, lonely years if he hadn't released her as abruptly as he had grabbed her.

He grinned. "You don't kiss like her, though. Next time I'd like to explore that a little bit further." And then he took off at a dead run that would have made the most spirited of horses envious and leaped over the hedge, disappearing into the night.

No sooner had he vanished than Alastair ran into the clearing, chest heaving. "What happened? Are you hurt?"

"I'm fine. My attacker fled when he heard your approach."

"Where is he?" he demanded, ginger-brown hair whipping about his face as his gray eyes glanced around.

"Gone," she replied, sinking down onto one of the stone benches. She pointed in the direction he'd run. "Don't worry, though, he'll come for me again."

"How do you know?"

He was her husband, that's how she knew. She knew him better than anyone—or rather she *had*.

Instead of saying just that, she touched her fingers to her lower lip, still warm and slightly moist from the kiss. "We have unfinished business, he and I."

In the waning hours before dawn, Five found himself in a pew in the back of a small church constructed of aged stone in varying—but otherwise unimpressive—shades of beige located within the area of the metropolis known as Square Mile—the original city of London.

It was dark inside the church, but the dark didn't bother him as it did most people. When shadows were so thick he could almost touch and taste them—that was when he felt the most at ease. So he didn't mind sitting there alone, though the church interior smelled of burnt candle wax and furniture polish, and he could hear rats scurrying in the corners.

The rats didn't seem to mind him either—a half-feral creature still a little twitchy from whatever Arden Grey had used to incapacitate him.

He had underestimated her—a mistake he would not make again. He was merely fortunate she hadn't decided to put a bullet in him while he was out. Although a bullet would have a hard time making it through his internal armor to pierce anything vital.

Absently, he rubbed his tingling fingers over the back of his other hand, feeling the metal-plated bones beneath. That was what the Company had done for him. Done *to* him. He frowned.

Familiar static crackled in his head. "*Status Report.*"

Five sighed and pinched the bridge of his nose with his thumb and index finger. Was it too much to ask for a moment's peace? He just needed to think, damn it. "It's not done."

A beat of silence. "*That is unaccepteable.*"

Instead of apologizing, or trying to explain, he chose another tactic. "She knows me. How?"

"*She's W.O.R. She's probably seen your file.*"

That could be, but it didn't feel right. "I feel like I know her."

"*Impossible.*"

Inexplicable anger rose within him. "You're lying."

"*You forget yourself.*"

Five laughed humorlessly, slightly mad. Fortunately there was no one else there to witness it. "I have forgotten myself for many years."

"*Do the job.*"

Five didn't reply. He had a mission—one that he had believed in until now. Perhaps the woman was toying with him, using what she knew against him, but that didn't explain the man whose face had been so much like his. There were things going on that the Company didn't know.

Or didn't want him to find out.

"*Five?*"

"She got the best of me with some sort of weapon. Next time I will not fail."

"*See that you don't.*"

The static gave way to the telltale click before he could tell the bastard to go shag himself.

He slumped in the pew, and leaned back against the hard wood, closing his eyes. He would kill Arden Grey, but he was going to get a few questions answered first. She knew who he was, and that put him at a disadvantage.

Her face was so clear in his mind, flawless and sad. Why did she seem so sad when she looked at him? Fear and anger he could understand, but not such sadness. The memory of her tears brought a viselike tightness to his throat.

Tears? His eyes snapped open. She hadn't cried to-night. She hadn't been wearing a peach gown either, but he could see her so clearly in his mind, tears trickling down her cheeks as she stood before him in a soft peach gown. She looked younger as well.

A memory. He did know her, or at least he had at one time. Turning his mind to trying to figure out how was pointless. He'd lost the moment, and trying to force it only made his head hurt.

Still, it was something. He would make the woman explain it to him the next time he came for her. She would tell him the truth before he took her life.

"You're certain it was Huntley?"

Arden snatched the tumbler of whiskey from Alastair's hand. They were at her house, in the library. "Now that I think about it, no. In fact, I'm quite certain it was Disraeli."

He grimaced at her sarcasm. "It's been seven years, Arden."

She downed the contents of her glass in one swallow. Oh, that lovely burn. It tasted like more. "You think I don't remember my husband's face? His voice? It was him, Alastair. Quite frankly I would expect you to be a bit happier at the news."

It was a low blow and she knew it. She knew how Alastair felt about her, though neither of them had spoken of it. In truth, she'd been too much of a coward. His friendship meant too much to her to risk losing it, so she pretended not to notice how he looked at her, pretended not to understand the things he sometimes said.

Now he looked at her with so many mixed emotions in his gray eyes she had to turn her head. "If Huntley is alive, Arden, there is no one who will be happier than me, save you." He spoke with such conviction that she knew he truly meant it. Alastair was one of those rare people who really possessed a noble and honorable heart.

A better woman would have handed him her own heart years ago, but Arden had never quite managed it. He deserved one without prior claim, one free to be given wholly.

"It was him," she said, forcing herself to meet his gaze. Shamefully, tears blurred her vision. "Oh, Alastair. It was Luke, and he tried to kill me." Her voice broke on a sob as she turned away, pressing the back of her hand to her mouth as hot wetness poured down her cheeks.

Damn and blast. She wasn't one of those women who cried all the bloody time. Were the situation reversed she doubted Luke would stand here bawling over her. Yet there was no denying her emotions. She'd dare Queen Victoria herself to remain stoic after facing death at the hands of the man she'd pledged her life and heart to.

Although Prince Albert was more machine than man now, so perhaps her majesty could relate entirely.

Warm fingers took the glass from her other hand. There was a soft thud as it was set aside, and then strong arms encircled her. Like a child she crumpled against the solid wall of his chest, grasping at his lapels as though they were the last vestiges of her pride.

He smelled like bay rum and male, with a sweet hint of pipe tobacco. Inexplicably, the feel of his hands on her back made it seem as though it was going to be all right. If she raised her head she knew he would kiss her. She also knew that kiss would provide ample distraction, give her something to lose herself in, but ultimately would do nothing more than hurt one of her dearest friends and make a mockery of her wedding vows.

And her husband trying to choke her to death hadn't?

Sniffing, Arden pulled away, smoothing her hands

over the marks her fingers had left in the lapels of his jacket. "Forgive me," she murmured, voice a horrid nasal thrum.

A handkerchief appeared before her blurry gaze. She took it gratefully and wiped her eyes. Then, because it could not be ignored, she also blew her nose. Her spaniel, Beauregard, who had been sleeping on a nearby chair, looked up at the noise.

"Please don't give it back," came Alastair's low, gravelly voice.

She laughed—not just because of the expression of mock horror on his face, but because Alastair always made her laugh. "I imagine there are scads of formerly distressed damsels across Europe who have one of these squirreled away in their lingerie drawers."

"They are legion," he replied drily. Then he grabbed the bottle of whiskey from the cabinet and poured her another glass. "Come, sit with me. Tell me everything."

Arden tucked the damp linen into her sleeve and followed him to the sofa.

He did not attempt to hold her, which said more for his character than any daring rescue or dangerous intrigue he'd orchestrated on behalf of the Wardens. He was not one to take advantage of a situation—or put either of them at risk of doing something they'd both regret. He thought too much of her—and too much of himself.

She told him about waking up to find Lucas in her room the night of the murder at Hammond & Sons, and about the poppy in the carriage, and finally how she'd gone out for a bit of air that evening suspecting that he might come for her again. Hoping that he might. The only thing she didn't tell him was about the kiss—not because she didn't wish to hurt him, but because that was private.

When she finished, Arden found Alastair watching

her with a deep frown on his lightly tanned face. "Mind control," he muttered. "Christ Jesus."

"You believe me?" How incredulous she sounded—pathetically so.

He nodded. "I don't want to, but I'd be a fool to do otherwise. I'd rather suspect the Company of doing the impossible than dismiss the notion and end up buggered."

Unlike Inspector Grant, Alastair did not apologize for his choice of words. Then again, he knew Arden could turn a coarse phrase when she wished.

"What do I do?" she asked.

"What do *we* do," he corrected her, pouring a drink for himself as well. "I'm not about to let you go through this alone—Huntley either, for that matter."

Her shoulders slumped with great relief. To have him believe her meant more than she could ever hope to articulate. "All right then, what are we going to do?"

"If he's been sent here to kill you, he's obviously going to try again to complete his mission. We will have to set a trap."

A frown pulled at Arden's brows. "He's strong, Alastair. Unnaturally so. I think he could have snapped my neck with one hand. And he's heavy—more so than a man his size ought to be."

Her friend did not seem surprised by this. "They've undoubtedly augmented him, probably with internal armor and metal plating on some of his bones. We've had success with it recently on some of our own agents as well."

With that statement the pair of them directed their attention at Alastair's right hand. It looked relatively normal except for the scars. His hand had been crushed several years ago. Dr. Evelyn Stone operated, laboriously replacing and reinforcing his bones with metal—

even the joints were delicate and complicated hinges. Arden knew this because she constructed those joints and assisted the smithy in forging the new bones. It had taken hours for Evie to work around the tendons and muscle, but the end result was that Alastair possessed a hand that was incredibly strong and dexterous.

"Isn't the procedure dangerous?" she asked, even though she knew the answer.

He nodded. "If Huntley survived it, no wonder they altered his mind as well. They wouldn't want to risk losing him—he's too powerful a weapon."

A human-automaton hybrid. Arden shuddered at the thought. She was all for the progression of science, but there were some things that seemed wrong—even to her. Saving Alastair's hand was one thing, but filling a man full of metal in order to make him a more efficient warrior was quite another.

Arden raised her glass to her lips and drank. Soon her muscles would become wonderfully languid and she would go to bed, slipping into a dreamless sleep. "We'd better make certain it's a good trap, then. If we fail it could end up costing both our lives."

"Do you own a pistol?" he asked.

"You know I have several."

"Keep one beside your bed—within easy reach. I'll be by in the morning. I believe I know exactly how to capture our boy without harming him."

Hope blossomed in Arden's chest. She reached across the short distance between them and took Alastair's scarred hand in her own. "Thank you."

His fingers curled around hers. She watched as he swallowed, a frown marring his brow. "You do realize that if the Company has tampered with his mind he may not be the man you married. He may never be that man again."

The truth was a hard and bitter lump in her throat. "I know."

He squeezed her fingers, his gray gaze strangely vulnerable. "I want you to know that I'm here if ever you have need of me, no matter what the circumstances. Or the need."

Oh *no*. No, after all these years don't let him do this now. "Alastair—"

She swallowed the rest of her words as his mouth claimed hers. It was a passionate kiss—one that should have weakened her knees and dropped her drawers—but she felt nothing, nothing but the horrid guilt of wondering what she had ever done to win his regard.

He released her, a flush across the top of his high cheekbones, regret dimming his gaze. "I should apologize, but I won't. If Huntley is back I know I'll never have another chance to kiss you again. I couldn't let the opportunity slip away."

Arden opened her mouth, but the words got tangled up in her tongue and refused to come out.

"Not a word," he said, rising to his feet. "We can pretend this never happened if you like, and I will do whatever you ask of me where your husband is concerned. He was my best friend and I will do everything in my power to reunite the two of you."

"Why?" she demanded, finally finding her voice.

The twist of his lips could hardly be called a smile, for it was completely void of humor. "Because I love you, Arden. That's why." Then he turned on his heel and strode from the room, leaving her reaching for the bottle of whiskey.

Chapter 6

Arden had been asleep for a grand total of four hours when someone knocked on her door. Loudly.

"What?" she yelled, stomach and bed rolling as though on the open sea. Most people would swear to never drink again at this point. Arden knew better than to make such empty promises.

The door opened. In the predawn gloom her bleary eyes made out the silhouette of Mrs. Bird. The older woman was in her nightclothes and cap. "I'm terribly sorry, my lady, but there's a gentleman here—"

Arden bolted upright, swallowing hard to keep her stomach where it ought to be. "Is he from the sanitorium?" Had her mother had another apoplexy, or worse?

The housekeeper's expression could only be described as sympathetic—perhaps with a little indulgence tossed in. "No, ma'am. He says Inspector Grant sent him."

Damn and blast. Another murder. "Tell him I will be down directly."

The older woman nodded, then hesitated. "Do you . . . do you require any assistance, Lady Huntley?"

Arden's lips twisted, her expression as unsteady and brittle as her constitution. "You're a love, Mrs. Bird. Take yourself back to bed. I can look after myself."

The housekeeper didn't look as though she believed that last part, but she dipped a curtsy and left the room. Arden crawled out of bed and staggered to the wardrobe. She used her nightgown as a chemise and pulled a gown of thin russet suede over her head. It had a built-in corset that laced in the front. She didn't bother with stockings, just shoved her feet into matching boots. Her head swam as she fumbled with the laces.

She had passed out with her hair up, so she didn't have to tend to that. She was a little steadier on her feet as she walked to the door. She opened it to find Mrs. Bird on the other side holding a glass of cloudy liquid.

"Your tonic, my lady. I thought you might have a need."

"You deserve a raise in wages, Mrs. Bird."

The woman's plump cheeks dimpled. "Indeed, ma'am. Drink up now."

Arden took the glass and downed as much as she could in one swallow. It was foul stuff, but it worked.

Another long swallow. With a grimace, she handed the empty glass back to her housekeeper. "Thank you."

"If I might be so bold, I worry about you, my lady."

Arden stifled an unladylike belch and brought her hand up to clap the other woman's shoulder. "I worry about me too, my dear Mrs. Bird. I will endeavor to alleviate both of our concerns in the future."

Mrs. Bird didn't look as though she believed that any more than Arden did. Arden took her carpetbag from where it sat beside the door and crossed the threshold.

Inspector Grant's man waited for her in the hall at the bottom of the stairs. He removed his cap when he saw her. "Beg your pardon, Lady Huntley. Inspector Grant bade me to tell you he wouldn't have sent for you at such an ungodly hour if he didn't have need of you."

"No need to apologize, sir. Let us not keep the inspector waiting any longer." She took a cape from the closet and allowed the young man to place it around her shoulders before leaving the house.

The police carriage was horse-driven—real horses, not automaton. Good lord, it was going to take forever to get where they were going. At least she would be as sober as she was likely to get by the time they reached the scene.

Thankfully the officer sat up front with the driver, leaving Arden alone in the coach. She rested her head on the hard cushions and closed her eyes, letting the tonic do its work. By the time the ill-sprung, rickety vehicle hobbled to a full stop she was as much herself as she could be.

She didn't wait for someone to open the door for her—it seemed such a silly thing given the circumstances. The steps weren't equipped to automatically drop, so she gave them a nudge with her boot and then descended to the damp pavement.

It had begun to rain since she left the house—and this time Mrs. Bird hadn't thought to make her take her umbrella. At least her cape would save her gown from ruin. She slipped the hood up over her head and trotted after the officer who guided her to where Inspector Grant waited. She had to dodge puddles already forming on the uneven cobblestones.

She didn't know where she was exactly. Given the direction in which they'd traveled and the smell, she guessed they were near the docks. Daylight was a sliver of gray on the horizon, but already there was activity around a few of the warehouses. The workers and middle classes were coming to life just as the upper and lower levels of society were going to bed.

Or being yanked out of them whilst still somewhat inebriated, as the case might be.

"Lady Huntley," the inspector said, doffing his hat. "My apologies for the hour, but we have a situation much like what we had at Hammond's, and I need your expertise."

Arden met his gaze from beneath her hood. "You want to know if it's the same man."

"Yes, ma'am."

She straightened her shoulders as rain pelted her back. Her cloak would be covered with dots of grime when it dried—the air down here was thick and sticky with coal dust, coal being a cheaper method of generating the heat needed to create steam than the gas and oil used in better neighborhoods. "You'd better take me to her then, Inspector Grant." Her stomach recoiled at the thought, but duty took precedence over the fact that she'd felt compelled to drink herself stupid over Alastair's kiss and declaration.

He led her to a narrow alley between two ancient buildings that seemed to have nothing more than spite holding them upright. There, on the worn stones, lay the body of a woman, already wet with her own blood. The rain and filth of the alley only served to spread the crimson stain throughout her clothing and skin.

It was not as bad as the girl at the factory, but bad enough. This woman—and she was just barely one at that—had been slit from belly to throat, her petticoats thrown up around her thighs.

Her stockings had been mended more times than Arden could count, and her petticoats—a dull gray beneath the faded, and too-short blue gown—were patched and frayed. Whatever sorrows and trials life had thrown her, poverty was not one Arden knew except by sight. It was a fact for which she was entirely grateful. How sad to have to sell oneself and still not have enough to purchase tooth powder or a bar of soap.

She crouched beside the body to get a better look, lifted the petticoats with one gloved hand, and saw a glint of thick moisture on the girl's thigh. Men were so free with the stuff. She'd seen it all manner of surprising places and locales. How unfortunate that there wasn't a way to trace the ejaculate to the man. They'd take care where they left it then.

"Did you rearrange her clothing, Inspector?" she asked, darting a quick glance at Grant.

He bobbed his head in a curt nod. "She may have been a dollymop, but she deserves a bit of dignity."

"You dear man." Obviously she was still a little drunk, but the compliment was deserved no matter how much it embarrassed either of them. "He used her then, before he killed her."

"I hope it was before," one of the younger officers commented.

Grant chastised the boy for speaking so in front of Arden, but she called him off. "I hope so, too," she agreed, before turning her attention back to Grant. "Did Dr. Stone deduce that there had been sexual congress with the Lynbourne girl?"

The older man gave a curt nod, his sharp gaze on the young officer. The poor thing was going to get a serious talking-to later, Arden suspected.

"No wonder you asked for me. The murder is very similar to that at Hammond's."

"Except this poor thing was a far cry from a debu-tante," Grant added.

"Indeed. Well, let's find out, shall we?" She opened her bag and removed her gear.

"Excuse me, Inspector?" One of the officers stood at the entry to the alley. "We have a potential witness, sir. I thought you might like to speak to her."

Grant turned to Arden. "Do you have need of me here, my lady?"

"None at all," she replied, slipping on her spectacles. In fact she preferred to do this sort of thing as privately as possible. She never knew what she was going to see or how it was going to affect her.

Three minutes later she was on her hands and knees retching against the wall of the alley. What had happened to this woman had been awful—some of the most vile images she'd ever had scorched into her mind.

Arden slowly pushed herself up so that she knelt in the alley. Rain dripped from the edge of her hood onto her face, and she welcomed its chill. Her hands shook as she removed the apparatus from the prostitute's head and returned it to her bag. Whoever had killed her was indeed a monster, but not the same monster who'd killed Baron Lynbourne's daughter. This man hadn't worn fancy clothes, and he was missing his front teeth.

And he'd raped her while he killed her—used her in so many awful ways before making the brutal cut. Then he'd delivered his final insult by spending himself on her leg after he was done, as her life flowed across the dirty stones.

A shadow moved across the alley as the lazy fingers of a wet dawn slowly crept in. Arden glanced up, expecting to see Inspector Grant.

Instead she saw a dirty man in need of a shave and a dentist. Her heart stopped at the sight of him. She knew him. She had seen him just a few moments ago through the prostitute's eyes.

Frantically, she groped for the pistol she always carried in her bag. The killer came at her fast. For a second she was too terrified to scream, her mind flashing through the gruesome catalog the woman's eyes had given her. Her normal calm, or facsimile of it, disintegrated like sugar into tea as his filthy hands reached for her. She opened her mouth . . .

There was a snap, and the killer crumpled to the ground beside his victim, his head turned at an impossible angle, sightless eyes bulging and wide.

She might have felt relief if she hadn't looked up and met her husband's bright gaze.

There were few people who could manage to look imposing and dangerous—and altogether too gorgeous—when dripping wet, but Lucas was one of them.

Inky hair fell over his forehead as water trickled down the lean planes of his face. Shadows deepened the lines around his eyes and mouth, made the grim smile on his lips all the more frightening.

Rain poured off the long leather coat that hung from the strong breadth of his shoulders—exaggerated by the leanness of the rest of his frame. He crouched before her, paying no attention to the body of the prostitute or the man he had just killed with the apparent ease of swatting a bug.

"What is it about you that makes people want you dead?" he asked, eyes glinting unnaturally bright in the gray morning.

Arden's fingers closed around the pistol in her bag. Now that the first threat to her safety was gone, she wasn't about to let this one get the better of her. "Part of my charm, I suppose." He chuckled and she added, "Why didn't you let him? He would have done the job for you."

His gaze locked with hers, and what she saw there sent a shiver down her spine. "You're mine," he growled.

"Yours to kill, you mean." It was tempting to let him do it. She didn't want to die, but the thought of him being able to kill her . . . Well, what was the point of going on when so much of her life had been about him and he was lost forever?

She needed a drink, or perhaps a good slap.

His hand came up, and she fought a flinch. Instead of grabbing her already bruised throat, he cupped her cheek. She had the pistol out of the bag.

"Are you going to shoot me?" he asked with a smile, fingers rough against her skin. "Do you think a bullet can stop me?"

Arden placed the end of the barrel against the underside of his chin. "I doubt they thought to armor you here."

He grinned, white teeth flashing in the fading gloom. "That's my girl."

She froze, gaze searching his face for some sign of recognition. "How do you know I'm your girl?"

His grin faded, the light in his eyes turned to ice. He dropped his hand to her neck, but instead of squeezing, he gently stroked the tender and battered skin. "I don't know. But you are, aren't you?"

God, it hurt to swallow; her throat was so tight—a condition that had nothing to do with the strength of his touch, but rather the gentleness of it. "Yes," she whispered, but she did not move the pistol.

His dark brows dipped. "Why can't I kill you? I remember . . . I know I've tried to do this before, but failed. I resolve to do it, but when I'm with you, killing you is the last thing I want to do."

The suggestive timbre of his voice ignited a flame inside her. It had been so long, but intimately she remembered all the times he had spoken to her in that tone—and what generally followed.

She opened her mouth. It was simple. All she had to say was "I'm your wife," but the words refused to come. What if she said it and he couldn't remember?

"Lady Huntley?" came a voice from the mouth of the alley. It was Inspector Grant.

Her husband sprang to his feet, leaving her mourning the warmth of his touch. "I'll come for you again," he promised her.

"I'd be disappointed if you didn't," she retorted coolly. Inside she trembled like a child.

She watched in awe as he scaled the side of one of the buildings using only the structure's windows and ledges for purchase. He climbed like a spider.

Inspector Grant rushed to her side. "Good Lord, what happened?"

Of course he would notice the new body in the alley— and the strange man fleeing the scene.

Arden's shoulders slumped. "The dead man is our murderer. He attacked me."

"The other bloke killed him?"

She nodded, numb.

"Broke the bastard's neck. Can't say that I'm sorry— though I'm going to have the head of one of my good-for-nothing constables for not being here to protect you. I should like to shake your rescuer's hand."

Something snapped inside her and laughter rushed forth like water over a broken dam. She felt like death warmed over; she'd just seen a vicious crime through the eyes of the victim, been attacked by the murderer and then saved by the man she loved who also wanted to kill her. And dear Inspector Grant wanted to shake Luke's hand.

What else could possibly happen next?

Alastair was waiting for her in the parlor, enjoying a cup of coffee, when she arrived home. It was the perfect continuation of the day, and exactly in keeping with Arden's opinion that fate was out to give her a royally good spanking.

He looked perfect, as he generally did. His steely gray
frock coat matched his eyes, and his ivory shirt warmed his
complexion. He might have at least had the courtesy to
look a little worse for wear, but then again he hadn't been
the one trying to drown himself in a bottle of whiskey.

His eyes widened at the sight of her. "You look awful."

The insult lessened the guilt she felt over his earlier
declaration of love. "How terribly convenient, seeing as
that's exactly how I feel."

Others might have flushed at her words, but Alastair
merely raised one cinnamon brow as he set his cup on
the table in front of him. "Imbibed a bit too much last
night, did you?"

"A tad," she replied with forced lightness.

He knew why—it was plain as the knot in his cravat.
The bounder didn't even have the decency to apologize
for admitting his feelings and ruining what, for Arden,
had been a perfectly lovely friendship.

Of course she'd gotten cross-eyed drunk after he left.
Her dearest friend loved her, and she was in no way de-
serving of that love. Lord, she was a proper mess. She
loved a man who wanted to kill her. She worked for the
government because her husband and father had, not
because she particularly enjoyed the work. She hadn't
even been a decent enough wife to pop out an heir
within the first year of marriage.

And then there was the fact that there was a very
good chance she might lose her mind one day, as her
mother had done and was still doing.

"Would you care to join me for breakfast, Alastair?"
she asked. Self-pity and a good brush with death did
wonders for the appetite.

He nodded and rose to his feet. "Mrs. Bird said you
were out with Grant. Was there another murder?"

Arden took his arm as he offered it, and shamefully leaned on him a little as they left the room. She stifled a yawn. "Yes, but not by our factory killer."

"You don't have to go every time he whistles, you know. I know Dhanya assigned you to Scotland Yard, but let the fellow solve his own bloody crimes once in a while."

"He wouldn't have sent for me if he hadn't believed the murders might be connected."

"Are you all right?"

Telling him about Luke sat on the tip of her tongue. She wanted very badly to tell him everything about that morning, but if she did he might see Luke as a threat and not be so keen to help her capture him. He would try to protect her, and that was the last thing she wanted right now. He couldn't be her hero anymore—that was her husband's job.

If he didn't kill her first.

"No," she replied honestly. "I'm not all right. But I will be after some coffee and eggs." That was true as well, to an extent. Physically she would feel better, and that would have to do for now.

"Did you bring the device?" she inquired as they ate. Mrs. Bird had set an extra place at the table upon Alastair's arrival, and the two of them sat across from each other at the breakfast nook in the Egyptian drawing room. They had done this before: taken breakfast together. It had never bothered her before, but now she was aware of the intimacy of the act and it shamed her.

How could Alastair have possibly fallen in love with her? It was such a ridiculous notion. Her, of all people. Lord, imagine the freckled little ginger children they'd produce!

He nodded as he smeared peach jam on his toast.

"Yes. I had the footmen take it up to your rooms when I learned you weren't at home."

"Why would you do that?" It came out a bit more suspicious than she intended, but he'd turned her upside down with his declaration, and things that would never have bothered her before suddenly seemed to take on much more meaning. Having something taken to her private rooms was so improper now that Luke was home. Now that Alastair had betrayed her by admitting his feelings aloud.

Nonplussed, Alastair took a bite of toast. He chewed and swallowed, forcing her to sit and wait for his answering, her embarrassment growing with every second. "Because I assume that's where Huntley will come for you, where he believes you to be the most vulnerable."

"Is that where you would choose to attack a woman, in her bed?"

He took a sip of coffee and slowly returned the cup to the table. Then he turned those damned stormy eyes of his to her, seeming to look right to the heart of her. "You're angry with me because of last night. I understand that, but I'm not the man who tried to kill you, Arden. If you expect me to apologize for that you will be sorely disappointed."

Arden massaged her forehead with her fingers, eyes closed in shame. "Forgive me, Alastair. I am a proper wretch this morning."

A slim smile curved his lips. "You are most mornings."

Despite herself and the day she'd already had, though it wasn't yet nine o'clock, a snort of laughter burst out of her. She reached across and wrapped her fingers around his with a gentle squeeze. "You're my dearest friend, Alastair."

Something flickered in the depth of his eyes. Pain—she'd seen enough of the emotion to recognize it. It disappeared as quickly as it had come. He turned his hand palm up so that he could squeeze her fingers in turn. "You've been mine as well. I will miss our friendship."

Arden straightened, heart sputtering. "Are you going somewhere?" Surely he wasn't going to run away just because she couldn't love him in the way he wanted?

"No," he replied with a hint of sadness. "But we won't be able to carry on like this once Huntley returns."

"Why won't we?" she demanded, pulling her hand away. Why did he have to continue bringing up these oh-so-vexing truths?

He fixed her with a stalwart gaze. "Because I have my pride. And because I will not play a part in making one of my oldest friends seem a cuckold." At her outraged scoff he added, "You must know there's been gossip about us, Arden. Even you, with your head filled with books and machines."

She did know, but she had ignored it because she hadn't wanted to lose him. He was her rock, the thing she'd clung to ever since Luke's disappearance. He had given her focus. Given her hope. As Luke's friend it had been as if she still had a piece of her husband with her.

To her great shame, tears sprang to her eyes. They would not have dared appear if she'd been at her best. "I've used you most terribly, Alastair."

He rose from his chair and came down on one knee beside hers. "You haven't done anything I haven't allowed you to do. No need for tears, love. Not for me."

That only made the hot wet pour all the harder down her cheeks. She threw her arms around his neck and buried her face in his shoulder.

"All right," Alastair murmured, planting a kiss on her forehead as he rubbed her back. "Go ahead and cry it all out then. . . . Jesus Christ!"

Arden jumped out of his arms. "What?" she asked. He

was already on his feet, face white as he moved to the window.

"Alastair? What was it?"

He turned his head toward her, steely eyes bright with shock. "Huntley," he rasped. "I swear to God it was Huntley."

Who the hell was he? Five raged as he tore through the streets of Mayfair on his velocycle. Who was the bastard who had the nerve to put his hands on *his* woman? And why had the sight of the two of them embracing—the man consoling her—felt like a blade in his heart?

It had felt like a betrayal, and that stunned him into stupidity. He never should have allowed himself to be seen. Now the man knew he was watching Lady Huntley, and that made him inconvenient. He'd rather not kill any more people than he had to, and instinct told him the man would not be easy to take down—not like the miscreant in the alley that morning.

Five should have let the greasy bastard do his job for him, but the thought of those dirty hands around Arden Grey's throat filled him with a deep, inexplicable rage. He told himself she was destined to die by his hand, but he hadn't allowed that to happen either. The perfect opportunity to snuff out the light in her eyes, and he hadn't been able to do it.

Why? He'd never failed in a task before. It wasn't because he was attracted to her. He had been attracted to other women as well, but if one of them betrayed him he'd snap her like a twig. What made this hungover, auburn-haired wench different?

Why had the sight of her in that man's arms, in that house, made his chest tight? Never in a million years would he have thought Alastair capable of such a betrayal.

Alastair?

The two-wheeled machine beneath him swerved suddenly. He had to jerk on the steering bars to avoid hitting a steam carriage. The driver yelled obscenities at him, but they barely registered in Five's mind. He drove the cycle down the street to his lodgings, parked and took the stairs to his rooms two at a time. His mind raced, a pulse pounding in his temple as he held on to the memory and struggled for more.

The man's name was Alastair. He was the Earl of Wolfred. He was three and thirty, the same as Five. They had been at school together. That's where they became friends. Alastair had stood with him when he married . . .

Pain split his skull, lancing deep into his brain. He stumbled into his room, barely slamming the door before his vision blurred and black swarmed the edge of his mind. He couldn't see his bride's face through the agony.

Her face was what brought the agony—he knew this. He fought to remember her even as his stomach threatened to empty itself and his body trembled. He knew this pain; it was as familiar as an old friend. This was like what the Doctor did to him when he visited, only he hadn't remembered it until now.

He wasn't supposed to remember. Someone had taken his memories away. Taken away his identity, his life.

They had taken away his wife.

Five's knees slammed into the floor, splintering the wood. He crawled across the worn rug, every inch bringing his skull that much closer to exploding. Her laughter rang in his ears, loud and unrestrained. Her skin had felt like a mix of silk and velvet. He remembered once she had tasted of peaches, and she smelled . . . she smelled of bergamot.

Something broke inside his mind. He felt it give like a

string pulled too taut. His temple struck the floor as he collapsed, and he lay there unable to move or make a sound—scarcely able to breathe. His ear felt ticklish and warm. Probably blood.

Darkness took hold and shook him like a dog with a rag doll. His last thought before letting that darkness take him was that Arden Grey smelled of bergamot as well.

Chapter 7

Henry arrived at four—just in time for tea. Arden was in her workshop, thoroughly distracted by a new invention that combined Mr. Tesla's work and her father's research in sending and tracking Aether wave transmissions. She had just attached the small mechanism to Beauregard's collar when Mrs. Bird knocked to tell her of her brother-in-law's arrival.

Arden was tempted to tell Mrs. Bird to turn him away, but they needed to speak. "Put him in the library, Mrs. Bird. We'll take tea there." The library was where she felt the most secure—other than her workshop, and she'd be buggered if she'd let Henry see the inside of her sanctuary. Books bored Henry, whose interests were of a more physical, to the hounds, sort of bent. Luke had been the same to an extent, but he'd never made her feel like an oddity because of her interests.

After wiping them on a small towel, she applied cream to her hands. Then she removed her apron and smoothed her hair. Henry already thought her half mad;

there was no need to strengthen that notion by cultivating the appearance of a harridan.

Beauregard, having none of her insecurities or vanity, ran from the room on his short legs, his entire hindquarters wagging in anticipation of the tummy scratching "Uncle" Henry was certain to perform. For as long as she'd known him, Henry preferred animals to people — or at least he preferred them to her. He hadn't thought much of his older brother marrying the daughter of a practically impoverished baronet. The former Lord Huntley—her father-in-law—had decreed that there were some connections worth more than money, such as Sir Frederick's political and government cronies within the W.O.R. To be honest, there had been moments when she wondered if that was why Luke married her, but she knew it was rubbish. He'd loved her. She was certain of it—even if his brother thought he was "settling."

Before she left the workshop, she couldn't help but check the small viewer on the workbench. A thrill raced through her as she saw the small dot of light moving up the screen. The device worked! Using radio waves she was able to track the dog's movements. While it wasn't sophisticated enough to show her the best path to take, it was better than nothing. She would have to check it to make certain it did indeed have the correct location, and if that worked she could take it to Dhanya. Surely this sort of apparatus would be useful to the Wardens.

And perhaps, in their gratitude, they would go easy on her husband. The idea of what they might do to him if they suspected him of treason . . . Well, there was no point in worrying about that now. It only made her snappy and short of breath, neither trait one she desired to exhibit in front of her brother-in-law.

Her stride was quick as she walked down the stairs. Her boot heels clicked loudly on the polished floor of the open hall, sharp and rapid. Her jaw began to ache, it was clenched so tight. This was what Henry did to her. He did it to her at the party the night Lucas tried to strangle her. In fact, she would rather go up against her physically enhanced, murderous-minded spouse right now than his younger brother.

It wasn't that she didn't like Henry. Once upon a time she quite adored him, but that was before Lucas disappeared, and Henry reverted to thinking ill of her. Before he started talking of having his brother declared legally dead so that he could fully assume the title of Earl Huntley rather than continue on as proxy. He treated her servants as his own, came to call whenever he pleased, and considered allowing her to remain at the house a gesture of his generosity.

It was enough to make her former adoration turn rancid. Never mind that she was probably unfair toward him in her estimation of his motives and assessment of his behavior, he was still *wrong*. She strode into the library with every intention of telling him just that.

Mrs. Bird, invaluable housekeeper as she was, had arranged for extra tea, sandwiches and cake to be delivered to the library. Normally Arden took tea alone, so the extra food must have been taken from what would normally be shared by the servants. Henry had better eat it then, if her household had to go without because of his uninvited arse.

Make that uninvited *arses*, she corrected as she crossed the threshold. Not only was Henry there, but he had brought a guest as well, an average-looking man of just-above-average height whom she recognized as Mr. Kirkpatrick, the family solicitor. How dare Henry ambush her like this! Luckily she hadn't had any liquor to drink—that would have made her relaxed, and she needed to be sharp right now.

Arden smiled, well aware it was probably more a baring of teeth than anything remotely pleasant. "My dear Henry, how lovely to see you. Mr. Kirkpatrick, this is an unexpected surprise; it has been too long."

The solicitor, gentleman that he was, cast an uncomfortable and somewhat tense glance at Henry. "Apologies, Lady Huntley. I thought you expected us this afternoon."

Watching Henry squirm afforded more pleasure than it ought. "Well, it is nice to see you all the same, sir. Will you sit? My cook makes an incomparable tea."

Mr. Kirkpatrick smiled and inclined his head. "How could I refuse? Thank you."

Arden's own smile faded as she turned to her brother-in-law. "Henry. Sit."

He had the good grace to look uncomfortable as he resumed his seat. He might not have much in the way of love for her, but he was intimidated by her all the same. Arden seated herself on the settee where she would be better able to play hostess, but also where she would be the most comfortable.

She poured three cups of tea, added the requested milk and sugar and prepared plates for herself and her callers. It might be petty but she resented having to wait upon them when they were there to make her life difficult. They made small talk as she went through this ritual. Then, when they all had refreshment at hand, she asked, "To what do I owe the pleasure of this visit?"

The solicitor cleared his throat. "Lady Huntley, Lord Henry has asked me to begin proceedings to have Lord Huntley declared dead in absentia."

"Has he?" She shot a dark glance at Henry, who met her gaze with a defiant lift of his chin. "Well, I'm afraid he brought you here for nothing, Mr. Kirkpatrick. You see, my husband isn't dead."

"My dear Arden," Henry began with a sigh, "I know you loved my brother, and your devotion does you credit, but it's been seven years. You can no longer maintain this pathetic obsession."

Pathetic? Oh, he was fortunate she didn't have her discombobulator on her. She'd send enough electricity through him to singe his hair. He'd have a hard time of looking like a dandy then, when all that pomade caught fire.

"It's not 'pathetic,' Henry. It's true. Lucas is in London. I've seen him several times." She hadn't meant to reveal all so soon, nor in this blunt manner, but he gave her no choice. He was going to have Lucas declared legally dead, and she couldn't allow that to happen, no matter whether her husband remembered himself or not.

The color ran from Henry's face. Mr. Kirkpatrick leaned forward, as though a closer inspection of her person might make her words more clear. "You've seen him, my lady?"

"Yes."

"Where?" Henry demanded. Blood had returned to his upper extremities and now his cheeks were positively florid.

"Here," Arden replied. "Outside the party the other night, and elsewhere in London."

"It wasn't him." Henry shook his head most vigorously. "It couldn't have been him. You are mistaken, Arden. Your grief makes you see what your heart wishes were true."

While his heart made him fervently deny it, she realized his own desire to see his brother again. Immediately her animosity toward him eased. Perhaps he found it

easier to insist that Lucas was dead than torture himself
with hope as she had all these years.

She wanted to scream that she'd been right from the
bloody rafters. All of London pitied her, thought her
touched in the head, and she had been *right*!

"It *is* true," she insisted—gently. "Lord Wolfred saw
him as well, earlier today."

The poor thing looked as though she had tossed tea
in his face. She would hug him if she weren't still
miffed.

"This certainly changes things," Mr. Kirkpatrick surmised, clearly thrown off-kilter. He probably didn't have
clients come back from the dead very often. "Do you
suppose Lord Wolfred would be willing to discuss the
encounter with me?"

"I do not see why not." Arden smiled at the man, but
she knew what he was thinking. If Lucas had returned to
England why was he not in this house, with his wife? His
gentlemanly ways kept him from asking in front of
Henry, but the solicitor would have many questions for
her in the near future.

"My brother is not alive," Henry maintained rather
heatedly. "I would know if he was alive."

Arden felt for him, she truly did. "He is, Henry."

"No!" He leaped to his feet, cheeks afire and eyes
blazing. "If Lucas was alive he would be here with you.
With me!"

Slowly, she rose as well, watching him as she would a
growling dog. "I promise you he is alive."

"Then why isn't he here? Why haven't I seen him?"

She stilled, and cast a glance at Mr. Kirkpatrick out of
the corner of her eye. She didn't want to have this conversation in front of the man who held her husband's
fate in his hands. "I'm sure he would be if he could." She

gave him what she hoped was a meaningful look. He knew his brother worked for the W.O.R.—it had been a point of contention between them. Henry didn't think Luke should put himself in harm's way when he had a responsibility to his family.

Henry shook his head. "I don't believe it." A hiccough of laughter escaped him. "I don't *believe* it."

At this point, Arden decided the best course of action was to keep her silence. Mr. Kirkpatrick, however, chose the alternative. "I think perhaps Lord Henry and I should take our leave of you, Lady Huntley."

"No," Henry protested. "She's wrong, or lying. My brother is dead, and I refuse to think otherwise until I've seen him with my own eyes."

"Had you joined me for a walk in the garden so we might continue our conversation the other night, you would have seen him." More than likely Luke wouldn't have shown himself, but there was no need to remark on that.

She might as well have been talking to a door for all the attention her brother-in-law paid her.

The solicitor rose to his feet. "Come along now, Lord Henry. We can continue this meeting at another date." He turned to Arden. "At a time that is convenient for you, of course, my lady."

She nodded. "Of course. Thank you."

The older man then added, "Perhaps his lordship will be able to join us."

Well, at least he hadn't called her a liar as Henry had, but there was an element of disbelief in his voice. She could hardly blame him. She wouldn't believe a word of it either if she wasn't living it.

"I hope so," she replied.

Mr. Kirkpatrick guided Henry to the door and gently

pushed him over the threshold; then he stopped in the doorway and looked over his shoulder at her. "It's not that he wants the title so badly, Lady Huntley, but rather that Lord Henry desperately wants to move forward and stop living in the past."

Arden tried to smile, but simply didn't have the heart for it. "Don't we all, good sir. Don't we all."

Five sat at the rickety table in his room eating the plain but hearty supper his landlady had prepared for him. His head felt like it had been kicked repeatedly by a foul-tempered mule, but at least he had an appetite.

The voice in his ear—in his head—had called to him earlier, after he woke up. He hadn't responded. More than likely he'd catch hell for it later, but for now he felt no remorse. Right now he was trying to sort out whether or not the Company had lied to him, or if his imagination was filling in gaps his memory couldn't.

He didn't like the thought of having been lied to and used. Undoubtedly he wasn't alone in that sentiment, especially when it came to having his trust betrayed. That aside, there was no denying that he had remembered things since being back in England.

Since his first encounter with Arden Grey. She was the key to all of this—his key to the truth. He could not kill her until he discovered just what that truth was.

Seeing her earlier, in such a private moment with that man, had awoken feelings in him that could only be described as jealousy, anger and possessiveness—with a dose of sadness tossed in.

He had killed other women—and men—agents who tried to play both sides, seductresses sent to acquire sensitive secrets. Never had he experienced the sort of trouble Lady Huntley shoved down his throat. Never had it taken him so long to complete this sort of mission; so what was it about her that made him falter?

Was it the fact that she smelled like bergamot, just as this mysterious "wife" of his had? Or was his fractured mind simply substituting her scent for the one his mind had lost?

It was going to drive him mad, this wondering.

He used a chunk of soft bread to mop up the rest of the gravy on his plate and popped it into his mouth. Now that he had eaten, his head didn't hurt quite so much—though the bloodstained handkerchief on the washstand, and the rusty water in the basin, were proof of just how bad it had been.

He was no stranger to his own blood, but knowing it had come from his ears was unsettling, even to him.

A firm rap came upon his door. Assuming it was Mrs. Brown come to collect his dishes, he went to answer without asking who it was. He realized his folly as soon as he pulled the door open and saw his visitor.

The Doctor.

"Hello, Five," the wiry man intoned. "How lovely to find you at home."

Five's eyes narrowed. The Doctor had never visited him before—at least not that he could remember. Truth be told, there were sections of his life even in the years since the Company had brought him in that were about as clear as mud. He used to think it was just the way his mind worked, after forgetting the entirety of his life. Now, noticing the heavy leather satchel in the smaller man's hand, he wasn't so certain.

He knew they had made other people forget things. Maybe they had done that to him as well. This leaden feeling in the pit of his stomach had nothing to do with his dinner and everything to do with his visitor. Instinct warned him to stay out of striking distance of the little man. In his years with the Company he'd seen bigger men than himself brought down by men and women even smaller than the one standing before him.

"Doctor." He kept his tone casual—with just a touch of surprise. "What are you doing here?"

Narrow shoulders shrugged as shrewd, bright blue eyes peered at him from over the wire rim of round spectacles. "Our mutual friend contacted me when you didn't respond. Is everything quite all right?"

A controlled smile curved Five's lips. "Right as rain."

The smaller man inclined his head. "May I come in?"

This was going to get messy, Five realized as he stepped back into the room. "Of course."

The Doctor crossed the threshold with a seemingly relaxed posture, but like all trained killers, there was a tension in him that came from being around another of his ilk. There was a very good chance one of them might not leave this building alive.

Five closed the door. The Doctor surveyed the room with feigned disinterestedness. He was looking for anything that could be used as a weapon or for defense if necessary. Five would do the same thing were the situation reversed. Fortunately, he already knew where all the useful items he owned were stashed.

"So, why didn't you answer when our friend called?"

Five rolled his shoulders, loosening the muscles there. "I was asleep." It was the first time he'd lied to a Company agent, and it rolled off his tongue like a Scot's r's.

"Asleep?" A sandy brow arched. The man had a face like a can of worms, scarred and pockmarked. "You sleep six hours a night, and that's it."

"Unless I'm knocked unconscious."

"Someone knocked you out?" That he sounded so surprised might have been taken as a compliment.

"I remembered something." He shouldn't admit it, but he wanted to see the reaction it got. He watched his companion carefully. "I remembered that I have a wife."

"Did you?" The leather bag was set on the table, the top of it open just wide enough for slim fingers to fit inside. Little bastard thought he wouldn't notice? "Who is she?"

Acting on a hunch, Five shifted his weight to a stance that would allow him to move quickly. "I'm not certain, but I think Arden Grey can tell me."

The Doctor went still, and that was all Five needed. The enigmatic Lady Huntley was right—she knew him, and he should know her. Five pounced. One arm went around the shorter man's neck, and the other came down to seize the wrist of the hand holding the syringe the "doctor" had taken from his case.

"You don't want to do this," the wiry man rasped, fingers of his free hand clawing at Five's forearm.

"You're right," Five growled. "What I want to do is kill you, but I don't want my landlady to find your body. So you're going to take a little nap instead." He squeezed his arm closed, cutting off the man's oxygen. It didn't take long for him to stop struggling and pass out. The man might have been a deadly adversary, but once it came down to sheer size and strength, there was no contest.

Five lowered his burden to the floor and picked up the syringe that had fallen to the rug. He studied it for a moment before taking his coat from the closet and slipping his arms through the sleeves. Then, he grabbed the Doctor's bag from the table and yanked open the door. The pounding in his head threatened to start again as he bounded down the stairs, images dancing in and out of his memory like the flickering of a candle. They teased him; coming just close enough that he could almost recall the exact moment, and then dancing away before he could tell what the hell it was.

His velocycle was parked on the street where he had left it. Frankly, it was a surprise no one had stolen it yet, but anyone who crossed his path in this neighborhood knew a predator when they saw one and knew better than to draw his attention. He set the bag on the back of the cycle and used the straps there to hold it in place. He straddled the machine before flipping the ignition switch, and releasing the kickstand.

He tore off down the street as the sun sank on the horizon, casting a pinkish halo over the city. He had no friends, no idea who he was. He had just rendered one of his brotherhood incapacitated—an act of sedition—and the one person who had any of the answers he wanted was a woman part of him still thought he should kill.

Well, at least he knew what to do next.

Arden retired early. She took a bottle of scotch and a glass with her, and instructed Mrs. Bird that she was only to be disturbed if the house was afire or someone was dead. The housekeeper eyed the bottle in her hand with pursed lips, but she nodded anyway. Dear thing knew to pick her battles.

In the sanctuary of her room, Arden entered the adjoining bath and turned on the water for the tub. After the day she'd had the only thing that could possibly get the knots out of her neck and shoulders—and dull the ache in her heart—was a hot bath and a stiff drink—or six. She undressed as the tub filled.

She drank too much. She knew it. Her servants knew it. Inspector Grant knew it. Hell, perhaps every citizen of London with one working eyeball knew as well. She didn't care. If it weren't for spirits she would have gone mad, or even killed herself, years ago. As she poured a hefty measure of scotch into a glass she recognized her weakness and took comfort in it. She would sleep well tonight.

After adding a few drops of bergamot oil to the water she turned off the taps and stepped in. The water was the perfect temperature and had warmed the back of the copper tub as well. Arden leaned back against the metal with a sigh and took a sip from her glass as she closed her eyes.

Poor Henry. His was the face she saw on the back of her lids. It was almost as if she was seeing him through someone else's eyes, like with the A.R.O.T.S. She'd only ever seen him so discomposed once, and that had been when Dhanya had met with the two of them and told them Lucas was most likely dead.

God, she hoped they could fix Luke. They had to fix him. It didn't seem likely that either she or Henry would survive if they couldn't. Her fingers tightened around her glass. She could kill every agent the Company had at this moment, and it still would give her no peace.

Such thoughts were not conducive to relaxation, so she pushed them as deep into her mind as she could. Soon, thoughts of Luke filled the empty spaces, reminding her of times they'd shared. He'd been gone longer than they had been together, and some of the time they'd shared hadn't been good. They fought a lot, about why he didn't want to have children right away, and when he would cut back on his work for the Wardens. It seemed so foolish now, when she'd give anything to have him back.

She took another sip of scotch. Its warmth slid down her throat to blossom like a flower of heat in her chest. The heat of the bath made its effects all the more potent, and by the time she'd finished the rest a delightful lethargy had taken hold of her limbs.

Her mind turned to more intimate memories. Luke had taught her things she never could have imagined. He was the kind of man whose pleasure was intrinsically tied to the pleasure of his partner. The more aroused he made her, the more aroused he became. These memories woke that familiar tension inside her, caused a delicious thrum between her thighs.

For seven years she'd gone without the touch of any man, not just the one she loved. It was a long time for a woman to go without, especially one who had enjoyed a rather passionate marriage. Arden had learned not only how to look after herself, but how to indulge herself in other ways too.

That was how her delicate little invention was born. Originally the small brass clockwork device that was worn over the fingers like a ring, but rested on the underside of the longer three, was meant to be used as a treatment for aching muscles and knots of tension.

However, curiosity led to experimentation, and suddenly Arden found herself with a discreet way of relieving *all* of her tension. She'd mentioned it to Zoe, who demanded to have one—and refused to take it until Arden agreed to let her pay. Then Hannah of all people had asked for one, and soon she had a surprisingly large clientele of upper-class women who did not want to go to a sanitorium to treat their hysteria, or were unmarried, or quite bluntly, wanted to give themselves what their husbands or lovers could not—at least not on a regular basis.

Best of all was the design. If anyone saw it they might think it an odd piece of jewelry or a trinket, unless they had one of their own. It certainly was more subtle than a brass phallus.

She had yet to perfect a waterproof prototype, so in the bath her plain and nimble fingers had to do the job. She slowly lifted her left leg—it felt as though it weighed five stone—and draped it over the side of the tub. Then she slipped her right hand between her legs, parted the curls there and began to stroke what Luke had called her "sweet spot."

In her mind it was Luke who touched her. In her fantasy he used his fingers and mouth to tighten her nipples to a point just shy of discomfort before sliding down and using his mouth to torture her. In the water she could almost pretend her fingers were his tongue, licking faster and faster as she gasped and cooed, the ache inside her building. She lifted her hips, matching the jerky rhythm of her hand until the protrusion of slick flesh beneath pulsed and spasmed, engulfing her in shuddering ripples of delicious liquid heat. She moaned aloud at the pleasure of it, the release.

Tension drained from her limbs and she sank deeper into the tub. It took a few seconds for her to realize that the leg draped over the side was cold and that her water wasn't much warmer.

She could run more hot water into the bath, but she was beginning to prune, so she pulled the stopper and reluctantly pushed to her feet. Languid from head to toe, her legs trembled slightly with the effort of keeping her upright. Carefully, she blotted her skin with a towel and stepped out of the tub onto the mat where she quickly dried her legs and feet. She hadn't the energy for it, but she hated climbing into bed damp.

Her Japanese silk dressing-gown lay across a brass apparatus that resembled a cross between a radiator and a quilt rack. The rungs of it were actually tubes that circulated hot water, warming whatever was placed over it with a gentle heat. Arden sighed as she slipped her arms into the heated silk, and used her big toe to switch the machine's boiler to the off position.

After cinching the belt of her gown, she retrieved the

scotch and her empty glass and carried both with her into her bedroom. Another little sip before slipping between the sheets, and she wouldn't have to wait for sleep to find her—she'd find it quick enough.

The carpet was soft and plush beneath her bare feet as she padded into the dimly lit room. A small fire crackled in the hearth, warm and inviting as it warded off the evening's spring chill.

"Don't scream."

Arden jumped, a strangled yelp breaking free of her throat. The glass fell from her fingers, thudding heavily on the carpet. It didn't shatter, but a few drops of leftover scotch speckled the top of her foot.

The bottle, however, remained safe in her grip. There was no way she was going to let go of it—not when it was the only weapon she had.

Lucas emerged from the soft shadows in the corner near the fireplace. He was disheveled—hair mussed, shirt open several buttons at the throat. There was a certain tension in his face that concerned her. It was an expression she'd seen before, usually when he was extremely agitated, trying to find the solution for a problem that just would not be solved.

"How about I won't scream, and you won't kill me?" How long had he been there? How had he gotten in without her hearing? She had only been in the next room with the door open.

He nodded. "I'm not here to kill you. I'm not certain I could even if I wanted to." He glanced around the room, as though trying to suss out exactly where he was. What had happened to him? The confident killer was gone, but that did little to console her. He was more dangerous now than he had been with his hands around her throat.

"Why are you here?" she asked softly, holding the bottle of scotch against her stomach.

The corner of his mouth lifted in a self-deprecating smile that seized her heart in her chest. She knew that smile. She *loved* that smile. "It seemed the right idea at the time."

It took every ounce of resolve left in her drink-addled mind not to return that smile and melt into a puddle of feminine goo at his feet. He wasn't the man she married, no matter how much he looked the part. She had to remain smart. Cautious.

He took a step toward her, more sure of himself now. "I heard you in there, fingering yourself. Who were you thinking of, me or the redhead?"

Shame threatened to overwhelm her, but he was the only man she'd ever shared a bed with, and she'd be damned if she'd be embarrassed in front of him. "I'd have to be pretty demented to do that while thinking of a man who wants nothing more than to kill me."

"There are plenty of things I'd rather do to you right now than kill you."

Heat blossomed in her cheeks, but Arden ignored it. She had to stay focused if she wanted to stay alive. "But here you are trying to decide whether or not to kill me."

"Actually, I'm here because I want to know why every instinct I have screams that killing you would be a tragedy. I want to know who I am and how you know me. But most of all I want to know why you smell like bergamot."

Her throat constricted so tight it hurt to breathe. She either seized this opportunity with all her might or let him go. "I smell like bergamot because you gave me a bottle, but I don't think you need me to tell you who you are. You're a smart man; surely you've figured it out by now?" She held her breath.

His gaze slid past her, and when his pale eyes widened she knew he had seen the photograph on her vanity. He brushed past her to get to it, picking it up by its ornate frame. Taken shortly after their engagement, it had started out as one of those awful things where the man sits and the woman stands behind his chair, but Luke hadn't wanted her to stand behind him, so he'd pulled her into his lap instead. The photographer—Henry—took the picture while the two of them were grinning at each other.

When Luke turned his head to look at her, his face was white and grim. The hand that held the frame trembled, but his gaze was sharp and clear. "I'm Lucas Grey, and you're my wife."

Chapter 8

It should be the happiest moment of the past seven years. Her husband was home. He had come back to her.

Arden felt as though she might be ill.

So many nights spent weeping for him, despairing for him, and sometimes cursing him. She'd clung to the dream of having him returned to her, only to have it mocked by the fact that the Company turned him into an assassin. Her assassin. Determined to save him, she could only hope that he would come for her again, because this time she was ready.

And now he stood before her telling her exactly what she wanted to hear, and she didn't know if she could believe him or not. Had he truly remembered, or was this just another cruel act on behalf of an agency that would have her head on a platter?

He set the frame down with a thud. "I have to go."

What the devil? She set the whiskey on her dressing table and hurried after him as he crossed the carpet toward the balcony doors. She hoped he planned to actually open them this time.

"Why?" she asked, hating the whiny edge to her voice. "If you've remembered who you are—"

He whirled on her, bringing her up so short she almost ran right into him. She could feel the heat radiating off him, smell his familiar scent. "They know I'm here." He pointed to his head. "They can hear everything."

"Oh dear," Arden murmured, horror taking hold. "You've gone mad."

Luke scowled at her, pale gaze blazing into her soul. "Don't be daft, Ardy. They put something in my head. They talk to me through it, and they can hear every conversation I have—everything I do."

A smile slipped over her lips—relief despite the tightness in her stomach. "You called me Ardy."

The furrows in his brow eased, giving way to an astonishment that could not be false. "I've always called you that."

A breath of laughter escaped her. She choked the rest of it back, afraid that once she started she wouldn't stop, and from there it would turn to tears. She opened her mouth to ask about the listening device when Luke suddenly turned white.

"Get out of my head, you bastard," he growled.

Arden's blood froze. Had they found him? Or was he, as she had earlier feared, mad as a hatter?

He hit the right side of his skull with the heel of his hand. "I said get the fuck out of my head!"

A high-pitched whine caught her attention. As it increased in volume, the anguish on her husband's face did as well, until he fell to his knees clutching his head, crying out in wordless agony.

Was that blood in his ear?

She pivoted so fast her robe tangled around her ankles, threatening to send her sprawling. She stumbled but didn't fall, her hands finding the standing lever of the contraption Alastair had delivered to her earlier. She pulled.

There was a humming noise followed by a loud thud. She turned to see Luke on his back, limbs splayed. He stared at her with a mixture of trepidation and wonder. She didn't blame him.

"The pain stopped," he said.

She nodded. "I know."

"I can't move."

"I know that too." The Calypso Magnetic Device was a large "floor" generally used to detain automatons, but both she and Alastair figured it would work on a man whose bones had been plated with metal—it worked on Alastair's hand. She had planned to use it only if Luke became violent, but the device proved to be more useful than first intended.

It had been her father who explained to her how magnets interfered with Aetheric transmissive frequencies. Over the years the W.O.R. had used similar instruments to interfere with Company communications and weaponry—and vice versa. Who would have thought she'd employ the same practice to keep her husband's brain from leaking out of his ears.

His gaze seized hers and refused to let go. There was no expression on his angular face. "What now? Turn me over to your friends? Kill me?"

His matter-of-fact tone weighed heavy on her heart. It shouldn't surprise her, and it certainly shouldn't put her on the defensive, but it did a bit. She expected him to trust her, even though she'd ask the same questions of him.

Slowly—more because her head was swimming and less because she thought she ought to be cautious around him—she sank to her knees on the carpet, and stretched out on her side next to him. She needed to be still, or she'd cast up all that glorious whiskey.

The Calypso had no effect on her, though it held him like some sort of exotic specimen on display. She could do whatever she wished with him and he would be powerless to stop her. A heady thought. An arousing one.

Did she want to make love to him or punish him for leaving her alone seven years ago? Both, perhaps. Right now she simply desired to be close to him. It felt so good it hurt, and she could enjoy it without fear that he might try to strangle her at any moment.

"I don't know what I should do," she told him, honestly. "I could alert your brother or the Wardens. I could summon Alastair, or lock you in the cellar. One thing I will not do, however, is let you go." She lifted herself up onto her elbow so she could see him better.

Luke frowned. His face was so close, and turned toward her just enough that she could visually trace the faint lines around his mouth in the firelight. "What did I ever do to deserve such devotion?"

Arden's mouth opened . . . then closed again. For those brief seconds her mind was blank. "You saved me from the man in the alley."

"Only because I planned to kill you myself." His direct gaze made her cringe inside.

"But you couldn't do it."

"No. Something stopped me, every time."

Thank God. "That was you at the factory, wasn't it?"

"I think so."

She frowned. "You don't know?"

He looked as though he wanted to shake his head, but it was held immobile by the Calypso. "A man called the Doctor has tampered with my memory. He's probably the one who took you away from me."

"So, you don't . . . remember everything?" What did he remember? And how much of it included her?

"No. I have images in my mind. Things that I know

without knowing how. The ginger—he's a friend of mine, isn't he?"

Arden inched closer to his warmth. The floor was becoming uncomfortable and a little chilly. She was wearing nothing but a robe, after all. "Your best. Alastair Payne, Earl of Wolfred."

"I had memories of him as well, back at my flat before I passed out."

Dear God, what had they done to him? "Do you lose consciousness often?"

"No. Seeing the two of you together earlier did something—like opening a door in my head. I remembered that both of you . . . meant something to me."

She fought the tears that threatened. "Yes."

"And I loved you?"

Arden ignored the way his voice went up ever so slightly, making the statement a question. Ignored the pain that came with it. "Yes."

Pale eyes met hers. "Of course I did. Intelligent, beautiful and now you're mine."

She went completely still, heart in her throat. He had spoken those exact words to her on their wedding night. Did he remember that night, or just the words?

It didn't matter. It was exactly the right thing to say, and exactly what she needed to hear to give her hope. And it was exactly the sort of sentiment that enabled her to bring her body against his, sliding over until she lay atop him. He looked surprised, but didn't say a word. His gaze warmed, glittering with anticipation. That was all the encouragement she needed. She lowered her head.

His mouth was warm—pliant and oh-so-familiar, yet exciting. Despite all her protests to the contrary, there had been a part of her that worried she might never feel his lips on hers ever again.

What a relief their warm familiarity was.

She slid the tip of her tongue along his bottom lip. Luke's mouth opened, letting her inside so she could taste him. Her hands braced on either side of his head, allowing her better leverage to press her hips against his. Through her robe she could feel him growing hard in response to her need. She rubbed against him, lifting her head just enough to gasp against his lips. He groaned.

"Turn this bloody thing off," he growled.

Arden arched from the waist, reaching for the lever that would free him to do whatever he wanted to her. She was so eager for him that she didn't even mind if he killed her, as long as he made her come first. She couldn't wait to feel his hands on her skin, inside her. She wanted to hear his breath, feel it hot on her ear and cheek as he pounded himself into her.

She froze, remembering the blood she had seen in his ear and what had caused it.

"I can't," she whispered, meeting his gaze.

His eyes hardened. "You don't trust me."

"I don't want to turn the Calypso off until I can be certain the Company won't try to hurt you again."

The harsh lines of his features softened, and his gaze warmed once again. "It's a risk I'm willing to take."

"But I'm not." She slid off him to kneel by his side. Every inch of her wanted him desperately—to the point that she was ready to throw caution and caring to the wind. But after seven years without her husband's touch, it would not be making love if she took advantage of his immobility without trusting him completely; it would be what was so crudely referred to as "fucking," and that was not how she wanted it to be between them, not after all they'd been through both together and apart.

Luke looked at her as if he understood. He obviously didn't like it, judging from the expression on his angular face, but he seemed to know her hesitation had to do with more than his present predicament.

They stared at each other for a few seconds. It wasn't uncomfortable, but it left her feeling stripped bare all the same. "You need to send for someone," he told her. "The Company will come for me if they think I'm alone with you."

Arden snorted. "This house would be the wrong place for them to attack."

"I've gotten in here with little difficulty."

She gave him what she knew had to be a slightly condescending smile. "Indeed." That was all the explanation she was prepared to give—just in case he was playing her for a fool. She hated to think it, but she'd be an idiot not to be careful at the very least. It didn't seem wise to remind him that he'd helped her improve security on the grounds and once knew the system as well as she.

"Send for someone," he pressed. "You know you have to, and I can't stay on this thing forever."

He was right. Regardless of what the Wardens might do to him, he would need their help. She couldn't take the transmitter out of his head—she was no surgeon. Only Evelyn could make certain the Company lost their way of spying on him. Only Dhanya would have the power to ensure Luke was treated fairly and protected to the best of W.O.R.'s ability.

If only they had some way—a humane way—to determine just where his loyalties lay. He seemed sincere, and she wanted to believe he meant what he said. But he had been with an enemy of the Empire for more than half a decade. Realizing that they had used and lied to him did not mean it would be easy for him to betray them. Luke would need the help of all his friends to undo the damage those bastards had wrought.

With a sigh, she rose to her feet and crossed the carpet to the small desk in the corner where she took care of all her personal business. An ebony and brass telephone sat on the polished mahogany top. She removed the portion for listening from the cradle—the metal was cold against her ear. She turned the crank on the side toward her rather than away. She did this three times—one long, one short, one long again.

The connection was made a second or two later. Static crackled. "Jabberwocky."

"Bandersnatch," Arden replied. The code words changed on an irregular basis, and Mr. Carroll's writings were excellent for them, as they weren't really words at all.

"To which number may I connect you, madam?" The operator inquired. There were six of these women who took turns running the Warden switchboard so that there was always an operator no matter the time of day or night.

"Oh-four-two-five-eight-three-nine, please."

"One moment." There was silence, followed by a click and then ringing in the same long-short-long sequence in which she had turned the crank. That would alert Alastair that the incoming call was from a fellow Warden.

The rings repeated once more before he picked up. "This had better be good," he growled, his voice thick with sleep.

She took a deep breath. "It's Arden. Alastair, he's come home."

His silence lasted two thumps of her pounding heart. "I'll be right there."

Five . . . er, rather, Luke, almost fell asleep on the magnetic pallet that held him hostage. This room—this house—filled him with a sense of security he couldn't remember ever feeling before. Despite not being able to lift his hand to scratch an itch on the side of his nose, he was content; filled with the naive hope that perhaps his life was not the raging shite storm he suspected it of being.

His wife—he was still trying to wrap his brain around that one—had left him after making her short telephone call. She promised to be back as soon as possible, saying that she was going to her workshop to get something for him.

For all he knew she could come back with a handsaw and a wheelbarrow, but he didn't think so. Not that a handsaw would do her much good against his bones.

His gut told him to trust her, and he had learned several years ago to trust that instinct. In fact, he was fairly certain it was not trusting his instincts that had gotten him into this mess to begin with. If only he could interpret the scant, chaotic images vying for attention in his mind, then he might know how he came to be in this position, but they were only fragments—nothing that made sense.

Trying to make sense of it all made his head hurt, and he'd had enough of that for one day. He closed his eyes and listened to the slight, pleasant buzzing in the back of his mind. It lulled him like the gentle whir of an airship motor, making his eyelids heavy and his muscles as languid as a cat draped over the back of a sofa in front of a sunny window.

There was no one in his mind. No one could eavesdrop on him or shout orders. For the first time in as long as he could remember—which given the grand scheme, wasn't impressively long—he was completely and utterly alone. The whirring was proof of that, caused by the powerful magnet pressed against his head. His eyes closed, and peaceful darkness drew him down regardless of the images swirling behind his lids.

He woke with the sensation of being watched. His eyes reluctantly opened as exhaustion tried to keep them shut.

The ginger man stood over him, watching with a curious expression. Had he not been incapacitated Luke would have leapt to his feet and ruined that pretty face. The pressure holding him to the floor wasn't so lovely anymore, when thoughts of this man holding his wife filled his head.

"Where's Arden?" he demanded.

The ginger arched a brow. "Her workshop. She'll be here in a moment."

Something in that statement ignited Luke's ire like a letter carelessly tossed onto the hearth. This man had been his best friend once. He knew that just as he knew Arden was his wife, but that knowledge aside, he could cheerfully rip the bastard's arms off. "Are you often in her bedroom?"

A groove deepened in Alastair's left cheek as his lips twisted grimly. "Only when her husband, long presumed dead by everyone but her, returns home intent on causing her death."

He didn't share the man's humor. "I have no intention of hurting her."

Alastair gave a slight shake of his head. "You'll understand if I don't take you at your word."

Luke would have shrugged had he been able. "Your opinion doesn't concern me." Actually, it did. And that pissed him off even more.

The other man crouched beside him, a dangerous glint in his gray eyes. "I could kill you right now just to keep her safe."

A cold smile took hold of Luke's mouth. He'd been

right to be jealous of this man who would kill to protect *his* wife. "Best make it look like an accident then. Killing me won't get you into her bed."

His old friend paled a little before his cheeks flushed a dull red. "You're as much a bastard now as you ever were." Then the damnedest thing happened—Alastair grinned. "It really is you. I'll be buggered."

"Not by me you won't," Luke shot back without thinking. The wonder in the other man's eyes told him that this was something that they used to say to each other, years before, when he knew who he was.

This man—Alastair—knew him better than he knew himself at the moment. Or rather, knew more about him. He tried to remember more, but the memories that had come back crowded his brain, crawling over one another, demanding to be recognized. It made him dizzy.

Christ, he hoped he didn't puke. He'd choke to death, pinned to the floor like a bug. Then Alastair could eventually slip into Arden's bed with a clean conscience.

"Are you all right?"

Through narrowed eyes, Luke stared up at the still-hovering ginger. "No."

As his luck—which had been described as being as good or bad as the shithouse rat, depending on how one looked at it—would have it, that was the moment Arden swept into the room. She had some sort of crown in her hand.

She took one look at him and her eyes widened. "Good Lord." Quickly, she crossed the carpet. Had she been wearing shoes he would have described her step as "stamping," but that might have more to do with his head than her stride.

The hem of her dressing gown brushed against his cheek, and he caught the scent of her. Sweet, with a hint of bergamot, and woman. He remembered the noises she had made in the bath, and how he had wanted to climb into the tub with her and give her something to really moan about.

Thankfully he was in enough discomfort that he didn't embarrass himself by getting hard.

There was a thunk as she shoved the lever, and then the humming in his brain stopped, and his body felt lighter—capable of movement. She had turned off the magnet, and any moment the Company would have at him again. This time they might kill him. He wasn't afraid to die—he'd come close so many times he'd begun to think death didn't like him much—but now that he remembered her, he found himself reluctant to give up his wife and her big, worried brown eyes.

"Alastair, help me get him up."

They were intimate enough that she called his old friend by his Christian name. Luke couldn't remember if it had always been that way. Had they become more than friends in his absence? He had no right to be jealous; he'd had lovers of his own. Knowing that he had broken his marriage vows made the sickening in his belly even worse. It didn't matter that he hadn't known he had a wife.

Arden took his left arm, and Alastair the right. Together, they began to pull him upright. The exertion turned both their faces red.

"Heavy son of a bitch," Alastair grunted. Arden did not seem the least bit shocked by his language. Luke couldn't remember if that was new or not.

He pulled free of their hands, sending both of them skidding backward a few feet. Then, head feeling as though it was being beaten by a brick on the inside, he slowly pushed himself to his hands and knees, then his feet.

"I've gained a few pounds," he explained to the three Alastairs wavering before his eyes.

The other man eyed him . . . warily? "So I've noticed."

"Come sit down," Arden commanded, then to Alastair, "Fetch a glass of water, please."

She came to Luke's side to help him as he moved toward a chair on trembling legs. Obviously she wished to help him, but if she couldn't pull him up with help, she certainly wouldn't be able to support him if he fell. He lowered himself slowly onto the chair—too fast and he might break the delicate-looking thing. When she shoved a clean chamber pot into his hands he was thankful. When she pressed a cool, wet face cloth to his forehead he clasped her hand in his and gently squeezed.

"Thank you," he murmured.

He couldn't tell if she smiled or not, because a second later he retched, stomach muscles clenching as the contents of his stomach burned his throat and hit the white porcelain bottom of the pot with a sick splash. He puked twice, holding the pot with trembling hands.

"Are you done?" she asked after a few minutes. She didn't sound disgusted in the least.

"I think so," he replied. He was weak to the point of helplessness. If he was attacked at that moment he doubted his own ability to defend himself, despite his superior strength. She took the chamber pot from him and set it close by.

Alastair returned with the water, which Luke drank greedily. It cleansed his mouth, soothed his throat, made him feel as though living might be a good thing. Arden removed the cloth from his forehead, and replaced it with something cold and hard. Something metal.

"It's not much," she explained. "A lesser version of the one that held you to the floor. It's weak enough that it shouldn't affect the metal in your body unless you touch it, but strong enough to interfere with the Company's device until we can get it out of you."

He glanced up at her—his eyeballs ached. "Can you do that?"

"Not me," she replied with a gentle smile. "But I know of a brilliant surgeon who will know how to go about it."

Luke frowned. A splinter of pain lodged deep in his skull—a hard pinch deep in his brain—but he ignored it. "Stone," he said. "Dr. Stone." Did he know this because he remembered, or because Stone's name had been one of many he had seen listed of known W.O.R. agents and collaborators?

"Yes," she replied with a smile so hopeful it damn near broke his heart. Looking at her was difficult. On one hand he wanted to grab her, throw her on the bed and ride her until they were both sore. He also wanted to hold her, just so he could smell her hair. And then there was part of him—a small part, but it was there—that hadn't accepted that she wasn't the enemy and that still wanted to choke the life out of her.

It was like being awake in a nightmare. He couldn't tell reality from deceit, and he didn't know whom he could trust. He couldn't even trust himself.

"We have to take him to the Director," Alastair said to Arden as he handed Luke a packet of powder. "For the headache."

Luke turned to him. "How did you know?"

The other man frowned. "Please. I've known you since we were eight. By the way, could you show me your right shoulder?"

The powder was bitter as Luke ripped it open with his teeth, but he washed it down with the water he'd been given. He wiped his mouth with the back of his hand before lifting his gaze. "Why?"

Alastair's lips thinned. "Just do it."

"Alastair," Arden admonished, but he ignored her, fixing Luke with a determined stare.

Sighing, Luke unbuttoned his shirt and pulled it down to reveal the tattoo he'd had since long before the Company found him. He had a few, but this was the oldest. The black ink was faded to a teal blue, but the image was clear enough: a gryphon pawing at the air with its talons, beak open in a fierce cry.

"Satisfied?" he asked.

Alastair nodded. "Yes," he rasped. He seemed oddly relieved, happy and yet saddened by the sight. Arden looked as though she was biting her tongue to keep from crying.

It struck Luke then that this was their irrefutable proof. Were it not for the fact that his head felt like it had an axe buried in it whenever he tried to think, he would have realized sooner that they would need to see this for their own peace of mind. And he needed to see their reaction for his own. These people truly knew who he was. After seven years of wondering—of almost reconciling himself to the idea that he might never know—he knew his name.

A name that felt less real to him than the number he had been assigned.

"I'll send for Dhanya in the morning," Arden said, her voice hoarse.

This Dhanya had to be the "Director"—W.O.R.'s commanding officer. She must be new, because he didn't recognize the name. It had been a man running things last he could remember. But these were modern times, and women were employed in many positions once held by men alone.

"You know it cannot be left until morning," Alastair argued as Luke rebuttoned his shirt.

"It can and it will," came her angry, flushed-cheek reply. Her back was as straight as a poker, and Luke couldn't help but notice how her impeccable posture pushed her breasts up and out. Wolfred noticed as well. The only one who didn't seem to notice was Arden. "She'll want to test him and interview him. She'll take him away and I—" Her voice broke, and she turned away from them both, moving to the dressing table where she braced both her hands and bowed her head. In the mirror, Luke could see her squeeze her eyes shut—fighting tears.

And still her back remained straight, her shoulders stiff.

Out of the corner of his eye he saw Alastair start toward her, and he came to his feet in protest. Blood rushed to his head, making him sway, but the nausea had passed and he no longer felt as though his skull was being chipped apart by a dull chisel. His old friend steadied him with a quick hand, which Luke thanked him for but brushed aside.

As though he could read Luke's mind, the earl backed off—not just from him, but from Arden as well.

What the hell did he do now? Comfort her? He hardly knew how. All he knew was that for the last seven years he hadn't known he had a wife, and that for that same seven this beautiful woman had been left wondering if her husband was dead or alive. He'd been out having adventures—granted on behalf of the enemy—and fucking whomever he wanted. Doing other things he hadn't wanted, but had been ordered to do. He'd thought they were the right things. . . .

She had been waiting for him. And he didn't have to be a bloody genius to see that she was afraid of losing him again.

As though he were some sort of prize.

One thing he did know—this was not a woman who took emotions lightly, nor shared them indiscreetly. She was barely holding herself together, and if he coddled her right now, or tried to comfort her, she would break down. She would never forgive him for it.

Instead, he lowered his head so that his mouth was close to her ear. "You know Wolfred is right."

She shot him a glare that made him reconsider the possibility of her dissolving into tears. Her ferocity did something queer inside his chest, deep beneath his ribs. "I know no such thing."

This was not the woman he married—he realized this though he had no solid memory to back it up. This woman was going to make his life very interesting, a thought that he relished despite himself. "You do."

When she straightened and drew back, he did the same. They squared off like opponents about to fire in a duel. She would fight him until she had no more fight in her. He enjoyed a good row as much as the next man, but he'd already made shite of her life. Besides, he didn't trust himself alone with her. Not to shag her and not to kill her. Those two choices made him a danger to her, and made him uncomfortable in his own skin. He had so much blood on his hands, but he couldn't remember a time when he questioned his own honor—at least not in the last seven years. He questioned it now, and she would try to convince him otherwise because she wanted to believe that he was the man she married. He was no more that man than she was that girl.

It was time to take her fight away. He smiled at her, and reached out to touch the silky warmth of her cheek. The sensation brought a rush of emotional memories with it—a million and one touches stored in the dusty cupboard of his mind. With it came a flash of pain that fled as quickly as it came. Arden frowned at him, but she leaned into his palm. So trusting.

Luke dropped his hand and turned to Alastair. The other man's face was void of expression, but his steely eyes betrayed the pain this reunion brought him.

Luke met that gaze unapologetically. "Take me to the Wardens."

Chapter 9

Both men were fortunate that Arden hadn't her Electrical Discombobulation Intensifier at hand, because she would have rendered them both incapacitated and twitching on the floor. And she wouldn't have cared if they soaked their trousers, either.

The nerve of both of them, disregarding her like that. Alastair was supposed to be on her side. And Luke ... was it too much to ask that he spend a few hours with her after seven years apart? Early in their marriage she would get down in the mouth when he'd work long hours without her—what could she do when England was his mistress? But right now she wasn't maudlin. Right now she was incredibly angry.

Of course she was going to accompany them. Luke had tried to persuade her otherwise, but she refused to cave. At least the pair of them were intelligent enough to wait on her rather than leaving her behind. Obviously she couldn't appear before Dhanya in her dressing gown. She needed all the armor she could manage.

She didn't wake her maid or any of the servants.

Beauregard had to be asleep on his bed in front of the kitchen hearth or he'd have been dancing around their ankles barking like mad at them all. This silence felt eerie and tense, not comforting as it normally did.

A little while later, she joined them in the foyer, wearing a teal gown with a corset bodice that laced up the front. Her hair was secured in a black snood and her boots were soft leather, worn to such a degree of comfort that they molded around her feet.

Luke stared at her as she approached. The blatant appreciation in his gaze should have filled her with warmth, should have given her hope. Instead she wanted to slap his handsome face so hard he would have to talk out of the back of his head.

He must have seen the anger and hurt in her eyes—how could he possibly miss it?—because he arched a dark brow. "You didn't look at me with that much venom when I tried to kill you."

"I think perhaps you're still trying," she muttered with a shake of her head. She'd forgotten her chains and her cheek felt oddly bare without the cool metal strands brushing against it.

Luke sighed—the same way he'd always sighed when she said or did something he thought irrational. "If you don't take me to the Director, both you and Alastair risk being accused of treason. I have to turn myself in if I want any hope of getting my life back."

"*Have* to," she repeated bitterly. He had almost won her over with his words, until he used that offensive four-letter one. "That's what you said every time you left this house—and me—to run off and play with the Wardens."

There was no denying his surprise at her vehemence. Arden was angry enough—and her tongue loose from the whiskey she'd had another glass of while she changed—that she felt compelled to remark upon it. "I see the return of your memory is selective at best." Tugging on her gloves, she brushed by him. "Let's get this over with, shall we?"

The men followed after her; Alastair last so he could no doubt keep an eye on Luke. Or perhaps he simply did not wish to be within striking distance of Arden. Once upon a time she would not have reacted with anger. She would have wept, perhaps. Pleaded a little. It was only this unfamiliar, deep-seated rage that kept her from doing both right now.

But she would rather lick one of Mr. Tesla's coil transformers than show just how afraid she was at that moment. For years she had clung to her belief that Luke was alive, that he would come back. Now, she was faced with the possibility of losing him once again to duty, or perhaps to the Executioner General.

Their driver took his perch on the front of the carriage while her husband sat across from her and his best friend took the seat beside her. Perhaps Alastair thought himself better equipped to protect her from that position. Perhaps he was staking a personal claim—she often thought men were like dogs that way. Provided Alastair didn't urinate on her all would be well. What she didn't bother to point out was that with him by her side, it would make killing them both all the easier. Luke could go for both their throats at the same time, and with metal-plated fingers it wouldn't take much pressure to crush both windpipes.

"Why are you being so agreeable?" she asked the man half shrouded by shadow across from her.

He might have arched a dark brow again at the question. Certainly his lips lifted in that lopsided manner that both broke her heart and made her want to strike him. With Luke it was almost impossible to tell if he was laughing with her or at her.

Odd, but while he was gone she had forgiven—

forgotten—most of his faults. Now her irritation with all those peevish behaviors came rushing back.

"How would you have me behave?" His rumble of a voice filled the interior of the carriage despite his quiet tone.

Arden shrugged. If she ignited the lamp she might see him better, but then he would be able to see her as well. She glanced at Alastair, noting how his eyes shone like a cat's in the dark—another augmentation courtesy of the W.O.R. The Wardens and the Company were more alike than she cared to ponder.

"You do not seem the least bit concerned about what might await you at W.O.R. headquarters."

"I'll decide whether or not to be concerned once I'm there." His deep voice filled the darkness. "Are you concerned, Ardy?"

She winced at the pet name, a pinch in her chest. "I'd be a fool not to be, given the circumstances."

Out of the darkness he came, leaning forward so she could see his face in the pale wash of moonlight peeking through the window. Beside her Alastair tensed. "Despite the fact that I don't deserve or require it, you are worried about me. Do you think the Director will execute me on the spot?"

"Or this might all be a ruse and you might not kill only me, but the Director as well."

He didn't seem the least bit put out by her suspicion. In fact he smiled at it. "So much for wifely trust."

"Can I trust you?" she parried. She wanted to, but she'd be a fool to give it so quickly—the Wardens had taught her that.

Luke came closer. He reached out and took the fingers she had fisted in her lap. Out of the corner of her eye she saw Alastair's hand move to the inside of his coat, where he often kept a weapon.

Glacial eyes locked with hers. "If you couldn't, you'd be dead by now."

She glanced down at his hand, wrapped around hers. His fingers were strong. Warm, and slightly rough. She wanted to lift those fingers to her mouth, press her lips against the back of them and let loose the scald of tears that seared the backs of her eyes.

She bit the inside of her mouth so hard she tasted blood.

"The Director will not be half so confident in your assurances," Alastair remarked blandly.

Arden looked up as Luke turned that unnerving gaze on his friend. "I think we both know that the Director's chief concern will be what sort of information I might impart," her husband said. "That should keep me alive long enough to prove myself worthy."

She blinked. He was right, of course. She hadn't thought of it in her irrational state—much to her annoyance— but it was little wonder he was so calm when the Wardens would certainly jump at the chance to know all the Company secrets her husband had stored in his mind.

Secrets that had taken her place.

Bitterness settled on her smarting tongue, and in her heart, sharp and unwanted. She hadn't realized just how angry she was at him for his absence—for so many things. She had been too bogged down in missing him, too smothered by regret to remember that the flaws in her marriage were not hers alone.

The truth was she had often hated the W.O.R. for being such a huge part of their lives. She had despised Luke at times—herself as well. It was only after she'd lost him that she found comfort in the agency, and dedicated herself so thoroughly to it.

She turned her head to find him watching her. His expression was neutral, but his gaze was anything but.

She knew just by the weight of his stare that he knew how she felt, the confusion and torment, and that he understood it as well. But, she supposed, that was the luxury of being the one who left rather than the one left behind.

Would he have waited for her as she had him? Or would she have returned home to find him married to another woman? Perhaps she might have succeeded where he failed and killed him in his sleep, never knowing that he had once been hers.

Luke's lips tilted with just enough of a twist that she knew he could tell what she was thinking. "Shine's already off the penny, isn't it?" His tone was vaguely amused—mocking even—but there was genuine regret in his eyes.

"It could use a little polish," she replied honestly. "But I wouldn't say it's completely tarnished. Perhaps a slight buffing?"

He smiled at that, and so did she. Warmth blossomed in her stomach, spreading outward. All concern and fear were obliterated in that moment. Her head swam pleasantly, and for one hot second she contemplated throwing herself into his arms and shoving her hand down his trousers. But that might distress dear Alastair, who had made his own feelings for her quite clear.

Thank God she had never taken advantage—not fully—of his regard. Alastair was precisely the sort of man a woman fell in love with were she not careful. While Luke . . . Lucas Grey was exactly the sort of man a woman wanted desperately to have fall in love with her. Even now she felt that desire to call him her own, to be the one to hold his heart, pressing down upon her. She wanted to possess a man who remembered even less of her than she had forgotten about him.

Just how much had he remembered? Not all of it, of

that she was certain. She had no way of knowing—short of asking—just how much of the past lived on in his mind. Did he remember the disagreements about duty to their country versus duty to each other, and children?

Perhaps she might have asked, but she didn't wish to do so in front of Alastair, and what was more, their carriage had just chugged to a stop, signaling their arrival at their destination. It was a pretty little street in Chelsea lined with redbrick and white-trim houses that spoke of elegance without pretention, and it was very quiet at this late hour, as any decent neighborhood ought to be. But one of these homes had a thin diamond glazing on all of its ground floor and street-facing windows. It also had special shutters and doors that would snap into place if the right alarm was triggered. And it was equipped with its own arsenal, a safe room, underground tunnels, and housed a series of pipes that could deliver sleeping gas into a specific room or rooms provided you knew the right code to dial on the control panel. One wrong number, and the gas would fill the room you were in instead.

It was the Director's quarters, and very few people in the W.O.R. knew its location. The agency was cautious to the point of paranoia.

"Now what?" Luke asked.

Before Arden could respond, Alastair struck. His fist flew with astonishing vigor into Luke's jaw. She gasped as her husband's head flew back, and the interior of the carriage filled with Alastair's imaginative swearing.

"Bastard's got a jaw like iron," her friend groused, flexing his fingers.

"Not iron," she argued. "He wouldn't be able to move. I suspect it's gregorite that protects his bones—the same metal used to rebuild your hand."

He scowled at her. "What would I do without you to tell me what I already know?"

It was an old argument between them—him saying she talked to him like he was simple, and her saying he treated her as though she was a delicate flower. She was accustomed to such things coming out of his mouth when he was brooding, but that didn't stop her from returning the scowl with one of her own.

"Did you also know that I could have spared your hand and used something less injurious to render him unconscious?"

"Of course you could have. I wonder why you keep me around at all."

Alastair was in fine form tonight. His nerves had to be as sharp and ragged as her own. They would apologize for things said later, but for now they were both open game.

"I keep you around," she said, glancing over her shoulder at him as her man opened the carriage door, "because I can't carry him on my own."

They hadn't tied him up. That was the first thing Luke realized when he regained consciousness. The second was that the "crown" Arden had made for him was no longer on his head. He reached up to touch it and it was gone. Then he spied it sitting on a rough table some seven or eight feet away.

"You don't need it," came a new, slightly exotic voice. "There's not a transmission in the world that can penetrate these walls."

He turned his head toward the voice and noticed that he was in a cellar, sitting in a thronelike chair with a high back and sturdy armrests. No wonder they hadn't restrained him; he was sitting in a Venom Chair. On the outer length of the leg supports ran a line of small needles. Similar needles were poised to snap into place over his neck and arms. If he made any sudden moves those needles would pierce his skin, and the pump attached to the back of the chair would flood the syringe tubes with venom extracted from the blue-whirled kraken off the southern coast of Australia.

It would kill him within a handful of heartbeats.

He'd best not make any sudden moves, then. Slowly, he lifted his gaze to his audience. Arden was there, trying not to look concerned, but he could tell from the way she kept running her fingernails beneath each other that she was nervous—for him. A foolish sentiment, but one that warmed the hollow space in his chest nevertheless.

Wolfred—yes, that was what he used to call the ginger-haired man, not Alastair—stood to Arden's right, square jaw clenched. Bastard packed one hell of a punch. He would have to in order to have knocked him out as he had. Luke couldn't blame them for taking precautions—every good agent did. They didn't trust him any more than he trusted them, and yet something deep inside him had complete confidence in both of them, even though Wolfred was obviously in love with his wife.

The other woman seemed familiar. Her striking features appeared older than he thought they ought—indicating that it had been a long time since he'd last seen her. She wore a long robe of bright orange velvet, and her inky hair hung heavy around her shoulders. She was like some sort of exotic bird—of prey.

"The Director, I presume?" he asked, centering his attention on her.

She took a step forward, expressionless. "You presume correctly. Do you remember me, Lord Huntley?"

He stared at her, picturing her younger, softer. His brain protested with a dull ache, but he ignored it. He could see her, laughing at something Arden . . . no, something that he had said.

"Withering. You're Duncan and Ashwina's daughter. Does she still run the bakery?"

She paled, and he knew he had been right in mentioning her mother. It proved that at least he wasn't pretending to have regained his memory. Unfortunately, it also could be interpreted as vaguely threatening. "Yes, she does."

Luke didn't miss the look the Director—he still hadn't remembered her first name—shot Wolfred. His memory was no longer in question—but his loyalties were. If she asked which side he was on, he would say his own. Perhaps Arden's as well, since he'd only allowed them to bring him here in order to protect her. She brought out the chivalry in him.

"Where have you been these past seven years, Lord Huntley?"

After years of knowing no other identity than the number the Company gave him, being referred to by another name felt wrong. Regardless that he'd had countless aliases during that time, he wasn't playing a part right now, and these people knew things about him that he did not.

"In the employ of an organization called the Company," he replied honestly. "One morning I woke up in Paris with no memory of anything before that day. The Company found me, told me I was one of theirs. I believed them because they seemed to know me."

"I imagine they had completed extensive research," the Director remarked, rather dispassionately, but there was a hard glint in her amber eyes. "Have you any idea how they managed to obliterate your memories?"

He shook his head. "No, though the Doctor often did something that required an injection of some sort. I recall it being painful. And when they first approached me I had a bandage on my scalp. They said I had been injured."

His wife gasped. It was as soft as a whisper, but he

heard it. She was so pale her skin had taken a slight bluish tint.

"You think they did something to my brain."

Arden nodded. "There's been much research into how the mind works recently. I've read papers on doctors performing surgeries that have completely altered criminal behavior. The same practice could be used on the area of the brain that masters memory."

What she didn't say hung heavily in the room. "I might never fully remember my life."

Now she shook her head, her expression a mix of horror and determination. "We'll need to do some tests, but Dr. Stone should be able to ascertain what's been done."

He'd waited so long to remember any detail of his past that he couldn't bring himself to be distraught. He remembered her, or at least enough of her to inspire a visceral reaction. He wanted to hold her, smell the warm skin in the hollow of her neck. He did not, however, want to hurt her in any way. The great joke was that he would probably hurt her very deeply if he couldn't remember their life together.

"Not exactly the homecoming you imagined, is it?" he asked her, forcing a slight smile.

"No." To her credit, her eyes were dry and her shoulders straight. "But it is preferable to the alternative."

Luke grinned. If the Company were the villains they appeared to be, then both he and Arden would be in severe danger, but at that moment he didn't give a rat's arse. Let the Company come. Let Miss Withering do what she would.

"You will be transferred to a W.O.R. facility," the Director told him. "You will be examined and debriefed. Our doctor will see about getting that transmitter out of your head. You will give us everything you have on the Company."

These were nonnegotiable terms, still Luke nodded his consent. "Fine."

"How long are you going to keep him?" Arden asked. The anxiety in her tone inspired an ache in his chest, though the others appeared not to notice that she was the least bit upset.

"For as long as it takes," he answered before Miss Withering could. "Until they are certain I am not a threat to you, or this country."

The Director inclined her head. "Well said."

Luke turned to Wolfred. "You will protect her, won't you? If the Company sends someone else after her?"

His old friend nodded. "I will."

Ignoring his wife's protests, he directed his attention once more to the dark-haired woman. "Then let's get started, shall we?"

Whenever emotions threatened to have the best of her, Arden found peace and control in rationality. That was what she had to do when Lucas handed himself over to the W.O.R. without so much as a blink.

The entire time he was in that infernal chair her heart had been in her throat, her emotions flailing all over the place. And when Dhanya asked Alastair to shackle Luke's hands behind his back in preparation for transport to the W.O.R.'s holding cells, hysteria threatened.

She was not going to be one of those women who came undone in front of witnesses. From a pocket sewn into her skirts she withdrew a delicate silver flask, and opened it with trembling fingers. She took a deep, quick drink before hiding it away once more. As she dragged the back of her hand across her mouth, her gaze locked with her husband's. He was standing now—away from the execution chair—and his hands were behind his back.

Perhaps it was merely the echo of her own conscience, but it seemed disappointment clouded his pale eyes.

Arden lifted her chin. Being that he was the one who had been sent to kill her, she reckoned he had no right to look at her like that. If not for him her nerves wouldn't need a little extra fortification. Alastair gripped Luke's arm and pulled him toward an iron door on the back wall of the cellar. She rather fancied him all restrained and vulnerable. She might slap him if not for the fact that it would hurt her more than him. She might kiss him too—or anything else she wanted. But she would definitely begin with a slap. She smiled at the thought. Her husband responded with a raised eyebrow.

"I apologize for the chains, Lord Huntley," Dhanya said as she unlocked the heavy door and pulled it open. The hinges screeched. "I'm sure you understand the necessity of them, however."

"You'd be a fool not to take precautions, Director." Luke glanced over his shoulder. "You should go home."

Arden shot him a droll look. He hadn't changed that much—still trying to protect his pride under the guise of sparing her seeing him lowered. "I'll forgive you for suggesting that since you don't remember me very well. I believe this is one of those 'for worse' situations I agreed to in front of God and all that."

His lips tilted. "I wouldn't want to stand between you and God. By all means, come along."

He wasn't mocking her, she realized, but teasing her. Odd. He didn't press the matter either. At one time he would have commanded her to go home and she would have listened. Was this a change for the better? Or did he simply not care?

Regardless, she followed behind them, stepping into

the darkened tunnel on the other side of the threshold. There was the sound of a hand crank being turned, a sputtering chug, and then small lamps on either wall flickered to life, filling the damp space with a warm glow.

"Ah, the Director's private rail," Luke remarked as they all gazed upon the small steam engine before them. It was clean and richly appointed, its black lacquer gleaming.

"Yes," Dhanya replied, her expression one of surprise. Arden had to admit to being somewhat curious herself. Luke had never mentioned the private rail before. Very few people knew of it. It was one more secret he'd kept from her that she had been forced to discover on her own.

Just as she'd been forced to discover Rani Ogitani. She hadn't known the woman had once been Luke's lover until the two of them were sent on an assignment together shortly after he and Arden returned from their honeymoon. Luke hadn't said a word. It had been Zoe who commented, saying that Arden was a more confident woman than she to allow her husband to go off with his exotic former mistress. And partner. They had often worked together for the Wardens.

She never admitted it to anyone, but Arden had spent the next fortnight wondering if her husband was sleeping with the gorgeous spy. When he returned home he told her nothing had happened, and she believed him. Two years later he told her he had to go off with Rani again. She tried not to worry about it, but then Rani was found injured and Luke wasn't found at all.

It might be irrational, but Arden had blamed the other woman for Luke's disappearance. She still did.

She turned her attention back to her husband. He glanced at Alastair, who still held his arm. "Not that I would have denied you the pleasure of knocking me out in the carriage, but it wasn't necessary. I have a hazy recollection of this place. I've been here before."

Alastair's gray eyes narrowed. "You're too kind." But Arden thought she saw his lips twitch when Luke grinned. Her shoulders relaxed a little at the sight.

The four of them climbed into the main car. The rail was so secret, even Dhanya's servants knew nothing of it. She drove the engine herself, and thanks to a boiler that kept a constant amount of steam circulating by recycling unvented steam back into water, the engine was prepped for travel at all times. All Dhanya had to do was throw a few switches and levers, and the metal beast roared to life.

Arden and the men sat in plush velvet seats behind Dhanya. To her surprise, Alastair did not sit between Luke and her, but rather put Luke in the middle. Her husband sat with his bound hands behind the seat back.

He turned toward her, effectively obliterating the rest of the world as their conveyance lurched forward, quickly picking up speed. There was nothing but him— sight, smell and warmth. Even her ears seemed deaf to everything but his voice.

"I'm sorry," he murmured.

She nodded, throat suddenly very tight. "You were right, this has to be done." The words tasted like dirt even though they were true. Any other action might very well have led to a conviction of treason for both of them—if he hadn't killed her first. Were these reminders of his mission the rational part of her brain talking, or the part of her that had gotten what it wished for—the return of her husband—and was now terrified by it?

"I would rather be back in your room," he added, his voice dropping to such a degree that it slipped down her spine as a delicious shiver. "I would have liked to join you in the bath and give you something to really moan about."

Oh dear God! Heat flooded her veins, rushed up her

cheeks and tingled between her thighs. Her nipples were so hard her whiskey-addled mind thought they might have petrified after years of neglect. If it weren't for Alastair—who had augmented hearing, she was mortified to remember—and Dhanya, she would ravish him here and now. It would be worth dying for if her trust in him proved misplaced.

Instinct demanded she trust him. Common sense, however, erred on the side of caution. Inebriation wished both would go to hell and let her feel a man inside her for the first time in seven years. *Her* man.

Against her better judgment, she raised her gaze to his. "That ought to give you something to think about later when you're alone in your cell."

His gaze brightened, the blue deepening in the lamplight. "I'm thinking about it now."

"Good," she retorted, cheeks hot. Her lips curved into a smile despite herself. "Perhaps I'll think of it as well, when I take my bath tomorrow evening."

She wasn't certain, but she thought she heard him make a growling noise low in his throat. They stared at each other, wrapped in a blanket of sexual awareness as bittersweet as it was arousing.

"Are we almost there?" Alastair demanded peevishly.

The spell was broken. Arden glanced away, uncertain whom she was more embarrassed for—herself or Alastair. Luke arched a brow, but didn't say a word. Did he wonder if she and Alastair were lovers? He had to suspect there was something between them. She couldn't stand the idea of him thinking she had been unfaithful. She reached over and put her hand on his thigh. When his gaze locked with hers, she shook her head, and squeezed his leg, feeling the hard muscle beneath her fingers. His expression told her he understood, and he gave a slow nod of his head, a smile tilting his mouth.

An ugly thought took hold of her then. He'd been away for years. Had no concept of her existence for all that time. How many women had he been with while she clung to the hope that he was still alive?

While she'd been alone, untouched and unloved, how many lovers had flushed and shivered beneath his strong hands, or worse, evoked the same response in him?

She needed a drink, but another swallow might just as easily send her to a pit of melancholy as keep her from the edge. No, what she needed to do was focus on the present, and everything that was positive about it. The negative would wait—it would always be there.

The remainder of the journey was spent in silence. When they finally came to a stop, Alastair led Luke off the train. The door of this tunnel led into the cellar "dungeon" of the Wardens of the Realm. It wasn't far from W.O.R. headquarters, but like the Director's house, wasn't part of the main compound. Less chance of prisoners escaping and killing agents—or stealing sensitive information.

The guards at the door snapped to attention when they saw Dhanya. Their eyes narrowed when they spied Luke, bound like a criminal.

"This man is a former W.O.R. agent," Dhanya informed them in that no-nonsense tone of hers. "He is to be treated with care and respect until I say otherwise. He will be held in W-one-C-four."

The guards nodded. "Yes, Director," they chorused, and stood back while she inserted the key into the lock.

Arden had never been in this part of W.O.R. properties, but she'd heard the stories of subterranean cells that were medieval in nature. Obviously those stories had been exaggerated somewhat. There were Spartan cells, with large, external-clockwork locking mechanisms, but they were far from cruel.

They walked down a rough stone corridor to a wide
set of wooden stairs. Each step was well worn, the middle sagging from years of use, but they were sturdy and
barely groaned in protest as the four of them—one with
a gregorite-plated skeleton—climbed to the top.

At the top, Dhanya inserted a key into a scarred and
dull lock and turned it. She withdrew the key and inserted another, turning it as well. Finally, she slipped a
punch card into the slot right above the lock. There followed a sound that was a cross between a slap and a
groan as the specially designed keys inside found the
proper punch sequence. A heavy thud, and then the
punch card was spat out. Dhanya took the card—which
looked none worse the wear for having been chewed—
and turned the heavy iron handle.

They entered a corridor, the floor of which was covered by a worn red carpet. Here the walls were paneled
and papered, both of which appeared to be at least a
century old.

"It looks like the home of an impoverished noble,"
Luke remarked as Alastair marched him along.

"Parliament sees no reason to waste tax monies on
renovating what is essentially a prison," Dhanya informed
him. "Be glad there's gaslight rather than candles."

Arden thought to remind her that a body didn't generally have to worry about candles exploding and taking
the entire building with them, but kept her lips firmly
shut. She also resolved not to think of this place as a
potential grave for her husband.

They continued on until they were almost at the end
of the corridor; then they stopped, and another guard
soon joined them to unlock the iron door. It swung open,
to reveal the chamber beyond.

Arden's mouth dropped. She'd be jiggered. This was
no ordinary cell. This was a bedroom worthy of a gentle-

man, even if from a previous era. The lamps on the walls filled it with warm light, illuminating the hand-painted wallpaper and four-poster bed. There was an armoire, a dresser with a washbasin, and a desk in the corner. The only thing missing was windows, and the air was slightly stale for their lack.

Luke was surprised as well. "It's nicer than the rooms I let." He stepped inside. "Do I get a valet?"

No one laughed at the joke, but he didn't seem to mind. Alastair stepped in as well. "Turn around. I'll unlock the shackles."

Luke didn't turn. Instead, he extended one arm out in front of him. The shackles hung from his hand. He had snapped them.

Arden's lips twitched. "That's a rather showy manner of making a point," she commented. "We're all aware that you came here of your own volition."

Luke grinned. He could have broken free whenever he wanted. He could have injured any, if not all of them, but he hadn't. The notion nursed the hope that lay tense and heavy in Arden's chest.

Of course, he might be toying with them.

Alastair took the shackles. "Impressive," he remarked before using his augmented hand to squeeze the restraints back into the proper shape. The locks would still need to be fixed, however—if that was at all possible. Arden almost rolled her eyes. The posturing had begun. Any moment one of them would start thumping his chest.

"I'd like a word with my husband," she said, tone crisp. She'd been perfectly agreeable—mostly—with all of their demands and decisions, but this was one upon which she would not concede. "Alone, please."

Alastair looked as though he might protest, but said nothing. Dhanya merely nodded. "Of course. We'll be right outside the door." Then she pulled a pistol from the small of her back—a warning to Luke.

Her husband was still smirking as the door shut, closing them in the clean but slightly stuffy room.

"Aren't you afraid to be alone with me?" he asked.

"Should I be?"

"Yes, but perhaps not for the reason you think."

She raised a brow. "Because you might ravish me rather than kill me? Trust me, my lord, when I say you might do well to be afraid yourself."

He chuckled, a flash of heat brightening his eyes, but it faded to regret as quick as it had flared. "I wish I remembered more of you."

"So do I." She swallowed against the tightness in her throat. "I won't allow them to hurt you."

Luke shrugged shoulders that were so much broader than she remembered. "Pain fades. I don't think your director wants to hurt me. She wants what I know. I'm a genuine piece of Company ingenuity. She'd be a fool not to use me."

It sounded so cold and devoid of caring, but it was practical and true.

"Tomorrow I'll bring you some clothes and toiletries."

He lowered his chin, regarding her with curious eyes. "You kept my things?"

"Of course." Did that seem silly to him? Perhaps she was silly to reveal so much, but after seven years apart, what did she have to lose?

He lifted a hand to trail the back of a finger along her cheek. His touch was so desperately tender, so gentle her chest constricted at it.

"I cannot believe I was such a virtuous man as to deserve so true a wife."

Arden caught at his hand. She pulled it away from her

face but did not let go. "You weren't," she replied honestly. "But I loved you regardless."

"You never gave up hope?" His brows drew together. "All those years and you never let go?"

She forced a smile. This situation was in desperate need of levity. And she was in need of a drink. "I believe tenacity to be a virtue, one which I possess in abundance."

Strong fingers tightened around hers. "You must have wondered if I was dead."

"Of course, but I never gave in to it."

He stared at her—as though she was some queer creature he'd never seen before. The lines between his brows and around his eyes deepened. She wanted to kiss them smooth. In that moment, she knew he was no danger to her—not physically at any rate. "No wonder he's in love with you."

Arden opened her mouth to protest, perhaps defend Alastair, but her words were silenced when he wrapped his other arm around her back and yanked her against him. "Oh!" His chest was so warm and firm.

His head lowered, bringing his mouth to hers. His lips were warm and firm as well, demanding and cajoling. She opened hers to the spicy taste of him, the sweet intrusion of his tongue. Her fingers gripped his biceps, feeling the hardness beneath her fingers. He had always had a lovely physique, but not like this. She didn't know what to make of it. She liked it, but it wasn't the way she remembered him.

He wasn't the way she remembered, and that frightened her. It was also intriguing. The man she married never would have kissed her so roughly, with so little finesse. He would have used his lips to seduce her and slowly build up to tasting her.

She had to admit, she found this new and urgent

method . . . *interesting*. She matched the strokes of his tongue with her own. When he pulled away, she stared up at him with eyes that didn't quite focus.

"Something else to think about when I'm in the bath?" Her voice was thick, slightly slurred.

He didn't smile, but his gaze was hot and bright. "Yes. Think of me. God knows I'll be thinking of you."

Her flush made a fool of her. "You don't really remember me and yet you say such things." But oh, she wanted him to tell her just what he might do to himself while thinking of her. And what he might do to her, in the privacy of his mind.

He pulled her close once more. "I remember enough, but I don't need memories to want you, Arden."

A shiver rippled through her, a little nip of disappointment underneath. She wanted him to remember her, to want her because she was his loyal wife, not just because she was a woman who didn't fear him. "Yesterday you wanted to kill me."

"I wanted to kiss you more."

"That's disturbing on so many levels."

He chuckled and lowered his head in that way he always had the few times she'd seen him flustered or embarrassed. "I suppose it is." A heartbeat passed before he looked up, serious again. "I don't want to hurt you."

She swallowed. His words resonated deep inside her. "I believe you."

"Good. Now, you'd better go. Make certain Wolfred takes you home, and have the Withering woman assign guards to your house. If the Company comes looking for me, you'll be the first place they look."

She would not let him see how much that fact actually scared her. She was not a woman who allowed fear to rule her, and more often than not, bullied the emotion into bowing to her. "I will. Is there anything I can do for you?"

He caught a lock of hair that hung near her cheek and stroked it between his fingers. "Wait for me. Just a little while longer."

This time there was no stopping it. A hot tear slipped down her cheek. God help her if he was a liar, because she'd been sucked in, and believed the words that seemed to drip from his lips as sweet and potent as honeyed cider. She could only nod, and force herself to move away. She needed to leave right now, or she would finally lose her mind. He did not try to stop her.

The door was heavy, but she pulled it open, and stepped out into the corridor where both Dhanya and Alastair waited.

"Are you all right?" Alastair demanded, spying her tears. "Did he do something to hurt you?"

She shook her head, and swiped at her eyes with the back of her hands. She turned to the other woman. "Promise me you'll do whatever's necessary to fix him."

Dhanya nodded. "You have my word."

"Good." But Arden would keep a close eye regardless, just in case Dhanya's duty to the Crown exceeded the boundaries of friendship. With that promise to herself firmly in place, she directed her attention to Alastair.

"Take me home please, Alastair. I'm quite done in."

Dhanya spoke up. "I'll have one of my men drive you both home, and have your carriage returned to you as soon as possible, Wolfred."

"Thank you," Alastair replied, and offered Arden his arm. "Let's get you home."

Arden could have hugged him. "You're a good friend."

It might have been her imagination, but she thought he winced. Regardless, he made good on his promise and saw her safely home. Dhanya sent a couple of guards along behind them to keep watch over her house until late morning when others would take their place. They wore dull metal and black leather armor that blended into the night, but allowed them to move freely. It was quite effective against blade and bullet, and also augmented the wearer's physical strength. Arden warned them about her own security androids so they could avoid an attack.

When she finally crawled into bed, her head was already beginning to ache. She took a powder and some water, and pulled the blankets up around her ears. Sleep came surprisingly quickly despite the excitement of the evening and the fact that she was indeed thinking of Luke.

But her thoughts weren't sexual. All she could think of was how he'd looked at her when he realized she had waited for him in every sense of the word. She wondered if he would still look at her that way when he finally remembered that she was to blame for the Company abducting him in the first place.

Chapter 10

They were going to cut open his skull.

It was the morning of Luke's second day in the luxurious cell, and he had naught to do but sit and wait for the guards to come for him.

Self-preservation told him to run. He even had a plan: When the guards came he would render them both unconscious and slip into the private rail tunnel below. There were all manner of escape routes down there, and other tunnels few people knew about. Somehow—conveniently—he knew about them, and he could use them to get to freedom. The W.O.R doctor had removed the device from his ear the day before, so he could make a run for it without worrying about the Company finding him that easily.

When they did find him, they'd most likely kill him. If he didn't kill them first—and he would certainly try his damnedest to do just that. They had sent him to murder his own wife. They had turned him into what he was with that goal in mind. For years he'd been their ... puppet, for lack of a better term.

That pissed him off. When he got out of this place he was going to make retribution a top priority. If he got out of there, that was. His other priority? His wife.

Christ, she was something. Equal parts wanton and priss. She could play the fine lady, but she didn't mind getting dirty, was frigging brilliant and drank like a man. He found her fascinating, confounding and humbling.

She had remained true to him, if he was to believe her. That must be a thorn in Wolfred's side. He'd seen the two of them together, and found it hard to believe that she hadn't let herself be seduced. Rationally, he knew he'd have no grounds on which to fault her. The world had thought him dead, and he hadn't known she existed. He'd certainly had lovers of his own.

Irrationally, he wanted to make Wolfred—or any other man who might have had her, or even wanted to have her—swallow every one of his bloody teeth. Arden was his. He'd known that the first time he tried to kill her.

Thank God he hadn't succeeded. The very idea of taking her life turned his stomach. And yet, there was a small part of him that continued to insist he do just that, and then go back to the Company where he belonged. It was the cowardly part of him that wanted to do this. It was also the cowardly part of him that wanted to escape.

Because this man, this Earl Huntley, no longer existed inside him. The man Arden had waited for was as dead as the world believed him to be. She was going to be so very disappointed when she discovered that, and yet he couldn't bring himself to run.

It was the possibility of having Arden for his own that kept him in this cell—that made it possible for him to let the W.O.R. literally inside his head.

Dr. Stone had examined him before she removed the communication device from his ear. She was a striking woman of mixed blood. Her accent was vaguely Irish, but she looked as though she might have Spanish and Jamaican ancestry as well. And she didn't seem to find him the least bit intimidating, though he noticed she had two automatonic Pulver rifles pointed toward him from either side of the room. The blast from just one would make a mess of most men. He knew from experience it would hurt like hell, but wouldn't kill him. It would, however, take him down.

Dr. Stone took photographs of the inside of his body using Rontgen's "X-ray" method, and seemed fascinated by the extent of gregorite plating on his skeleton.

"You don't have any of the scarring usually associated with this sort of procedure. I've heard that Company surgeons have developed a way to inject gregorite into the body, along with a catalyst that makes it adhere to bone, but I've never seen it done." She glanced up at him with an expression that looked like a cross between awe and disgust. "Extraordinary."

Then she showed him the photograph of the inside of his head. His skull was covered with plates of metal, each molded to the bone. One plate in the front of his head had a hole in it, revealing the bone beneath.

Dr. Stone tapped the plate in the photograph. "If they altered your brain, this is where they did it. They removed this bit of bone and made a sort of door. Unfortunately I won't be able to get in there and take a good look, but I think I can see enough to determine what procedures might have been done. I would like to do the surgery as soon as possible."

It wasn't a request, so Luke didn't bother with granting consent. "I want to see my wife beforehand."

The handsome woman watched him with doelike eyes. He couldn't tell, nor did he care, what she was thinking. "Of course."

So now he sat in his cell doing the same thing he had

done most of the day before when not being debriefed by the Director herself—writing down every name, every mission, every fact no matter how minuscule he could remember about his seven years in the enemy's employ. It was a lesson in humiliation. Every page of vellum he filled was another stone of shame laid upon his shoulders. How could he have allowed himself to be taken? Surely the Director wondered the same thing. Wolfred, and especially Arden, must wonder as well. The Company had buggered him senseless, made him their whore, and made him fucking oblivious to the fact that they were the ones responsible for the theft of his life. Like a green recruit he had believed everything they told him because he wanted to believe it.

They took everything from him. The best revenge was to get it back. So shag the humiliation, let them root around in his head. He would do whatever it took to personally bring the Company to its knees.

He touched his right ear, and his fingers came away with tiny specks of dried blood on them. It didn't hurt, though it probably ought to. If not for the blood, and the fact that he had seen the device with his own eyes, he would never know the communicator had been removed.

Not that it mattered in here. The whole place was like a collection of "cages" similar to the one Mr. Faraday invented, designed to interfere with transmissions.

He put down his pencil and raised his arms above his head in a stretch. A loud ripping sound followed as the seams in the shoulders of the shirt he wore surrendered.

"Bugger," he muttered. The shirt was apparently his, made of the softest linen he'd ever . . . that he could remember ever touching. Arden had brought it for him yesterday, along with some trousers that were a bit loose in the waist and tight in the thigh. The Company obviously had a different training regime for their agents.

Either that, or he had been somewhat lazy seven years ago. Perhaps that was what got him caught.

Wolfred was in good shape. Strong and fit. He was a handsome enough bloke—charming when he wanted to be. He certainly didn't have a nose that looked sharp enough to cut cheese. It said something about Arden that she hadn't fallen into his arms—something that honored her, and scared the shite out of him.

A knock and the sound of keys rattling outside his door took him from his thoughts and scribbling. Slowly, he rose to his feet as the door opened. One of the guards stuck his head in. "A visitor for you, sir."

It was Arden. She swept into the room in skirts the color of paprika under a long violet silk frock coat. Her hair was haphazardly piled on her head with auburn tendrils hanging around her face, and a single gold chain ran from her ear to her nose, rather than the multiple silver strands she'd worn before.

Luke stared. All she was missing was a halo of sunshine. She was a goddess, right down to that smattering of freckles across her nose.

She glanced at the door when it clunked shut, leaving them alone, then back at him. "You wanted to see me?"

Was she even half as impressed by him as he was by her? Doubtful. He hadn't shaved that morning. In fact there were many mornings when he couldn't be bothered to drag a razor over his cheeks. He was rough and crass—a killer. He had consorted with the enemy, and while she was happy to have her husband home, she had to know that he was not that man. Not anymore.

"Yes."

"Was there something you wished to discuss?" Her clipped tone was edged with something so sharp it cut, but didn't hurt. Fear. She was afraid for him, and he could have kissed her for it, even if it was misplaced.

"No."

She frowned. "Then why did you ask for me?"

He chuckled, feeling every inch the ass. But he did not look away. "I wanted you to be the last thing I saw before they cut me open."

Blood drained from her cheeks, leaving them white as chalk. She was a little dark under the eyes—bruised-looking. She'd woken up this morning with a headache, he'd wager. How much did he figure into her reasons for numbing herself with liquor?

"You're going to be fine," she said, teeth clenched. She sounded as though she was trying to convince herself of that as well. "Evelyn is a talented surgeon."

He thought of the Doctor. "So were the people who did this to me. I came out of that not knowing who I was."

"That's different. The Company is evil."

He laughed again, but it was humorless and raw in his throat. "That's what they say about the W.O.R. Good or evil is a point of view, Arden. The Company used me, but don't fool yourself into thinking the Wardens wouldn't do exactly the same thing to a Company agent if they thought it would benefit their cause."

She stared at him as though he was speaking in tongues. Perhaps to her he was. Perhaps he oughtn't challenge her idealism. Sometimes a little black and white was refreshing after a palette of gray.

Her gaze dropped. "You ripped your shirt."

As a change of subject it wasn't exactly subtle, but he'd take it. "Sorry."

The corners of her lips curved delicately upward. Whiskey-colored eyes glittered as they met his. "Did you do it intentionally?"

"No." That would be ridiculous. "It was too tight across the shoulders—" He stopped when her smile became a grin. Damnation, but she was pretty when she smiled.

"That's it," she said. "It's the shirt's fault you have the shoulders of David."

Luke arched a brow, unable to stop his own smile. "The shoulders of David? I'll take that as a compliment."

She flushed—a dark peach filling her cheeks. "It was meant as one. When you come home we'll have your tailor come in."

"When I come home." He was beginning to sound like a damn parrot.

Her eyes were wide, her cheeks flushed as only a redhead's could be. "Why, yes. I assumed you would come home when Dhanya is done with you."

What an interesting choice of words. "Yes. I should come home." With her. Where she slept and pleasured herself in the bath.

She lifted her chin, exposing the delicate, pale flesh of her neck. He watched her throat as she swallowed. He wanted to kiss her there. "I can stay elsewhere, if that is what you wish."

Luke's gaze flew up, brows clamping together in a scowl. "Why the hell would I want that?"

The puffy shoulders of her jacket lifted—absurd balloons trying to pull free from their moorings. She seemed genuinely confused—which either made her totally unaware of her own charms or stupid. His guess was the former. "You didn't know you had a wife until a few days ago."

"I didn't know I had a fucking name until then either. It's your house."

She winced, and he knew he had said the wrong thing. "It's your house. I've just lived there the past nine years."

Nine years. He'd been gone from her longer than they'd been together. "It's *our* house," he amended. That was decidedly gentler than demanding that she remain there or he'd tie her to a bedpost. "And if I survive this procedure with my mind intact—and your Director allows me to live—I want you there when I come home."

Her wide eyes took on a glossy sheen—tears, he realized. "Christ, I didn't mean to make you cry."

Gloved fingers dabbed at her eyes. "You didn't. It's just that I cannot believe you're really here. Your brother will be so happy."

"My brother?" His heart gave a hard thump. A hazy face swam in his mind, slowly coming into focus, a headache hot on its heels. "The man I saw you talking to at the party that night."

She nodded. "Henry. He's missed you too."

"I'm surprised he hasn't had me declared dead."

"Of course not." Her gaze flitted away from his. "He didn't believe you were dead any more than I did."

She was lying, and doing a piss-poor job of it. Usually he'd be angry at it, but it was oddly sweet that she wanted to spare his feelings. "I'm very fortunate to have such a brother. And such a wife."

"Yes, well, there were those who said I was delusional." She smoothed her palms over her hips, still not looking at him.

"Was one of those people Wolfred?"

Arden actually looked affronted. "He looked for you. He went all over Europe searching, paid all manner of bribes. When that turned up nothing he lost hope."

"He's in love with you."

She stiffened, wide-eyed expression narrowing to something just short of a glare. "Don't say that."

"It's true."

"I know, but it makes me feel like I took advantage of his friendship, and there were days he was the only friend I had."

During his years under the Company's control he'd met several women who thought nothing of exploiting a man's affections for their own gain. Hell, he had thought little of turning the tables on a few of those same women. Perhaps that said a lot about the sort of person he was. He hoped, for the sake of this woman, that his old friend hadn't shared his callousness.

"I never should have left you." It was the only apology he could think to make.

Her clear, brown gaze was hard. "But you did."

"Why?" That was the question that had niggled at his dodgy memory ever since it first began to return. "Selective" she had called it. "Was it an assignment?"

Arden tugged on the bottom of her jacket. "That had a great deal to do with it, yes. To be honest, I do not know the whole of it."

Strange. They seemed to have had a good relationship, something of a partnership. Why hadn't he told her what he was up to? Unless, had he been under direct orders not to?

"Withering's predecessor, what happened to him?"

The fair skin between her brows furrowed. The woman frowned so much it was a wonder she didn't have a furrow as deep as a ditch there. "He suffered an apoplexy and died. Why?"

Balls. "I thought he might be able to provide some details of my last mission."

"Oh." Her expression softened. If she gazed at him in pity he just might have to kill her after all. "This all must be damnably frustrating for you."

Luke chuckled. His wife was a master of understatement. "Mildly."

They stared at each other for a moment. Then he said, "You will stay for the procedure?"

She nodded. "I won't be in the operating theater, but

I'll be here when you wake up." She smiled then, and it was damned near impossible not to smile back. She obviously had complete faith in Dr. Stone—or she was a better liar than he thought.

There was a knock on the door, and the guard stuck his head in once more. There was no such thing as privacy in his posh prison. "It's time, your lordship."

It didn't feel the least bit odd to be deferred to by that title. Or rather, it felt oddly *right*. "Thank you." Luke straightened his shoulders. He'd gone up against assassins, been in situations so tenuous it was a wonder he made it through unscathed, yet he was nervous about this. What if it all went wrong? What if he woke up as he had in the Company hospital with no memory whatsoever?

Small, warm fingers entwined with his. He looked down to find Arden standing beside him, holding his hand. She smiled reassuringly. "I'll walk with you, if you don't mind."

"Not at all," he replied. Damn, his voice was hoarse.

The guard put the shackles on him before leading him down the corridor to the lift and up one floor to the operating theater. Arden remained by his side the entire time. She even stood by the operating table as Dr. Stone applied chloroform. His wife's face was the last thing he saw before blackness pulled him under.

He hoped when he woke up he'd remember her.

"Damn it, Dhanya! He's jumped through all your hoops. I want my husband back!" Two days of seeing him as a prisoner had made Arden realize she trusted him more than she thought. And nights of wishing he was there to make good on his promise to give her "something to moan about" only added to her frustration. Perhaps it was incredibly slatternly of her, but she wanted her husband at home, in her bed, and bugger the rest.

Her friend and superior drew her spine straight, her face an imperious mask. "You would do well to remember just who it is you're talking to."

Arden's own shoulders snapped back. "In this place your word may be law, but don't think I won't petition the Queen herself. My husband is a Peer of the Realm."

"And a traitor."

If anyone else had called Luke that, she would have jabbed them with the pronged end of her discombobulator.

"Not a willing one." Arden met the other woman's amber gaze and held it. She was nothing if not willful. Her stubbornness was legendary; without it she would have given up hope for Luke's return years ago. She'd be illegally married to Alastair right now, or at least be his lover. It was only sheer determination that kept her pious, and it had worked out in her favor.

Dhanya folded her arms over her chest. She wore black trousers with a shirt of violet silk and a black waistcoat embroidered in gold. Her long black hair hung down her back in a loose braid. She looked beautiful and impenetrable. Two minutes ago, Arden had found a piece of copper wire in her own hair—left over from a glovewarmer she'd been working on for a client earlier that morning. It wasn't as though she needed the funds such work brought in, but it kept her mind sharp and occupied, and it also gave her access to ladies who knew all the latest gossip. It was in her best interest to know what was going on—especially with a poor girl murdered. There were still no leads, but Arden shamefully had to admit that since finding Luke in her bedroom she hadn't given the murder her full attention. "He's not going anywhere until I am satisfied that you and the rest of Britain is safe from him."

Arden picked up the notepad from the desk and held

it up. The pages were covered with writing in her husband's hand. "He's given you pages of information already. Surely that gives you some degree of confidence."

Elegant shoulders shrugged. "I've yet to confirm any of that. And you shouldn't be reading it."

Arden tossed it back on the desk. "I don't want to read it." She didn't want to know the things he'd done for those monsters. "I want my life back. I want my husband."

Dhanya appeared unmoved, but then she had never been married. She had no idea how it felt to have Luke returned just to lose him again. "I am sorry, Arden, but I will not sanction his release one second before I am ready."

Arden's temper flared into hot pettiness. "Then I'm afraid I won't have that device for you until I'm ready."

The Director flushed. "You said we wouldn't speak of it. And you're being a child."

Her first came down on the desk. "I want my husband!"

A moment passed as silence settled between them, neither prepared to look away first, or even blink. Then Dhanya began to chuckle. Arden followed, much to her own chagrin. Oh, but it felt good to laugh. She sank into one of the chairs in front of the desk and the other woman did the same. Their chuckles faded, leaving both of them wiping at their eyes in silence.

Having regained her composure at last, Arden said, "I need him, Dhanya. I need to have him at home with me. I've waited so long I fear I may go mad if I have to wait much longer."

Resting her elbow on the desk, the Director regarded her with a sympathetic gaze. "You know he's not the man he once was."

Arden nodded, her fingers toying with the bit of wire that had fallen from her hair. "I'm not the same woman.

I'm not sure that's entirely a bad thing." Though that was a lie. If they weren't the same people, would they still love each other? She had been shocked when Luke said there was little difference between the Wardens and the Company. Why, he'd been all about his duty before he disappeared. He believed the W.O.R. to be an instrument of good against Company corruption.

She'd also been surprised at the way he looked at her when she lied to him. She was a very good liar, but she was certain he could sense her deceit. He had never caught her in a lie before—not that she knew of. Of course, she'd never really had anything to lie to him about before.

"A few more days," Dhanya assured her. "Let us monitor his recovery from the procedure, see what he might remember about his last assignment and how he was taken. Then you can take him home—with some provisos, of course. You never know, returning to his home and to you just might trigger memories."

She referred to his spy work. Personally Dhanya would want Arden to be happy, but what mattered to the other woman was uncovering what had happened to Luke, whether or not he had been betrayed. What really gave her pause was Dhanya's mention of his last assignment. No one seemed to know what it was. If Dhanya didn't know, then the former director had taken it to his grave. That meant it involved something extremely sensitive. But what? It had been so secretive that her father had been forbidden to discuss what devices he supplied for the operation. And when Luke disappeared, he'd been taken into headquarters for a private meeting with the former director—a meeting he refused to speak of, but Arden had seen the sadness, and fear in his eyes. He refused to tell her anything, even when she begged him on her knees, sobbing for her husband.

Her heart broke a little at the thought of Papa. Luke had yet to inquire after him, but he would eventually, and she would have to tell him that Papa was gone, and that Mama had fallen to decline.

As soon as her mind turned to her mother she shut it down. That was more heartbreak than she could take at the moment.

"Thank you," she said. "I know you have the Empire to worry about, so I apologize if my wants seem petty in comparison."

Dhanya's full lips curved. "I cannot imagine what you must be going through, so I will apologize if I seem cold in my motives. But threaten me with Her Majesty in the future and you'll never taste Mama's sweets again."

That was a threat that hit home. "I would rather die." It was said with humor, but when Dhanya fixed them tea on the little burner she had in the corner of her office, and brought out a plate of her mother's delicious concoctions, Arden thought perhaps she should keep such threats to herself in the future.

She was on her second cup of tea and fourth sweet when Evelyn arrived. It had only been a little more than two hours since she put Luke under. The sight of the darker woman launched Arden to her feet, dread heavy in her chest, food and tea revolting in her churning stomach. "Is he . . . ?"

Evelyn looked horrified. "Oh, luvvy, no! He's fine. Brilliant, actually. Sleeping now, but you'll be able to see him in a bit."

Choking back a sob, Arden sank into her chair before her knees could give out. "Oh, thank God." When she reached for her empty teacup, Dhanya splashed some whiskey in it from the bottle she kept in her desk drawer. It was the bottle she kept for special or dire occasions. Which of those she considered this, Arden had no idea.

"Evelyn?" Dhanya held up the bottle. When the doctor nodded, she poured some whiskey in a cup for her as well. "Tell us everything."

Evelyn took the whiskey with a tired and grateful smile. Arden couldn't remember ever seeing the woman when she looked as though she was rested. "I made a small incision on Lord Huntley's forehead above the small section of bare bone in his skull. When I inspected the opening I found a small mechanism inside, which I managed to extract intact." She took a sip from her cup.

Arden exchanged glances with Dhanya. "What sort of mechanism?"

"The sort normally used in asylums to release medication into patients in regular intervals."

Dear God. "Did you find anything inside it?" Arden asked, swallowing hard against the horror and disgust twisting inside her.

Evelyn took another drink. "Yes. I need to run a few more tests because I wanted to talk to the both of you first, but I think a chemical compound was being used to inhibit Lord Huntley's long-term memory. Just having the device implanted in his brain would be damaging enough."

The thought turned Arden's stomach. She took another drink regardless. "Will he recover his memory now that it's been removed?" Did she want him to recover?

Her friend shot her a sympathetic look. "I'm not certain, luv. With the gregorite in the way, it's difficult to see just how much damage has been done. Plus, there's so much we don't know about the brain. Add to that the damage that the chemicals have done over years of continued use. . . . I think you should prepare yourself for the possibility that he will never fully regain his memory."

Arden caught her top lip between her teeth. So much of his life—of their life together—lost forever. How could they ever hope to regain what they once had? "Thank you, Evie."

"I wish I could have brought you better news."

She cleared her throat. Sympathy was well and good, but it could quickly become pity, and she would rather hack off her own hands than be pitied. "Is his mind otherwise sound?"

Evelyn rolled the cup between her palms. "The procedure was completely without incident, so I've no reason to suspect otherwise."

"That's all I can ask. The rest will be what it will be."

Arched brows from both women met her statement. "That's very . . . calm of you," Evelyn allowed.

Arden shrugged, careful to keep her inner turmoil to herself. "It's why God made whiskey." She forced a chuckle when her friend looked even more shocked. "I'm just happy he's remembered who I am and stopped trying to kill me. Honestly, you two. Right now it's enough just to know I was right."

To her great relief, both of her companions believed her lies and laughed. Dhanya raised her cup. "To husbands not trying to kill their wives."

"I'll drink to that," Evelyn agreed, lifting her cup in toast as well. Arden followed suit. She suddenly felt lighter—a combination of the whiskey and the good news about Luke. She still had hope. After clinging to it for the past seven years, she would not abandon it now. After all, it had served her well.

She sat with the women for a little while longer—enough to enjoy a second cup of Dhanya's whiskey and make use of the loo. She was just about to take her leave when Mr. Chiler's voice came through the orophone on the desk. "Pardon me, Director?"

Dhanya moved the device—which looked like a miniature gramophone horn—toward her so she could speak into the flared mouth. She removed a piece of cork from it. "Yes, Chiler?"

"I have Chief Inspector Grant on the telephone. He's looking for Lady Huntley. Would she like to speak to him?"

Dhanya looked to Arden for consent. Arden nodded. "It must be important for him to call me here."

"Ring him through to this station. Thank you, Chiler." A second later the telephone in the office began to ring. Dhanya put the piece of cork back into the orophone before answering the other device. "Certainly, Inspector. Lady Huntley is right here." Dhanya passed the telephone to Arden.

"Inspector Grant?" Arden said into the mouthpiece, holding the listening part to her ear. "What is it?"

"Sorry to trouble you, my lady, but I was of the hope that you might have the time to call upon me at Scotland Yard today."

Arden hesitated. She wanted to see Luke before she left. "Is it important?"

There was a pause on the other end. "My lady, would I call you at this location if it wasn't?"

Whatever it was, Grant obviously didn't want to discuss it over the telephone. No matter that it was a marvel of modern innovation, it was all too easy for operators to listen in on otherwise private conversations—a favorite pastime of many, despite one of W.O.R's telephone exchange operators having been charged with treason for sharing something she'd overheard. "I'll be there as soon as I can, Inspector." She didn't add that it had better be worth forcing her to leave her husband.

He thanked her and she disconnected the conversation by placing the earpiece in its "switch."

"Has there been a break in the investigation of the baron's daughter?" Dhanya asked.

"He didn't say," Arden replied, rising from her chair. "Ladies, I'm afraid I must take my leave of you. Evie, may I check upon Lord Huntley before I depart?"

"Of course." The darker woman made a face that said she hadn't needed to ask. "He's in the infirmary. The nurse will let you in."

She hugged both of the women before leaving, and carried her hat in her hand. She had to ask Mr. Chiler for directions to the infirmary, but found it easily enough. The ward was closed off by a metal door with a slider that opened a few seconds after she knocked. The nurse let her in as soon as she identified herself. Dr. Stone had left her name as a temporary visitor to the locked facility.

Luke was at the far end of the short row of beds, the majority of which were empty. His color was good, and aside from the snowy bandages wrapped around his head, he looked perfectly normal. Peaceful. She couldn't help but smile at the sight of him. Hopefully Evelyn's procedure had severed the last of his ties with the Company.

The armed guard watching over him nodded at her as she approached, and moved a discreet distance away to give her a little privacy, but remained close enough should anyone—herself included—make trouble.

Arden lowered herself to the edge of the narrow cot, sitting on her hip so as not to disturb Luke's slumber.

She reached down and smoothed back the hair that stuck up above the top of the bandage wrapped around his head. It was soft and silky, and brought a lump to her throat. If she had a pound for every time she'd come close to, or had cried since his return, she'd be an extremely wealthy woman. God, someone ought to horsewhip her for this sentimentality.

Dark lashes twitched, then slowly opened. Glassy

pale eyes stared up at her as his lips curved into a lazy smile. "I know you. You're my wife."

Arden grinned like an idiot. It felt as though a huge mass had been lifted from her back. How could she not have been consciously aware of just how afraid she'd been that he would wake up with his memory gone once more? "Yes, I am."

His lids drooped. "Nice wife. You want to crawl in here with me?" One of his hands clumsily patted the side of the bed. "There's plenty of room."

There wasn't enough room for a breath in that bed, let alone her entire girth, but if time had allowed she would indeed attempt to stuff herself in there. "I'd be delighted, but I can't stay. I have an appointment."

Luke frowned, then grimaced when the expression tugged at the stitches on his forehead. It seemed to be a struggle for him to keep his eyes open. "Where?"

"Scotland Yard."

His frown eased, and he lost the battle with his heavy lids. "Duty then. Can't ignore that."

"No," she replied, spine straightening. His words were like a sharp cut to her heart despite being an echo of their past. "I can't."

He didn't speak again—he was sound asleep once more, his chest rising and falling in an easy rhythm. She envied him the escape.

Arden placed the back of her fingers against his warm cheek, feeling the sharp edge of his cheekbone against her knuckles, the scratch of stubble. Quickly, she rose to her feet and walked away, refusing to let the irrational part of her mind wander into all the places it wanted to go. There didn't have to be some foretelling of doom in his words.

Though as she left the infirmary she had to wonder if

it would be Luke's sense of duty that caused friction between them once more, or her own.

The man stepped onto the dirigible docking platform and placed his beaver hat upon his head. Hyde Park smelled of horse shit and airship grease, just as it always did. He'd never understand why so many people insisted on clinging to such antiquated notions as horse-travel, but he didn't care. Let the mindless chattel do as they would. He had more important things to occupy his mind.

It had been almost three days since they lost contact with Five. The Doctor had been unsuccessful in his attempt to subdue the operative and had the injuries to prove it. Five had not returned to his rooms since, and the last information gleaned from the communicator in his ear had placed him at his former London home—with his wife.

Earlier today his contact at the W.O.R. confirmed that Five was in their possession, and orders had been given to detonate the device in Five's brain. As valuable as he had been, he was a liability now and could not be allowed to live. He would be a great loss to the Company, and give the Wardens a glimpse not only into Company technology, but into years of missions and subterfuge.

It was his job to clean up any mess, find out what the W.O.R. knew, and finish Five's original mission. And, in case they were unsuccessful in immediately eliminating Five, he was to do that as well. It was a distasteful business, but he would not rest until Arden Grey, Lady Huntley—and her husband—were dead.

Chapter 11

Chief Inspector Grant was standing outside the Scotland Yard building when Arden arrived. He was smoking a pipe, and judging from the little mounds of ash at his feet, had been doing so quite prodigiously for a while.

"I thought you gave that up because your wife detests the smell," she said, by way of greeting as she stepped out of her touring carriage.

"I did," he replied grimly as she lowered her goggles. A plume of fragrant smoke rose around him in the steam-damp air. "But she'll just have to forgive me for it."

His face was pale, the skin beneath his eyes dark and bruised-looking. She'd seen him look haggard before, but it seemed worse now, as though his position was finally wearing him down.

"There's been another murder, hasn't there?" She didn't wait for him to respond before digging her bag out from behind the driving bench.

"Yes. Another girl with her heart ripped out. We've gotten some of the findings back on the first girl as well. I didn't want to call you, but . . ." He took one last haul off the pipe. "Two girls in less than a fortnight. I need your help to find this bastard."

That he didn't mind his language—and didn't apologize for it—proved just how tired and stretched thin the inspector truly was. Arden drew a deep breath, filling her lungs with the smell of pipe tobacco, which she didn't mind in the least. She drew calm around her like a warm blanket. "Where's the latest victim?"

"Here at the morgue." He tapped the bowl of his pipe against the dingy gray stone wall. Scientists might have discovered a fairly clean-burning coal alternative, but there was no undoing the decades of soot ground into every pore of London's buildings and streets. "Didn't want the press to catch wind and put her photograph in the *Times*, soulless vultures."

Arden wasn't surprised by his vehemence. She'd worked with Grant long enough to know that he believed the press to be on par with the lowest of criminals. She didn't quite share his opinion, but she had also worked with him long enough to understand where it came from. They'd almost lost the Ripper because of the press.

She pulled back her shoulders. "You'd better take me to her, Inspector. Perhaps she can give us what her predecessor could not—the identity of her killer."

"I hope so, Lady Huntley." He slipped his pipe into his jacket pocket. "Some of the lads are likening these to the Ripper murders, but I didn't feel half so horrible for those poor souls as I do these dear little girls."

Grant's shoulders were hunched as she followed him to the door exclusively used for Scotland Yard staff. He inserted his punch key in the box on the wall and waited as it finished its sharp clacking before withdrawing the card and turning the heavy, spoked wheel on the iron door. There was a hissing sound, like that of train brakes, only not as loud, followed by a thunk, and then he pushed the door open.

"After you, Lady Huntley."

Arden stepped over the threshold. Given her association with the police force, this wasn't the first time she'd been allowed access to the inner workings of Scotland Yard, and it probably would not be the last. It wasn't a cheery place, though the odd chuckle punctuated the din. The men and women who worked here had that dull-eyed look of people who had seen every possible human evil there was. All of their shock and horror—even sorrow—had been all used up, and there was nothing left.

She inclined her head in greeting to those whose gaze caught hers. No one was surprised to see her. Though Grant took pains to conceal her involvement in Yard business, she was still a known asset to many. The rest simply didn't care.

It wouldn't be that scandalous for society to find out about the work she did for the Yard, only slightly more so if it was discovered she was a W.O.R. agent. The real scandal would be caused by the devices for ladies she made in her workshop. Such was the way—the general populace barely blinked at violence, but sexuality was a different story.

The morgue was in the basement, of course, where bodies were kept cool in the storage area using small amounts of solidified carbon dioxide. It was a dangerous substance, and Arden had seen more than one morgue attendant who had lost a finger or two to frostbite because of it. Still, it was effective.

She pulled her shawl tighter around her shoulders to ward off the chill as they descended the stairs, Inspector Grant carrying her case. She took her flask from her reticule and allowed herself a small sip. She'd always enjoyed a nip now and again, but over the past few years she'd come to depend on spirits more and more. She knew it, and wasn't nearly as bothered by it as she supposed she should be.

It wasn't as though she was a drunkard. It wasn't as though she *needed* it to cope. It just made doing what she had to do so much easier.

The whiskey warmed her from the inside out. She opened her tin of cloves and popped one in her mouth, letting the sharp spiciness roll over her tongue and perfume her breath.

Only the *Curator Mortuorum* was present in the morgue when they entered. She was a tall woman—over six feet—with a sturdy build and thick curly red hair. Arden was thankful for her presence, as Mrs. MacNamara considered herself a caretaker of the dead, and tried to make the viewing experience as pleasant as possible.

"Lady Huntley," the woman said in a deep Scottish brogue. "Good to see you."

Arden slipped her gloved hand into the woman's much larger one. Mrs. MacNamara had an incredibly strong grip. "You as well, though perhaps someday we'll meet in pleasanter circumstances."

The older woman nodded solemnly. "God willing. You're here to see the girl Grant brought in earlier?"

"That's right," the inspector answered. "Would you be so kind as to fetch her? Also, I'd like you to repeat your findings on the Rathbone girl to Lady Huntley."

Rathbone? Ah yes, Arden remembered. That was Baron Lynbourne's family name.

Mrs. MacNamara went into one of the large cooling chambers used to store London's "done in." Newgate had its own morgue for prisoners, so the only bodies that fell into Mrs. Mac's capable hands were those who had suffered a wrongful death. Though on occasion the denizens of Newgate ended up on her table as well. Men with nothing to lose didn't have much respect for human life.

Arden had an awful feeling that one day her own body would end up in the Scottish woman's care. She might have already if Victor Erlich had been a tad bit faster, and she hadn't been able to reach her discombobulator. She hadn't meant to kill him, but she hadn't been about to let him rape her either. Alastair was meant to find the bastard, but she'd been the unlucky one. It was the last time she worked in what they referred to as "the field." She hadn't the love of danger that Alastair and Luke shared, though there were times she'd rather face the wrong end of a pistol than witness the last moments of another person's life.

When the *Curator Mortuorum* returned, she pushed a gurney in front of her. One of the wheels squeaked, and the shroud covering the body had seen better days, but Mrs. Mac took care with her cargo. She brought the gurney to the center of the room, beneath the operating chandelier, before gently peeling back the sheet.

Arden gritted her teeth as her gaze fell on thick chestnut hair—its elaborate coiffure ruined. Next, the deathly pallor of a smooth forehead, a fringe of still lashes, followed by a slack, round cheek. When the entire face had been revealed she gasped, horror sending a rush of tea and whiskey up from her belly. Only sheer fortitude kept her from humiliating herself. Embarrassment burned in the back of her throat, acrid and raw.

Grant whipped his head around to stare at her with those sharp eyes of his. "You know her?"

She nodded, averting her eyes long enough for the nausea to fade and her composure to return. "Cassandra Millingston. Earl Farnsworth's daughter."

The inspector swore—so well and in such detail that Arden could almost see a cloud of blue around the words. She didn't blame him, and she certainly wouldn't ask him to apologize for it. She understood, and agreed with him.

It wasn't just that she knew the girl, or that the victim was an aristocrat, but she knew as Grant did that once word got out that another peer's daughter had been murdered, there would be a panic amongst the upper classes. The Season might very well be called to an early end.

Their killer was undoubtedly of the aristocracy, and if the Season ended prematurely, their chances of finding the bastard would practically disappear with it. If he was indeed of the upper class, he would drift away to the country, and even if he killed again, they might never track him down.

"We have to keep this as quiet as possible," Grant said.

Arden arched a brow. "Rather impossible, don't you think? The moment you tell her parents the rest of the Mayfair set will know within an hour at the most." She didn't point out that a mass exodus would be soon to follow. "The girl's parents are undoubtedly concerned if she went missing last night."

"I shall have to think of something," Grant said in a low voice, gaze flinty. "I'll not let *this* one slip away."

Perhaps the Ripper investigation had affected Grant more than he let on. Arden turned to the *Curator Mortuorum*. "Mrs. Mac, would you be so kind as to show me the rest of the body?"

She was prepared for what lay under the sheet, though her stomach insisted on turning itself inside out at the sight. This young woman had been split open just like Lynbourne's girl, her heart brutally ripped from her chest.

"He's got a sense of anatomy, but I don't think he's a medical man," the Scottish woman informed them.

"Why not?" Arden inquired.

Mrs. Mac gestured with her finger toward a splintered rib, then past to the tattered tissue beneath. "Most with medical training are fastidious, brilliant and arrogant. This monster has no finesse. Even Saucy Jack had to show off his skill with a blade—to an extent. These girls weren't cut; they were torn open."

"I beg your pardon?" Arden frowned. "How is that possible?"

"There's not a knife mark to be found, but look at the bruising." Arden forced herself to look where the coroner pointed. If not for the whiskey her mind might better comprehend what the woman was saying. Oddly enough, the whiskey was the only thing keeping her from casting up her accounts all over Mrs. Mac's boots. "He shoved his hands into their torsos, pulled their ribs apart and tore the hearts from their chests."

Arden swallowed hard. "So the killer had to be uncommonly strong."

Mrs. Mac's expression was full-on incredulous. "Without a doubt, my lady. He had to have gregorite hands to do something like this."

Her first thought was Luke. He was strong enough to do this. And the first night she'd seen him had been at the site of the first murder. But he'd been locked up in his W.O.R. cell last night. He couldn't be the killer. Relief dropped her shoulders just as shame filled her with its dirtiness. How could she think him capable of such madness—even for a second? Never mind that he'd been sent to kill her—that was a mission. This . . . this was just lunacy.

"I found traces of gentleman's hair pomade under her fingernails," Mrs. Mac continued, gesturing toward a

small vial on a nearby tray. "I haven't been able to identify the brand yet."

"May I?" Arden asked. At the other woman's nod, she
took the vial, removed the stopper and sniffed. A flood
of memories rushed at her, tightening her throat and
burning her eyes. "Wexell's Best," she murmured, replacing the stopper before tears actually escaped.

Inspector Grant's expression was one of terse hope.
"Are you certain?"

Arden smiled sadly. "Yes. My father used it. I'd know
the scent anywhere." The thought of her father, on top of
everything else, threatened to send her over the edge,
but she mentally dug in her heels and forced all of her
emotions into a far corner. They'd come for her later, but
for now she was safe.

"Surely there can't be that many men of the peerage
with augmented arms who use that particular pomade?"
Grant scribbled in his notebook.

"I dare say there will be a number more than you
hope," Arden advised. "It is a very popular brand—most
ladies quite like the scent of it. Plus, it doesn't make a
man's hair feel like grease."

The inspector grimaced. "Never understood the stuff
myself. If a man wore his hair short as is proper, there'd
be no need to slick it all back."

Arden and Mrs. Mac traded amused glances as he
scribbled in his book once more.

"Inspector, where did you happen to find the body?"
So much easier to refer to the deceased as a thing.

"Hyde Park. We're fortunate the watchman who
found her knew better than to make a fuss. Managed to
keep all very discreet."

"Hmm. You could narrow your search by concentrat-
ing on young or very charming gentlemen." Arden stared
at Cassandra Millingston's dead face. Bless Mrs.

MacNamara—she had pulled the sheet up once more so the grisly wound was covered. "He had to be winsome enough for these girls to go off with him. First to the factory and then to Hyde Park."

He didn't look up from his book, but kept writing. "Odd that he would kill so close to where he probably lives, isn't it?"

Arden shrugged. "It might be the only place he could convince her to go. I'll know more once I've seen through her eyes. Would you assist me, Mrs. Mac?"

With the larger woman's assistance, Arden quickly outfitted both herself and the corpse with the Aetheric Remnant Oscillatory Transmutative Spectacles. She took a deep breath as she turned the key, then wished she hadn't. The room reeked of death, and she was soon going to be unable to escape it.

It only took a moment for the device to begin showing her the last few minutes of Cassandra Millingston's life. It was dark, but the moon and a nearby lamp made it possible for her to see the shady outlines of her surroundings. Lover's Walk, that's where she was. She was on the dark path famous for providing the proper concealment for romantic trysts.

From the lazy way she looked around—slowly and slightly unfocused—Arden realized Cassandra had been somewhat intoxicated. She hadn't been fall-down drunk, but tipsy enough that going to the park with a man seemed like a good idea.

Stupid girl. Meeting a man in the dead of night was *never* a good idea, not when reputation was all a girl had to recommend her. Still, Arden couldn't pass judgment. She'd had her own share of kisses—and sometimes a little more—in the dark.

She spun around—Cassandra that was—the world tilting and sliding around her. She had probably laughed out loud. Her hands waved about in the air. She was dancing.

Suddenly, she was pulled into the arms of a man. Her own arms wound around his neck. Arden saw a flash of his jaw—strong, clean shaven—and part of his ear. She couldn't tell the color of his hair in darkness, but it didn't appear to be black.

"Come on," she snarled between clenched teeth, not caring that others could hear. "Show me his bloody face."

But all she saw was the cravat pin—onyx in the shape of a horseshoe. It slipped slightly out of focus. Then, her hands braced against the man's broad chest. She pushed, struggled, turned her head—probably to scream—and then . . . oh, God.

Cassandra Millingston had looked down. She had seen her killer's hand in her chest. She must have felt him break her ribs. Had she felt her heart beat in his grasp just before he . . . ?

It all went black. Arden ripped the spectacles from her head and tossed them at Mrs. Mac. She half ran, half stumbled to the sink in the corner before the sweets, tea and whiskey in her stomach came rushing up. She retched until there was nothing left, and when she was done, she turned the tap to wash it all away, and splashed some water on her cheeks.

She turned to face Mrs. Mac and Grant in humiliation. "Forgive me."

"Here." Grant shoved a brass and leather flask in her face. "Drink."

She had her own, of course, but she didn't feel like whiskey right now—it didn't taste as good when it came back up—so she took the brandy he offered and swallowed a generous amount.

"What did you see?" Grant asked after she'd taken another drink and passed the flask back.

"Not his face," she allowed with a ragged, bitter chuckle. She swiped the back of her hand across her mouth. "His hair isn't black, if that helps. He's clean shaven. Tall, and well built." Most of this they already knew. "And Mrs. Mac is right, he shoved his hand into her chest like she was no more substantial than pudding." Oh, God. She'd never eat pudding again.

She heard the inspector writing it all down as Mrs. Mac patted her softly on the shoulder. When the scratch of pencil on paper stopped she hazarded a glance at Grant and said, "I'm so sorry I couldn't see more."

The gruff Scotland Yard agent looked surprised. "You saw what she did. I don't expect I could ask much more than that from someone who wasn't even there."

Arden shook her head in frustration. "I should be able to build something more helpful. Perhaps if I go through my father's catalog again I will find a solution— something that could prove more efficient and helpful."

A kind and heavy hand came down on her shoulder. Grant stared into her eyes and gave her a firm smile. "My lady, you've already proved your worth to me. Do not diminish it by punishing yourself for things beyond your control. Only God was meant to see everything. To know everything."

Normally she despised when people threw God into the conversation. God was no excuse for her own ineptitude, but this time she let it go. Unless she devised a way to know what a person heard before they were killed, it was doubtful she could have done any more.

She thought of Luke and the listening device the Company had put in his ear. Was it even possible to capture the sounds a person heard before their death? Perhaps if she could access the actual portion of the brain responsible for memory . . . Oh, the things she could do.

Had the Company inventors responsible for the thing

in Luke's head once thought the same thing? Of all they could achieve if only they had the proper bits and pieces? Was she really any better?

"So we're looking for a young, fit gentleman of the upper classes with hair that isn't black, but is pomaded, and hands that have been augmented." Grant looked up from his writing. "That gives us a bit more to go on than just the cravat pin."

Arden wouldn't forget that pin—not even after she was dead would she forget it. She glanced at the dead girl. Her family would be beside themselves. London society would panic. There was very limited time to find this monster.

And as a lady invited to almost every societal function, Arden knew she was the only one who could do it.

She had better find him before he killed again.

Dhanya Withering hadn't become Director of the W.O.R. by being sentimental or by being soft. Contrary to what many believed, it also wasn't because she was supposedly the bastard of a Royal Duke either. She had risen through the ranks by being smart, by putting the welfare of the Empire ahead of her own, and by being a proper bitch when the circumstances demanded it. She had never given priority to her personal feelings.

Until now.

"Are you certain it's wise to let him go?" Alastair asked. They were on the floor above the infirmary, watching Lucas Grey get his bandages changed through the glass.

"No," Dhanya replied, her gaze focused on Grey. "But I'm going to do it regardless."

Beside her, the tall man stiffened. Mentally, Dhanya braced herself. Was this going to turn into one of those unfortunate times when a peer reminded her of her low birth? Would he believe birth made any difference in this place, where she ruled? She was answerable only to the Prime Minister and Her Majesty. Only once had a peer gone over her head to the queen.

Dhanya had won, but it didn't change the fact that most of these titled brats thought themselves above her. She had never gotten that feeling from Lord Wolfred, and she hoped he wouldn't lower himself by doing it now.

"I am worried for Lady Huntley," he informed her.

"Of course you are, as am I." The only difference was, she wasn't in love with Arden. Wolfred thought he concealed his feelings, but one only had to see him look at her once to know the truth.

"We do not know for certain that he will not try again to kill her, as much as I want to believe otherwise."

His words spoke to her own fears, but she reminded herself that a part of the earl hoped that Huntley proved to be a traitor; then he might still have a chance to win the man's widow.

"My instinct tells me he won't hurt Arden, but that's not the sole reason I'm letting him go. The Company's first attempt to assassinate her failed, but that doesn't mean they won't send another." She turned to him. "Lord Huntley is more than equipped to protect his wife."

The slightest wince passed over Wolfred's handsome features—for which Dhanya was sorry—but the man had to reconcile himself with reality and what was right. Arden's life might depend upon it.

"I know you think you can protect her, my lord, but you cannot be with her twenty-four hours a day without drawing notice and causing a scandal. Her husband is our only option, even though he too is bound to be a target."

"He won't be able to protect her at all if he's dead."

"I do not believe Lord Huntley is all that easy to kill, though you are correct. If anyone knows how to kill him it is the Company. That is why I'm putting you in charge of making certain he is as safe as possible. The two of you are old friends; no one will think it odd to see you hovering around him as much as possible."

"You expect me to put all my trust in him?"

Dhanya sighed. "With respect, Wolfred, I don't believe for a moment that it's Lord Huntley whom you do not trust. Tell me honestly, if one of those nurses caring for Grey right now tried to kill him, would you try to save him or let him die?"

A dull flush appeared high on his cheekbones. "I would save him."

"Good." She turned back to the window. "He's given us extensive information about the Company, but I want you to question him as often as possible, see if he's forgotten or seems to be concealing anything. Pay particular attention to anything relating to inventions. The Company seems to have outdone the W.O.R. when it comes to scientific innovation. I want to rectify that. Let Lady Huntley in on that as well. The woman has a brilliant mind for anything machine-related."

"As you wish, Director." There was no denying the coolness of his tone.

Dhanya paused, then lifted her head and turned her body toward his. "Am I asking too much of you, Lord Wolfred? Will it take too much effort for you to pull your head out of your own arse long enough to protect the man who has been your longtime friend, and the woman for whom you have long carried a torch? Because if you're not up to the task of trying to keep both of them alive, I can always find someone else."

Wolfred looked as though he could strangle her with

a smile on his face. "I believe I can pull my head out of my arse long enough to do as you ask, madam."

She sighed. "It's not punishment, for God's sake! I'm asking you to do this because you're the only person I trust to do it besides myself and possibly Zoe. As I've said, you'll raise the least amount of eyebrows, and you probably won't arouse the Company's suspicions. If you want to sulk or despise me for it, go ahead, but remember that I have no compunctions about letting you go if you cease to be of use to me." Perhaps it was a tad bit harsh of her, but she needed to be certain—needed Wolfred to be certain—that personal feelings would not interfere.

He raked a hand through his thick hair. "I appreciate your trust, and I can honestly promise you that I will do everything in my power to protect both Lord and Lady Huntley." There was real conviction in his voice this time, and that eased the weight on her shoulders.

It wasn't fair of her to demand he keep his feelings out of the matter when it was her own friendship with Arden that made it so imperative to let Lucas Grey go home. His presence might bring even more danger down on Arden, but the conviction that he could dispose of any foe that came their way was ample justification. She was forced to trust a man who had spent the last seven years being mesmerized and God-knows-what-else by Britain's greatest enemy.

"Thank you," she murmured.

"How long have you known?"

Dhanya's head whipped up. "What's that?"

He looked indignant. "How long have you known that I . . . have feelings for her?"

Poor thing. This was probably the closest he'd ever come to admitting those "feelings" to anyone, even himself. "A few months," she lied. She'd known ever since she first saw them in the same room years ago. "Don't worry; I'm sure no one else has noticed." Another lie, because she was dead certain that if Lucas Grey was half the man she suspected him of being, he had already figured it out as well.

In fact, he had probably known it before he ever disappeared.

Lord Wolfred nodded. He seemed relieved. Poor bastard. She truly felt for him. He actually thought he could conceal his feelings. He was excellent at playing any part that was necessary in an assignment, but Arden Grey was his Achilles' heel. She was Huntley's as well.

Surely the two of them together could put jealousy aside to protect Arden. If they couldn't, and anything happened to the one friend she had, Dhanya would personally kill them both.

Chapter 12

He was going home.

The thought sat heavy in Luke's stomach, as ominous and unsettling as a disturbed grave.

"You look as though you're going to the gallows," Alastair remarked as they drove through the bustling streets in his touring carriage. It was a slightly boxy vehicle, black lacquered, with brass pipes as big around as a man's wrist coming up each side in sets of two, funneling the steam that made the beast capable of traveling at great speeds. It had a soft top that could fold down like an accordion, but was up today to protect Luke from view — of gossips and potential assassins.

"I'm going to a place where practically everyone knows more about me than I do. And I'm being taken there by a man who knows me better than any of them."

Alastair smiled slightly. "I can see where that might be unsettling for someone accustomed to being in control and prepared for any eventuality."

"Yes," Luke replied drily. "I wager you can see it very clearly."

His companion chuckled and silence fell between them for a few moments as Luke stared out at the city rolling by. It all looked familiar but strange at the same time—like images from a dream he couldn't quite recall. It was annoying.

"Does she even know that I'm coming?"

"Not at all. Arden would have wanted to plan for your arrival, which means she would have alerted the servants. Even if she didn't tell them what was going on, they'd talk. More important, they'd talk with other servants and tradesmen. Someone would have found out when you were expected. This way, there's little chance of someone lying in wait for you."

But of course there were no guarantees. "I'm not sure I like you calling my wife by her Christian name."

Alastair kept his gaze on the street—a good thing given all the traffic. His face was devoid of expression. "She calls me by mine."

"Don't much care for that either." He looked out again at the passing city.

"You had no problem with it seven years ago."

Luke turned his head, maintaining his calm despite the emotions raging inside him. "Did I wonder if you were trying to shag her seven years ago?"

The carriage swerved to avoid hitting a dog barking in the street. Alastair's knuckles were white on the steering bars. "Your wife's fidelity has never been something you've had reason to question."

There was no mistaking the affront in his tone. Luke didn't care. "That wasn't what I asked. Before I disappeared, was I aware of the fact that you, to put it politely, coveted my wife?"

A muscle in the other man's jaw visibly clenched. "It wasn't like that."

Luke didn't give him time to explain—it didn't matter,

did it? "Which begs the question, did you offer me up to the Company so I'd be one less obstacle between you and Arden?"

The vehicle swerved suddenly to the side, careening down a side street before jerking to a halt. Alastair whipped around to face him, and he brought his fist with him.

Luke's head snapped back with the impact, but this time he did not pass out. He came back with a swing of his own. Alastair ducked, and Luke's fist went right through the back wall of the carriage.

Alastair gaped at the hole as Luke pulled his scraped hand free. "You could have killed me, you bloody bastard!"

"If you touch Arden, I *will* kill you." Damn, he was bleeding. He began to untie his cravat with his uninjured hand. He shouldn't have reacted like that. He really could have killed the man, while Wolfred would have knocked him out at worst.

"I have no intention of touching Arden." Alastair shoved him. "And you're paying to have that fixed. You mad bastard."

Luke wrapped his cravat around his bloody hand. "Send me the bill."

"I will." Alastair steered the carriage back into traffic toward Mayfair. "If you were so concerned about someone else making a bid for Arden's affection, perhaps you shouldn't have left her alone for seven years."

"I'm fairly certain I didn't intend to be gone that long," Luke replied drily. He knotted the cravat. "Why did I leave? Was it an important assignment?"

His companion's face tightened. "You never shared all the details with me. You were certain there was a Company spy amongst the Wardens. When you left, you said it was to follow a lead in Paris."

"Did I find the traitor?"

"I don't know. You were pretty closemouthed about the whole thing. Then we lost contact with you." He shot Luke a glance. "That's all I know. You made me promise not to speak of it, not even to Arden. I never have."

That Wolfred didn't break his promise said much about their former friendship—enough that Luke felt like a sack of shite.

"Arden says you looked for me." He refused to feel guilty for trying to hit him regardless.

Alastair shrugged as they made a left turn onto another street. He pulled out to go around a slow-moving cart and slipped back into the lane, narrowly missing being struck by a pair of automaton horses pulling a fancy carriage. Luke raised a brow in admiration.

"You were my friend. Of course I looked. You would have done the same for me."

"Would I?" He couldn't stop the words from falling out of his mouth. When Alastair shot him a questioning glance, he continued. "I remember events, but I don't remember what sort of person I was. Would I have honestly gone after you?"

His companion nodded, eyes on the road. "I'm certain of it."

"Good." Nice to know he hadn't been a right proper bastard. "Child!"

The vehicle swerved again, Alastair cursing the air blue as he missed the boy, who had chased a clockwork doll into the street, by scant inches.

"This is why I prefer velocycles," Luke informed him, grateful for Alastair's quick reflexes. "They're easier to maneuver."

Alastair snorted, his expression dubious. "You like velocycles because they're fast, reckless and entirely too dangerous. You always have."

"Well, it's nice to know I haven't changed completely."
And it *was* oddly comforting to know the Company
hadn't managed to rob him completely of himself.

"Not completely, no." His friend shot another glance
his way. "But enough."

A scowl pinched the skin between Luke's brows.
"Enough how?"

The touring carriage turned once more, this time into
a long, gravel drive. Luke recognized the house not just
as Arden's, but as a place that meant a lot to him. Tiny
snippets of memory raced across his mind, few of them
making sense, but all of them in this house.

It was home, and he knew it in his bones.

Alastair cut the engine when they reached the house.
Angling his body toward Luke, he snatched his hat from
the seat between them. "Enough that I don't know if
we're friends or enemies."

"Not enemies," Luke replied immediately, certain of
the words. "Not sure about friends, but we're not enemies."

White teeth flashed in the other man's tawny face.
"Good enough. Now, shall we give your wife a surprise
that will make her want to kill us both?"

Mrs. Bird fainted when she saw him. Arden could hardly
blame her. She felt rather vaporish herself when Alastair
and her husband walked through the front door. Although her reaction might have had a fair bit to do with
the fact that he had removed his cravat, leaving much of
his throat bare to her gaze. His neck had been a favorite
place to bury her face and breathe in the clean, spicy
scent of him. She'd kiss him there, dip her tongue in the
salt-sweet hollow . . .

She swallowed. Ronald had caught Mrs. Bird before
she hit the marble floor, thank God. But who was going

to catch her when she fell down the rest of the staircase because her knees were too weak to support her? This was foolishness. He was only a man, after all.

But he was the finest man she'd ever seen—even finer than he'd been before—and a woman shouldn't have to go so long without her man. She might try very hard to be a woman of rational and scientific mind, but she was still a woman, and she'd been raised to indulge all curiosities, to believe that no knowledge was bad knowledge.

Luke had been very happy to educate her when it came to sexual congress—filling in what the books left blank, giving practical experience to what had been simple theory before.

In short, her husband was arousal on legs, and though part of her thought herself silly for it, she wanted him oh-so-badly. And now he was home. Hers.

He couldn't have come at a better time. She'd just returned from the home of Earl and Countess Farnsworth, where she had gone with Inspector Grant to ask the family and staff not to discuss Cassandra's death. They'd done their best to appeal to the household's sense of justice. Everyone seemed heartbroken over the tragedy, so hopefully their desire to see the killer caught would silence even the loosest of tongues. It had been very difficult to witness Farnsworth and his wife's grief. She could only hope that they would behave as the Lynbourne household and keep silent. The less gossip, the less likely it was that the killer would flee.

"What are you doing here?" she demanded, finally finding her voice as she reached the bottom of the stairs. It was as though she couldn't talk and descend at the same time.

"I've come home," he replied, directing a glance at Alastair. "We thought it best not to preannounce the fact."

Yes, she understood. They hadn't wanted to risk an assassin waiting for him. She should have anticipated such a move; then she wouldn't be so off-kilter. She had thought she'd have time to prepare—and that Dhanya would keep him longer than a few days.

Her friend had kept her promise after all. Arden supposed she ought to be ashamed that she had expected otherwise, but she couldn't quite manage it.

The poor servants. They looked as though they had seen a ghost. Dear Mrs. Bird was just beginning to come round. She felt for the poor woman, as she had grown up in this house the same as Luke. They had known each other for most of their lives.

Arden turned to them as a few more servants trickled in. They hadn't expected this, of course, and so when one of the new maids spotted him through a window, she mentioned it to another woman who had been there longer. Word spread fast that Lord Wolfred had arrived with a dark-haired, blue-eyed man. Then, one of the footmen saw him, and chaos ensued.

"Everyone," she said, venturing toward the assembled household, "Lord Huntley has returned." It was overstating the obvious, of course, but some would need to hear it as much as she needed to say it. Saying it aloud, in front of witnesses, somehow made it real.

A loud cheer went up as they fell into line. Arden gestured for Luke to join her and took him through the procession, familiarizing him with old staff, and introducing him to new. They all gazed at him in wonder. Mrs. Bird burst into tears, and Luke actually embraced the slightly older woman, patting her affectionately on the back. "Hush now, Birdy. It's all right."

But the dear soul sobbed with renewed vigor when he referred to her by the pet name he'd used since he'd been a boy. He gazed helplessly over her head at Arden, who couldn't help but smile. She could tell the affectionate name had simply popped into his head. It must be so frustrating to know so much yet not be able to recall it.

He looked fatigued. He had a small bandage on his forehead where Evie had operated, and underneath his eyes was smudged with blue. He was in desperate want of a shave—she'd have to hire a new valet for him. He had a fading bruise where Alastair had hit him, and a red mark over it that looked as if he had been struck again. She glanced down at the cravat wrapped around his hand, and could guess what happened.

"Alastair ducked, did he?" she inquired sweetly after they'd gone through the servants.

Luke glanced down at his hand before grinning sheepishly at her. "He's going to send me the bill."

Rolling her eyes, she shook her head. What was it about men that made them insist on reacting to almost any sort of situation with violence? "I don't understand why the two of you take such pleasure in hitting each other."

"Don't you?" He arched a brow in a manner that told her not to be so obtuse. "I would think it obvious."

Mortification flooded her cheeks. She grabbed his arm and pulled him away from the servants and their sensitive ears. "Not because of me?"

His pale gaze roved over her with predatory interest. She shivered in response—which he acknowledged with a smug grin. *Men.* "History is filled with wars fought over beautiful women."

"I'm not beautiful." She'd spent her entire life being most comfortable and at peace with the fact.

"A woman so intelligent should not be so dim when it comes to her self-worth. Now say good-bye to Alastair so we can talk and I can familiarize myself with my home."

She was halfway across the floor before she remembered how much she despised being ordered about. As much as she wanted some time alone with him, she was nervous about it as well—agitated. This did not mix well with indignation.

"Would you care to stay for tea, Alastair?" she asked sweetly.

Her friend looked over her head, and she didn't have to turn to know whose gaze he sought. Traitor. She could just imagine Luke back there, shaking his head—and none too subtly either.

"Thank you, my dear, but I must be off. I shall leave the two of you to your happy reunion."

Was she being overly sensitive, or did she detect a trace of irony in his tone? Regardless, she walked him to the door, Luke a few steps behind. Alastair kissed her hand and departed. She turned to find her husband watching her closely, a curious expression on his face.

"What?" she demanded. Most of the servants had dispersed now. Mrs. Bird had mentioned making certain Cook prepared "His Lordship's favorite" for supper, as she dabbed at her eyes and smiled like she'd just seen the sun for the first time. Ronald went with her, his arm about her shoulders.

"I just realized that you really aren't attracted to Wolfred."

"I told you he was my friend," she retorted sharply. "Nothing more. Perhaps now the two of you will stop treating me like some bone caught between two hungry dogs."

He actually had the gall to look affronted. "I think both of us would agree we only want what's best for you."

Arden's back straightened. "And I don't think either one of you is the least bit equipped to know what that is.

I have lived without you these past seven years. I have contributed to the Wardens. I have brought in an income of my own. I have assisted Scotland Yard, and *I* killed Victor Erlich—that is why you were sent to assassinate me, remember? So, I am very sorry, my lord, but for years I have lived by no other counsel but my own. I am not about to give my free will over to a man who has forgotten more about me than he knows."

If she thought her bold words would silence or lower him, she was wrong. He stood there, staring down that sharp nose of his at her as his lips lifted in a lopsided smile. "Refresh my memory—have you always been so bossy?"

She folded her arms over her chest. The toe of her right boot tapped in irritation. "I am not bossy."

"Yes you are." He took another step closer, until she could see nothing in front of her but him. "You're acting like a governess again, reprimanding me as though I were an incorrigible child, and I must say . . . I like it."

Arden trembled—literally trembled like a nitwit—as his pale gaze burned a trail from her head to her toes and back again. "Had I known that when we married I would have ordered you about a long time ago."

"So you weren't this bossy back then?"

"No." Perhaps a little, but she'd been a girl then.

"Good." He gave her that lazy, lopsided grin again. "I'd hate to think I'd forgotten that as well. Shall we continue our tour?"

Arden took the arm he offered and set off on legs that wobbled beneath her, damn things. When had he become such a shameless flirt? He had always been charming, but this . . . this made her mouth dry and her heart pound like a debutante at her first ball.

"Where would you like to begin?" she asked as they crossed the great hall.

"Wherever you want to take me," he replied, that amused lilt of his clinging to every word.

The bedroom. That was where she wanted to take him. Then she'd show him just how bossy she could be. Her cheeks heated at the thought.

"The library," she said, ashamed at how hoarse the words came out. "Let's start with the library."

After luncheon—during which the entire staff seemed to appear just to watch Luke eat—Arden suggested they take a walk around the garden before continuing on with the house. She said it was so she could show him improvements to the grounds, but really she wanted to talk to him in private.

He looked tired, but he didn't argue.

"When we return you should rest," she told him as they stepped outside from the back terrace. The breeze carried the scent of lilacs and roses upon it. "You look exhausted."

"Just a headache," he replied a bit too lightly for it to be "just" anything. He touched the bandage on his forehead. "I suppose having someone digging in your brain will do that."

She inclined her head in sympathy. "Dr. Stone says the Company used some sort of chemicals on you."

Luke nodded, squinting against the watery afternoon sun. "She told me."

They walked along the path away from the house. "I'm surprised Dhanya let you go," she admitted. "I thought she'd hold on to you awhile yet."

Hands behind his back, Luke seemed even taller as he walked beside her. Did the metal in him prevent him from slouching? "She might have, were she not so afraid of the Company's retaliation."

Frost breathed along Arden's spine. "You mean they'll come for you."

He shot her a narrow glance, but she didn't fool her-self that it was because of the sun. "I believe she's more concerned about them coming for you."

Her heart stopped—just for a second. Just long enough to hurt. Long enough for her to almost give in to the fear. "You failed your mission. They'll want us both now."

"She let me come home so I could protect you."

Arden kept her gaze fastened on him. "Did she tell you that?"

"No." There was a touch of humorless laughter in his tone. "But I'm not stupid."

That was the last thing she would call him—on most days at any rate. "Who's going to protect you?"

Luke turned his head to favor her with a languid grin. "I suppose that would be you."

He said it as though it was a joke, but Arden wasn't stupid either, and she heard what he didn't say—that Dhanya wasn't so concerned about his safety. "I'm sure she believes you can protect yourself. She knows what you're capable of."

"No, she doesn't." He shrugged. "But she knows I'll protect you, so it's a start. They're not going to execute me anytime soon."

"Speaking of death," she began rather lamely, wishing they didn't have to speak of it at all. "We need to discuss your brother."

"Harry?"

"Henry."

"Right." She knew from the set of his jaw that he would not forget his brother's name again. "What of him?"

She sucked in a lungful of breath. There was no easy way to handle this. "I haven't told him you've returned."

"Because he might tell someone, or because you fear it may put him in danger?"

"Because he's going to have you declared dead." She was going to go to hell for being such an awful person, but she simply could not find it within herself to trust Henry, no matter what excuses Mr. Kirkpatrick made for him.

Luke looked confused, and slightly caustic. "Could that not be stopped by telling him I'm back?"

"Without you standing beside me he wouldn't believe it. He's thought you were dead right from the beginning."

"Ah, now I've got it." He actually smiled. "You kept it from him for spite."

"That's not it at all." Perhaps it was, just a little. "He's never believed me when I insisted you were still alive. If I said you had returned without giving proof, he would think I sought to postpone the proceedings."

"Invite him for tea tomorrow." It was a suggestion to her ears rather than an order. "He doesn't deserve to hear it from gossips."

"I'll invite the solicitor as well." When he gave her a questioning look she added, "Just in case Henry thinks you're an actor I've hired, or a hallucination."

"Surely he'll know me when he sees me." Incredulity hung on every word.

"He's mourned you and moved on. That's not easy to come back from."

He regarded her thoughtfully. "Then I suppose it's lucky for me you didn't mourn me."

She smiled, but didn't reply. Perhaps they were both lucky.

They turned around then, and walked back toward the house. The garden was lovely, but not terribly fascinating.

"I'd like to see where the automatons come up."

Arden paused. "You remember them?"

"No," he replied with a shake of his head—a lock of black hair fell over his forehead, stark against the white bandage. "I saw them one night I was here."

It was said casually enough, but it still sent an unpleasant shudder down her spine. She'd almost forgotten how easily he'd gotten past her security and had entered her—their—home with the intent to kill her.

And now he didn't have to sneak in at all.

She pushed the thought from her mind. He was no threat to her—at least not physically. "You see that statue of Pan? It's standing on a movable platform. At night I enter the proper code on the surveillance apparatus control panel and the statue lifts slightly and moves out of the way to allow a patrol automaton to rise out of its holding cylinder. There's another under a specially designed grass lid. The machines then follow their predetermined route, which changes from night to night."

Luke nodded in approval. "So it's impossible to watch the house one night and know the protocol. Smart."

She preened a little under the praise. The randomness of the path had been one of her upgrades to the system. "Thank you, though now that you have shown me the weaknesses in the arrangement, I shall have to make improvements. Despite the system having been implemented while you were here, you were right that it shouldn't have been so simple for you to get into the house." She reached up to touch her chains but found only bare skin. She dropped her hand. "Perhaps steam vents that are triggered when an intruder gets too close to the house."

"That's definitely a deterrent." His brow furrowed—an indicator that he was trying to remember. "Your father installed the automatons, did he not?"

"Yes." She smiled at the memory. "As a wedding present. You asked him if he might not have come up with something a tad more extravagant. It took him a moment to realize you were joking."

Beside her, her husband chuckled—that hadn't changed. "That's the only memory I have of him. How is your father?"

Arden swallowed against the tightness in her throat. She had known he would ask eventually. "He passed three years ago."

The smile melted from his face. "Oh, Ardy. I'm so sorry." When he held out his arms, she stepped into their surprisingly gentle embrace. He could have crumpled her like paper with his strength, and she wouldn't care. Death was a small price to pay for something that felt this good. Her arms went around his waist, and she placed her forehead on his shoulder. So many emotions warred within her—anger that he hadn't been there at the time, and sadness too. But she was also glad he hadn't had to see it. And she was glad to have him here now.

It took a moment, but she managed to fight back the tears. She was already entirely too vulnerable to him, and she had to guard herself against his next question.

He asked it a moment later. "What of your mother?"

Yes, if she had already been crying this would have made it worse. Instead, she drew back, dug her nails into her palms and said, "She's in the country." That's all she was prepared to divulge at that moment. "Let's go inside, shall we?"

If he thought her change of subject odd he didn't mention it.

"I'll show you to your rooms," she said after leading him through the house to the main staircase. "Do you need a powder for your head?"

"No. I generally avoid the things."

"Really?" She paused on the step and turned to face him. "You used to take one whenever you had an ache or pain. And you took one from Alastair the other night."

That seemed to bother him. "The Company used massage and Chinese needle medicine for such things. Meditation as well. It was imperative to keep the mind clear at all times. Opiates are a last resort."

"Fascinating." She started up the stairs again, her brain already turning the information over and over. Could she use one of the small engines in her Personal Hysteria Dissolution Mechanism to create a device to massage the muscles in the neck and shoulders? At least that would be an invention she didn't have to wrap in plain paper and personally deliver under the guise of a social call, like some of her others. Although it might not be as popular. A sanitorium in France had purchased five of the hysteria treatments from her a few months ago, and applauded the effectiveness of the device.

Still, she couldn't shake the thought that her father would have wanted her to use her skill to create something more beneficial to the world. She told herself that women's health was very important indeed. Just because she had a talent for invention didn't mean she had to become the female equivalent of Mr. Tesla, or that Edison fellow.

Personally, after the last few hours she craved a drink more than she wanted to contribute to the scientific community. Or a bath. Perhaps a nap instead. Just a little time to think and be quiet. She had wanted her husband home—for so long—and now she had no idea what to do with him.

Well, that wasn't entirely true. Thoughts of her little machines and paroxysms of pleasure had given her several ideas, but she was too much of a coward to implement any of them. Still, she'd spent so much time thinking about sexual intercourse she was beginning to think she was turning into a fourteen-year-old lad.

When they reached the top of the stairs, she led him down the corridor past her own room to the master suite. It was connected to her own through the shared bath. Her fingers trembled slightly as they curved around the ornate brass doorknob.

"Here you are," she announced so brightly she winced. "I took the liberty of ordering some new toiletries for you, but we'll inquire with the agency about a new valet. Roberts left five years ago to work for a baronet in Kent. Also, as I said before, we'll need to schedule an appointment with your tailor. I presume there's no way of collecting your belongings from that lodging house?"

"It would all be gone now," Luke replied, gazing around the room. Arden had always liked this room. The walls were covered in a rich cream paper that looked as though it would feel like velvet to the touch, and trimmed in ebony. The furniture was simple, but of excellent quality—also made from ebony. Lightweight ivory curtains hung from the windows, but the centerpiece of the room was the large four-poster bed with its stark white pillows and quilt.

"Do you want me to show you where everything is? Or would you like to see how much you remember?"

"I'll do it myself . . . Thank you." His pale gaze held hers. "How did you get the staff to ready my room without out telling them I'd returned?"

"I didn't have to tell them anything. The maids just did their regular cleaning of this room yesterday. It's been done once a week, but now that you are back it will be done daily."

He frowned, gaze roving around the room once more, as though taking in the sheer size of it. "You kept it ready for me?"

"Of course," she replied. Why wouldn't she? "I wanted it ready for when you returned."

He wore an unreadable expression when he faced her. His lips were parted, his eyes fierce. When he moved toward her, all grace and strength, she didn't know whether to run to him or *away* from him. Instead, she held her ground.

When he reached her she was caught up in a swift embrace that lacked both finesse and tenderness, but set her heart racing regardless. She fancied she could feel the metal in his grip. His fingers shoved into her hair, pulling at the roots, scattering pins. His other arm was around her back, holding her against him so tightly that, had she remembered how to breathe, she would have been robbed of all breath. Her hands braced against his chest, fingers curving into the fabric of his coat.

His mouth took hers, hard and insistent. She clutched at his lapels. Were there any space between them she would have pulled him closer.

The hooks at the back of her gown let go, one by one, under the nimble attack of his fingers. Arden made no move to stop him. She had no intention of stopping this, even though part of her brain screamed that it was a mistake—that it was too fast, too soon. When the gown gaped around her, she dropped her arms and stepped back from his embrace to let it fall to the floor around her feet. She stood before him in her drawers, chemise and a violet satin corset that pushed up her breasts and nipped her waist in a most flattering fashion.

Luke stared at her, eyes bright as crystal caught by the sun as he shucked off his jacket and waistcoat. The fine linen shirt beneath was another of his old ones, and it pulled tautly across his shoulders. He grabbed two handfuls of it and pulled it over his head.

Moisture leeched from Arden's mouth—and she had a pretty sound idea of where it was going. His chest was as smooth as she remembered, but his abdomen was more muscular, his waist narrower. His shoulders were broader with heavier muscle. She was wrong—he didn't have shoulders like David.

David should be so bloody lucky.

He reached for her and she went willingly, trailing her fingers down the fine line of hair that drifted downward from his navel. Her lips brushed his with the lightest of touches before she turned her back to him. "Unlace me?"

Those agile fingers went to work on her stays. She shivered, gooseflesh covering her arms as his teeth nipped at her bare neck. The corset fell to the floor, but before she could kick it aside, Luke's hands slid up her belly, over her ribs to the ribbons of her chemise. Two tugs and it fell away as well. Those same warm fingers cupped her breasts and gently squeezed her nipples, bringing a tormented moan to her lips.

Too long. It had been far too long.

As the thin fabric slid down her arms she heard him make a low sound in his throat. His hands stilled, still holding her breasts.

"What?" she demanded, annoyed that he had stopped.

"When did you get this tattoo?" His voice was soft, and hoarse.

He must mean the small wing on her right shoulder. It was the only decoration she had other than her chains. "On our honeymoon in India. You wanted me to have something to remember it by forever."

"It seems you were with me even when I didn't know it." He dropped his hands and she turned around as he did, presenting her with his bare back.

Arden made a sound that was somewhere between a gasp and a sob. There, on the back of Luke's left shoulder was a tattoo of a wing. The ink wasn't as faded, and it was larger by design, but there was no denying that it was the mate to hers, right down to the number of feathers.

"I got it four years ago when I was in India on assignment. An old woman in—"

"Calcutta," she finished, tears blurring her vision. The same old woman who had done hers.

He turned. "Yes."

She threw herself at him and he caught her, lifting her. She wrapped her legs around his waist as she kissed him with all the emotion she couldn't possibly put into words burning in her chest, threatening to split her apart.

Part of him had remembered her.

Luke turned and took a few steps. The ivory wallpaper was cool against her bare back, and Arden dug her shoulders into it for support.

His hand came between them, slipping easily through the slit in her drawers so that he could touch her. Arden gasped at the contact. She wanted his fingers inside her—anything that might ease the ache. He slid one inside and she moaned, her head pressing into the wall as she arched her neck. His other arm slid underneath her, holding her so that he could tease her into a tense spiral of wet heat while his mouth sucked hard on one of her nipples.

Arden rode his hand, bringing herself to the brink of orgasm just before his fingers eased away. She opened her mouth to demand that he put them back, but then she felt his forearm against the inside of her thigh and she realized he was unfastening his trousers.

When he returned to her it was with something bigger and smoother than his fingers. The blunt head pressed against her dampness, making her tense with anticipation. Slowly, he pushed forward, and her body opened to him, stretched with such a delicious ache as he filled her.

"Open your eyes." His voice was rough, low.

Her lids were heavy, but she pushed them open to stare into the bright, clear depths of his eyes.

Then he pushed and filled her completely, driving her shoulders farther up the wall.

"Do *not* close your eyes," he commanded. "I want you to look at me."

Arden's belly tingled at his words, the need inside her twisting and churning. She kept her gaze glued to his as they began to move together, instantly matching rhythm. The intensity of his expression, the stark desire in his eyes aroused her far more than anything she'd ever experienced before. It was like making love with a stranger who was somehow so very familiar. Exciting yet comfortable, dangerous yet completely safe. She could do anything with this man, and let him do anything to her, even though it was as if they'd never done this before.

She clung to him as the tension in her mounted, gripping him with her thighs as they thrust and pushed. Faster and faster, harder and harder. She didn't care when she banged the back of her head on the wall. He grunted when she dug her fingernails into his shoulders, but it only made him thrust deeper.

She came with a loud cry of triumphant thanks to whatever gods were in charge of carnal bliss. Luke followed shortly after, pressing her hard against the wall as his entire body stiffened. She held him tightly as the spasms rocked through him, and then draped herself limply over his shoulder as he carried her to the bed.

She smiled at him. "Thank you."

The lines of his face were still a little harsh, but there was humor in his eyes. And heat. So much heat. "Thank me later. I'm not done with you yet."

Chapter 13

Luke woke up alone.

He glanced over his shoulder at the expanse of bed at his back, then propped himself up on his elbow to survey the room, but Arden wasn't there. All that was left of her was a single silk stocking hanging limply from the footboard.

He'd never had a woman leave him before. "Arden?" No reply. She was well and truly gone then. The realization left a strange hollow feeling in the pit of his belly. If she'd left a few quid on the bedside he didn't think he'd feel much more whorish than he did right then. He'd scratched her itch and now she was off doing whatever it was she did in this mausoleum of a house all day.

Although it was apparently his mausoleum. No wonder it had felt familiar to him. No wonder he'd climbed to her bedroom so easily that first night—instinct had taken over.

Just as some part of him had known to get that tattoo. He could still feel the soft brush of Arden's lips against the ink feathers. He shivered. She had wanted him with a ferocity that matched his own. He'd never wanted to be inside a woman so desperately in all his life—not that he could remember anyway. Perhaps it had always felt like that with her. God help him, but he didn't think he could manage three goes that close together again on a regular basis. Usually he liked to take his time, make the climax as good as possible, then pass out. But with Arden, he felt like a boy again—randy and eager. He came too quick but was ready for business again in a few moments. She hadn't seemed to mind though, her orgasms outnumbering his.

Christ Automaton, but she was a sexual machine. She matched him thrust for thrust, against the wall, on her knees, on top of him. When he'd let sleep claim him he had thought for certain she would do the same, but if she had, she hadn't slept for long.

He glanced at the clock on the mantel. Four o'clock. He'd been asleep for a little over an hour. At least his headache was gone.

Perhaps his wife had taken that with her.

His wife. It was the first time he thought of her that way without immediately feeling a sense of surprise. It was as though shagging her had somehow made it all more real. She was his now, and she would never belong to anyone else so long as he lived.

He had to make certain they both lived. That meant defeating the Company, a task far easier said than done, but if they could survive this immediate threat, there was a good chance they could have a future.

The thought of spending the rest of his days with one woman, in one place, used to scare the shite out of him. Before he had remembered who he was, he couldn't stay in one place longer than a few weeks before the urge to roam came upon him.

Perhaps that urge had simply been homesickness, only he hadn't known it at the time.

Tossing back the covers, he slipped out of bed and walked naked to the wardrobe where he found, in addition to several shirts, a vast collection of waistcoats, a few jackets and a thick velvet robe that he slipped on. At least it fit better than the rest of his old clothing.

He went to the shared bath and turned the faucets for the tub before turning the crank on a strange radiator-like device he deduced was to warm towels or clothing. He placed a heavy towel on it once the tub was full, and slowly sank into the bath. It was a decadent luxury he enjoyed until his skin began to wrinkle.

A little while later, he was dressed in another pair of trousers and a shirt that fit tolerably well. He shoved his feet into a pair of boots that felt like they had been expressly made for him, and realized that they probably had been. Then he went downstairs looking for his missing spouse.

The first maid he stumbled upon stared at him as though he was a ghost—all wide-eyed and pale. She told him that it was most likely Lady Huntley was in her workshop around the back of the house, as that's where she spent much of her time. Then she gave him directions, and when he asked, replied that she would indeed ask Mrs. Bird to send along tea and sandwiches.

When he reached the building he assumed to be the workshop, he knocked and waited for her to grant him entry before walking in. It was a large room and neat as a pin. It had to be, for there were so many bits of machines, strange devices and tools that it would be an indecipherable mess were it less organized.

And in the middle of it was his wife. Arden stood at a long table on the right wall of the room tinkering with something that looked like a Roman centurion helmet made for a Cyclops.

She looked up, her cheeks flushing softly when she

spied him. She looked softer to him—less stern. "I thought you were sleeping."

"I was until I woke up alone." He smiled at the "governess" clip to her words, and closed the distance between them. "What are you working on?"

"Nothing, yet," she replied, glancing down at the helmet. "But when it's done I hope it will be a sort of memory receptacle."

"For me?"

She shrugged. "If you want."

There was something in the way she said it. "Why wouldn't I?"

"Its design is more for storing memories than reviving them, and not all memories are pleasant—as I'm sure you know."

"How could I possibly have unpleasant memories after spending the last seven years under the control of an agency whose sole purpose was to use me as an instrument of death?" He hadn't meant to sound quite so bitter—or amused. Those things he'd done were very real, and yet they seemed to have been the acts of another person. Regaining even just a little of his memory had changed him. He wasn't the Lucas Grey she remembered, but he wasn't Five anymore either. In fact, it was a little overwhelming just to know he had a name.

Arden lifted her head and turned those big brown eyes of hers to his. "Did they make you do many horrible things?"

"I've got blood on my hands, yes. Whether or not the Director will hang me for it remains to be seen." At that moment, looking at her and seeing no judgment in her expression, he realized that he did not want to die. After years of not caring, it felt oddly terrifying to suddenly have a reason to want to live.

"You're not going to hang." She used a wrench to tighten a bolt on the side of the helmet. "I won't allow it."

Luke chuckled. "Break me out, will you? Ferry me away to the far corners of the earth where they'll never find me?"

Her jaw was set as she turned to him. Such a fierce little warrior. "If necessary, yes."

"Why?" He was genuinely confused, and didn't bother to hide it. "Why would you risk so much for a man you barely know anymore?" There, it was out in the open. They were more strangers than anything else. Strangers who were practically obsessed with each other. "Surely not just because you think you owe me anything?"

The helmet fell on the bench with a clatter as the full force of Arden faced him, hands on her hips. "Because you are my husband. Because you could have killed me on several occasions and yet you did not—not because I stopped you, but because you couldn't do it. And because even though the Company tried to obliterate me completely from your mind, you got a tattoo from an old woman in Calcutta that matches that of a woman *you* barely know anymore."

Luke stared at her, a peculiar tightness in his chest. "I don't see how a man could ever entirely forget a woman like you."

She caught her breath. "You say these things and all I want to do is take you inside me and never let you go."

He understood, even as his body reacted to her words. Theirs was such a strange and unique situation that it was difficult to know how either of them felt, let alone understand it. Physical attraction was the one thing they had that needed no explanation or apologies. And maybe if he made her come hard enough, often enough, she'd stop being angry at him.

Because she was angry—even if she didn't know it. He could see it in her eyes, feel it when she had dug her nails into his flesh. She was so very angry, and he couldn't blame her. He was angry too. He'd lost seven years of his life—seven years that had been taken from her as well. The only difference was that she had been aware of it every damn day.

He could take her again now and they'd both like it, but while that might be what they both wanted, it wasn't going to fix anything.

"I'll never say no to shagging you," he replied honestly. "But given that Birdy will come bustling in here any moment with tea, perhaps we should try something less . . . startling instead."

She appeared charmingly indignant. "I didn't mean I wanted to . . . not now!" She scowled at him. "You're not irresistible, you know."

"Only when I say those *things,* then?" He couldn't help but smile at her. He'd smiled more at her in the last few days than he had smiled in the past seven years.

"I should never have told you that," she replied haughtily, but there was a sparkle in her eye that softened her words.

"Is this what we were like before I left?" he asked, toying with a bolt on the workbench.

Arden stilled. Then, she went back to her helmet. "Of course. How else would we have been?"

"I don't know." What he did know was that Arden was lying to him. And he had no idea why.

But he was going to find out.

At what point should she cease to be a coward and stop lying to her husband? This thought plagued Arden long after she left her workshop, into the days that followed. Why did she not simply tell him that she wasn't that same girl he'd married? It wasn't as though he remembered. Wasn't as though he had expectations. Did he? And what of her expectations? How could she articulate that she was afraid to talk of the past because they might never feel that way about each other again?

She had both loved and resented him back then. She'd been angry that she couldn't have her own way, and enraged that the W.O.R. was more important to him than she was. And yet, she cherished every moment they had together before he rushed out to defend his country.

They had been together forty-eight hours, and he was still under the same roof. After seven years of being alone, she wasn't quite sure what to do with him. She wanted to talk to him, spend time with him, but she was afraid of doing just that. What if they had nothing to talk about? Or worse, nothing that the other wanted to hear?

She had sent word to Henry that morning asking him to come visit. Alastair had called upon them earlier, and Luke had given him yet more information he had remembered to write down, but that was it. In fact, Luke seemed far more interested in what she was doing—her inventions, even the naughty ones, enthralled him. He'd never been all that interested before. Usually it annoyed her having someone under her feet while she worked, but he'd been pleasant company.

"You're bloody brilliant," he'd told her, and the awe in his voice humbled her. And last night, he'd come to her room and done things to her he'd never done before. The memory made her knees tremble.

She refused to think about who he might have done them to while she was there alone, wondering if her womanly bits might wither from inattention.

He was a man who could kill her with little effort— and who had killed with little thought—yet he treated her as though she was the extraordinary one. And when she told him about her work with Scotland Yard, she'd been prepared for him to insist that she give it up because he thought it dangerous, or beneath her. Instead he asked about the killings.

"That's why you were in the alley that day," he surmised now as they sat together in the parlor having a glass of whiskey. They were waiting for Henry to arrive. "You thought the whore was another victim."

She nodded. She was becoming accustomed to the fact that his language was sometimes a little rough. So was hers. "But she wasn't. Our bloke kills noble girls." She thought of Cassandra Millingston, and the skill with which Grant—and she—had managed to keep her death quiet. Word had gotten out of the girl's demise, of course, but society believed it to have been an accidental death rather than a murder. That wouldn't last, of course. Eventually, her grief-stricken parents, or the servants, would say something to someone with a big mouth and word would leak out, but for now they had a little bit more time to look for the killer.

"You arranged this meeting with my brother to hasten my reintroduction to society, didn't you? So you can hunt the bastard down."

When he put it like that it sounded rather cold. Unfortunately it was fairly accurate. "And so Henry doesn't find out from gossip, and because you are his brother and he loves you. And because I cannot stand keeping it from him."

He arched a brow, and she scowled in return. "Yes, and because I want to get out into society and find the monster, and if you're with me I know I won't be in any danger."

His gaze brightened. "You trust me with your life?"

"Of course." And she meant it, despite common sense insisting she should not.

Luke's lips curved in a slow smile. "You say these things and I want to bury myself inside you."

How many times was he going to throw that careless remark back at her? She didn't mind—not really. It was just that . . . she was new to this open sexuality. She'd been brought up a lady, and intercourse was something between a husband and wife, hardly discussed, and done only in the dark. Usually in one position. Luke had disabused her of that notion early in their marriage, but he was even more sensual now—demanding, even. And he made a wanton out of her. She wanted him with a ferocity she couldn't remember possessing seven years ago. She was practically shameless with it. Next time he came skulking by her workshop she was going to make certain there was a clear bench.

He wasn't the only one who had changed, but perhaps he didn't feel as though she was quite the familiar stranger she thought him. Instead of clearing the confusion about their marriage cluttering her mind, sex had only thickened the fog. He didn't seem the least bit unsettled at the notion of having a wife, though she was very much aware that she now had someone to answer to after years of independence.

"I admire and appreciate your loyalty," he told her, suddenly serious as he took a sip from his glass. "And just so we're on even ground, I would never allow anything to happen to you. I'd kill anyone who tried to harm you."

His words sent a shiver down her spine. They were so darkly possessive, and yet so incredibly lovely. For that moment she believed she was the most important thing in his world. Perhaps that would change as memories came back and he became more comfortable in what must seem like a new life, but for now, she would simply enjoy it, and not think about how soon it might end.

"I would do the same," she informed him, honestly.

He looked very pleased with himself. "I believe you would. I thought you were going to use that electrical shock device of yours on the tailor this morning."

She shrugged. "He kept poking you with pins."

"He was nervous."

"Nervous?" She snorted. "What's he to be nervous of? He's been doing that job for twenty-five years."

"And I'm the first customer he's ever had come back from the grave."

"Then he should know better than to let it show."

"Perhaps you think he should have had a stiff drink and pretend disinterest?"

Arden froze, like a fox when it first spies the hound. She wasn't a fool, and no one could ever accuse her of not being self-aware. She'd have to be a top-notch idiot not to understand.

"Perhaps. If the stiff drink enabled him to do what had to be done."

His expression was neutral—completely so. He must be one devil of a card player. "If he needs a drink to do his job, perhaps he should find another vocation."

Her smile was brittle. "A valid point, but no one really cares if he drinks, because he is a man." To make her point, or perhaps just for spite, she swallowed the remainder of whiskey in her glass in one go and rose from her chair to stamp toward the liquor cabinet.

"There's no need to be defensive."

"I'm not." She slanted a glance at him as she set her glass on top of the cabinet's polished top. She wanted another drink, but that would only make him right, wouldn't it?

"You drink. A lot."

"Are we really going to have this conversation with your brother due any moment?" she demanded, fingers gripping the cabinet ledge.

Suddenly he was there beside her, looming over her. "It would be better if you didn't imbibe quite so much."

"You know what would be better, Lucas?" Bitterness so thick she could taste it dripped from her tongue. "If you didn't come back here after seven years of not knowing you had a wife and pretend to be someone who knows what's best for me. If you had known that you wouldn't have left in the first place."

Now it was he who went perfectly still. "You've expressed disappointment several times, Arden, but you haven't exactly told me what it was I did that pissed you off so badly you've held a grudge for seven years."

There was a dangerous note in his voice, but she ignored it. He was right. She was pissed off, and there would be no going forward for them until they confronted the past. No matter that he couldn't remember and she would dearly like to forget, it could not be ignored.

"You left me. You went off to do the bidding of your precious Director." That had been Dhanya's predecessor, of course.

"Alastair said I was on the trail of a traitor."

Arden shrugged. "He would know better than I. You rarely discussed the W.O.R. with me."

He frowned. "But you are a Warden."

"Now I am. Back then I was merely the daughter of their chief inventor and the wife of their golden boy. I wasn't one of them. I joined after you went missing. I naively thought I might be able to contribute something, do something that could bring you back."

"You killed Victor Erlich," he said roughly. "That's what made them send me back."

She chuckled—harshly. "I did something right after all."

Warm hands came down heavily on her shoulders—a

little too heavily. All he had to do was squeeze, and her bones would snap like dry tinder. For a second—and only one—she thought he might do just that.

Perhaps she didn't trust him as much as she thought.

His eyes glittered—cold as diamonds with just a hint of blue. "Stop stalling, stop lying and tell me what I did to hurt you so damn badly."

"I don't want to tell you." What a mess she was. Afraid he might not be that same man, and yet just as afraid that he was.

"Why not?"

Her gaze whipped to his. "Because I'm afraid if I tell you, you'll stop looking at me like I'm the most important thing in your life." It came rushing out in one breath, half hysterical, and oh so freeing.

Luke stared at her. He removed his hands from her shoulders, and stood there, arms at his sides. She didn't need her sentimentometer to know that he was frustrated—it rolled off him in waves so thick it was practically tangible.

This was the point when he began to withdraw from her. She knew it. How could he not when she was obviously a bedlamite? Her emotions changed like the weather, as did her behavior. One moment she writhed against him like a snake and the next she pushed him away.

Her father used to do the same thing to her mother at times. She glanced down at the empty glass on the cabinet. Her mother blamed her father's moods on drink. He had liked a whiskey now and again.

If she was honest with herself, he'd liked more than one.

"Luke, I—" Whatever she might have said was cut off by a knock on the door. Mrs. Bird stuck her head in.

"Beg your pardon, my lord and lady, but Lord Henry is here."

Arden smoothed a hand over her skirts. "Have tea sent in, Mrs. Bird. And please see that we are not disturbed while Lord Henry is here."

"Of course, my lady." She directed a small smile at Luke as she closed the door.

"We'll finish this discussion later," he promised once they were alone again, a dangerous note in his voice. Arden knew there would be no avoiding it. Perhaps it would be a relief to get it all out. After all, he was the one who'd pointed out that they were both drastically changed people. If she was really a different woman than the girl he'd married, then she ought to prove it by behaving like the woman she wanted to be rather than a spoiled child stamping her feet because she hasn't gotten her own way.

She met his gaze evenly, chin lifted. "All right."

The door to the parlor opened and in walked Henry. Whatever he'd expected, his brother alive hadn't been it. He turned white as death when he saw Luke, and approached him like a child approaching a large, possibly dangerous dog.

"Luke?"

Luke was the taller of the two, so he had to look down to meet his brother's wide-eyed stare. "Hello, Henry."

Later, all Arden could remember of the moment with any certainty was that Henry Grey threw the first punch.

Chapter 14

Had he known his brother meant to hit him, Luke would have spared the younger man the pain of such action. As it was, Henry's howls were matched by Arden's spaniel Beauregard to form one of the most god-awful rackets he'd ever heard. He'd heard victims of torture who hadn't made such a fuss.

"You broke my damn hand!" his brother cried, cradling the appendage, which did look as though it was badly done in.

Luke tapped his finger against his forehead. "Gregorite plating." Was he a complete arse for finding this situation a little amusing? The runt was lucky he hadn't instinctively hit him back.

Henry stared at him, his face contorted in pain. "You don't have any scars."

"New procedure. Wouldn't recommend it." Out of the corner of his eye he noticed Arden watching him. He didn't want her to know how painful the process had been—he had remembered some of it as well. The last thing he wanted was for her to see him as weak. Though perhaps a better way of making certain that didn't happen would be to step up and resume the role of Lord Huntley.

But he was beginning to think Lord Huntley was a bit of a twat. Or rather, had been, especially if he'd been anything like this younger sibling.

Henry cast a glare at him before slumping into one of the wingback chairs. He had something of a sullen look, but then part of that was undoubtedly pain, and the realization that he had hurt himself far more than he could ever hurt Luke.

"This is rather convenient," his brother commented, turning his petulance toward Arden. "The lord of the manor returning just days before he's to be declared dead."

Luke stiffened, but to her credit Arden showed no reaction to his words. "I couldn't have planned it any better myself."

Henry's chin—so similar to his own—jutted in Luke's direction. "You expect me to believe that this is my brother? That he chose to return now rather than before?"

Arden shrugged. "He had little choice in the matter, I assure you." Then she turned her lovely face to Luke, her expression wry. "Did I not tell you he'd wonder if you were an actor?"

"How much did she pay you?" the younger man demanded of Luke, as though he hadn't heard her—or didn't care. "I'll double it if you renounce her as a liar."

"Watch your mouth, runt," he growled, standing up straight. "I'll break more than your hand." It didn't matter that Arden had lied to *him*. Nobody else was going to accuse her of falsehood, especially this little wanker.

Blue eyes blinked. For a moment, all of Henry's anger was replaced with amazement, but it quickly disappeared under the onslaught of deepening distrust. "Did she tell you to call me that?"

This was ridiculous. Perhaps he'd have more patience if it wasn't for how heated his interrupted conversation with Arden had been.

"I'm Lucas Grey," he informed his brother. "The Earl of Huntley. Either you believe that or you don't, but not believing won't give you the title."

Henry's spine snapped straight, and he jumped to his feet, still cradling his hand. He was pale, but angry red splotches appeared in his cheeks. "You dare accuse me of title-grubbing when you claim to be a man dead these seven years! I should call you out, sir!"

Luke's fists clenched at his sides. He knew he was supposed to love this man as his sibling, but right now he couldn't summon anything more positive than sheer dislike. "Please do. I hope you're a good shot, because you'll have to be."

Arden stepped between them, though there scarcely was need. There was still a good ten feet between the two of them, and though Luke could close that distance very quickly, he wasn't feeling *that* violent at the moment.

"This is not the reunion I had hoped for," she told them both. She turned to the younger. "Henry, what will it take to prove to you that this is indeed Lucas?"

He turned his baleful glare on Luke. "What did you do to the puppy father gave me when I was six?"

Luke had no bloody idea. His memory was weaker the further back he tried to go, and what he had remembered often came to him unbidden. "I sincerely hope I didn't kill it."

Henry's brow lowered in disgust, and his lips curled into a sneer. "I knew you weren't my brother. I'll have Scotland Yard on you. You'll hang for impersonating a Peer of the Realm. Both of you will swing for it."

"Oh, for pity's sake! You're the one who belongs on a stage." Arden fisted her hands on the sweet curves of her hips. "Henry, Lucas has suffered an injury that impedes his memory."

"Again, very convenient."

If he didn't wipe that sneer off his face . . . Luke's head was beginning to ache from trying to remember what had happened with Arden, and now trying to recall something that could prove he was who he was.

Christ, if it wasn't for the fact that he'd remembered the things he had, he would wonder if he was really Huntley as well.

He hadn't killed the puppy. He might be a changed man, but he was never cruel to animals, he knew that. He liked animals, even the foolish, foppish Beauregard who'd tried to make love to his leg just that morning.

"I dressed it up in a pair of your short pants and taught it to sit at your place at the table. Mother didn't find it nearly as amusing as Father and I." He met his brother's gaze. "You cried."

A dull red stain spread across Henry's cheeks. "One of the servants could have told you that."

Luke pinched the bridge of his nose. "Fine. You don't want to believe I'm your brother, then don't. Get the hell out."

"You cannot order me about as though you were master of this house." The younger man's eyes blazed with fury. They looked so very much alike, though Henry was a little heavier. Was the resemblance not enough? Or would his brother rather believe he was dead and gone than accept the truth?

"He is master of this house," Arden informed him. "He hasn't and cannot be declared dead, and once he's out in society, everyone will accept that he is Huntley — alive and well."

"We shall see about that!"

As Henry whirled about, ready to march out, Luke pushed to remember something—anything. If asked, he wouldn't be able to say why it was so important that this man, who looked so much like him but didn't feel like family, believed him. But he needed him to believe.

"When you were ten years old you caught Father with one of the maids. You were so upset you ran and told Mother. I remember that you didn't understand the next day when we found out the maid had been let go. Her replacement was a homely little thing, and Father began spending more time away from home. I told you that you should have kept your mouth shut."

Henry stopped, back rigid. He didn't look over his shoulder. "You said all men of rank had mistresses."

Luke didn't remember that part, and the words made him wince. How jaded had he been at twelve? But that didn't matter so much as the expression on Arden's face. She looked disappointed.

He'd been a top-notch twat indeed.

"I was an idiot," he said, casting his wife a meaningful glance. "And wrong. You never forgave him. Not even when he asked you to while on his deathbed."

Henry gaped at him. It was obvious now that he believed Luke was who he claimed to be. But the wonder in his face quickly gave way to something more disturbed. "Are you quite all right?"

Luke frowned. Then he felt moisture above his lip. He reached up and touched it with his fingers. They came away red. His nose was bleeding. Damnation. He pressed the ball of his hand to his forehead, but it did little to ease the skull-splitting pain—it only made the incision hurt.

"I told you his memory had been impaired," he heard Arden admonish. Slender, but capable hands gripped his shoulders, guiding him.

"Sit down, dearest."

Dearest? How could she use any endearment with him? He was broken, perhaps beyond repair. No, she loved who he used to be, who she thought he was, and he'd do well to remember that, even if the former Lord Huntley didn't deserve it. Still, he did as she commanded.

"Is he dying?" Henry asked. Luke might have laughed if he didn't think to do so might make his head literally split open.

"No, he's not dying!" Arden's sharp tones made him both wince and smile. He opened his eyes so he could see the ferocity in her expression. Henry was suitably cowed.

Such a governess.

She held her hand out to the other man. "Give me your handkerchief." She snapped her fingers. "Now, Henry."

Henry reluctantly obliged, and within seconds the snow-white cotton was shoved under Luke's nose. "Hold this," his wife instructed. "Tilt your head back a little."

He knew what to do for a nosebleed—he was a man, after all, and had been hit in the nose often enough to know the procedure—but he liked having her fuss over him. No one had fussed over him in a very long time, and his chest was tight with it.

"I'm going to send for Dr. Stone," Arden told him, her brown eyes filled with concern. Her fingers combed softly through his hair, and it was all he could do not to close his eyes and lean into her soothing touch.

"I want Dr. Vincent to examine him," Henry announced, in a tone that might have been imperious were it not for a hint of reticence.

Arden paused in the act of pulling the bell for one of the maids, and fixed the other man with a gaze that could freeze Lucifer's bollocks. "Now that you know it's him, you're going to try to have him declared incompetent, are you?"

Henry's shoulders straightened. "If he's my brother I want the family physician to examine him."

"He is your brother, and you want your doctor to claim he isn't mentally or physically fit to be the earl."

She was an astounding woman, Luke realized. At times she seemed almost afraid of him, but back her into a corner or challenge her and she developed a backbone more rigid than the metal covering his bones. Henry was bigger than she, stronger too, and yet she stared him down as if he were no more than a spoiled child. Perhaps that was how she saw him, but Luke saw a man caught up in duty. Henry's apparent callousness wasn't out of a lack of fraternal love—not really—but out of his sense of duty to family, and to the title.

Henry didn't want to believe, because then he'd have to accept that he had buried a ghost, and all the pain that came with that would rear its head.

"It's all right, Ardy," he told her, removing the handkerchief so he didn't sound like a nasal git. The bleeding seemed to have stopped. "If it gives the runt peace of mind, let him have his doctor."

Her face tightened in displeasure, and she hesitated before giving a curt nod. Napoleon couldn't have been so imperious. "Fine." Then to Henry, "You will speak to me beforehand. I won't have you descend upon him whenever you wish."

A flush swept up Henry's neck to fill his face. "You talk to me as though you are my better. This is my family home and I will call on it whenever I please. I let you stay in this house because you were my brother's wife, but you will never be anything more than an impoverished baronet's daughter who got caught fucking an earl and forced him to marry her."

Luke sprang from the chair, lunged toward his brother, and caught the younger man by the throat. He lifted him with one hand, so that his toes dangled just above the ground. Henry sputtered and gasped, clawing at the fingers around his neck.

A chill settled over Luke as he met the other man's bulging gaze, but he knew his anger had to burn in his eyes like a raging blaze. "You may be my brother, but if you insult my wife again, you little twat, I'll crush your windpipe and watch the life drain out of you. I promise you I won't feel the least bit bad about it either."

"Luke. Luke!" It was Arden. He turned his head toward her. "Let him down."

His fingers twitched around the throat in their grasp. It wouldn't take much more than a gentle squeeze—not with his strength. And he knew how to dispose of a body so that no one ever found it.

But that wouldn't win him Arden's trust, and it wouldn't look good to the Wardens, who would probably kill him. He could run. Arden might come with him. He turned his attention back to Henry, whose face was turning a most amazing shade of plum.

The memory came like a flash of light—he was standing in front of this man, but they were both little more than boys. There were four other boys there as well, all of whom had been picking on Henry. They had hit him until he was bruised and bloody. Luke had stopped the fight, and he was prepared to take on all four of those boys to protect his little brother. He did take them all on, and took quite a beating for it himself. This boy had loved him back then. Looked up to him.

He lowered Henry to the ground and released his grip on his throat. His brother gasped for air, wheezing.

"You're an animal," he rasped.

Luke nodded. "But I'm still your brother, and you will

treat my wife with respect. She's the only one who believed I was alive all these years. How long was it before you gave up hope, Henry? How long before you first tried to take what is mine?"

The other man's face was still so purple it was difficult to tell if he was ashamed or not. "I have looked after the accounts, the holdings and everything else associated with the Huntley title."

"Did you look after my countess?" Luke asked in a quiet tone. Henry's averted gaze said more than words ever could. "I'll see your doctor, let him poke and prod me, but now you need to leave, because I don't like you very much, and for the past seven years that's been all the reason I've needed to kill a man."

Henry didn't need more prompting that that. Cradling his injured hand, he tore from the parlor as though the hounds of hell champed at his very heels.

"Well, that went perfectly smashingly, don't you think?"

His mouth curved at Arden's dry tone. "The genuine brotherly love was quite humbling."

She sighed and came toward him, capable and slightly calloused hands cupping his cheeks. She turned his head from side to side, all the while studying his face. It was a little disconcerting knowing she was practically looking up his nose. He was torn between shoving her hands away and kissing her. Instead he asked, "Is it true what he said?"

Her gaze lifted to his as she lowered her hands. "You mean about why we were married, or that I'm a liar?"

"About how we came to be married."

She smiled—an oddly sad expression. "How will you know I'm not lying about it, though?"

"Because a woman who didn't care about her husband wouldn't have waited seven years."

She swallowed, and for a second, her composure cracked. "I suppose not. We were caught together at a lecture my father gave at the Royal Society. You had already asked me to marry you and we were ... uh, celebrating perhaps a little too enthusiastically."

Luke grinned. "I imagine we were." Damnation, but he wished he could remember it. "How old were you?"

"Oh, nineteen I suppose. You would have been four and twenty. Your mother wasn't impressed that you wanted to marry so young. She thought it was a mistake."

"Obviously I knew what I was doing."

Arden blinked. "Yes, I suppose we both did. Although there were times when I thought you agreed with your mother's sentiments."

Raking a hand through his hair, Luke tried to remember something—anything—that would make him think better of his old self, and couldn't. It hurt too much to push, and he didn't want to risk another nosebleed. "When's my birthday?"

"September twenty-third."

In a few months he would be four and thirty. It might seem a small thing, but this information made him inexplicably happy. Slowly, he was beginning to think of himself as a person, not just Five. And the Earl of Huntley was beginning to feel less like an assumed identity and more like who he really was.

Except for the part about being a complete arse.

"Tell me the rest of it," he commanded. "How did we go from enthusiastic to me deciding the mission was more important than you?"

She sighed. "Fine. Since you're not going to give me a moment's rest...." She turned away, her hands coming up to rub the back of her shoulders. "We had been fighting about whether or not to start a family. I wanted a child, and you thought it was too soon."

A child. He'd never thought of children, not once in all those years with the Company. He'd wondered if he had family, but never if he was a father. What if he had returned here to discover he was a father? Could a child ever understand a father who had tried to kill its mother?

"Was it?"

"Too soon?" At his nod she shrugged. "At the time it felt right, but now ... Perhaps I was a little young to rush into motherhood. You wanted to distinguish yourself with the W.O.R. You wanted adventure, and you wanted me to join you on those adventures, which I couldn't do if I were confined. You didn't understand how I could possibly want to stay here and raise a family when there were so many injustices in the world that needed righting." She smiled ruefully. "And I couldn't understand why you felt compelled to risk your life all the time when you had responsibilities at home—mainly to me."

"So that was it? I walked out because you wanted a child?"

"Not quite. I ..." She frowned, and he caught the longing glance she directed at the liquor cabinet. "I missed my monthly and was so very excited. I told you I was pregnant and you reacted ... Well, you were angry. You had already accepted a new assignment—something you wouldn't discuss even with me."

Luke swallowed. "I was on the trail of a traitor." He didn't want to believe he was capable of being such a spoiled tit. He wanted to at least have a seminoble reason to leave this woman alone at what must have been such a vulnerable time for her. "At least, that's what Alastair tells me."

"He would know. Anyway, my monthly came and you went off to save the empire with your partner."

The way she avoided his gaze made him uneasy. "Alastair?"

"No. You left with a woman named Rani Ogitani."
Finally her gaze locked with his. "Your mistress."

The Cavendish party was practically a mob when Arden
and Luke first arrived. Word had spread that he had "returned from the grave," and the entire city was like a
hive of bees over it—droning incessantly. It was all anyone could talk about. She'd had literally dozens of callers, most of whom she had to be "not at home" for. And
it was impossible to go anywhere because everyone
wanted to know about her husband and how she felt
about his miraculous return.

This would be the same husband who hadn't spoken
to her more than he had to since the mention of Rani
Ogitani. It had only been two days, but she felt his
withdrawal—and the sting of the last thing he had said
to her. He had muttered something about being a "twat"
that sounded apologetic. Twat was such a foolish-
sounding word, but that wasn't what upset her. What
bothered her was that he obviously withdrew because he
assumed he had slept with the woman—which was exactly what Arden had been scared of when it all initially
happened. It wasn't that she hadn't trusted him—not really. It was because Rani Ogitani was essentially a female
version of him. She lived for danger and adventure. How
could Arden ever compete? She was so petty where the
exotic spy was concerned that she'd harbored a secret
satisfaction when the woman returned from the mission
missing an eye. That satisfaction soured when she learned
Ogitani had suffered the injury while trying to fight the
men who took Luke.

She wished he could have told her that he hadn't slept
with Ogitani, that he didn't find her more satisfying and
desirable than Arden, but he couldn't. Her only consola-
tion was that he didn't remember the woman at all. Or

so he claimed. She didn't think he was lying. He looked too disgusted with himself to lie on top of it.

Then he had looked at her and said, "I wish I wasn't Huntley." He left the room immediately after.

How was she supposed to take that? She told herself she had nothing to do with the proclamation, but she couldn't quite believe it. A little voice that had always popped up whenever she wanted something told her she wasn't good enough to keep him, that all the changes wouldn't be enough to hold his interest, and that the parts of her that were the same no longer attracted him.

She had a glass of whiskey and told the voice to shut the hell up. Still, she felt bruised and stung inside. This was not how she imagined their reunion would be. Lord, had she truly believed everything would just fall into place and they'd go back to how they were before he left? Before she realized she might not be enough for him?

How were they ever going to rebuild on a foundation so shaky? She'd fooled herself into thinking that everything would be perfect if he just came back to her, and now she was faced with just how naive an assumption that had been. In this crowded ballroom, her husband might as well have a target on his back the way the women attacked him. If she hadn't been enough for him when he claimed to love her, why would she ever think she would be now when he barely knew her?

It all made her head hurt, and quite frankly she wasn't at this event to fret and ruminate over her marriage. She was there because it gave her an opportunity to look for the monster who killed those two girls.

Inspector Grant had visited her earlier—after she filled Luke in on everything she knew about his relationship with Rani Ogitani. It hadn't been a long conversation. She didn't tell him how jealous she had been of the woman, or her fears that they had resumed their affair. He didn't remember, and she was surprised to realize it didn't matter anymore. Not as much as it once had. The look of horror on his face at the idea of knowingly breaking his wedding vows had been all she needed.

Perhaps the changes that had overtaken the both of them would have some advantage after all.

Grant had arrived before they could discuss the matter further, and that was just as well. Luke left the room without needing to be asked. As much as it pained her to exclude him, he had not yet been reinstated into the Wardens, and was not privy to W.O.R. information.

"I've compiled a list of suitors that flirted or showed an interest in both girls," Grant informed her, handing her an envelope. "There's half a dozen names on there, all from aristocratic families."

Arden removed the paper and scanned the list of names. In her chest, her heart sank like a stone. There was a lot of breeding and blue blood behind each of these names. "And these are only the ones the parents knew about."

Grant frowned. "You think there may be more?"

A dry chuckled escaped her throat. "I'd wager my left arm there are at least three more. I was once a young girl, Inspector. The secret ones are always the most exciting— the sort you'd recklessly run off with."

"Foolish girls."

"Did you never sweet-talk a girl into sneaking away for a kiss, Inspector?" She couldn't help the edge to her voice. At his flush, she continued. "I doubt any of them thought she was in danger of losing her life with you. Her virtue, perhaps, but not her life. These girls might have chosen the wrong gentleman to sneak away with, but they are not to blame for their deaths."

"A good point, Lady Huntley, and one well taken at that. 'Tis the father in me speaking."

Arden clapped him on the shoulder. "Your girls will grow up all the more world-savvy because of you."

"What sort of man fathers a boy who turns into a killer?" The inspector's face pinched with both pity and disgust. "What sort of tyrant raises such a child?"

"I'm not certain," Arden replied, "but chances are I know him."

Those words haunted her as she stood in the crowded ballroom later that evening. There was very likely a killer in this crush, perhaps that awful father of his as well. So she stopped watching Luke, who stood in the middle of a large group of men and women vying for his attention, and turned her eye to the rest of the gathering. She ignored Henry, who stood on the far side of the room looking sulky and favoring his hand, and his wife, Marianne, who glared at Arden as though she was a monster herself.

Yes, because it was all Arden's fault that Henry was an idiot and punched a man with a gregorite-plated jaw. Obviously she should have seen it coming and thrown herself in front of Henry's fist to spare him the pain.

Every man that passed by her she checked for a horseshoe pin on his cravat. Thus far, she'd counted five—none worn by one of the names on her list. Lord Thomas Fenton was on the list, but he wore a simple diamond stickpin. Lord Elton James was also on the list and wore such an elaborate mess of lace and silk round his neck she couldn't see if he wore a pin at all. She had yet to cross paths with the others.

And even if she were lucky enough to discover one of them wearing the horseshoe, she would then have to discover whether or not he had automatized hands.

"I'm surprised you're not watching your husband," came Alastair's voice as he appeared at her side.

"I could say the same about you," she remarked

lightly, scanning the nearby gentlemen, hoping for a glimpse of a horseshoe cravat pin. "In fact, I'm surprised Dhanya hasn't had you living in a tree outside our house."

He grinned at her. "If you see a very large nest, just ignore it."

Arden smiled back, but it was brief. "Is she concerned that Luke is a traitor, or that the Company may try to kill me again?"

"Both. Have you noticed anyone suspicious skulking about?"

"Nothing. Though I must confess to being a tad distracted."

"How is it?" His tone was low, and soft. Her throat tightened in response.

"Fine."

"You're a lousy liar, Arden."

"No, I'm a tremendous liar, especially to myself. It's telling the truth that gives me trouble." She took a sip from her glass of champagne and grimaced. It was warm. That didn't stop her from downing the remainder in one gulp.

"What has happened?"

"I'd really rather not speak of it, Alastair." She snatched another champagne from a passing footman with a tray, trading it for her empty glass. "If you happen to see a man with a horseshoe-shaped cravat pin would you be so good as to alert me?"

"Of course." He didn't ask why. He rarely did when he assumed a request was work-related. Alastair only worried about her when it came to personal matters.

"Arden, may we talk? Privately?"

She cast a glance at Luke, who hardly seemed to know she was alive. He looked so lovely in his tailored black suit and white shirt. It was amazing what clothes that fit

properly could do for a man, even one already as handsome as her husband. It was hardly fair that women had
to primp and crimp and stuff themselves into corsets and
shoes that often pinched one's toes.

"Of course." She linked her arm through his and allowed him to lead her toward a balcony where they
could take a little fresh air and speak without being
overheard. They had to walk by the automaton "orchestra," which so many upper-class houses now employed.
The musicians were like overgrown dolls in appearance,
with pink "skin" and wide eyes. Arden often imagined
one of them coming to life and murdering them all in an
emotionless rampage. It had never happened, of course,
but the creatures unsettled her all the same. They played
their programmed music beautifully, and only needed to
be wound once during the course of an evening, but they
lacked the depth of feeling a human could bring. Though
she was scientifically minded, Arden preferred music
and art with a human touch.

Outside on the balcony, the evening was cool—a refreshing change after the warmth of the ballroom. The
music was softer, the lighting dimmer; everything was
altogether more agreeable than the stuffy ballroom.
Lanterns illuminated the balcony and the garden below,
and made Alastair's hair a rich tobacco.

To Arden's surprise they were completely alone. Obviously everyone was too busy fawning over her husband to make a break for the out-of-doors.

"If you want to talk about Lucas, I don't," she informed him, gripping the stone balustrade in her gloved
hands as she stared out into the shadowy garden.

"I think he's already getting enough attention for one
night. I want to talk about you. About us."

It was as though an icy hand wrapped around her
spine. "What of 'us'?"

Alastair leaned his elbow on the railing next to her. Relaxed as his posture was, he was still much taller than her. He wasn't as tall as Luke, but he was a little broader through the shoulders and chest. She might be intimidated—or perhaps swoon—if she hadn't known him so very long.

"I owe you an apology." He glanced down at his hands. "I let myself believe Luke was dead because that allowed me to think that there might be hope for the two of us. I would get so angry at you for hoping he'd come home, when I was right there, alive and eager."

He looked at her as though he expected her to argue. Oddly enough, she didn't feel the urge. "There were times when I wanted to share your feelings, Alastair, but I simply could not. I never meant to hurt you."

"I know. My behavior has not always been as it ought, nor have my motives always been strictly based in friendship, and for that I apologize."

"Accepted." She smiled at him. "Aren't you glad now that we never did become involved? What a mess we'd be in right now."

His stormy gaze locked with hers. "Yes, because I would have killed him the first night he came for you."

"Oh." There wasn't much else that could be said. "I wouldn't want you to have blood on your hands, Alastair."

"And I don't want him in your bed." The curve of his lips was familiar, but the regret behind it was not. "At least one of us will get what we want. Good night, Lady Huntley." He lowered his head and gave her a chaste kiss on the cheek before straightening and walking away. Arden was left alone on the balcony, face hot.

She truly was an awful person to have let things get so out of hand with Alastair. She'd known he cared for her—fancied himself in love with her—but not to this extent, not to the point that he would have killed the man who was once his best friend for her.

Just what had Alastair meant when he bid her good night and called her by her title? It had sounded so final. There were so many assumptions she might make, but Arden knew in her heart that this was the end of their friendship. He would come if she needed him, but they would never again be as close as they had been these last few years.

Drawing a deep breath of cool night air, she squared her shoulders and headed back inside to the party. She had a killer to find, and she wasn't going to find him moping on the balcony. Plus, there were easily a dozen women inside just dying to ask her about her husband's return, and another half who had expressed interest in one of her devices. The discombobulator was almost as popular as the anti-hysteria machines.

But these thoughts abandoned her as she stepped over the threshold and caught sight of her husband. He was exactly where she had left him, wearing the exact same expression of frustration and amusement, only now the people around him had stepped back to clear a path for the stunning woman in a bloodred gown and matching eye-patch heading straight toward him.

Rani Ogitani, his former partner and mistress.

Chapter 15

He was surrounded like flies on shite, but Luke became aware of two things at once: the crowd around him parting, and his wife.

Being able to finally draw breath without tasting someone's cologne bitter and pungent on his tongue was a blessing, but the look on Arden's face when his gaze found her stole all the air from his lungs. He'd seen predatory women in the past, but the possession in his wife's eyes ignited something very primal deep inside him. He wanted to go to her, take her to a place where they could be alone without some idiot asking him how he was "enjoying being home, har har," and shag till they were both too weak to move.

It would have nothing to do with sexual arousal, love or even attraction. It would be about possession, stark and primal—like a wolf offering his throat to his mate.

After the things she'd told him—that she suspected he was unfaithful, that he went on assignment with a former lover, leaving her alone . . . he couldn't for the life of him figure out why she thought him worth waiting for.

But he had gotten the same tattoo. Having her with him even when he had no idea of it, that had to mean something. Even if it didn't exonerate him, the glint in her eye told him why she had waited.

Because he was hers.

Then he saw her gaze move past him, and her porcelain features turned hard as stone. He turned to see who or what she was staring at, and caught a whiff of perfume that reminded him of incense, danger and sex—and not in what he would call a pleasant manner.

The woman was tiny, but she walked with the grace and confidence of someone whose body was as lethal as any weapon. Her hair was jet-black and fell in a thick, straight curtain to her waist. Her gown was a rich red with a Mandarin collar, tight, corseted bodice and long full skirt. Her ivory arms were bare, and as she walked an occasional flash of leg peeked through a slit in the fabric. He caught a glimpse of garter and red leather boots that came up over her knees. One of her legs was automatonic—he spied a flash of a filigree brass thigh as she moved toward him, her gait purposeful and extraordinarily even, despite the prosthetic.

Over one eye she wore a black leather patch adorned with diamond rivets. Was it actually bolted to her face? A gaze almost as dark as her hair met his, and full lips curved into a seductive smile. He was supposed to be impressed—it was expected of him. Instead, the spot in his head that Dr. Stone had patched up itched as though something had slipped inside and tickled his brain.

"Lucas Grey," she purred, standing right in front of him, so close her jutting breasts brushed his torso. "Lord Huntley returned from the grave. It is *very* good to see you, my lord." Her accent was posh, with just a touch of the Orient.

"I'm sorry," Luke said smoothly, pasting a disarming

smile on his face. "Have we met?" He had a pretty good idea of who she was, given the look Arden had given her, but if he hadn't been told her name it wouldn't have come on its own. She had to be the mistress. He rather liked not remembering her, even though he was certain that made him an even bigger arse.

A few people tittered nervously. Others chuckled at the slight, but most just stood in silence and watched. Her smile drooped. She honestly had expected him to know her, even though she had to have heard about his "amnesia." All of London was talking about it. It had been in the papers for Christ's sake.

"We've done more than meet," she informed him saucily, and a few onlookers sniggered.

"Perhaps if you told me your name," he suggested. It wasn't gentlemanly to embarrass her, but she obviously didn't care about embarrassing him, or Arden. He might deserve it, but Arden didn't.

A slender arm slid through his, and then his wife was at his side. "Huntley, this is Miss Rani Ogitani."

Christ. He'd rather be in the scope of an Aether cannon than caught between these two women. "My apologies for not remembering you, Miss Ogitani. I'm afraid I've had trouble remembering almost every detail of my past, except for Lady Huntley, of course." He must have said the right thing, because Arden squeezed his arm.

The two women stared at each other, but while Ogitani's expression was wary, Arden's was one of patently false pleasantness. Only her eyes betrayed just how angry she was; they glittered like amber under the chandeliers. Truth be told, his wife looked slightly mad, and it was all he could do not to grin at the sight.

"We should get you home soon," his wife said sweetly. "But first, that dance you promised me. Will you excuse us, Miss Ogitani?"

"Of course." The little woman didn't look at all pleased, but short of making some kind of scene—which she'd already done—there was nothing she could do.

The automaton orchestra—which would give a child nightmares—had just started playing a waltz as Luke and Arden joined the other dancers. People watched them curiously, waiting for gossip fodder.

Did he even remember how to waltz? Yes, it appeared so. His body fell easily into the movements, and as they began their dance he pulled her closer. His body remembered what his mind could not. "Shall we smile and pretend all is well?"

The grin she gave him was like a shark about to strike. "Do you really not remember her?"

"Nothing. In fact, I'm not sure what I saw in her to begin with." He didn't mean any insult, but it was true. There was no mystery to such a woman, only a battle of wills and empty sex.

Five would have fucked her, got any information he could and then moved on. It wasn't lost on him that perhaps Five had been a bit of an arse as well. So why hadn't he returned to his former self when his memories began to return? What had changed? He wasn't quite Huntley, but he wasn't Five anymore either.

Who the hell was he then?

Real satisfaction brightened Arden's face. "Good. Because I won't be made a fool of a second time."

He grinned at the promise in her voice. "Have I mentioned that I find bossiness arousing?"

"Have I mentioned that I find being ignored for two days off-putting?"

Luke laughed as he whirled her around. The metal lining his bones increased his strength, and he lifted her off her feet without any thought or effort whatsoever. "I thought perhaps you might not want me in your bed."

"You thought wrong. For what it's worth, I despise having an argument hang over my head. In the future, I would prefer to clear the air rather than to let things fester. I find it most vexing and distracting. I've thought of little else since."

By God, her directness was refreshing. He should have stayed to talk things out, but he had been too fixated on his own shame—and the fact that he wasn't sorry for no longer being the man she married—to think straight. "Forgive me."

Arden nodded, unflinching gaze still locked with his. "It is forgotten." Then a small smile curved her lips. "Next time, however, I use the magnet and force you to talk to me."

On that magnet, he would be helpless, completely at her mercy. The thought should be terrifying, but it was quite the opposite. "Let's go home," he suggested, voice low.

Heat flickered in the cinnamon depths of her eyes. "We finish the dance, otherwise people will talk."

"I don't really care."

She tilted her head, as though his words were unexpected. "All right."

Heart pounding in anticipation, Luke led her from the dance floor. He was only going home with his wife, and yet he felt as though he was about to embark on a dangerous mission, the exhilarating kind.

They didn't say good-bye to anyone. They simply cut through the curious crowd, gazes fixed straight ahead when they weren't looking at each other. Luke instructed one of the footmen to have their carriage brought around, and offered him several pound notes to do it quickly. They collected their outerwear by punching the number they'd been given on the keypad on the wall.

The mechanized belt growled to life and moved at a steady pace of coats and wraps until it stopped at theirs.

They were almost at the bottom of the steps when a voice called out, "Lucas!"

Luke stopped and turned. Rani stood at the top of the incline, an intense expression on her flawless face. She didn't speak; she just stared at him with that one dark eye.

A sense of dread washed over him. In that second he knew that she was no friend, and that she had only called out to delay him—separate him from Arden.

He whirled around just in time to see Arden at the bottom of the steps, and a horseless carriage careening toward her, faster than he'd ever seen one travel before. He raced toward her. If the vehicle hit her it would kill her—that was no doubt the intent.

The machine sped closer. He wasn't going to get there in time.

"Arden, move!" he shouted, his feet a blur over the steps.

She didn't look at him, didn't question him. She must have seen death approaching. He watched out of the corner of his eye as his trusting wife dove out of the way. The vehicle swerved toward her. . . .

Luke pounced, thrusting himself between Arden and the speeding carriage. He barely had time to brace himself for impact, but he turned his head away.

Then the vehicle wrapped around him.

Arden had seen many horrific things since joining the W.O.R., but nothing had prepared her for seeing her husband get hit by a carriage, and vice versa.

It was the quintessential unstoppable force and immovable object—or at least it seemed so in her frozen mind. She could only lie there on the steps—the edge of one digging into the flesh between her corset and underarm—and watch as Luke stretched out his hands a fraction of a second before the vehicle struck.

The front of the carriage caved under the force of his strength, and the velocity at which it hit, with a metallic screech of agony. The carriage drove Luke backward even as he did the same to part of it. Steam billowed around them as the destruction groaned to a halt, melting and moaning.

Luke was bleeding.

Somehow, Arden managed to scamper to her feet. Her ribs ached, but she ran to the twisted mass that held her husband prisoner, and when the man driving the carriage tried to crawl from the vehicle, she pulled her discombobulator from her reticule and shoved it hard against his grimy exposed throat. He spasmed and twitched like a fish flopping on a dock, but he could not escape.

The smell of burnt hair and urine filled the air—an unpleasant side effect of using the device on a higher setting, but at least she knew it was in working order.

She turned toward Luke. A flicker of movement in her peripheral vision made her head snap up in time to see Rani Ogitani hop on the back of a velocycle and roar away.

Arden's jaw clenched. Someday she and Ogitani were going to meet again. But that didn't matter right now. Luke was all that mattered.

He had saved her.

Alastair arrived as she reached Luke. There was a crowd gathered on the steps now—partygoers gawking at her husband's battered form. Alastair looked at the scene in horror.

"Help me," she said.

It took the two of them, despite Alastair's augmented

strength, to help Luke from the wreckage. He was awake, but bloody and unsteady. His hands were a sticky red mess, and there were cuts on his face and neck from flying glass and metal.

They helped him to the steps, where he collapsed on the stone. "Arden . . . are you unharmed?"

She hovered over him, using the handkerchief she'd pulled from inside his coat to dab at the wounds on his face. There were shards of metal and glass embedded in his skin. "I'm sore but unharmed, you great stupid article. What were you thinking?"

Pale eyes met hers. "Of you."

Wonderful, now she was going to start bawling. She sniffed and tried to fend off the blurring burning behind her lashes. "We're taking you to Evie."

"I'm fine. Alastair can stitch me up."

Alastair seemed surprised that Luke would have faith in his abilities. He flashed Arden a guilty glance. Perhaps he was thinking of his earlier claim that he would have killed Luke if she'd been his.

"I've seen Alastair's stitches, and you're going to Evie," she informed him in crisp tones that kept her voice from trembling. "I'm not taking you home until I know for certain you're fine."

"Bossy." His lips curved up on one side. He turned his head toward Alastair. "That one-eyed bitch was involved."

The other man's expression turned grim. "We'll deal with her later. Can you stand?"

As they helped Luke to the carriage that was now waiting for them, Arden turned to Alastair. "Thank you for coming so quickly."

"I heard him scream for you to move. I'm sorry I didn't get here faster."

His eyes flashed like mirrors in the lamplight. Sometimes she forgot that Alastair's hearing had been augmented as well. After Luke disappeared, Alastair had volunteered himself for several W.O.R. experimental "improvements" to make him a better agent.

Is that what the Company called what they did to their agents? What they had done to Luke? Improvements?

Arden settled in with Luke stretched out on the padded bench, his head in her lap. Alastair remained behind. "I'm going to make sure the bastard driving is taken to lockup. I'll meet you at Evie's."

One thing Arden had always admired about the Wardens was that they were like a family, so familiar and intimate, always looking out for one another. In the beginning that devotion had made it difficult for her, because she'd felt outside of it despite her father's lifelong service, and because she felt as though perhaps they pitied her because her husband had gone missing. Now, she was very happy to be a part.

Alastair closed the door and gave her driver directions. Within moments the automaton horses were galloping along the cobblestone streets faster than any real horse could. She cradled Luke's head, her bloodstained fingers gently stroking his face.

"That feels nice," he murmured. His eyelashes tickled the side of her thumb.

Since it seemed that he wasn't in any immediate danger, she allowed herself to think of things other than the moment. "I'm going to go out on a limb and assume that was no accident."

He chuckled, then winced. "The Company trying to tidy up loose ends, I reckon."

She affected a sniff. "Well, they're terribly sloppy at it."

Another chuckle—softer this time. The flesh around his eyes crinkled. God, how she fancied those lines, etched so carefully into his skin by years of smiles and laughter. "I love how you hide your true emotions behind wit."

"Really?" She ran her fingers through his hair, both massaging his scalp and searching for more shrapnel. "My mother always used to say it was highly annoying and very unladylike, and, further, that I would never get a husband if I insisted on saying whatever clever thing was on my mind."

His eyes opened. "And then you got me."

She smiled. "Exactly. You can be sure I made her eat crow then." She hadn't, of course. She just wanted to see him smile again.

He didn't. "I wasn't much of a catch, I'm afraid."

"You seem to labor under the delusion that I was," she drawled with an arched brow. "Neither of us was or is perfect, although I like to think that we're both a little less self-involved than we once were."

A frown creased Luke's brow and she immediately set to smoothing it with her thumb, carefully avoiding the myriad of tiny cuts there. "This may sound like an excuse, but I don't think I went to that woman just because we fought."

Did it say ill of her that she was thrilled to hear him refer to the gorgeous Rani as "that woman"? "I have to confess, after seeing her on the steps tonight I wondered the same thing. Do you honestly think she tried to kill you?"

"Ardy," he began in a low voice, "I think we both know I wasn't the target, at least not immediately."

Arden swallowed. The carriage had been heading straight toward her. "It seems we were correct in assuming the Company would come for you—for both of us. What makes you so certain Ogitani is involved?"

"I don't know, but Wolfred didn't seem all that surprised when I told him my suspicions." He paused. "Speaking of Wolfred, what did you and he do when you disappeared out onto the balcony earlier?"

She appreciated that he didn't push discussing that she was the initial target. "Saw that, did you? I thought you were too caught up in your admirers to notice if I came or went." She sounded petulant despite the forced lightness of tone.

"Woman, I knew where you were every minute of the evening whether I wanted to or not."

There was just enough humor in his gruff tone that she knew he didn't really mind. The realization made her as giddy as a girl. "Alastair wanted to apologize for making presumptions regarding our friendship."

"That was big of him," he drawled.

"He's a good man."

"I hear sainthood is eminent."

Arden grinned. "Jealous?"

"Deservedly so." Luke sighed. "I suppose I can't blame him for falling in love with you."

Oh. She didn't know how to respond to that. To be frank, the statement raised too many questions she didn't want to ponder, ask or obsess over, such as whether or not he loved her, or she loved him. She knew only that he had put himself in danger for her, and that if she lost him now she might not survive it. She didn't understand the depth of her emotion where he was involved, and at that moment she didn't care. There was just the two of them in this carriage. No one asking questions or watching them. No expectations, just them.

When they reached Evelyn's modest three-story townhome, Luke was able to walk in with just a bit of help from Arden and Gibbs. Arden sent the coachman downstairs to have tea and bread with Evelyn's staff.

The medical rooms were in the back of the house. Evelyn had Luke lie down on a table while she took photographs of his internal workings. It was a process that never ceased to fascinate Arden. To think that it had been an accidental discovery made it all the more amazing.

"I don't see any internal injuries," Evelyn told her as she examined one of the panels detailing Luke's ribs. "Though I'm not certain what it would take to hurt him. A sniper, perhaps. But it would have to be a damn good shot—look, even his heart is encased in metal. Brass, I think."

Arden looked at the ghostly image and saw where her friend pointed. There was indeed a metal casing around her husband's heart—almost like a cage. Knowing what she did about Luke's skeletal plating, she hadn't expected him to be badly injured, though she'd certainly been afraid for him. On one hand it gave her great peace to know how difficult he was to kill. On the other, she didn't want to know all the things that *might* do the job.

"They made him virtually indestructible." The darker woman's awe was obvious. How long before Warden agents started getting the same augmentations? Perhaps Luke hadn't been so wrong when he said there wasn't much difference between the Wardens and the Company. Not much at all, just different views of good and evil.

"But *they* know how to destroy him," Arden said. "I need to keep that from happening."

Evelyn looked away. "You said Rani Ogitani was involved. You know that the W.O.R. has been investigating her?"

"We assumed as much. Why?"

Her friend sighed, and folded her arms over the bodice of her serviceable white blouse and black waistcoat. "I'd be speculating based on gossip if I told you. You must know there are going to be those who wonder if Huntley isn't in league with her, especially since they were seen speaking this evening."

"How the devil did you know they spoke to each other?" Her jaw tightened. "Alastair." How the devil had he gotten word here so fast? Did he have a telephone in his carriage that operated on Aether waves?

"Don't be angry. You know he's acting on the Director's orders. We all want this to have a happy ending, Arden, but we're not going to risk your life for it, or the safety of this country."

Arden pointed at the photographs of her husband's insides. "That man stepped in front of a speeding carriage for me."

Evelyn shrugged, dusky features impassive. "Anyone with his sort of augments would know he'd be in little danger if he braced himself the right way, which Huntley obviously did."

Arden opened her mouth to argue, but was cut off. "I'm not saying that's what happened; I'm just advising you to be prepared for people to wonder."

"She's right."

At the sound of Luke's voice, Arden turned. Her husband limped into the room bare-chested and in bare feet. His arms had been wrapped in temporary bandages from the elbows down and little red slashes dotted his face and chest. Without braces, his trousers hung low on his hips, and she could see a large bruise had begun to form over his left one.

"Where are your shoes?" Arden demanded crossly, because it was the only thing she could think of to say that didn't involve swearing.

He gestured at Evelyn. "She took them."

"Were you afraid he'd run off?" she inquired darkly, not bothering to temper her tone or her expression.

Evelyn flushed, and retreated a couple of steps. "His left foot was cut." It was a lame excuse and Arden didn't believe it for a second. "If you would take a seat, Lord Huntley, I'll get you stitched up and take care of those fragments."

Luke gingerly hoisted himself up on an examination bed. He looked tired, and in pain, which he had to be despite being so incredibly strong. He was still flesh, after all. His gaze sought hers. "She is right, Ardy. The Wardens will wonder at my loyalty even more now, and no doubt that's exactly what the bitch intended."

"What she didn't intend," said Alastair as he closed the door behind him, "was for you to be the hero and step in front of that carriage. Regardless of your capacity for damage, that will earn you favor with many of the Wardens."

"Such as?" Luke asked drily.

Alastair lifted his chin. "Me."

Heat seeped into Arden's cheeks. Would it be so terribly difficult for Alastair to conceal the depth of his feelings? Maybe just for a little while? He'd done a tolerable job of it before Luke's return. "Did the driver give you any information?"

"He's barely coherent." Alastair turned to her. "What did you do to him?"

"I used my discombobulator on him. He should recover all of his faculties before morning."

"I certainly hope control of his bladder is among them. Good work, though. He might have gotten away if not for you."

"My wife is a most capable woman," Luke remarked, with perhaps a little extra emphasis on "wife." And then to Alastair, "Thank you for your assistance."

The two men stared at each other for what seemed an eternity. Finally, Alastair gave a slight nod and turned his attention elsewhere. "Do you want a hand, Evelyn?"

"You?" The doctor laughed. "You sew like a blind man. Thank you, but no. Lady Huntley can assist me."

Arden stepped forward. Her gown was already ruined from the evening's adventure, so what was a little more blood? Though she was tempted to throw a blanket over her husband's naked shoulders to shield him from Evie's gaze.

"Dr. Stone, I would like for you to examine my wife before we take our leave. She took a nasty fall earlier."

Evelyn shot her a narrow look as she removed one of the temporary bandages from Luke's left arm. "You failed to mention that."

"I didn't think it was important." Arden made a face at her husband. "But I'm in no mind to argue, so I'll submit to an exam when we're done."

The cut on Luke's arm was deep, so deep Arden thought she caught a glimpse of gregorite. She swallowed hard. Mercifully, it wasn't terribly bloody. She washed her hands in the nearby basin and assisted by holding the edges of the wound together while Evelyn used a small stitching apparatus that closed the cut from both sides with two needles that drew the thread back and forth through the skin. Arden made a mental note to discover the name of the inventor and give the man or woman her personal thanks.

Luke barely made a sound as they worked, though she knew from experience the procedure was unpleasant. When they were done, she swabbed the area with Lister's antiseptic liquid, and set to work cleaning the smaller cuts that marked his skin. Using tweezers she assisted in plucking pieces of debris from the wounds as well. She was fine, her hands steady, so long as she didn't look at him. Looking at him—in his eyes—reminded her of what he'd done for her, and the memory of it made her shake.

She wasn't ready to shake. She'd do that later in the privacy of her own room.

"Do you have any idea where Ogitani might be hiding?" Alastair asked, bracing his hands on his lean hips.

Luke shook his head and sucked in a sharp breath when Arden pulled a particularly deep bit of glass from his shoulder. "Sorry," she murmured.

He gave her a brief smile. "I'll survive." Then to Alastair, "I don't remember a damn thing about her, mate. If I do, you'll be the first to know."

"You must admit it's a little convenient that you don't remember."

Arden glanced over her shoulder at the other man, scowling. "This is becoming very tiresome. He's the one who was hurt, remember? Perhaps I think it's convenient that your 'guard' duties lapsed long enough for Luke to be injured."

Anger flashed in Alastair's gray eyes—and hurt. "That's not amusing."

"It wasn't meant to be," she shot back, forcing herself to hold his gaze.

Luke's hand settled over one of hers, blessedly drawing her attention away from Alastair, because she didn't know how much longer she could hold his stare. "I appreciate your faith, but Wolfred's not the one who has to prove himself. I am."

"I wasn't insinuating that Alastair intentionally allowed you to get hurt. I'm merely pointing out that this constant distrust has reached a threshold of foolishness. Do you have to be killed before the W.O.R. will even entertain the notion of your innocence?"

She stared at Luke, but out of the corner of her eyes she saw Alastair and Evelyn exchange a guilty look. Good. She hoped the pair of them felt awful.

"She smelled of incense," Luke said, frowning. "The kind they use in the opium brothels."

"Sandalwood," Alastair replied. "It's a stretch, but it could be she's hiding out in one of them."

"Or it could be that she likes sandalwood," Arden commented, looking between the two of them. "I won't bother to ask how you're both able to identify the incense used in those brothels."

"I'm going to alert the Director," Alastair informed them, cheeks flushed as he avoided making eye contact. "I'll call upon the two of you tomorrow. Evelyn."

When he was gone, Evelyn smiled at her. "I think you embarrassed him. Well done. Lord Huntley, you can get dressed. Arden, come with me so I can examine you. Then I'll give you both something for the pain you're going to have come morning."

A little while later, after confirming that she wasn't seriously hurt, and armed with a bottle of some sort of opiate, Arden found Luke—now fully dressed—and departed. Gibbs was already in his perch when they exited the house.

It was after two a.m. when they arrived home. Arden was in her bedroom, dressed in her nightgown, thanks to help from Annie, when Luke came in. He had stripped down to just his trousers again. She could grow accustomed to having him walk around like that all the time. Even with the cuts and bruises he was still the finest thing she'd ever seen. Modesty was not a virtue Arden could remember ever owning, and it certainly wasn't one she intended to claim anytime soon.

"Did you take some of Evelyn's pain medicine?" she asked, openly admiring the muscles of his abdomen and upper chest.

He shook his head. "No. Makes my head feel like it's stuffed with cotton. You?"

"No. I was just going to crawl into bed." She hesitated. "Would you care to join me?"

"Yes." He walked around to the other side of the bed and removed his trousers. He slipped between the sheets in his small clothes, the thin linen low on his hips.

Arden didn't have any hopes of intimacy as they slid between the sheets, both of them groaning as their battered bodies protested every moment. He pulled her into the warmth of his arms and didn't say a word. Neither of them spoke at all. Their lips found each other, hungry and insistent. Desperation clawed at her from deep inside. She ached all over, but she wanted him.

Needed him.

He lifted the hem of her nightgown, fingers sliding immediately between her thighs. He teased her to the point of aching before draping her knee over the crook of his elbow.

"Put me inside you," he commanded, breath hot against her cheek.

She reached between them and her trembling fingers wrapped around the hard length of his erection. Tilting her hips, she guided him to the entrance of her body and pushed herself forward so that he slowly slid inside.

Even her breath shook it felt so good.

He held her leg away from his injured hip as they rocked together. Their breath mingled, foreheads pressed together. Arden had never needed anything like she needed *this*.

"You feel so good inside me," she whispered, and whimpered when he ground his pelvis harder against hers. Her body ached—inside and out—but even were she dying she wouldn't have stopped.

"So tight," he murmured. "So fucking tight and wet."

She shivered at his words. She'd always liked talking during sex, and so had Luke. "Just for you. I'm wet just for you," she whispered in reply and was rewarded with a shudder, and a deep thrust that made her gasp.

They continued to whisper heated, wanton things to each other, the intensity increasing with their fervent motions. She came hard, a long, shuddering spasm that wrung itself out of her in a low cry. She clutched at Luke's shoulders as he stiffened, groaning as his own orgasm hit.

Afterward, they lay pressed against each other, stroking each other's skin.

"I'm so glad you weren't seriously injured today," she murmured. "I was so scared."

"When I saw that carriage coming at you . . ." He squeezed her, but not tight enough to hurt. "I don't ever want to feel that way again."

Arden wanted to promise him that he wouldn't, and she wanted him to promise her the same, but that wasn't a guarantee either one of them could give. The Company and its agents were out there, and they wouldn't rest until both she and Luke were dead.

Chapter 16

Luke felt as though he'd been hit by a train rather than a horseless carriage. His bones might be unbreakable, but the tissue surrounding them wasn't impervious to injury, and even though he'd stopped the brunt of the vehicle with his hands, his left side had taken a nasty bash, and his forearm had been cut open.

He and Arden had the devil of a time trying to get out of bed the next morning, and each took a bit of Dr. Stone's pain medicine. By the time they were bathed and dressed, Luke didn't feel quite so shite. He even managed to hobble downstairs to the dining room for breakfast. Just what was in that glorious little concoction of the doctor's?

The morning paper was beside his plate. This Lord of the Manor business was odd, yet familiar, and he was more unsettled by the fact that part of his brain accepted the head of the table, the paper and a valet as "usual" than by the things themselves. He'd feel much more comfortable if it were all a surprise.

Then he saw the morning's headline, and that was surprise enough.

MAN OR MACHINE? LORD HUNTLEY DESTROYS
RUNAWAY CARRIAGE WITH BARE HANDS!
WHISKED AWAY BY VIRTUOUS WIFE

"Mrs. Bird says they've been turning away callers and press all morning," Arden informed him as she entered the room. She wore a kimono-style gown in rust silk with a teal corset over it.

"I'm not surprised. Are you comfortable in that?"

She nodded. "The corset's tight enough to keep me from moving in ways that might be painful, but not so restricting that it hurts. Still, I'd prefer the pain to death."

"You've obviously never been tortured," he remarked before digging into his eggs.

"Have you?"

Luke glanced up to see her standing beside her chair, knuckles white as her cheeks as she gripped the back. "Yes." As he spoke his mind was filled with a barrage of images of things he'd never realized he'd experienced. The Doctor's face filled almost every one of them. The Company had tortured him to get information, and when that hadn't worked, they'd destroyed his memory and made him their puppet.

If he ever got his hands on that bastard Doctor again, he'd kill him.

Arden must have seen the rage and shame on his face, because she wrapped her fingers around his wrist as she sat down on his right, and squeezed. "I'd do anything to take that away from you."

His gaze locked with hers. "I've lost too much of my life as it is. I appreciate the sentiment, however. We don't need to discuss it any further." He didn't want to talk about it. It felt as though it had happened to someone else—just a snippet from a play he'd seen a long time ago.

She nodded and reached for the pile of correspondence between them. "Invitations to parties, balls, dinners and teas. We've become very popular, it seems."

"Everyone wanting to see for themselves if I'm man or machine." It was ridiculous, really. "They don't seem to realize that inviting us means inviting an assassin into their midst as well."

Her expression of dry amusement was so good he almost believed it—but it didn't quite reach her eyes. That was where he saw the glimmer of fear. "Or perhaps they do. The aristocracy is terribly bored, you know."

This time it was he who reached out to her, wrapping his fingers around her slender, cool ones. "I won't let the Company win."

She nodded—a stilted gesture that didn't say much for her confidence in him. Or perhaps she simply had too much confidence in the Company. "I know you won't."

"Rani Ogitani may have been my lover once, but never after I married you. I need you to know that."

Arden helped herself to the coddled eggs with a frown tucked between her cinnamon brows. "She's gorgeous. What man wouldn't want her?"

"Gorgeous as a cobra," he retorted. "No man who held his bollocks in any sort of esteem would go within ten feet of her."

Astonishment slackened her features as she glanced at him while reaching for the salt cellar. "Really? Every woman I know who has seen her remarks on her beauty."

"I'm not certain what I ever saw in her. There was no emotional attachment, I'm certain."

"You don't sound certain."

"I don't remember much about her."

"Then how do you know you weren't . . . lovers after our marriage?"

"I know. I don't need my full memory to know that I might have been an arse, but I was a faithful one." At least when he knew he had a wife.

She stared at him for a moment, eyes wide, before dropping her gaze to her plate. "I never expected that you would return without the memory of our life. I know it's unfair of me to be angry for things you cannot remember, but I can't seem to help it. You are not the same man, and yet sometimes you are. I don't know how to feel or think."

Luke rubbed his hand over his mouth. If he could take that from her he would, but there was nothing he could do. He wanted her with him for the rest of his days, but was it because of old feelings, or new ones? He had the benefit of seeing all her newness, while she couldn't seem to see beyond their past. "It seems we're both victims of our memories."

Her head turned. "So, what do we do?"

"Damned if I know," he replied with a harsh laugh. "Make some new ones? I really don't want you telling our grandchildren that I betrayed you or tried to kill you." He meant it as a bit of joke, but she looked as though he'd struck her.

"Grandchildren?"

He couldn't say anything right this morning. "Have you changed your mind about having children?"

"I . . . I haven't allowed myself to think about it much at all."

"And don't have to right now." In fact, it was the last thing they should be thinking about while the Company was trying to kill them. Afterward, when he'd sent every one of their agents home in a coffin, then they could discuss children.

They ate in silence. It seemed that he had shocked his normally verbose wife into losing her voice. Whether that was a good thing or bad remained unknown, like much of his life.

The doorbell rang several times during the course of their meal, but it wasn't until Luke was finishing his third cup of coffee that Mrs. Bird entered the room, a rather harried expression on her face, one that made Luke remember a young girl with a similar expression. It took several seconds for him to realize that it was a memory of Birdy in their youth. She'd grown up here, her mother the housekeeper before her. The two of them had played together as children.

She had known him longer than Arden. Longer than Alastair. She seemed to like him well enough, so perhaps he hadn't always been a wanker of the first order.

"Beg your pardon, but Lord Henry is here, my lord."

"We're not at home this morning, Mrs. Bird," Arden replied.

It was obvious that the housekeeper was accustomed to her mistress's clipped way of speaking because she didn't flinch at all, though others might have. "I know, my lady, but he has Dr. Vincent and Mr. Kirkpatrick with him."

Luke had no idea who Mr. Kirkpatrick was, but he remembered Henry mentioning Dr. Vincent during his previous visit. From the way Arden closed her eyes and pressed a hand to her forehead, Kirkpatrick was not a welcome addition.

"Your family solicitor," she murmured, as though reading his mind. "Put them in the blue drawing room, Mrs. Bird. I think we must see them," she said to him.

He agreed. "How do I look?"

"Like a bedlamite," she replied with a slight grin. It seemed they were to find solidarity once more in facing Henry and his companions. "Me?"

"A roughhoused wench." Pushing back his chair he

rose stiffly to his feet. Christ, it hurt. "Think they'll believe I'm not an automaton?"

She groaned as she stood as well. "Automatons are usually made of brass, and wouldn't have survived such a collision with their cogs intact. There would be pieces scattered all the way to Hyde Park."

"So that's a yes?"

"Yes." Together they walked to the door. "Your brother has to have heard what happened last night. He has a lot of nerve showing up with this foolishness this morning."

It was actually noon, but Luke didn't bother to correct her. He suspected that Henry's visit was entirely due to last night's intrigue. It could hardly be seen as proper—or sane—for an earl to cleave a speeding carriage in half.

At a snail's pace, they made their way to the blue drawing room—Luke had no bloody idea where it was, so he let Arden lead. He was still learning his way around the house. Sometimes he knew exactly where to go, and other times he was lost.

It was bloody frustrating, this knowing and not knowing the progress of his life. Bits and snatches came and went, a confusing barrage of images that often made no sense whatsoever. He knew it did him no good to get angry—that made remembering all the more difficult—but sometimes it was impossible. Sometimes things hovered so close, yet just out of his mind's reach, and he had to face the fear that he might never get it all back.

Their journey was peppered with curses, groans and hisses of pain. They shared a glance in the corridor that set them both to laughing, which made the pain both worse and bearable. They were still chuckling when they entered the room.

Two of the gentlemen stood right away, Henry a bit

more slowly. Once again Luke was struck by the resemblance between them. Did they take after their mother or father? Their parents were like ghosts in his mind—half-formed images that told him nothing. Surely there had to be paintings of them somewhere in the vast recesses of this house?

"Gentlemen," he said in greeting, offering his hand to the man closest him. "Please excuse our appearance. I'm sure you heard about the adventure we had last night."

"Adventure?" The man chortled. "I heard it was something much more sinister, Lord Huntley."

At least the man used his title. "Perhaps, Mr. . . . ?"

He looked surprised, jowls jiggling as he jerked back. "Vincent. I delivered your mother of you, my lord."

Luke grinned to ease the doctor's discomfort. "I thank you for that, sir. I'm sure my brother has informed you that I have a sort of amnesia." He shook the other man's hand as well. "Please, sit."

"May we offer you any refreshment?" Arden asked. Luke didn't miss her use of "we." With that one little word she declared them a unit. A matched set. At that moment he didn't care if she meant it. It was enough that she had said it.

The three of them declined, which instantly set the tone for the meeting. It was to be all business, then. They were here for one thing alone—to determine whether or not he should be allowed to own the title that was his by birth.

He wasn't attached to it, but it was one more thing that had been taken from him by the Company. He wasn't about to let his brother take it from him as well. He was going to reclaim his life if it was the last damn thing he did. He'd most certainly regret it later when he had to deal with tenants and rents, but for now it was something he could at least hold a degree of control over.

He waited for Arden to sit before leaning back against the small writing desk. He didn't want these men to see how much pain he was in, and trying to sit would reveal just that. Plus, standing gave him a height advantage, which was a timeless intimidation tactic. He crossed his arms over his chest and caught a glimpse of himself in a mirror on the side wall.

Good lord, he did look like a bedlamite—one that had been lobotomized. His hair was back from his forehead, revealing the healing wound from Dr. Stone's surgery. Little wounds from last night made tiny angry red slashes on his skin, and around his left forearm was a snowy white bandage that he should have pulled his sleeve down to conceal.

"The three of you are here to decide my fate, are you?" he asked gruffly, making eye contact with each one of them. One thing Luke did remember was how to pin a man with his gaze and stare him down. Wasn't that part of being a peer?

"Lord Henry has expressed concern for your health, Lord Huntley," the man he assumed to be Kirkpatrick, the solicitor—no one had introduced them—said convivially. "We are here to offer whatever assistance we can."

"Concern for his inheritance, you mean," Luke corrected. "You needn't speak to me as though I was a child, sir. I assure you that while my memory might be spotty, the rest of my mind is perfectly sound and capable of knowing when I'm being patronized and treated as a half-wit."

The solicitor flushed. Luke cast a glance at Arden and found her practically gaping at him. He fought the urge to grin.

"Why don't you gentlemen just go ahead and line up whatever hurdles I'm to jump over, or ask whatever questions you have so Lady Huntley and I can get back to our life?"

"The life that someone is obviously trying to end," Henry interjected. "Good lord, think of what this scandal does to the family."

"Aren't you a peach." Luke couldn't help but sneer a little. "Your brother is injured, your sister-in-law almost killed, and all you can think of is the scandal. Our mother would be so very proud."

Henry turned crimson but didn't back down. "Our mother would be humiliated by you and your behavior."

"Would she? I've been a prisoner these past seven years, of an enemy of England, and now I've returned, doing everything within my power to bring that enemy to its knees. Do you really believe Mother would be ashamed of her son being one of the few peers in England doing more than arse-warming a bench in Parliament?"

Arden looked as though she was about to applaud. Meanwhile, the men in the room looked heartily ashamed, which had been the point of his impassioned speech. He had no bloody idea if his mum would be proud of him or not. He couldn't even remember her name, and her face was nothing more than a wisp of dream.

But he couldn't think of that now. He had them where he wanted them. He stood up straight even though his battered muscles protested, and used his impressive height to even further advantage. He kept his expression firm, eyes hard. "I am Lucas Harris Stratford Grey, the Earl of Huntley, and if my brother wants the title he can get in line and kill me for it, or wait for someone else to do the job. Meanwhile I have read the correspondence from my stewards, have written to them, and my wife and I plan to visit each of my country estates once the Season is over so that I may resume my responsibilities."

They all stared at him—even Arden. He hadn't told her what he'd been up to those couple of days when he'd been trying to sort out how much of an arse he'd been to her.

"Henry, I thank you for taking care of things in my absence. I only wish you had included my wife in that care, but since she's not part of the earldom I suppose she slipped beneath your notice."

His brother looked as though he might choke—or actually attempt to throttle him. Henry's hand was bandaged from their last encounter, so Luke suspected the younger man wouldn't try anything so rash. "I paid her bills and her staff, which is more than most would have done. I allowed her to live in our family home."

"It is her home—and mine. All you did was oversee the fortune attached to the title. How much of it did you use as your own?"

"Are you accusing me of stealing from my own inheritance?"

"I'm accusing you of being a heartless bastard," Luke shot back. "You couldn't even give her the kindness due your own brother's wife."

Henry didn't respond. He glanced down at his feet, but only for a second before shooting Luke a dark look. Christ, but the runt was angry. Angry at him, and at the entire world.

Luke could relate.

"What say you, Dr. Vincent?" Luke asked, turning a hard gaze to the old physician. "Am I sound? Or am I bound for Bedlam? Before you decide, I think it only fair to inform you that I've received a written thank-you from the prime minister for the sacrifices I've made for this country. Would you care to see it?"

Their horrified expressions revealed that he had won, although he was going to have to answer for it to Arden, whom he hadn't told about the P.M.'s note. First Vincent, then Kirkpatrick took their leave.

"I think you should go as well, Henry," Lucas told his brother. Perhaps he would feel a greater sense of betrayal if his memories were clearer. As it was, he was more annoyed than anything else. "Perhaps we might talk again when you're not so angry."

To his surprise, Henry nodded. "Perhaps. But I shouldn't hold my breath were I you." Even more surprising was the disappointment Luke felt at those words. Surely at one time there had been a measure of brotherly love between them? Some sort of regard or loyalty?

When they were alone once more, he turned to Arden only to find her on her feet, watching him with an oddly amused expression. "Not too many people can say they've gotten personal correspondence from the prime minister."

He shrugged. Even his shoulders ached. "She probably had her secretary write it." That had been one of the biggest surprises of his return—discovering that England had its first female political leader. It shouldn't be that astounding—after all they had a female monarch—but he'd never thought the Tories and Whigs would stand for it, the bunch of old curmudgeons.

"Still, it should go a long way with the Wardens."

"The fact that someone thinks I suffered when really I did it all willingly?" Harsh laughter crawled from his throat. "It doesn't matter that they altered my mind; I thought I was doing the right thing. I believed that I was on the proper side."

She regarded him thoughtfully, yet with an odd sort of impartiality. "You know, it occurs to me that you've punished yourself more than the Wardens ever could. Perhaps you should just admit that you were taken advantage of and start fresh. Or does self-flagellation make you feel more like a man?"

Damn that tongue of hers. She knew just where and how to best strike with it. It stung all the worse because she was right. "The Company made a fool of me."

"And if you're lucky, they'll be the only ones in the span of your life."

"You're so bloody blasé. They robbed me of seven years. Robbed *us*."

"They could have simply killed you," she retorted, "but they decided to use you, and when it came time for you to do what they ultimately wanted of you, you didn't. If anyone should feel foolish, it's the Company. You're alive, we've been given a second chance, and there are worse things in life than losing seven years."

"Such as?" he asked with a scowl. "Have you any idea what it's like to be betrayed by your own mind?"

Arden held out her hand, her lips tight. "Come with me."

The Featherstone Sanitorium was situated in a picturesque location on the western fringes of the city. In the interest of comfort, they took the touring carriage with its superior spring and wider wheels that would hamper the jostling of their aching bodies. Honestly, Arden didn't know how Luke was even able to move, let alone drive, which he had insisted upon doing.

God bless Evie and her magic potions.

She didn't even mind him driving, she was so caught up in her own thoughts and anxieties. Not about Luke, not really. Today with his brother and the other gentlemen she'd gotten her first real glimpse of the man he now was. The old Luke would have tried a bit more charm—smiled and cajoled them into bending to his will. This man simply told them how it was going to be, and dared them to challenge him.

Best of all, he had spoken for her—acknowledged that she had been alone for the past seven years. She hadn't wanted or even needed Henry to look out for her, but neither had her brother-in-law ever offered. Oh, he let her stay in the family house, but without declaring Luke dead he couldn't kick her out. Besides, he and his wife had their own town house. She'd had access to money, and all the bills were paid. She made extra money on the side with her work for the W.O.R. and her inventions, so she never wanted for anything.

Except perhaps the friendship and support of the family she'd married into. The joke of it was that Luke didn't seem to know how much his words had affected her. He hadn't said them to earn her goodwill; he'd said them because he meant them. He might one day forgive his brother for trying to usurp him, but he would never forget that Henry hadn't done right by her.

Luke had never been more beautiful to her than he had in that moment. She loved every little bruise and cut, line and shadow on his gorgeously sharp features. In fact, after all the time and pain, there was part of her that still loved him. There was an even bigger part of her that was in danger of falling in love with the man he was now. There was no artifice to him, no polite veneer. He spoke his mind and offered his emotions freely. He laughed with real delight, raged with raw anger, and when it was impossible to tell where her body began and his ended, he looked at her as though she was the other half of his soul.

Good lord, when had she become so bloody romantic? Where was her rationality now? Laughing at her from some place far away, no doubt, for there was nothing the least bit rational about her feelings for Luke.

She wanted to throw herself over that precipice, but common sense held her back. He remembered little of their life together, so he didn't have those old feelings. What if he couldn't love her now? There was no denying the attraction between them, but that had never been an issue. What if he didn't fall in love with her? Or worse, what if he stayed with her because she was his strongest link to the past he couldn't quite remember?

They passed through the gates at the foot of the sanitorium's drive. When Luke saw the sign with the name of the place on it, he turned his head to give her a questioning look. He was the only man she'd ever seen, with the possible exception of Alastair, who could wear driving goggles and still look good.

Did he wonder if she planned to have him committed?

Judging by the amount of vehicles parked out front, they were not the only visitors who chose to call on this sunny and pleasant day. They parked near the front door, behind a wine-colored carriage pulled by four gleaming brass horses. It was a frivolous display of wealth. An automaton horse could do the work of four, and cost about as much. To have this many was just ... showing off, though a touring carriage such as her own wasn't cheap either. Her only excuse was that her father had built it.

They removed their goggles, and Arden checked to make certain her broad-brimmed hat was as it should be on her head. She smoothed the front of her peacock-blue driving dress and held out her hand as he came round to her side. Luke took it without a word, offering the comfort of his touch without knowing just how badly she needed it. She'd never brought anyone here—not Hannah, not Alastair.

The sanitorium was an imposing old estate dating back to Henry VIII. Red stone, dark trim and spires that reached toward the sky. Only the bars on the windows betrayed that this was a fortress and not a home.

They climbed the shallow stone steps to the heavy front door. Arden lifted the earpiece from the hook and placed it against her ear. When a voice inquired as to who was calling, she leaned toward the voice amplifier on the wall and said, "Lord and Lady Huntley."

There was a pause and then, "Identification verification, please."

From a small holder inside her glove, Arden extracted a round bit of metal that was notched around the perimeter—resembling a completely unsymmetrical cog—and placed it into the slot of the mechanism on the wall beside the visitor audio phone. The piece fell into place and immediately set the rest of the clockwork device into motion. It rotated clockwise, then clicked back, then forward once more, before it stopped and spit the tiny cog out into a small receptacle, from which Arden retrieved it.

"Come right in." The voice crackled in her ear. "She's in the solarium."

Arden thanked the woman and hung up just as a loud clunk filled the warm air. Slowly, the large doors split apart, sliding open with a low, grating noise. She gripped her husband's fingers tightly now, urging him over the threshold with her.

Luke glanced around at the stately foyer, and the guards all dressed in black, cudgels in their belts. "This is where Henry would have me. Tucked away like a dirty secret."

She stiffened. "Featherstone's not like that. These people need to be here to get the care they need."

He glanced at her, but she ignored it. She'd answer his

questions later. Right now, she just needed to get through this.

"What's in the bag?" he asked.

"A surprise," she replied, hefting the satchel in her right hand.

"What are we doing here, Arden?"

She sighed. His patience was obviously reaching its end. "You asked if I knew what it was like to be betrayed by your own mind. You also asked me why I waited for you. I'm going to answer both."

Silently, he walked alongside her as they continued down a wide, sunny corridor to a large, glassed-in area at the back of the building. There weren't bars on the glass in this area—those were used to keep people from jumping out of windows, and from escaping. All of the furniture in the solarium was bolted to the floor so it couldn't be thrown through a pane.

Here it was warm and bright, and patients sat on padded reclining chairs and enjoyed the day, while staring out at the gardens beyond. Patients walked out there, most with staff escorts, but the people in this section were those for whom actually experiencing the out-of-doors might be more frightening than pleasant, or more dangerous.

Arden spotted her immediately, her graying auburn hair bright in the sun. Her throat tightened as she approached, her fingers slipping free of Luke's. A face the color of cream, freckled across the nose, softly lined and creased, lifted at their arrival. Wide brown eyes crinkled at the corner.

"I know you," the woman said—her words an echo of what Luke had said after Evelyn opened his skull.

Arden smiled. Today was a good day. "Hello, Mama."

"Arden!" The days her mother realized she did indeed know her were often the most difficult. The pleasure in her voice, the bright recognition in her eyes were even more painful than the blank stares that had become more commonplace. The first day her mother asked her name was forever burned into her memory—one she would gladly lose.

A thin hand clutched at hers with surprising strength. "Sit down, my darling. It's so good to see you, dear girl."

Arden blinked away the tears, and braved a glance at Luke. He stood a few feet away, watching them with a startled and heartbroken expression. Oh yes, she was going to love this man whether she wanted to or not. "I've brought you a surprise. Do you remember him?"

Clarinda Chillingham turned her head expectantly. Her brow furrowed as her dark gaze fell on Luke. "Huntley?"

To her surprise, Luke bowed. "Lady Chillingham. You look as lovely as I remember."

Clarinda giggled and switched her attention back to Arden. "Your husband's very handsome, Miranda."

Arden didn't bother to correct her. Miranda was her aunt, her mother's younger sister. "He is, yes. I brought you something else. Do you remember that silly hat you wore last time I visited?"

Her mother smiled. "I love hats. Is it the one you're wearing? I would look good in that one."

Arden chuckled. "You would. Perhaps you can try it on later. I meant this hat." From the satchel she withdrew the helmet she'd been working on—the one designed to store memories much the way the A.R.O.T.S. stored visual moments, only on a lesser scale. The helmet recorded the process of the memory, though not the images of it—data rather than pictures.

Her mother made a moue of dislike. "Why would I want to wear that ugly thing?"

"Please? I brought you sugar biscuits."

Eager hands reached out. "Put it on me."

Arden grinned, and placed the helmet gently on her mother's head before handing her one of the biscuits she'd brought wrapped up inside the satchel. As her mother ate, she asked about various things that had happened in her mother's life. As usual, more recent events were lost to her, but she could recall seemingly mundane things that had happened in her childhood. Arden asked about things that had happened later. Her theory was that her mother's memories were disappearing in reverse chronological order. If she could store the newer memories in the helmet, she might be able to then give them back to her mother at a later date—when the older woman had forgotten them. It wasn't a cure—there would never be a cure—but it might allow her mother to hold on to her life a little longer, and allow Arden to hold on to her.

Soon, her mother would reach the point when Arden no longer existed in her mind, and Arden didn't know what she'd do when that day came.

They visited for a little while. Luke had come forward and sat down with them to listen to Clarinda's stories. He even had a biscuit at her urging.

"My soul, you're handsome," the older woman said, gaze bright as she looked at him. "Did you get into a row?"

Luke touched the healing stitches on his forehead. "Arden hit me," he told her with a grin.

When her mother turned to her—looking like an aging Roman goddess in her bizarre helmet—her gaze was blank for a split second and then exploded into brilliant recognition. "Arden! When did you get here? I'm so happy to see you, dearest girl."

Arden smiled. "I've been here a little while, Mama. I

didn't want to interrupt your visit. I know how much you like to flirt with handsome men."

Clarinda laughed. "I do." She jerked her head toward Luke. "Is he well hung?"

Luke's eyes bulged, and for a moment she thought he might choke, but when he saw her smile, he grinned back. She'd long ago given up being embarrassed by the things her mother said. It was no reflection upon either one of them, merely a common side effect of the dementia. "Now, Mama, you know a lady doesn't speak of such things." Then, in an exaggerated whisper, "I'll tell you later."

Her mother laughed, and things continued on this way for almost another quarter hour, when Clarinda's mood began to wane and she grew increasingly agitated and sharp. It was their cue to leave.

Arden gathered up the helmet that she had removed from her mother's head earlier, and packed it away along with the now-empty square of linen that had held half a dozen biscuits when they arrived. Clarinda wouldn't let Luke go without him giving her a kiss first. He barely managed to kiss her cheek—she turned her head fast and tried to catch him on the mouth.

"Good-bye, Miranda. Give my love to John and the children. And if you see Frederick, tell him I need my blue slippers."

It was the mention of her father that made Arden's eyes burn, not just that her mother was confused again. "I will. Good-bye, Mama." She kissed her mother on top of the head, drew her spine up straight and walked away as an attendant arrived to take her mother back to her room for a nap. Luke fell into step beside her.

"So you do have some idea of what it's like not to remember."

"No. I know what it's like to be someone who isn't remembered, although I suppose I can sympathize more than the average person with your plight. But now you also know why I remained in the station of countess. As much as I believed you would return, I needed to be able to afford the quarterly payments to make sure my mother stayed in Featherstone, where they take such good care of her. Lord knows I wouldn't be able to do it."

He didn't seem the least bit bothered by the fact that her motives had been less than completely pure, that she hadn't "just" been waiting for him. "You were very good with her."

She laughed softly. "A half hour visit isn't the same as day after day of it. I was losing patience before I had to put her in Featherstone, and she was much better then. Does it bother you to know I had other reasons for waiting?" She couldn't help but ask.

Luke shook his head, a reluctant smile shaping his lips. "I feel better, truth be told. It's good to know you're not some kind of saint. It makes me feel less an arse for the things I've done." Then, to her surprise, he reached down and took her hand in his. "That helmet of yours won't help me, will it?"

"No. The best it could do is store the memories you already have. I'm sorry. I'm trying to find something that will help you."

He shrugged. "Maybe it's best if I don't remember it all, though I do wish I could remember more of you. Our first kiss. Our wedding night."

Cheeks flushed, Arden squeezed his hand. "We'll just have to make some new memories."

His gaze locked with hers, bright and clear, as pale blue as spring sky. "We will." His smile grew. "We'll start with the bath."

They laughed together. She felt happy—hopeful. It was the first time she'd experienced either of those emotions whilst leaving this place. Normally when she departed she had to sit in her vehicle for several minutes fighting back tears—or giving in to them. Today, she left smiling, and when they reached the touring carriage, Luke went to the left side and left her to drive.

"I want to look around," he said, but she took it as more than that. She didn't know what, but his "giving of the reins," so to speak, meant something.

It was late afternoon by the time they arrived back in London, and both of them were hungry. They hobbled through the door and were met by the housekeeper.

"Ah, tea please, Mrs. Bird," Arden instructed. "We're famished."

The woman wrung her hands in front of her. "Lord Wolfred is waiting for you in the library, my lady. For you and his lordship. He seems out of sorts, if you don't mind me saying."

Arden rolled her eyes as she stripped off her gloves. "That's his way as of late. Include him in the tea, please." As if to punctuate the need for food, her stomach growled.

Alastair was indeed in the library. He stood near the shelves, a leather-bound book in his hands and a scowl on his face.

"Where the devil have you two been?" he demanded as he looked up.

Arden started, drawing back from the anger in his voice. "None of your business," she retorted hotly. He didn't know the extent of her mother's illness, and she meant to keep it that way. "What's the matter with you?"

He sighed and shoved the book back into its place on the shelf. At the same time, he ran a hand through his thick reddish hair. "Rani Ogitani was fished from the

Thames this morning. She'd been murdered." He couldn't quite look at either of them as he said it.

Indignation swept through Arden's veins. "And you were sent here to see whether or not Luke is responsible." She swore, drawing startled glances from both of the men. "There is no way Luke could have done it. For Heaven's sake, Alastair, he can barely move."

"I know. It's not Luke I'm here to see, Arden." His stormy eyes were apologetic but unflinching. "Where were you last night?"

Chapter 17

"Have you gone completely barking mad?" Luke demanded, caught between incredulity and anger. "Arden wouldn't kill anybody."

Alastair did not look convinced. In fact, he looked very much the opposite. "She killed Victor Erlich, and did a good job of it too. Toasted his brain with that discombobulator thing. That's why you were sent to kill her, remember?"

A low scowl cramped Luke's brow. "There's something of a difference between defending oneself and murder."

His old friend turned his back on him to address Arden. "I have to ask, where were you last night?"

"Here," she told him crisply, but she didn't seem the least bit put out that he thought her capable of murdering a woman in cold blood. "We came home from Dr. Stone's and went to bed." Luke watched a soft flush filled her cheeks, and he knew she was thinking about the fact that they hadn't gone immediately to sleep. There was nothing like realizing you were mortal to arouse the libido.

Alastair directed a carefully neutral gaze toward Luke. The bastard was excellent at hiding his emotions when he wanted, Luke would give him that. "Did you take any pain medicine before bed?"

"No. There's no way she could have snuck out without waking me."

"You're certain?" There seemed to be a large amount of challenge in that question. Did he suspect Arden of drugging him? Using some device to keep him asleep while she snuck out of the house to kill a woman she would have to go to a brothel—or worse—to find? Arden was brave, perhaps recklessly so at times—he remembered her facing him alone in the garden when she "discombobulated" him—but she was not stupid.

"When was the last time someone moved without waking you?" Luke asked haughtily. When Alastair didn't immediately concede, he continued. "How was Ogitani killed?"

"Shot to the head."

He chuckled—it was more relief than humor. Perhaps he hadn't been as sure of his wife as he thought. "Well, that proves Arden didn't do it."

"How do you reason that?" Alastair folded his arms across his chest. For a man who was in love with Arden, he certainly seemed hell-bent on finding her guilty. Did he want her to be a killer? Would that make it easier for him to walk away from her? It wouldn't for Luke.

Luke smiled. "Good lord man, have you ever known this woman to use something as straightforward as a gun? She'd use some sort of fantastic gadget." He looked at his wife. "Do you even know how to shoot?"

"Not well," she replied with a slight smile. "You know, for a man without much of a memory, you possess an uncanny ability to predict my behavior and know my mind."

Luke almost grinned back, but then he remembered that Alastair had practically accused her of murder—and was standing there rolling his eyes at them.

"Do you have any evidence implicating Arden?" Luke asked. That was the important question, and one he should have asked before this.

The other man shook his head. "Nothing concrete, of course, but enough that I came here directly. Ogitani had a device implanted in her mind that was similar to the one in yours, only Dr. Stone believes it was used to control the woman rather than affect her memory. She was shot in the exact spot—by someone who knew where to shoot. Also, we confirmed that she was hiding out in an opium brothel in Covent Garden."

"I would never go to an opium brothel," Arden insisted, lips curling with just a hint of disgust. "Do you think me to be a total imbecile, Alastair? I may have rushed headlong into danger on occasion, but really. An opium brothel? You must think I have bollocks the size of Buckingham Palace—or a brain the size of your big toe."

Luke tried not to smile. There was nothing the least bit amusing about this conversation or the circumstances surrounding it. Someone had killed Rani Ogitani—most likely because she had failed in her mission to kill either Arden or him. Or both of them. But his wife had a way of plain speaking that was delightfully blunt, concise and drier than a whore in the middle of a sandstorm.

"The Company would know all of that as well," Luke said, pushing his amusement aside. "In fact, they would know exactly where she was hiding. It seems to me that they shot her where they did to destroy the device as well, and dumped her body so you'd find her immediately. Perhaps they killed her because she failed her mission, or perhaps they did it just to prove a point."

"But you must have already theorized that," Arden commented, frowning. "I would think you would immediately come up with that conclusion, so why are you here? What did you find that made you come to me?"

Alastair reluctantly reached into his coat and pulled out a small wrapped bundle. Luke frowned. So, Wolfred had evidence after all. Why had he not brought it up before this? Whatever it was, Luke knew it meant nothing, because he knew that Arden had slept either in his arms or curled against him all bloody night.

Wolfred peeled back the wrappings to reveal a small brass compact with a poppy engraved in the top. Luke didn't know what the hell it was, but he'd seen Arden with something similar. She loved poppies. He had left one for her in her carriage when he'd been stalking her, though at that time he had no idea why the flower seemed the obvious choice with which to taunt her.

She'd had them in her wedding bouquet. He put one in her hair before making love to her the first time. The memory was like a kick to the chest, it came back so vibrant and real. Along with it came the emotions he'd felt at the time. He might have been an arse at times, but he had adored her.

Quickly, he pulled himself together, shaking off the overwhelming sensations. Arden was looking at the delicate piece in Alastair's hand, her face white. "It's a sentimentometer. May I?"

Alastair nodded and she took it from his palm, opening the top. "It is yours, is it not?"

"What is it?" Luke asked. He couldn't recall—not that it meant anything—ever hearing of such an invention before.

His wife tossed a quick glance at him—she was engrossed in studying the device. "It's an apparatus for determining a person's emotional state. Very useful in an investigation. Alastair, you have to make certain I have access to the body."

"Arden, you know the Director's going to balk at that." He shoved a hand through his hair. "Just tell me if this is yours, and how it came to be with the body. Please. I'll go to Dhanya with you and plead your case. You know she'll show lenience given the circumstances."

"Lenience?" Luke drew back. "There's nothing to be lenient for. Arden didn't do it."

But neither of them paid him any attention, and Arden didn't do as Alastair asked. She scowled at him instead. "You do not agree that Dhanya will have a great interest in Miss Ogitani's last moments?"

Luke's jaw dropped. She could do that? Bloody hell. What had they ever talked about when he courted her, when they married? Perhaps he'd been comfortable being brawn to her brains. Regardless, he was going to have to start reading a lot more if he wanted to keep up with her. And he was going to spend much more time in that workshop of hers.

Wolfred didn't appear nearly as impressed as Luke was, but then he was accustomed to Arden and all her "toys." "You can ask her yourself, but she'll probably want one of the agents who isn't involved to use the spectacles—or do it herself."

Arden made a face. "No one else knows how to use them—nor have they tried. Besides, one wrong adjustment could delete the images altogether. No, Dhanya will want me to do it, and me alone. And we're going to keep it just between the four of us."

Alastair sighed. "You know that appears suspicious, yes?"

Her frustration was palpable—like a child trying to communicate with adults who just smiled and patted it on the head. "Alastair, *this*"—she held up the sentimentometer—"is one of the first I built, and it's been in a W.O.R. vault for four years. A Warden gave this to Ogitani. A Warden with vault clearance."

Realization and horror dawned on Alastair's face. "Damnation."

Even Luke was smart enough to understand what that meant. The traitor. Whoever had given the device to Ogitani was a high-ranking officer in the W.O.R. He wondered if it was the same person who had given him over to the Company seven years ago.

If so, he dearly wanted to meet the son of a bitch.

Rani Ogitani would have been just as beautiful in death as she was in life were it not for the ragged hole in the middle of her forehead. The ghostly pallor of her skin only made her more striking, her hair all the darker. Arden stood over the petite body on the table and stared at it with a surprising lack of feeling. She wasn't sorry for Ogitani, nor did she take any satisfaction in her death. This woman had played a part in trying to kill her, and Luke. Shouldn't she despise Ogitani for that? It was as though any emotions she might have felt toward the woman had died with her.

"This is what's left of the bullet I took from her." Evelyn showed the three of them a distorted piece of metal in a small glass jar.

Luke held out his hand. "May I?"

Evelyn handed it over without hesitation. "Notice the markings that are still visible. They match several bullets we've seen in similar killings over the years. Whoever the assassin was, he makes his own ammunition. I've never seen anything quite like it. It has a fine point that penetrates the flesh and then the bullet spreads, doing even more damage. Small but terribly efficient when it comes to killing."

"The Wasp." Luke peered into the bottle with an intensity that Arden found as unsettling as the flatness of his voice. "He's a Company assassin. This is his calling card. His work. He uses a specially designed rifle inspired by African blowguns that fires with incredible velocity and is accurate from a great distance."

He and Ogitani were the only people in the chilly morgue who weren't surprised. "Until today we didn't have a name," Alastair revealed, regarding him with an expression of cautious wonder. "Are you certain?"

Luke handed the bottle back to Evelyn. "Absolutely. I worked with him on occasion."

"So you'd know him if you saw him." Alastair's excitement was obvious. Arden was still trying to come to terms with the fact that her husband had worked with a Company assassin. He *was* a Company assassin. Dear God. How many W.O.R. agents had he killed?

He didn't know better. . . . He is no longer that man. . . . Hell's bells, stop thinking about it!

And then she thought about Victor Erlich, and the expression on the bastard's face as she shoved enough electrical current into his body to kill him. It had had taken more than one go. It hadn't been simple self-defense, or she would have been content to incapacitate him. No, she'd intentionally killed him. At the time she hadn't thought of it as such—she just couldn't seem to stop herself. He had hit her, tried to rape her.

And in return she killed him. On purpose. That made her a killer too. Perhaps Alastair hadn't been so wrong to suspect her of killing Ogitani. Perhaps she and Luke weren't so different after all.

Luke shot the other man a wry glance. "I won't see him. His victims never do. But yes, I would recognize his face." His gaze flicked to Arden, and she saw what he wasn't saying in his eyes.

"The Company sent him to finish the job you didn't. He's here to kill me. Us." Her voice sounded oddly calm in her own ears, despite the icy fear that gripped her heart.

His expression darkened. "Not if I kill him first."

"How do you plan to do that?" Alastair demanded. "You might recognize him, but he'll take extra care to conceal himself from you. Hell, he doesn't even have to get close to kill you both."

"He has a transmission device in his ear, same as I did." He gestured to the corpse. "The same as Ogitani still does. Let Arden look at it. I wager she can come up with something to intercept transmissions—if she hasn't already."

"But they won't be sending her any more messages," Arden interjected, pleased that he thought so much of her intelligence. She had been working with transmissions in making Beauregard's new collar. "They know she's dead. Trying to find them without that originating signal is next to impossible. It would all be guesswork."

Luke's frown eased. "What if they think she's alive? If they think she's not dead, they'll send a signal to drive her out—or at least to listen in to the noise around her."

"They could be listening now," Arden remarked. "In which case, they'll know our plans."

"They're not listening," Luke responded with bitter conviction. "They're too sure of themselves. That's why they didn't have Wasp dig the thing out of her. They don't care if the W.O.R. finds it because they're sure it's inactive. But if they suspect he failed in his mission, they'll not only try to flush Ogitani out, but the Wasp as well."

They were all looking at her now. "Can you do what Lord Huntley suggests?" Evelyn asked.

Arden shrugged. "Yes. It won't be easy, but if the Company does open up the communicative channel I should be able to isolate it. I don't know if I can tell you where it's coming from, but we could eavesdrop on their transmissions."

"I'm married to the most bloody brilliant woman in all of England." Pride shone in Luke's eyes as his lips curved into that lopsided smile that made her knees quiver.

She flushed, but not before she caught the expression on Alastair's face. He was looking at Luke as though he were speaking in tongues. But then, Alastair had always treated her talent for mechanical devices as a given, not as something special. Whereas Luke . . . well, he'd always admired the things she and her father created, but this verbal praise was new.

"Thank you," she said, meeting his gaze. Time stopped for a second, closing in around just the two of them, blotting out everything else.

"Right." Evelyn clapped her hands, breaking the trance. "I'll remove the device as soon as we know what our girl was up to when she died. Arden?"

She started. "Yes. Of course." She hid her embarrassment by turning to the corpse on the table. She took the A.R.O.T.S. from her bag and set each pair into place. As she wound the key she heard Luke ask Alastair what she was doing, but she didn't hear the other man's explanation, as images began to play out in front of her eyes. As the scene unfolded, she reported it to her companions.

"She met him in her room at the brothel. At least I think it's hers—it looks lived in. He's wearing a hat pulled low over his face." She squinted. "I can't see his face. He's wearing a long black greatcoat and carrying a walking stick with a brass ram's head at the top. She's just picked up her coat and they're leaving together." She paused, waiting for them to reach a destination. "They're in an alley behind the building. I think they're arguing, she's gesturing angrily at him, grabbing the front of his coat, and then . . . bloody hell."

"What?" Alastair demanded.

Sighing, Arden removed the spectacles. "That's it. She grabbed the front of his coat and then everything went black. I'm assuming that's when she was shot, but she wasn't killed by the man she was with."

"You didn't see his face at all?"

She shook her head. "I'm afraid not. And of course, I have no idea what he sounds like. But . . ." She looked at the corpse. "Evie, did you look in her left hand?"

"No." The doctor came forward, the starched white of her apron brushing against her boots. Carefully, she uncurled the fingers of the dead woman's hand. Inside was a shiny brass button. Evie held it up, and Arden's stomach dropped at the sight of it. It had a gryphon wearing a crown of roses on it.

"The Warden crest," she whispered.

Both Evelyn and Alastair looked grim at the discovery. Alastair massaged the back of his neck with one hand while the other balled into a fist. "Since no one's come forward saying they were with Ogitani at the time of her death, we have to suppose her companion was also a traitor."

"Or also dead," Arden added. Perhaps she was naive, but how many traitors could there be within the Wardens' ranks? She thought of how many spies she'd met through her father who had infiltrated the Company and decided she didn't want to know.

"Perhaps it's the same bastard I was onto years ago," Luke remarked, a dark edge to his voice. Arden shivered at the sound of it. He'd been so sweet to her that sometimes she forgot how very dangerous he could be. There was a glint in his eye that told her he yearned for revenge. How many years would it take for him to have it?

Another seven? Would he be lost to her once again as duty and vengeance took over?

She wouldn't wait for him if it happened again. She would not be a fool twice. She would remain his wife, but she would live her own life. Perhaps she'd move to Paris or Greece and have affairs with charming men who spoke languages she didn't understand but liked the sound of.

The thought made her chest hurt, so she pushed it aside for the time being. Getting overly emotional never solved anything.

"You'll want to check the Warden tailors," Luke told Alastair. "Make certain they alert you if anyone brings in a coat to have a new button sewn on." When his friend shot him a startled glance, Luke smiled. "I'm sure you would have thought of it eventually."

Arden almost grinned at the sight of them, so like she remembered. They'd always had a good partnership—one remembering what the other had forgotten, thinking of what the other had missed. Working with Alastair, being friends with him, had allowed her to feel close to Luke during his absence. She thought again that it hadn't been fair of her to use him like that.

"To have gotten away with it for this long, to have vault clearance . . ." Alastair's voice dropped off as he turned his stormy gaze on each of them. "It has to be someone high up."

"And male," Arden reminded him. "That was definitely a man I saw talking to her."

"Were they involved, do you think?" Evie inquired. "I didn't find any evidence of copulation, but I did find a sandy-colored hair in her clothing."

"He was wearing a hat," Arden replied. "I couldn't see his hair clearly, but I don't think it was dark."

"So we're looking for men in higher offices of the

W.O.R. with light hair and a missing button, and a cane with a ram's head on it." Alastair shrugged. "We've worked with less."

Arden packed up her spectacles and snapped the case shut. "If that's everything, I believe I'll take my leave. Evie, if you could get that transmitter out of her ear I would appreciate it. I'll take it with me to analyze. Hopefully someone will try to use it." She turned to Luke as the other woman went to work. She had no desire to watch the potentially bloody procedure. "Will you return home with me, or do you wish to remain?"

He seemed surprised that she would even ask, which didn't paint a pretty picture of her, she supposed. She had been ordering him around a fair bit, but only because she wanted to protect him. That hadn't been good form on her part. He was a man, not a child, and treating him as the latter would only drive him away from her all the faster.

"Why don't you stay for a bit?" Alastair suggested. "I'd like to go over that old investigation and see if anything triggers your memory. There might be useful information in the notes you wrote for the Director. Perhaps we'll unlock a clue."

Luke seemed eager at the prospect, and Arden had no desire to interfere with the rebuilding of an old friendship, no matter how much she wanted him to come home, and to bed, with her. She forced a smile, said goodbye to the three of them and strode quickly to the morgue exit, her boot heels clicking sharply on the tile. The stiff ache in her muscles only made her steps all the more clipped.

"Arden." Luke's voice stopped her at the door.

She paused, made certain nothing of how she felt might show in her face, and turned as he limped toward her. "Yes?"

His reply was to cup the back of her head with one hand and pull her to him in a fierce kiss that more than made up for with passion what it lacked in finesse. When he lifted his head, he stared down at her with an amused tilt to his lips. She must look like a dumbstruck idiot, because that was exactly how she felt.

"What was that for?"

"To give you something to think about until I get home." He released the back of her head, to run his palm down her arm. "I won't be long."

Arden forced a smile. That was what he'd always said, and it had almost always been a lie. "I'll see you then."

"Don't forget this." He pressed a square of linen into her hand. Inside it was the device from Ogitani's ear. That was fast. It wasn't as bloody as she expected, though there were smears of crimson on the cloth. She left him to his excitement and intrigue, and had one of the Warden drivers take her home, where she immediately went to her workshop and set about tinkering with the device, studying it, dismantling it and putting it back together. Work always kept her mind from tiresome, angst-ridden thoughts.

Tonight had felt like old times: Luke and Alastair working together on Warden business, filled with excitement about catching their villain of the day. She had spent so long waiting for the man she had loved to come home, and now it seemed that he might still be that man she . . .

She wasn't certain that was the man she wanted after all.

Neither Luke nor Alastair wanted to remain while Dr. Stone examined the body. It seemed wrong and disrespectful to stay—not that Ogitani deserved their respect, the cold-hearted wretch. Still, it wasn't right, and there was strong evidence to suggest the seductive woman had been under the Company's control rather than operating under her own free will. That made her a pawn, and that was a little too close for comfort for Luke.

It also made it slightly less easy to despise her. What if she had been trying to stop them both when she said his name on the steps that night? But no, he had to be honest. She had tried to save him, but not Arden. She might have retained some sort of sentimentality where he was concerned, but she had been prepared to allow Arden to die, and for that he could never forgive her, no matter how much of a puppet she'd been.

Instead, they took the button with them—Alastair pocketed it, of course—and set out to visit the two tailors who worked exclusively for W.O.R. If the man Ogitani met was smart he'd take his jacket elsewhere to be repaired, if at all. But that would only succeed if he had extra buttons at home. The only places that had those particular buttons were the secretly sanctioned tailors who took care of everything from buttons to braces, drawers to disguises. A Warden's clothes might look fine and ordinary, but there were a myriad of hidden pockets and places to conceal weapons and gadgets—tools of the trade. A "regular" tailor could not be trusted, so there were two men in all of London whom the Wardens relied upon, and they belonged to families who had shared this duty for decades.

The first was a Mr. Gabriel, whose shop was located near Bond Street. As they approached the door, Luke thought it looked vaguely familiar, as though he'd been here before.

"Not quite Poole's and Company," Alastair remarked as they approached, "but no one makes a concealed pocket quite like Gabriel."

Poole was Lucas's tailor. He had a shop on Saville

Row. He knew this because Arden had the man come to the house. "Is this the man who made you that dark blue jacket with the dagger sheaths in the sleeves?"

"The same." The red-haired man glanced at him in surprise. "You're remembering."

"Pieces. Mostly useless stuff." Luke shrugged. It was insignificant. He couldn't even work up much pleasure over the fact. "I wish I could remember more of my marriage."

Alastair paused, his hand reaching for the doorknob. "Perhaps not remembering is a sign to concentrate on now and what's to come rather than the past."

Luke raised a brow. "Meaning I shouldn't want to remember what a prick I was."

"Exactly," came the chuckled reply as the door swung open.

The shop was small but well organized. The worn floorboards were buffed to a high shine and there wasn't a speck of dust on shelves that had seen obvious years of use. The air smelled of chalk and lemon, and vaguely of pipe tobacco.

"Lord Wolfred," greeted the gray-haired man behind the counter. "Good day."

Alastair doffed his hat. "A good day to you as well, Mr. Gabriel. Do you remember my friend Lord Huntley?"

"Of course. A pleasure to see you home once again, my lord. Are you gentlemen here for a fitting?"

"Information," Alastair said with an engaging smile. It was all Luke could do not to show his amusement. The man looked positively friendly. But then, he imagined neither of them would ever be considered jovial by any stretch of the imagination.

They approached the counter. Luke glanced around them, carefully searching the shop for spies or suspicious devices. Unfortunately, it was too easy these days to conceal such apparatus, such as the lens of a small camera in a lapel, the body of the device then being sewn into the lining of the coat.

His hip and arms ached. The cut on his forearm stung and itched. He should have gone home with Arden. He missed her—not that he would admit it aloud. That was why he'd stayed behind. He was coming to depend too much on her. And she was very accustomed to getting what she wanted. It was true that she was bloody brilliant, but he had his own intelligence, and it was time he started using it, else they'd both end up like Rani Ogitani.

Plus, he craved a degree of independence. He couldn't cling to her skirts forever, and it was his own fault that he'd started. He didn't know this world—not as he ought. Not as well as it knew him. That put him at a disadvantage, and he hated that. It was time to start trusting his own judgment.

Wolfred set the button on the counter. "We found this, and came to you in hopes that the owner might have come in to have it replaced."

Mr. Gabriel's dark gaze moved between the two of them. Luke didn't bother trying to be charming. He'd leave that to Alastair. He kept his own expression impassive, his gaze direct.

"You gentlemen know I cannot give out Warden-related information, not even to Wardens, without permission from the Director."

Alastair sighed. "How long have we known each other, Gabriel? This is important. Very important."

"I don't doubt that it is, my lord. But you've known me long enough to know I don't do anything without going through the proper channels. You come back with her permission, or have her contact me, elsewise I'm not going to tell you anything. My apologies."

Luke frowned. "Not even if it means a traitor walks free?"

Gabriel didn't even blink. "In that case, especially not. In those situations, my lord, it is best to do everything by the letter."

"Fine." Alastair took the button from the counter with manicured fingers. "We'll be back with the Director's permission."

When they left the shop, they stood on the street for a moment, in the sunshine.

"Why didn't we get permission in the first place?" Luke inquired, squinting at the gentlemen out shopping.

Alastair tossed him a quick glance as he lit a thin cigar. "I was hoping we'd have something before we involved her. She's going to have her own idea of how this should be handled. Want one?"

Luke shook his head at the offered smoke. "And her way of doing things doesn't always agree with yours, I wager."

The other man grinned around the cigar as he tucked the silver case inside his breast pocket. "Not usually, no."

"Are you going to meet with her?"

"Of course, and you're coming with me. We have to talk to her about getting you reinstated."

They began walking toward the carriage, Luke's hands curled into loose fists at his sides. "I'm not sure I want to be a Warden again."

Alastair came to a dead stop, wisps of smoke curling around his head. He yanked the cigar from his mouth. "What? You can't not be a Warden. You wanted to be a Warden since you were a lad of ten. You told me so."

"Did I?" Luke didn't remember. "Being a Warden led to me losing seven years of my life. I'm not about to repledge my allegiance to an organization which didn't bother looking for me—with the exception of you."

"Fair enough." Alastair crushed the cigar beneath his boot. "You're going to concentrate on your marriage then."

"Wouldn't you?" Luke didn't expect a response—it wasn't necessary. He already knew what Alastair would do.

And that was why Luke didn't trust him—not completely—because Alastair would take Arden over the W.O.R., too.

Chapter 18

"What if Wolfred's the traitor?"

Arden placed her soldering iron in its holder and lifted her goggles so that they sat on top of her head. She felt guilty for not giving more time to Scotland Yard and had been working on a device that was something of a gamble, but might help find the man nicknamed the "Debutante Killer." It was based in chemistry—something she had needed Evie's help with—and was attuned to the scent of Wexell's Best pomade. It was also a metal detector. If she could find a man wearing that pomade, and God help her, a horseshoe cravat pin that would be wonderful, but that wasn't enough. She needed to find a man with those two traits who had also known both victims and had metal-enhanced hands. She was overly warm and grimy, and not in the sort of mood required to play a spy's equivalent of a parlor game. "I don't think I heard you correctly. It sounded as though you just accused your oldest—and only—friend of being a double agent." She glanced up from the device—which she disguised as a fan.

He had the nerve to smile — the bugger — as he leaned indolently against the door frame of her workshop. He was wearing a pair of black trousers held up by matching braces and a white shirt open at the neck. His hair was damp and fell over his forehead, hiding most of the scars there. The little marks on his face had already begun to heal. Unfortunately the both of them were still a little stiff and sore from their adventure.

"He accused you of murder," he reminded her. "You have to admit it's a theory worth considering. He was the one who supposedly went looking for me but never found me. He was the first to arrive after the incident with the carriage. He knew where to find Ogitani, and yesterday he conveniently didn't bother getting the proper permission to speak to anyone about the button you found."

It *was* a theory worth considering. Were it not for the fact that she had known Alastair so long she might even do more than consider it, but the idea that he might have played a part in Luke's disappearance . . . "No. It's not him."

Luke's expression hardened. "If he came in here right now and told you that somehow I was behind it all, you'd believe that, wouldn't you?"

She scowled at him. "Don't be a jealous idiot. I would not believe it, and if you are so very concerned about my affections straying, why don't you give me a good reason to keep them with you." She hadn't meant to say it aloud, but his jealousy of Alastair was tiring, and she was still smarting over the fact that he hadn't come home with her the day before.

Slowly, he straightened and came toward her. She felt a little like a gazelle eyeing an approaching lion, and didn't know whether to run or simply accept her fate and offer up her throat.

His gaze held hers until he stood mere inches away.

His hand reached out and curled around the back of her neck, pulling her closer. "You're mine," he told her. "I'd kill any man who tried to take you away."

His words both terrified and thrilled her. "What of you?" Her haughty tone was ruined by a slight tremor, but she doggedly held his gaze. "Are you mine?"

"If you'll have me, I am yours alone."

Arden shivered. Her hands came up to press against his chest. The heat of him permeated the fine cotton of his shirt. "I'll have you," she whispered.

His eyes darkened, and his mouth came down on hers with a ferocity that stole her breath. His tongue slid between her eager lips to taste hers, and she devoured him in kind, pouring all the things she couldn't quite say into the kiss.

She was falling in love with him. It wasn't simply that she had never stopped loving him, despite all the heartache. She was coming to love the man he was. It didn't matter that his memory was dodgy. He was good to her mother, and laughed at her jokes. He liked that she was smart and didn't seem the least bit threatened by it. And he made her feel like she was the most desirable woman in all the world.

He turned her so that her back was against the workbench.

"The soldering iron!" she yelped, just as he was about to lift her up.

Luke peered around her at the bench. Their torsos pressed together as he reached over, disconnected the power to the heated device, and moved it out of the way.

"What is this?" he asked, picking up a prototype she'd finished the day before. It was an engine that strapped to the arm and had wires running down to rubberized pads that fit over the tips of the index, middle and ring fingers of the wearer.

Arden flushed a little. They had done such intimate

things together, but talking about her inventions embarrassed her, even with him. "You put the tips on your fingers, and when the engine is engaged, the tips vibrate."

"What's it for?" He was all seductive mock ignorance.

"Massage," she replied—lamely. "It helps cure headaches, stimulates the muscles."

"What else does it stimulate?" He strapped the control box to his forearm and slid his fingers into the tips.

Arden swallowed, the interior of her mouth suddenly bone-dry. "Any part of the anatomy you wish to apply it to."

"Interesting." With his other arm he circled her waist and easily lifted her to the surface of the bench. His gaze held hers as his right hand slipped beneath the rust-colored skirts of her gown. One nudge was all it took to make her thighs fall open.

She should be embarrassed. A lady would be. The kind of woman his mother had wanted him to marry never would have dreamed of inventing such a scandalous device, let alone using one.

The engine hummed to life. Goosebumps slid down Arden's arms. Her nipples tightened. She jumped when he touched her. It was the lightest stroke—a teasing vibration along the cleft of her sex.

"Is it stimulating?" he asked, voice little more than a rumble.

"Yes," she whispered, hoarse. To hell with being a lady. If he'd wanted a lady he would have bloody well married one. She spread her thighs wider to give him better access.

Luke took the hint. Smiling that crooked smile he brought his second finger to her dampness as well, gently rubbing the opening of her body as his first finger eased between the lips to tease the bud of flesh that tightened eagerly. She moaned.

"I love watching your face when you're aroused," he told her, a delicious roughness to his low voice. "Your eyes are like warm whiskey." He wiggled his finger and she gasped in delight.

His other hand braced against the small of her back, holding her in place as she squirmed beneath his ministrations. He didn't kiss her, didn't touch any other part of her body. He just kept his attention locked on her face as his skilled fingers and the magic of the machine built a delicious tension between her legs. It was so incredibly intimate, even though they were fully clothed. She stared into his eyes as her breathing quickened. Her fingers dug into the edge of the bench, allowing her to arch her hips upward to grant him better access.

She matched the rhythm of his touch, pushing against his fingers. The ache grew and spread. She could feel it coiling inside her, urging her to move faster, open wider.

"Come for me," he commanded roughly. "I want to feel you hot and wet on my hand."

That was all she needed to push her over the edge. Her head fell back and she came in a great rippling spasm that tore a long, loud cry from her throat. Luke gave her one more stroke that made her shudder before removing his hand from beneath her skirts.

The low hum of the engine died, and he began unbuckling the straps that held the device to his arm. "That worked well."

She chuckled, sated and limp. "You were right. I am brilliant."

Luke laughed as well. "Was that good enough for me to keep your affections from straying?"

"Almost," she replied, reaching for the buttons of his trousers. He was hard beneath her fingers. "I think I still need a little convincing."

A moment later he slid completely inside her. She felt

her body stretch and wrap around him, instinct demanding that she take him fully.

"Tell me you're mine," he whispered against her lips as he withdrew and slowly filled her again.

"I'm yours," she replied, wrapping her arms around his neck. "Always and forever, I'm yours."

His mouth silenced hers, and his arms wrapped around her, holding her tight as he quickened his thrusts. They came together in a mix of heat and swallowed moans, and as they collapsed against each other, Arden was fully, and happily, convinced.

"Thank you for coming with me." Arden stirred sugar into her cup of coffee. Too bad she hadn't brought any whiskey with her—she could Irish it up a bit.

Odd, that was the first thought of drink she'd had in a while.

"I could hardly allow you to come alone," Luke replied, taking a sip from his cup.

Arden's spine stiffened. They were at the coffeehouse to spy on two suspects in the debutante case; Fredrick Fitzhugh and Maurice Willet. She'd already ruled Willet out, as he was almost as pale as an albino, and the killer was not fair. "If you could not have come, would you have forbidden me to do my job?"

Her husband paused before slowly lowering his cup to its saucer. "I would have asked you to postpone until I could accompany you."

"Why?" Her spoon hit the delicate china sharply. "Because now that you've returned I cannot possibly be equipped to perform the tasks I've successfully done without your assistance these last few years?"

His brows rose ever so slightly, but his expression was carefully blank. "No, because I would worry about you investigating on your own."

"I used to worry about you as well, but you always considered having me along on an assignment more of a hindrance than help. I'm every bit as good at my job as you were." Where was all this anger coming from? It bubbled deep inside her, frothing toward the surface, threatening to spill all over the table.

"I would never suggest otherwise."

"No one's ever captured me and turned me against my country." As the peevish words spilled out of her mouth, she couldn't look at him. She watched Fitzhugh instead. His build fit what she had seen through the dead girls' eyes, and he bore faint scars on his left hand from where it had been crushed in a riding accident. The killer had both hands augmented, didn't he? She'd only seen him use one, and then slide the other into the girl's chest. Had it been his left or right . . . ?

"You're angry at me for being nabbed?"

Her gaze went to her husband, unflinching. Anger made it easy to look him in the eye. "If you hadn't run off after some secret assignment—traitor or not—we could have had these last seven years together."

"I didn't get caught on purpose, Arden."

"You knew the risks."

"As did you. You still do. Did you ask me not to go?"

Her jaw tightened. She was beginning to get a headache. "No. It wouldn't have done any good. You would have patronized me and told me not to worry, that you had a duty to the Crown. And now you'll forbid me from doing the same. You want me to give up my work, don't you?"

Luke watched her as though he thought her a mad woman. "I have no intention—"

"Don't lie to me, Luke," she sneered. "I know you."

His face hardened like stone. Arden found herself staring into the eyes of Five. "You don't know *me* at all, and you've shown no interest in rectifying that."

Arden opened her mouth to defend herself, but nothing came out. He was right. She didn't know him—she only knew the things that weren't as they used to be.

But Luke wasn't done. "You are angry at me for things I have little memory of, that I cannot change. We can't have a future if you can't let go of the past."

"I do not dwell on the past." Lord, she was sputtering like an overly full teapot.

He gave her an exasperated—and slightly amused— look. "You waited seven years for a man who no longer exists. You put your life on hold. I know you think you've done so much, but you haven't. You spend all your time trying to prove yourself to me, to your father, to the W.O.R. You make machines so your mother can hold on to her past, you were jealous of a woman who might have mattered to me almost a decade ago. All your friends are from your past—or mine. Everything you do is linked to something in the past, with the possible exception of your female gadgets. Even your involvement with the Wardens is because you couldn't let go of me."

Arden ground her teeth. Her molars might crack, but she would not give into a fit of girlish tears. "Perhaps I should have let go."

"You should have, but I'm glad you didn't." He reached across the table and offered his hand. "Let the man you married go. The one with you now will never leave you or make you feel second in any way."

She stared at his open hand. He had a tiny scar on the pad of his index finger. He could crush every bone she had with those five digits. Taking it would mean giving him her trust, her heart—perhaps even her soul.

But he offered his in return. He was a lot braver than she was, she realized. Then again, he had little past to cling to. Today and tomorrow were all he had. They could make new memories, a new past, together. It might not work, but what had she spent all those years waiting and hoping for if not this?

Arden placed her hand in his, heart in her throat as their fingers entwined. Their gazes locked over the table. Luke smiled at her—confident, gentle, possessive. He wanted her—not the girl she'd been, but the sharp and prickly woman she'd become. She loved him for it.

She squeezed his fingers tight. And then, she let go.

When Hannah called later that day, Arden was frowning over the newspaper. Someone had told the press that there was a murderer targeting aristocratic young ladies, and the front page was ablaze with the kind of journalism that was certain to cause a panic amongst the upper classes.

She'd known it wouldn't be long. They had been fortunate that it stayed as quiet as it had, but she had foolishly clung to the hope that they would find him before the vultures got their claws into the story. Even when confronted with fearmongering in black and white, she still hoped they might find him before he fled the city along with his potential victims.

There was a party the next night that she and Luke had been invited to. She would make certain she studied all the men in attendance, especially Frederick Fitzhugh. They had to go. Luke wanted to avoid crowds because that would make it easier for their would-be assassin, but he understood the sense of duty and obligation she had where this monster was concerned.

Their rather heated discussion in the coffeehouse the day before had been such an awakening for her.

"Can I say how delightful it is to see you wearing color?"

Arden looked up, and brightened at the sight of her

friend. It seemed an age since they last spoke. "Hannah! What a lovely surprise. Come in. Would you like coffee?"

"I would indeed." The brunette pulled the pin from her wide-brimmed hat and swept it from her head. "How are you, dearest? I tried to call the morning after your horrible accident, but Mrs. Bird was quite adamant that you were not at home. There's no lasting damage, is there? You're not in pain?"

"A little bruised, but that and the stiffness are passing. Come, don't just stand there, sit with me."

Hannah started toward the table. "Where is your husband? If I were you I wouldn't let him out of my sight."

"He's not far," Arden replied with a smile as she poured a cup of coffee for her friend from the silver pot on the warmer. "He's with Wolfred. They're sparring or some other manly pastime."

"Ahh, men and their violence." Hannah plunked down on the chair to her left. "They don't seem to outgrow it, do they?"

"No." And if it made Luke and Alastair friends again, she hoped they never did. Of course, she didn't add that Luke was hoping to take his violence out on this "Wasp" character when he found him.

Perhaps she should be intimidated by the fact that her husband could literally tear a man limb from limb, but she found the knowledge oddly comforting. Now, if he would just forget this foolish distrust of Alastair, she'd be even happier.

"So," Hannah began, cradling her cup in both hands. "How are you enjoying having him home again? Is it all you hoped for?"

"Better, in some ways. In others . . . well, we're still getting to know each other again." Her friend fixed her with an odd stare. "What?"

"This does not sound like marital bliss."

"Hannah, he doesn't even remember most of our marriage, and neither of us are the same people we were seven years ago."

Hannah leaned back in her chair. "I expected to find you over the moon with happiness. At least tell me that he's fulfilling his husbandly duties."

Arden almost choked on her coffee. She had to cough several times before she was at rights again. "I cannot believe you said that."

"This coming from a woman who makes the most scandalous and wondrous toys." Hannah's eyes sparkled. "Surely you're not going miss-ish on me."

"Miss-ish" was not a word Arden ever thought could apply to her. "Of course not. The bedroom is the one place I know exactly where I stand with Huntley."

"I could make a witty remark about 'standing,' but I do not believe you're in the mood for jokes." Hannah set down her cup and covered Arden's hand with her own. "You know it will all work out. You've been given a second chance—your love returned from the dead. Surely if anyone deserves a happy ending it is the two of you."

"I'm as fond of fairy tales as the next person who was ever a little girl, but this is life, Hannah, not a story. I wish it were. But enough of that nonsense. You are positively glowing this morning. You must tell me what has been going on with you."

Hannah actually blushed, a most becoming shade of pink. "I have a beau."

"How could you have not told me that immediately? Here I am droning on while you've been sitting on such a wonderful secret! You must tell me everything." Her enthusiasm was not false. For years she'd wished that Hannah would find someone to make her feel wanted and desirable.

Her friend giggled like a schoolgirl. "It's Lord Thomas Clivington, Viscount Elwood's heir."

Arden raised her brows. "A future Viscount no less. I'm not certain I know Lord Thomas. Is he quite tall with brown hair?"

"Yes. And the most beautiful blue eyes." Some of Hannah's happiness dimmed. "You would probably know him better if I reminded you that he was in that terrible carriage accident four years ago that claimed the life of his fiancée."

"Oh, now I remember. Tragic. Lucky for him that you came along."

"He hasn't been much in society. It took many months for him to recover from his injuries—it required many surgeries, the poor thing. But now he's perfect. Absolutely perfect."

"Thank God for modern medical science. I'm in awe of the things they can do these days." Arden grinned. "I am so happy for you, my friend."

"Oh, thank you." Hannah's smile brightened the room. "He's going to be at the Dawtons' party onboard the *Albion* tomorrow night. Are you planning to attend?"

"Yes. Luke and I both."

"Wonderful!" She clapped her hands. "Then I will be able to introduce you. Oh, Arden, I just know you're going to approve of him."

"I've no doubt."

Her friend's hands were at just the right level that Arden's gaze fell on the delicate ivory scarf tied around Hannah's neck. She felt the blood drain from her face—it seemed to pool in her stomach and curdle there. "That's an interesting piece of jewelry."

Hannah's fingers went to her throat. "Do you like it? Thomas gave it to me. He said it was so I would think of him. I know it was forward of me to accept it, but I couldn't help myself. Arden, I think he might be the *one*."

He certainly was, Arden allowed, valiantly trying to keep the contents of her stomach where they ought to be. She prayed that Thomas Clivington was *not* the one—at least not the one she sought.

The cravat pin Clivington had given Hannah was horribly familiar. It was onyx stones set in gold, and it was shaped like a horseshoe.

She had to be wrong. She could see several such pins at any social event. Her dearest friend's beau was *not* the Debutante Killer.

"You're *certain* this Clivington is the killer?" It wasn't that Luke doubted her, but this was a serious accusation.

"No." Arden pressed her hand to her mouth and then yanked it away. "Luke, it was just the pin. I saw a similar pin through the eyes of those poor murdered girls. I will never forget it. And now I can't help worrying that the killer is courting my dearest friend!"

They were in his bedchamber. She'd come to him the minute he returned from sparring with Wolfred—whom he truly hoped was not their traitor, because he was starting to like the man. Again.

He stripped off his sweat-soiled shirt, wincing as the muscles in his side pulled. He was healing, but not fast enough for his liking. Wolfred had managed to get in a few blows that never should have landed because of it.

"Have you contacted your inspector?"

"No. I wanted to talk to you first."

Like a partner. A husband. He doubted she even realized the significance of what she'd just said.

"Your fear could be irrational, or it might be your instincts telling you something." He tossed the shirt into the laundry-lift in the wall. With the toss of a switch the steam-powered engine lowered the basket of dirty clothing to the laundry room, and also allowed the maids to send laundered items up, eliminating the need to carry heavy baskets up and down stairs. "Did he know the girls?"

"I don't know."

"Does he have augmented hands or use that awful hair glue?"

She rubbed the back of her neck. "I don't know that either, although I have Mrs. Bird inquiring after the former."

"Birdy?" He frowned. "How would she know?"

Arden looked at him as though he was daft. "She's a servant. Don't you know how servants love to gossip about their employers? She was going to discreetly ask Clivington's housekeeper if she saw her at the market this afternoon."

Servants and spies. Who would have thought they could be so similar?

"Have Inspector Grant keep an eye on him if Birdy comes back with confirmation. He's already watching the Fitzhugh fellow, correct?"

His wife nodded. "Yes." The anxiety and fear in her countenance wrapped around his chest like a vise. He would do anything to make her feel safe—to take the fear away. The depth of his attachment to her made no sense when there was so much of their past he couldn't remember, but in his heart he knew he would die for her, whether he understood it or not.

"It's probably not him. Your friend is hardly a debutante, is she?"

That eased the strain in her features. "No, she's not."

"There, no reason for concern."

She began pacing. "What if we can't prove who the killer is? What if he kills someone else? What if we find him but he gets away? It's almost impossible to convict a peer."

"If you find him and he gets away, I'll make certain he doesn't hurt any more girls." He didn't say how, of course, but there could be little doubt.

Arden went completely still—a deer that's heard the cocking of a rifle. Any moment she'd bolt.

Slowly, her face turned toward his. Her wide gaze searched his face—probably to see if he was jesting. "Are you serious?"

He should lie. He should say no, chuckle and pretend he wasn't a madman. "Yes."

She frowned. "You would do . . . *that* for me?"

"If you asked it of me. I would do it without hesitation."

"I . . . I don't know if that knowledge is terrifying or arousing."

"I'm not certain myself," he replied honestly. He shouldn't have said anything at all. He wouldn't blame her if she thought him a complete monster, without any sort of conscience. But it was true. If she asked him to kill, he would do it without an ounce of remorse.

Maybe he was a monster. After all, there was a part of him that was still Five. Had the Company made him a killing machine, or had he always had that potential, just waiting to be unlocked?

"How would you do it exactly?" She glanced away. "Theoretically, of course."

Was she truly considering it? Or did she merely want to gauge the depths to which he would plummet? "I'd sneak into his home, break his neck and toss him down a flight of stairs—make it look like he fell."

"An accident. He'd never be able to hurt any more girls." Arden frowned. "But then no one would ever know what manner of devil he was."

"Is that really that important?"

That frown turned on him. "Of course."

"So you'd ruin his family as well as him. That sounds more like vengeance than justice."

Her cheeks darkened, but she didn't look away. "Who's to say that his family aren't equally evil?"

"That would be like someone thinking you must be as demented as your mother."

She looked as though he'd slapped her. And this time she did look away. "Someday I could be." Then she added, "And you're a bastard for reminding me."

"Yes. It was a cruel way to make my point and I am sorry for it."

"But it was a point well-taken," she replied, no longer angry, it seemed. "It would be wrong of me to punish the killer's family for his sins. And if we find him I would be eternally grateful if you sent the man straight to the devil, but I would not ask you to become like him. I won't allow you to become like him."

Luke was silent for a moment, weighing his next words carefully. "Arden, this man has already ruthlessly killed two girls. I respect the work you do for Scotland Yard, but you should leave the actual apprehension of the bastard to Grant."

She stiffened. "I thought we agreed that you don't get to order me about?"

"I'm not ordering, I'm asking. But since we're on the subject, since I've been home you've done nothing *but* order me about. Unless English law has changed, you're as much my possession as this house. I'm the master here."

Her eyes flashed—russet fire. "Don't you dare compare me to a . . . a chair! I am your wife. I am your equal."

"I would never call you otherwise, but if you expect me to do what you want, you have to be willing to give in to my wishes as well, especially those that involve your safety."

Her jaw was mulish, but there was an air of sheepishness about her. "I'm not accustomed to having to answer to anyone."

He smiled. "I'm not accustomed to any of this. I think we've muddled through fairly well thus far. Or do you have regrets?"

"If I have any regret it's that I didn't ask you to stay with me. I was prideful and foolish, and look what it cost us. We don't even know each other now."

That stung, though he knew it wasn't intentional. A few weeks ago his only goal had been to kill this woman; now he was prepared to kill *for* her. At times he wondered if she'd unmanned him or if he felt all the more a man for having had her devotion.

She drove him to distraction, frustrated him, amazed him and made him want to be better.

Why? What was so special about her that, even when he had no notion of her existence, he got a tattoo that matched hers? The Company had erased his memories, but they hadn't managed to dig deep enough to get rid of her.

They regarded each other in silence for a moment. How did he measure up under her scrutiny? A man who didn't want her bossing him around, but would kill for her if she asked.

"Do you think it's safe to go to the party tomorrow night?"

Luke turned to the armoire and pulled out a clean shirt. "No," he replied, "but we have to. Both Clivington and Fitzhugh are going to be there. If we're going to figure out if one of them is the killer, then we need to go."

She smiled faintly. "We?"

"I'm afraid you're stuck with me." He tucked the shirt into his trousers. "You fine with having a partner?"

Arden walked over to him and adjusted the collar of his shirt, smoothing her hands over it and down his shoulders. Her touch soothed him. "Very. We should keep Alastair close as well. He can look out for a Company threat while we keep our eyes on Clivington and Fitzhugh."

That was a sound plan, provided Wolfred wasn't the one trying to kill them in the first place. Now Luke would not only have to watch his "friend" but two other ponces as well.

It was becoming increasingly difficult to ensure that he could keep himself and Arden alive.

Chapter 19

Evelyn Stone, Arden discovered later that day, was not a woman who took no for an answer.

"I need to see Lord Huntley," the doctor insisted, holding her leather bag in front of her with both hands. They were in the library, where Arden had been re-searching just how much evidence was needed to try a peer for murder. "Director's orders, Arden. You know I wouldn't insist otherwise."

She did know. Evelyn's vocation elevated her social stature to a degree, as did her reputation for being one of the best doctors in the country, but the fact remained that she was middle class at best. She never seemed to forget that, even when those around her did.

"What's Dhanya doing, sending you here without warning?"

The darker woman smiled. "I reckon that's exactly why she sent me, so the two of you wouldn't have time to prepare."

Arden sighed. God grant her patience. Reaching for the bottle on the desk, she poured a measure of whiskey into a glass. Luke's words about how much and why she drank whispered in the back of her mind, but she ignored them. He should be glad for the whiskey. She'd be a raving lunatic without it.

"Can I pour you one as well?" she asked her colleague.

Evelyn shook her head. "Thank you, no. I've found drink and medical procedures do not mix."

"Are you going to be performing a 'procedure' on my husband?" She fought to keep alarm from her voice. What if Dhanya had her do something that damaged what memory Luke had?

Full rosy lips parted, and dark eyes took on a sympathetic light. "No. I'm going to ask him a few questions, have him perform a few tasks and then go home because I've been wearing these clothes for almost thirty-six hours."

Arden frowned. "What happened?"

She was answered with a grim expression and head shake. "Nothing I'm at liberty to discuss. Let Huntley know I'm here, my friend. Let's get this over with as quickly as possible for both of us."

"Dhanya and I are going to have a little chat about this," Arden muttered as she removed the earpiece from the phone on the desk. She pressed the button for the stables, where Luke was apparently making a few mechanical improvements to her touring carriage.

"Dhanya's on brief leave," Evelyn informed her stiffly. She was always so protective of the other woman.

Arden's gaze lifted to the doctor's as she waited for an answer from the stables. "Is she to whom you've dedicated the past thirty-six hours?"

Evelyn didn't respond, and that was answer enough. Enough to alarm Arden and make her forget she was miffed at Dhanya. "Is she going to be all right?"

The other woman gave a curt nod. "For the most part."

"Is there anything I can do?"

"No." When Arden continued to stare at her, Evelyn sighed. "You did not hear this from me. Dhanya was attacked in her home the night before last."

Arden stifled a gasp. "Was she harmed?"

The doctor gave her a hard look, one that broke Arden's heart. "Oh, poor Dhanya. Was it a random break-in?"

"It wasn't a break-in at all. Her attacker let himself into her house. He had a key. He knew all the security measures."

"The traitor."

Evelyn shrugged. "It would seem so, and rumor has it he's making his move before your husband can turn him over to the authorities. You understand why it's imperative that I speak to Lord Huntley? The Wardens are on me to find out if he's remembered anything else—or if he's still on the Company's side."

Arden's defense of her husband was silenced by a voice in her ear. "'Ello?"

"This is Lady Huntley. Is Lord Huntley still there?"

"Yes, ma'am. Would you like me to fetch him for you?"

"No. Please ask him to return to the house as quickly as possible. Dr. Stone is here to see him. Thank you." She hung up. "Have a seat, Evie. You're hovering."

Her friend eyed the sofa with obvious longing. "I'm afraid if I sit down I won't be able to get back up."

"You're exhausted. I'll have Mrs. Bird bring you some tea. That will invigorate you."

Luke arrived at the same time the tea tray did.

"Who is in charge while Dhanya is on leave?" Arden asked Evelyn after passing her a cup.

Evelyn shot a sharp glance at Luke, as though she expected him to suddenly grow horns. He caught the look and returned it with a sardonic smile. "Wonderful, I can finally put my plan of world domination into motion."

At least the doctor had the grace to look sheepish. "Forgive me. This speculation of a traitor within the W.O.R has us all on edge. Mr. Chiler is taking care of the office as usual, and Lord Wolfred is acting as Director."

Arden didn't miss how Luke's face hardened ever so slightly at the mention of Alastair. Did he still suspect him of being the traitor? Perhaps if she were him she would wonder as well; after all, Alastair had known about Luke's investigation seven years ago, and he had made a grand effort of looking for him when Luke disappeared. But Alastair's grief over the loss of Luke had been real, and Arden was certain his loyalty to his country was incorruptible.

But then she'd also been certain that Luke had gone to Rani Ogitani because he loved her. He'd never breathed a word about the woman being suspected of treason, which he must have known. She had doubted him, believed the worst, and had been wrong.

She did not want to be wrong about Alastair.

Evelyn said she could stay for her examination of Luke, so Arden did. The doctor checked his healing wounds, prodded him where he'd been injured after the incident with the touring carriage, and checked his reflexes and strength. He broke the squeezing device she used to measure his grip.

"Any improvements to your memory?" Evelyn asked with a wry smile as she put the broken apparatus in her bag.

"I've remembered a few new things," he replied.

"Such as?"

"I remember the first time I saw Arden."

Arden gaped at him. "You do?" This was the first she'd heard of it.

Luke smiled slightly. "I don't remember where it was, but you were wearing a yellow gown and had a poppy in your hair."

"Drury Lane," she informed him, voice thick. "It was a production of *A Midsummer Night's Dream*." He remembered her. Tears stung her eyes and she blinked them away.

"Anything pertaining to what you were investigating prior to your disappearance?" Evelyn's impatience cleaved the tender feeling in her chest.

"Not really. There are bits, but they're fuzzy."

"Might I have your permission to attempt mesmerism on you, my lord?"

Luke's gaze rose to the woman hovering over him. "It's that imperative, is it?"

"It is," Evelyn replied, face grim.

"Then go ahead. I'm not certain how well it will work on me."

She held up a syringe. "This will relax you and help overpower any safeguards the Company might have implanted in your mind."

"Evie . . ." Arden's voice trilled upward.

"He'll be fine, luvvy. Don't you worry. I won't hurt him a bit."

Luke turned to her, confidence in his countenance. "It will be all right. And you can stay and watch, right, doctor?"

Evelyn smiled. "Of course. Why don't you set up that contraption of yours to record what he says?"

It soothed her to feel as though she was part of the solution. Arden quickly went to the library where she kept her sound recording equipment. She returned within minutes and set the cylinder machine up on the table near Luke's chair.

The device was of her own design—a modification of that Edison bloke's. While many used wax cylinders, Arden had discovered that a substance called celluloid provided much better quality, though the cylinders could not be shaved and recorded over as wax could. She withdrew one of the sturdy plaster-core cylinders from its protective tube and carefully set it on the mandrel. Then, she wound the large brass key on the machine's carved oak side and positioned the sharp, precise stylus in place for etching Luke's words into the celluloid. All she had to do was flip the switch to engage the gears that powered both the mandrel and stylus.

She tilted the sound amplification horn toward her husband. Evie's drug was working. He flashed her a languid grin. She couldn't help but smile back. If they survived all this intrigue, she was going to make certain she treated him better. She was going to get to know him as well. It was shameful to think that his favorite color might have changed and she wouldn't know.

Evie used her small pocket watch as a pendulum upon which Luke could concentrate as she talked him into a relaxed state. She gave Arden a nod when she was ready to begin questioning him, and Arden flipped the switch on the machine. The soft whirl of the engine and delicate swish of the stylus whispered around them.

"What's your name?" Evelyn asked, pocketing the watch.

"Lucas Harris Stratford Grey, Earl Huntley."

"Are you married?"

"Yes."

"And what is your wife's name?"

Luke smiled. Arden's heart kicked against her ribs. "Arden."

"Lord Huntley, I'd like you to tell me what you remember of the night you disappeared. Before the Company took you."

Luke's brow furrowed. "I was at Rani Ogitani's house."

"Who was Rani Ogitani to you?"

"We worked together at the W.O.R. We had been lovers."

"Were you lovers the night you are at her house?"

Arden shot Evelyn an indignant glance, but the other woman didn't acknowledge it. Arden turned her attention to Luke once more, anxious to hear his answer even though her heart already knew it.

"No. Arden's the only woman I want."

And she had it on recording! Was it foolish to feel so happy for what she'd already known?

Evelyn continued her questions. "What are you and Ogitani doing at her house?"

"I've dropped a few hints that I'm unhappy with the Wardens because I suspect she's a traitor. I'm trying to get her to confess."

"What does she say to you?"

"That she knows how I feel, that she's unhappy as well. She says the Wardens are outdated and foolish to protect an archaic country that still has a monarchy. There's a man she wants me to meet."

"Does she tell you his name?"

"No, but he's on his way there now."

"Do you see him when he arrives?"

Lines creased his scarred brow. "Yes. I can see his face but it's hazy. It's not Wolfred."

She would never in a million years admit it, but Arden secretly sighed in relief. Not Alastair, thank Heaven. How could she have ever doubted him, even slightly?

"Do you recognize the man?" Evelyn was frowning

now as well. If she was surprised by his mention of Alastair she didn't show it.

"No, but I might recognize him if I see him again." Luke's face hardened. "I hope I do see the son of a bitch."

Evelyn patted his shoulder. "I hope so too," she replied, surprising Arden. She'd never known Evelyn to be the least bit bloodthirsty, but this traitor had orchestrated the loss of many Warden lives.

"Do you remember anything else?"

"The man said he'd been looking forward to meeting me and then there was blackness. I don't remember anything else."

Apparently satisfied, Evelyn brought Luke out of the trance. Arden turned off the recording machine and stared at it. Luke had seen the traitor. He knew the man's face. This would all be over soon.

The examination continued for another half hour—until Evelyn was satisfied. "You're healing, regaining your memory, and showing no signs of ill effects—physical or mental—from your years in Company custody. I believe you'll continue to regain memories, though I cannot say for certain that they will all return."

Luke shrugged. "At least I know who I am. For the last seven years I didn't even have a name. Not a proper one."

There was no self-pity in his tone, but Arden's heart broke for him all the same. She cleared her throat. "Evie, can you send a copy of your notes to Dr. Charles Vincent?"

Her friend seemed surprised. "Of course. Has he examined Lord Huntley?"

"He's the family physician," Arden replied. "My husband's brother has some . . . concerns."

"Ah." Understanding dawned in her coffee-colored

eyes. "I believe I understand. I would be happy to send on my findings, though I'm not certain how much weight they'll have if Vincent subscribes to the archaic notion that women shouldn't be doctors."

"He'll accept them, like it or not. We have a female P.M. for Heaven's sake. Everyone knows Victoria herself has sung your praises."

Evelyn's cheeks pinkened as she packed up her satchel. "If you say so. I'll send my notes to Vincent later today. Lord Huntley, perhaps you might write down everything you remember about the man you saw at Miss Ogitani's house. You should also work with one of our artists, see if they can draw an accurate likeness of the man."

"I will."

"I hope you enjoy the party tomorrow night. I understand it's to be a grand affair. An airship, no less."

"I'm looking forward to it," Arden replied. "Were you invited?" Evelyn might not be upper class, but she had treated enough aristocrats to occasionally warrant an invite to such functions.

"No." She had a strange expression on her face. "I have an aversion to airships. You'll have to tell me all about it."

Arden promised to do just that and then walked her friend to the door. "Did you mean it?" she asked once they were alone. "Will he continue to remember?"

Evelyn nodded. "I believe so. Make no mistake, the toxin did its damage, but the mind is an amazing thing. Honestly, I do not believe he'll regain his entire life, but he will remember more of it as time progresses."

"Thank you for helping him."

The other woman turned to her. They stood together in the front hall, the faint drone of a cleaning automaton adding a degree of privacy to their conversation. "For what it's worth, I'm inclined to believe you that he's not a threat. The Wardens will see that he gets justice."

Arden hugged her and they said their good-byes. Then she returned to Luke. He was on his feet, staring out the window at the pleasant day beyond. His arms were folded over his chest and his shoulders were rigid.

She knew that stance. Her blood turned cold at the sight of it. That was how he would always stand before he told her of an assignment he had taken—one that he might not come back from.

"What is it?" she asked when she found her voice and could make it strong.

He half turned, the expression on his face grim. It wasn't an expression she remembered, but it wasn't quite Five either. It was new. "Tomorrow night's soiree is on an airship."

"Yes. I thought I had mentioned that."

"You didn't." There was no censure in his voice, but she flinched at it all the same. "We need to send word to Alastair to make certain there's a strong Warden presence attending. They'll have us—and a large number of Britain's most powerful citizens—cut off from the rest of the world, unable to get to help. Isolated."

"You think the Company will make their play at the party?"

A muscle in his jaw flexed. "I think they're going to try blowing the damn thing right out of the sky."

Of course Luke didn't know exactly how the Company would come for them, but he had a good idea. They would wait until they were in the air, when medical assistance would be next to impossible. If they were lucky the Wasp would have orders just to take out him and Arden. But he knew those bastards, and he knew without a doubt they would take the path of the most carnage. The assassin would be there simply to make sure Luke and Arden didn't somehow escape.

He informed Alastair of this a short time after Dr. Stone took her leave. The three of them—Luke, Alastair and Arden—were in the room that had apparently been his study once upon a time. It was a good room—decorated in rich, comfortable colors. More important, it was soundproof, and built to resemble a Faraday cage, with metal mesh built into the walls, ceiling and floor. It had no windows. Luke didn't want to take any chances of their conversation being overheard.

"Dr. Stone will have to overcome her fear of air travel," Luke commented. "We'll need her to tend to the injured." And there would be people injured, no matter how this played out.

Alastair rubbed his chin. "I will tell her. How many spies do you reckon they'll have onboard?"

"Only as many as they need. Two, perhaps. Three, tops. They'll have another two in a small vessel that will fly alongside our ship to rescue their own if they decide to destroy it. The Wasp will be in one of those. Once he's done his job, they'll fly off in the panic." He didn't have to remind either of them what the Wasp's "job" was.

"We can use the sparrows attached to the ship to give chase."

Luke nodded. The small flying machines were standard on most air vessels now in case of an event that required evacuating the ship. There were larger "airboats," but the sparrows were for crew to aid in the procedure.

"We could just stay home," Arden suggested.

"No longer an option," Luke replied with a sympathetic gaze. "They'll know we're onto them and bring down the ship just to make a point. No, we have to end this."

"I have a gown Zoe—Madame Cherie—made for me during the Erlich affair. The bodice has thin sheets of gregorite sewn into the fabric. I'll wear it."

"Delicate armor." Luke almost smiled. "You're to stay inside the ship at all times."

She stiffened. He knew she would fight him on this. For someone who hated the danger he had put himself in, she certainly seemed to have a knack for diving head-first into it herself. "That won't deter them."

"I won't concede on this, Arden."

Her chin came up at a mulish angle, and her lip came out in a pout that he found surprisingly arousing. She didn't know how difficult it was for him to let her go at all. But she had been a Warden for years, and she knew what she could and could not do. Hadn't she taken him down with one of those contraptions of hers?

"Fine," she agreed. "But if you go off acting like a fool hero, I'll shoot you myself."

He grinned. "Fair enough. Whatever gadgets you have that might help us, now's the time to assemble them. Wolfred, how many Wardens will we have onboard to-night?"

"Seven," the red-haired man replied. "Chiler will be there. He's the son of a viscount, so he was invited. I'll arrange for Dr. Stone—she'll be in demand as the doctor who treated you. Then there will be the three of us and St. John Crane."

"Crane?" That was a name he hadn't heard in a while. "When did he get back?" And why the hell was it that he could remember a man who meant absolutely nothing to him but not his own wedding?

"A year ago," Alastair informed him, seemingly unsurprised that he knew who the man was. "India changed him."

That, Luke reckoned, was an understatement of grandiose proportions. "Is he still as mad as a French-pocked hatter?"

"Without doubt."

"Excellent. He'll be a good addition then."

Alastair smiled, but it didn't quite reach his eyes. "Should I take this to mean you no longer suspect me of being the traitor?"

Luke ignored his wife's gasp. Wolfred was not a stupid man; he had to know Luke would suspect him—just as Wolfred had been suspicious of him. "I suppose so."

"We have another problem," Arden reminded him. "The man who killed those two debutantes may be aboard the ship."

Alastair swore harshly beneath his breath. He raked a hand through his hair. "What in the name of holy hell am I supposed to do about him?"

"Nothing," Luke replied before Alastair could. "He's Arden's to apprehend. I'll watch her back." He'd have to be blind to miss Arden's surprise and obvious pleasure at his words. The thought of her going after a killer scared the piss out of him, but he wouldn't try to stop Wolfred or any other agent from doing their job, and he wasn't going to earn her resentment by stopping her. No matter how much he wanted to do just that.

"I've already contacted Chief Inspector Grant of Scotland Yard," Arden informed the other man. "He's been working the assignment with me, as you probably already know. He has his officers watching both suspects. Which reminds me, I should inquire as to whether or not he can have men on the ship since we cannot keep our own eyes on Fitzhugh and Clivington at all times."

"You do not think the monster will try to harm anyone onboard the ship, do you?" Wolfred asked, incredulous.

"He killed one in a factory with the owner upstairs,

the other in a public park. I'm not going to put anything past him." She rose to her feet. "The two of you will excuse me?"

"Of course." They both stood as well, and did not sit until she had left the room.

"She seems to be handling this very well," Alastair commented once the door had clicked shut.

Luke ran a hand over his jaw and mouth. "She hasn't been drinking as much." The moment he said the words he wanted to take them back, but Alastair merely nodded.

"Good. I'd begun to worry about her. I reckon that decreased dependency on spirits can be attributed to your return."

He snorted. "I would think that would make the habit worse, not better."

Dark gray eyes met his. "I think you underestimate yourself, my friend. And her regard."

"Perhaps, but one thing I don't underestimate is the mess I've wrought."

"You've given us pages of notes on major Company operations, names and addresses. And now we are closer than ever to apprehending a known Company assassin and possibly our traitor."

"Arden told you I remembered his face?"

Alastair nodded. "And that she found the frequency the Company uses to contact all agents. You were right — they did try to contact Ogitani when I let it slip that she was still alive. He's a Warden. All we have to do is find him."

"Before he finds us," Luke amended. "Or rather, before he kills us."

The other man frowned. "Are you worried about that?"

"He's gotten the best of me once — I'd be a fool not to

be concerned," Luke replied. "I have no intention of letting the bastards take me out, but if something should happen . . ." He trailed off. Surely there was no need for him to speak it aloud?

His old friend stared at him in surprise. "Nothing's going to happen."

Luke was touched. Things hadn't exactly been smooth between them since his return, yet Wolfred wanted to keep him around. "Just tell me you'll do it *if* something should go wrong."

"Fine." It was accompanied by a reluctant and somewhat stiff nod. "If we don't all go down in a flaming ball of death, I will look after Arden."

"Thank you. She's lucky to have you as a friend."

Alastair smiled. This time it glinted in his eyes as well. "Huh. That didn't take very long."

"What?" He could make a dozen assumptions, but hadn't a clue as to which might be closest to truth.

Slowly, Alastair rose to his feet. He crossed to the liquor cabinet and refilled his glass. "For you to fall in love with your wife."

Luke started. "That's none of your concern." Good Christ, could it be? "I suppose it could be that I never stopped, but I can't remember."

"She tends to inspire devotion in all who meet her. You're very fortunate in that yours is returned."

He didn't want to have this conversation. They were discussing a woman Luke would kill for and Alastair adored. He didn't want to see just how much the other man cared about his wife, even though he had taken advantage of that emotion when he asked Wolfred to look after her.

"She loves the man I was. She doesn't know the real me yet. Hell, *I* don't know who I really am."

"My God, man. I've seen how she looks at you, and

I've wanted to bash your face in for it. Sort it the hell out, get your head out of your arse and be the man both of you deserve."

Luke stared at his friend's scowling face. "You should be a politician."

Alastair tossed back the rest of the whiskey in his glass. "And you, sir, were right. You shouldn't come back to the W.O.R.—not now anyway. You should take Arden to the country and get started on making fat, brilliant babies."

Had there been even the hint of mockery or bitterness in his tone Luke might have taken offense. Instead, he regarded the other man with remorse. "How can you possibly like me when I've ruined your hopes?"

"Because I wanted you back more than I wanted her, I suppose." He smiled ruefully. "And you can't imagine wanting anything more than her, can you?"

"Nothing," Luke replied honestly. Christ, he meant it. He didn't even want his memory as much as he wanted to spend the rest of his life with Arden.

"And that's why nothing's going to happen to you tomorrow night, because I'm not going to be the one to tell her that the only man who can love her as she deserves is dead. Am I understood?"

Luke nodded. "Completely." And he meant it—because after seven long years of not giving a damn, he finally had something to live for.

Chapter 20

The *Albion* was a beauty of an airship, with a full, pristine balloon hovering above a ship constructed of rich, glossy oak that was the size of any private seafaring vessel.

Arden and Luke were among the last guests to board at the Hyde Park dock. The area was lit with bright lanterns that illuminated the ship in the dark spring night. Specially designed magnets placed on the sides of the ship locked with those on the docking mechanism, keeping the ship in place as the balloon was filled with buoyant gas.

They climbed a portable set of wooden stairs to the door of the ship and crossed the threshold into an interior as grand as most Mayfair homes. Arden glanced around with feigned indifference for familiar — Warden — faces, and immediately spotted Alastair and Mr. Chiler in the crush.

Her "armored" gown was surprisingly light, and fit perfectly. It was a deep moss green with black trimmings. The sleeves were little more than strips of fabric that barely covered her shoulders, and the plunging front showed a shocking amount of décolletage. The bronze satin of her corset peeked out from the low neckline, accentuated by the Huntley yellow sapphires that hung heavily around the base of her throat. Matching earrings dangled from her lobes, and one thin gold chain swung gently between her nose and right ear—if she and Luke survived the night she might add another. Her hair was piled on top of her head in an elaborate style that concealed a small dagger, and her fan was made of sharpened blades that appeared to be nothing more than harmless jet. And in her reticule was her trusted discombobulator.

Beside her Luke was dressed in immaculate evening clothes—black and austere white with an ebony cravat. He looked gorgeous despite the scarring on his forehead. Fortunately a little hair fell over his brow and hid most of it. The little marks from their "accident" had faded thanks to Evelyn's salve, and his face was almost as she remembered it.

He was more handsome to her now than he had been when they first met. She'd always thought a gentleman looked better with a few lines on his face. She'd also always had a bit of a preference for what her mother used to call a "good nose," which Luke possessed.

She had become accustomed to him looking slightly lost, with the odd flicker of wonder as he remembered something, or wearing a flirtatious smile. Tonight he had a predatory expression that took her breath, pale eyes glittering with anticipation. It was the look of a warrior going into battle knowing he would win or die trying.

It was the dying part that terrified her. She had just gotten him back. She could not lose him, not again. Her heart couldn't take it.

She reached down and twined her fingers through his. Gloves separated them, but she felt the warmth of him regardless. He turned his head to look at her and the predator was gone, replaced by a man who looked at her as though she was the most beautiful woman he'd ever seen.

No, he was no longer the man she had married, but she believed perhaps she liked this new version even better—this man who would kill for her, who called her "love" and didn't seem to care if anyone heard.

Now a slow smile played about his lips. He didn't speak, but the fingers wrapped around hers gently squeezed. It was hardly a declaration of love, but by God it felt like one.

Please, she prayed silently. *Don't let anything happen to him.*

A footman passed by with a tray of champagne and she reached for one, then caught herself. She wanted a drink so badly her entire body cried out for it, but she would not give in. Not tonight, when she needed every wit she had as sharp as it could be. Never mind that her knees were trembling. She had killed a man, for Heaven's sake. She was not a stranger to intrigue and danger, and tonight there were more lives at stake than just her own.

Arden dropped her hand and turned away from the temptation, and caught her husband watching her intently.

"I'm very proud of you," he said, his voice so low it was little more than a rumble.

I love you, she replied in her head. Now was not the time to make such revelations, especially not with an audience, but she wanted to—almost as much as she wanted to find a secluded spot and ravish him. Instead, she smiled in pleasure and kept walking.

They didn't get far before they were stopped. Luke's popularity hadn't waned since his first public appearance. In fact, the incident with the touring carriage had only served to make him more in demand. Everyone wanted to fawn over him and tell her how lucky she was, how happy she must be, etc. Arden didn't mind the attention, as the gaggle of well-wishers and busybodies made it virtually impossible for a sniper to take a clear shot.

However, the crush would make it easier for someone to walk right up to them, stab or shoot one of them and then walk away.

Her corset was too tight. She couldn't draw a deep enough breath. Her heart struck hard against her ribs. Blast it all! This was not a time to panic and fall apart like a stupid, vapid waif. She sucked in breath through her nose and out her mouth, silently willing herself to be calm.

It worked.

Alastair nodded to them as they passed—a greeting and also a subtle confirmation that all was in place as they had discussed. Another man nodded and said hello. St. John Crane, she assumed, since he was a tall man, tanned and weathered, with a mad glint in his eye. He didn't stop to chat.

At midnight the pilot's voice crackled over the auditory amplification box to announce that they were about to "set sail." A cheer went up from the crowd. She spotted Fitzhugh among the revelers.

Arden's throat was too dry to cheer.

The ship lurched slightly as the docking mechanism was released, and then slowly began to lift. The motion was delicate, and the ship so large that it was barely noticeable, but Arden felt it in her stomach. For a moment it seemed unavoidable that she would empty her stomach all over her new black boots, but then it eased.

Alastair was to have made arrangements with the pilot to keep the ship on a wide circular pattern rather than a line out and back, so that they wouldn't stray too far from the dock if they needed to land quickly. He also arranged for there to be a small Warden medical crew on the ground. Evelyn was onboard.

They'd been in the air approximately twenty minutes, and Arden was speaking to Lady Waterford, a client of hers who wished to purchase a new anti-hysteria device because she'd worn out the one she purchased last year, when she heard someone cry out, "Arden!"

It was Hannah. She bustled toward her with the glow of a woman in love, and behind her, equally as glowing, was Clivington.

Looking at him, Arden wondered how she could have suspected him of being a killer. He was perhaps in his early thirties, boyish and charming with sparkling eyes. He didn't look as though he could hurt a fly, let alone rip a girl apart.

She didn't have to force a smile onto her face. "Hannah! How delightful to see you. You know Lady Waterford, of course."

Niceties were exchanged, and Hannah introduced Clivington.

"Delighted," Arden said, offering her hand. He wore gloves to cover his scars.

"The pleasure is all mine, Lady Huntley. My dear girl has told me so much about you, I feel I know you already." Even his voice was pleasant.

"And I you," she replied. "I do not recall the last time I saw Hannah quite so happy."

"Would you care to take a walk around the promenade deck with us?" Hannah asked.

"Actually, I promised Huntley I'd reintroduce him to some old friends." She couldn't very well tell them she wasn't allowed to leave the main room, could she?

"Please," Hannah begged. "I should so love to see the

view, and Clivington won't go unless we have a chaper-
one." She flashed him a grin. "He's entirely too proper."

The man actually blushed. "I would hate to bring
scandal upon you, my dear."

She should have had that champagne! The look on
Hannah's face was too puppyish to resist. "All right, but
only so you can see the view, and then I'm coming back
in." As she spoke she saw Fitzhugh heading for the exit
as well.

Hannah clapped her hands. "Wonderful!"

As the three of them strode toward the exit to the
deck, Arden glanced over her shoulder. Luke was talking
to Alastair and another man and didn't so much as
glance in her direction. He was going to kill her when he
found out she snuck out, but it would only be for a moment, and she'd stay close to the door. She couldn't let
the chance to try her invention on Fitzhugh get away.

They stepped out into the cool night air. Arden kept
to the shadows as she fumbled in her reticule for the
device she'd made specifically to track the killer. Tonight
was not a night to take reckless risks and make foolish
mistakes. Only the chance to catch a monster could have
made her break her word to Luke.

She walked up behind Fitzhugh. The needle on the
device whipped toward the section of the viewer attuned
to the metal detector, but that was it. Damn. She had
used one other component from the crimes to track the
murderer—a small sample of the skin taken from beneath Baron Lynbourne's daughter's fingernails. Arden
moved to stand beside Fitzhugh as he lit a cigarette and
pressed the small, handheld device against the exposed
wrist of his hand that rested on the ship's railing.

"Ow!"

"Oh, my apologies, sir," Arden gushed. "I must have
caught you with my compact. I am so very sorry."

The gentleman peered down at his wrist where her invention had pinched it. "It's nothing, my lady." But he moved away from her so she couldn't do it again.

Arden checked the device, and her heart fell. No match.

As she turned, she bumped into Hannah, and dropped the device to the deck floor. "Oh! Arden, how clumsy of me." She sounded so much more sincere than Arden had in her apology to Fitzhugh.

"I'm unharmed, dearest. It's nothing." She moved to retrieve the device, but Clivington beat her to it.

"Here you are, Lady Huntley. I think it might be broken. I seem to have pricked my finger on it."

"It's of no concern, Lord Clivington. I feel responsible for your injury. . . ." Her voice trailed off as she took the invention from him. It was open, and the needle swung wildly through the different sections.

It was him.

"It's so beautiful!" Hannah enthused, leaning against the rail. Beneath them, the lights of London glittered like jewels in a polished tiara. "Oh, Clivington, have you ever seen anything so breathtaking before?"

"Only you, my dear."

He meant it. The realization hit Arden like a slap on an already numb cheek. It was then that she knew Clivington was not a man who killed for sport, but rather because he had a compulsion. Not because he wanted to, but because he had to. Something inside of him made him do it, and those two poor girls had "flipped the switch" to his demon. That made him more than terrifying—it made him pathetic. He might kill Hannah, or he might not, but one truth remained—he would kill again.

"Oh no," Hannah said, lifting her left hand. "I forgot my reticule inside. Excuse me while I go and fetch it."

"I'll come with you," Clivington offered, but she brushed him away with a smile.

"I'll be right back. Lady Huntley will keep you entertained in my absence."

Arden opened her mouth to say they could all go inside, but Hannah was already gone, leaving Arden alone with her lovely bedlamite. What the devil was she supposed to say to him? And was it wrong that she now wished she'd had Luke kill him so she wouldn't have to see this . . . *human* side of him?

She drew a deep breath. Right now she had to be calm. Had to be smart. The man had no reason yet to toss her over the side. "My friend certainly seems taken with you, sir." She moved a little closer to the door.

Clivington grinned foolishly. "Do you really think so? I adore the ground she treads upon. She is so without artifice. Her every emotion is plainly written on her face, or truthfully expressed in words. Deceit is not in her repertoire."

"No," Arden agreed. "It is not. Hannah does not believe in hiding her feelings, sometimes to her own detriment."

He shook his head. "Which only shows the mean-spiritedness of the world we live in, the dual nature of it. Do you know, Lady Huntley, that I once offered my affection to a young lady only to find out she was using me to, as she put it, 'form a better acquaintance with the ways of the world'?"

"That's somewhat harsh."

"Indeed." Clivington didn't look quite so boyish now. Arden's stomach fluttered nervously. "Another only wanted to make her lover jealous. I offered the both of them my heart and had it tossed back in my face."

"Is that why you took theirs?" Arden asked, the words tumbling out of her mouth as though she had no control over her mind or tongue. Where was calm? Where the hell was smart?

He staggered back a step as though she had shoved him, the surprise on his face turning to anguish, and then to anger.

Clivington's monster had just shown its face. Blast it all to Hades.

His fists at his sides, he came toward her. Screaming would do no good. Arden shoved her hand into her bag, released the device and reached for her discombobulator. Her trembling fingers closed around the invention just as he reached her. Then there was a soft noise—a sharp bark followed by a cross between a thud and a squish.

Wetness sprayed Arden's face. Had Clivington spat upon her?

Then she saw the hole in his forehead. A rivulet of blood ran down his nose as he crumpled to the ground. He'd been shot.

The door opened, and there was Hannah, who began to scream as soon as she saw Clivington's corpse. Arden flew toward her as another shot whizzed by, embedding itself in the wall where she had just been standing.

"Hannah!" she shouted. "Get back inside!"

But her friend wouldn't budge, and didn't seem to hear. She just kept sobbing and screaming. Suddenly, Luke was there. He hauled Hannah inside and reached for Arden when another shot rang out.

Arden dove to the floor of the deck, where she would be hidden from view by the boards that filled the space between floor and rail. Luke dropped beside her.

"Are you all right?" he demanded.

Arden nodded, trying to ignore Clivington's dead gaze staring at her from down by her feet. She swiped desperately at her face, trying to wipe the man from her skin. He was the killer. "I thought it would feel good—knowing that he was dead. It doesn't."

Her husband's expression was as sympathetic as it was grim. "It never does, love. Now start crawling. We need to find another way back inside. Alastair's gone to the flying machines to take after the shooter."

"How did you know?" she asked as she began to inch forward on her elbows. "Did you hear the shot?"

"Your theory about the frequency of the transmissions was correct. He intercepted a message just before the shot. Alastair's trying to find who sent it. When I didn't see you inside, I knew you were the target." He didn't look at her, but his mouth thinned.

"I'm sorry." It wasn't good enough, but it would have to do for now. "I didn't know how to refuse Hannah." And now her poor friend's world had been torn apart. The practical side of her insisted that it was better to have it done now than for Hannah to find the truth years into their marriage when she did something to inadvertently release the monster inside him, but the more emotional side of her also knew that it didn't matter now.

Hannah would never know what Clivington had been capable of. No one would. He would never stand trial, never be exposed as a monster. No, he would be remembered as a minor hero, struck down by tragedy in his prime. There would be some who might even blame Arden for his death. Hannah would—at least for a while—because the man had simply gotten between Arden and a bullet.

Arden clenched her teeth against that thought to keep it from going any further. Right now she had to concentrate on staying alive, and not on whether she had bits of Clivington's mad brain in her hair.

They continued to crawl farther down the deck. There

was another door, but it seemed to be miles away, and not getting any closer. In the distance, she could hear the whirling of the sparrows as they launched from the ship to chase after the shooters. Not much longer now, and Alastair would have the assassin in custody.

The door ahead of them opened, and they both froze. A man stepped out onto the deck and closed the door behind him. When he turned, they saw it was Mr. Chiler. Arden sighed in relief.

"Mr. Chiler, get down," she urged, coming up onto her hands and knees. Luke tugged at her, but she ignored it. "You might get shot."

"Arden," Luke said sharply. "Get the fuck behind me, now!"

She glanced at him. For a moment—a second really—she thought that this was the moment where he betrayed her and proved her a fool. Then, she looked into his eyes and saw his fear. He recognized Chiler.

As the traitor.

She turned astonished eyes back to the man whom she had grown fond of these last few years. Dhanya's trusted clerk—or perhaps not-so-trusted. Dhanya had made certain he couldn't hear one of their last conversations.

Chiler stood before them, a pistol held in his mechanical hand and a small box with a switch in the other. He wore a victorious smile on his face.

"I'm afraid my last name isn't Chiler, my dear," he told her in a slightly accented voice. "It's Erlich. Not very good with anagrams, are you? Victor was my brother. Now, to take care of you two before I destroy this ship and everyone on it."

Luke yanked her backward just as Erlich pulled the trigger. Arden watched in horror as the bullet struck Luke in the center of the forehead—the one spot he was vulnerable. He collapsed to the deck, blood trickling from the wound.

Arden screamed, but it was cut short by a searing pain exploding in her upper chest. Another shot hit her side. It didn't penetrate her armor, but it hit hard enough to knock her to the floor. She reached for Luke, fingers grasping. She didn't want him to die. She didn't want to die. Not like this.

"I love you," she rasped. She thought she saw his eyelashes flutter.

Then everything went black.

Chapter 21

"I love you."

Luke's eyes opened to see Arden beside him, her pale chest covered in blood. It darkened the already inky fabric of her gown, dripped to the boards beneath her.

"Arden?" He reached for her, his fingers going to her throat. She had a pulse beneath the sticky warmth. It was weak, but it was there.

"How the hell are you still alive?"

Luke froze. Then he turned his head to see Chiler staring at him. "I shot you exactly in the spot that should have killed you."

"Maybe you're just a lousy shot," Luke replied, slowly moving into a crouch. Blood trickled into the inner corner of his eye, but he ignored it. All of his attention was focused on the man he intended to kill.

"They did something to you." Chiler raised the pistol once more and fired. It hit Luke in the stomach—another spot that should have been vulnerable, but was protected by a gregorite-enhanced waistcoat that Alastair had made him wear at the last moment. The shot knocked the wind from him, but his heavy, reinforced bones kept him from falling backward.

Chiler swore, and this time aimed for his throat, but Luke sprang just as the pistol fired. The bullet tore through the fabric of his coat and gouged his shoulder. He barely felt it.

With the sweep of his hand, he managed to knock the gun from the other man's mechanical fingers. His own fingers caught Chiler—Erlich—by the throat and swept him back, into the side of the airship cabin so hard plaster fell around them. The entire ship seemed to tremble. The switchbox fell to the deck. Luke had seen one like it before. It would send a detonation signal via radio waves to a bomb somewhere on the ship. They had to land. Now.

Erlich gasped for breath. "Huntley . . . Five. Do not . . . do . . . this."

The blood froze in Luke's veins. He knew that voice. He had heard it in his head off and on for seven long years.

"You son of a bitch," he snarled. "I ought to rip out your fucking throat."

"You won't," Erlich goaded. "You're one of us, Five. Whether you like it or not. The Wardens don't want you. They don't trust you. If I tell the Director you did all of this, she'll believe me over you."

"She won't believe you over Arden."

The other man's thin lips formed a cold smile. "I think we both know your wife isn't going to live long enough to tell anyone anything."

Luke punched him in the jaw. It gave beneath the force of the blow like a chicken bone, breaking with a satisfying snap. Erlich made a noise like a wounded animal—which Luke supposed he was.

"I don't care if the Wardens hang me," Luke informed

him. "Killing you will be worth it. You destroyed my life."

"You were just another of their lackeys." Erlich's words were deformed by his misaligned jaw. "They never cared if you lived or died."

"I cared," came a voice from behind them. Alastair. How had he gotten back so quickly?

Luke glanced over his shoulder to see his friend approach. "Where'd you come from?"

Alastair gestured to the rail with his thumb. "Crane dropped me off. What's going on, Luke?"

It was the first time since his return that the man had referred to him by his Christian name. "Chiler is Victor Erlich's brother. And your traitor." He used the toe of his boot to nudge the switchbox closer to his friend. "There's an explosive device onboard."

Disappointment, shock and disgust crossed Alastair's face. Then he glanced down and saw Arden. Luke had never seen such horror on anyone's face before.

"Is she . . . ?"

"She's alive," Luke replied. "Get her to Dr. Stone. I'll take care of Erlich."

"I'd love to let you do just that, my friend." Alastair's voice was dark. "But your place is with Arden. I'll take care of our traitor."

Luke glared at Erlich. The smugness on the man's face made him tighten his grip. That made the bastard a little more humble. "Let me kill him."

"You know that's not how it works."

"It's how it should work."

"Luke! Arden needs you. Take care of your wife."

His words cut through the fog of rage surrounding Luke's brain. Slowly, he eased his grip and released Erlich's neck. The man sagged but did not fall. He merely chuckled. "I knew you wouldn't be able to kill me."

Luke did the next best thing—he grabbed Arden's discombobulator from where it had fallen near her hand, and shoved it between Chiler's legs. The man couldn't even scream; he just twitched and pissed himself. He slid to the floor with the sound and grace of a balloon losing its air, spasming like a dying bug.

He tossed the device to Alastair, then left his friend to take care of things while he attended to Arden. He scooped her unconscious and bloodied body into his arms and carried her into the ship where stunned guests gasped in horror. He ignored them and went straight to Dr. Stone, who stood by herself near a door.

"Help her."

He wasn't allowed inside while Dr. Stone performed the surgery.

The ship had a small medical ward that the doctor had been able to turn into a makeshift surgery. The onboard nurse assisted by setting up the equipment for a transfusion, and Luke made himself useful by donating blood. Arden had lost so much already.

The damned dress had saved her life. She would have had a nasty wound in her side had she not being wearing the gown. As it was she was badly bruised. The wound in her shoulder, however, was the bad one. The bullet tore into her just below the collarbone and fragmented. Erlich had been aiming for her heart.

Luke sat in a chair outside the ward, hand curved over his mouth, rubbing his jaw. Waiting. He might have even prayed, though he'd never admit to it.

"I'd like to tend to your wound, Lord Huntley."

He glanced up at the nurse standing before him with a tray of equipment. "Wound?"

She pointed a hesitant finger at his head. "That one, sir."

Luke reached up. It was scabbing over, but he felt the hole in his flesh where the bullet had hit. Was it in there, slowly working its way to his brain? He had a bitch of a headache, but he didn't feel as though he were dying. Might be good to make certain.

"All right."

The girl smiled and set the tray on the table beside him, where his glass of whiskey sat. He hadn't touched it.

He sat perfectly still as she cleaned the area, even though the liquid stung. When she finished wiping at it, she frowned. "You have a metal skull."

"Only on the outside," he replied dumbly.

"The bullet broke the skin but bounced off the plating."

"But there used to be bone there—that's why he shot in that spot."

She shrugged. "It's not there anymore. Good luck for you, I'd say. It looks like it might have been designed to be a vulnerable spot."

Luke didn't respond. He didn't say another word while she worked. Evie Stone had suspected the Company would use that small target as a way to kill him, and had saved his life without knowing whether or not he could be trusted. It would have been one of the few ways the Wardens would have to take him down as well. The nurse tended to his shoulder also—it required stitching. When she left, he got up and began to pace. The ship was safely docked once more and all the passengers had been ushered off, despite their desire to hear firsthand whether Arden lived or not. He'd dismiss them all as vultures if he hadn't seen genuine concern on some faces.

One of the Scotland Yard blokes took Hannah home, and Clivington's body had been carted away. His being killed was a good thing, but there were several people who were going to feel a lot of pain over it. Better that than knowing he was a monster. If there really was a judgment waiting for them all, then Clivington would be answering for his crimes to a power higher than any court in England.

Still, he understood that Arden had wanted to see him pay for his crimes. Luke wanted desperately to make Chiler—Erlich—pay for all that he had done to him, and to Arden and everyone else involved.

Finally, Dr. Stone appeared. She had been sweating a bit around the hairline and her striking face was dewy. Her apron was smeared and stained with blood. Arden's blood.

Luke straightened. "Well?"

"I took the bullet out and stitched her up. It didn't hit any bones or arteries, fortunately, but there was extensive tissue damage from the fragments. She'll heal, but it will take a while."

The air whooshed from his lungs. "So she's going to be all right?"

"I won't lie—I've seen people die from less, but Arden is very strong and she has a lot to live for. I believe that she'll be fine provided infection doesn't set in. I will give you instructions on how to prevent that. Would you like to see her?"

"Is she awake?"

"No, and she won't be for some time. I'll see about making arrangements to take her home. I don't know if any vehicle travels smoothly enough to take the risk."

"What if I carried her?"

She frowned. "You mean in a carriage?"

"No, I mean what if I walked home carrying her?"

She appeared astonished. "I hadn't thought of that. It's a fair bit of a walk."

"I can do it, even with a wounded shoulder. She won't weigh more than a sack of potatoes to me." It was true.

The Company had made him very strong, and his endurance was as high as a man's could be.

"Yes, your strength. My apologies, I had forgotten. All right, then. If you want to take her home I'll make up a list for you and follow behind in a hack."

"Take our carriage," he said. "It has to come home anyway, and it will be safer than a hack."

She smiled, as though amused by the idea that he thought of her safety, or perhaps at the idea of traveling in an earl's private conveyance. "Thank you, my lord. Follow me."

Luke did. She led him into a very clean room that smelled of blood and disinfectant—smells he'd encountered too many times in his years with the W.O.R. and the Company.

On a table in the center of that room was his wife, her skin almost as white as the sheets that covered her. Her face was tinged with dried blood and gore. Dr. Stone had redressed her, and the gown that had looked so beautiful on her just hours before now looked garish and morbid.

He couldn't see her chest move. "She's dead," he whispered, a sudden burning striking the back of his eyes.

A firm hand came down on his arm. "She's only in a deep sleep, my lord. Take her home and I'll follow. I promise I will not leave her side until I know for certain she'll be fine."

Without another word, Luke gently scooped Arden off the table, cradling her against his chest like a child. His battered flesh protested, but his gregorite-plated bones did not. The wound in his shoulder stretched but didn't give, and the bruised area in his stomach ached like a son of a bitch, but he ignored it all. Nothing—absolutely nothing mattered more than Arden at that moment.

Making certain the sheets were tucked around her, he

carried her down the ramp of the ship into the cool spring night. He walked as quickly as he could, with as smooth a stride as he could manage. It was perhaps one half mile to their home, and when he arrived, the entire household was gathered in the hall. Somehow they'd heard about the shooting.

Birdy rushed forward with a horrified look on her face. One of the men had been comforting her—the tall one who worked in the stables. "Is there anything we can do, my lord?"

"Dr. Stone will be here shortly. Have a room made up for her, please. I also expect Lord Wolfred will be by—have some food prepared. Cold meats and bread should do." He hadn't given many commands since moving back into this house, because he hadn't thought it his place, but it felt natural to do so now.

He carried Arden to her room and carefully set her on the bed. He peeled back the sheets and slowly unfastened her gown to slide it off. He unhooked her corset as well, and then removed her blood-stained chemise. He ripped the seams apart on the fragile garment to avoid moving her as much as possible, and tossed it on the floor to be discarded. Then he eased the already turned-down blankets over her naked body. The bruises on her pale skin turned his stomach, and the dried blood made his throat unbearably tight.

What if Erlich had killed her? His eyes burned at the thought, and his chest pinched. He shouldn't think of what-ifs. Erlich hadn't succeeded in his plans, and the man who had stolen so many years of his life was now in the hands of the W.O.R.

Luke sat down on the edge of the bed and watched her sleep. "I heard you," he whispered hoarsely. "When you said you loved me, I heard it. You better wake up soon so I can tell you how much I love you. I don't understand how it happened so fast, but I do love you. You make me give a damn."

He swiped at his eyes with the backs of his hands. "I will not let you leave me. I'm not like you; I couldn't carry on without you. I don't *want* to carry on without you."

"Ahem."

Luke turned. Dr. Stone was in the doorway. "Forgive me, your lordship. Wolfred is here, and I thought you might like to talk to him. I can sit with Arden."

"I can't leave her."

She rubbed the back of her neck with one hand. "What if I told him to meet you in your rooms? You'd only be a few feet away then."

He could do that. "Fine."

The doctor left the room only to return a few minutes later. Reluctantly, Luke rose from the bed. "You'll get me if she wakes?" Now that the rage and shock had worn off he felt . . . lost. Vulnerable. He didn't like it. This was not how his father had told him a man should feel. A man was supposed to be detached at all times.

That was a damn useless memory to recover.

"Of course."

Alastair was waiting for him when he entered his bedroom through the door to the shared bath. He was pacing, but stopped when he saw Luke. "How is she?"

"Good. Asleep, but Dr. Stone thinks she'll be all right."

"Thinks?" The anguish in the other man's face inspired a multitude of emotions in Luke. He wanted to punch him. He also wanted to comfort him. He felt guilty, as though he had stolen Arden from him.

"She's as certain as she can be given the circumstances."

Alastair nodded, as though that sounded more satisfactory than "thinks." "Evie said you carried her home."

"I did." That was all he was going to say. There would

be no sharing of feelings tonight, not when his were so raw. What he needed right now was a good, old-fashioned stiff upper lip. "What of Erlich? And the bomb? Did you catch the Wasp?"

"We did. He was a little surprised to see us board his ship, and tried to take out Crane, but he soon saw the error of his ways. By God that Crane is a madman. After a few moments of Crane's 'persuasive' techniques, the Wasp offered us Company secrets in exchange for his life. We'll put him in the holding cells."

"They will send someone to end him."

"Most likely, but he'll give us everything he knows before then."

"And Erlich?"

Wolfred's reply was interrupted by the arrival of Mrs. Bird, who had a tray laden with various cold meats, cheese, boiled eggs and hearty bread. There were also two pints of ale. A workingman's supper.

Luke thanked her and sent her off to bed with the promise that he'd send for her if they needed anything at all. He turned his attention back to Alastair to find the other man chewing on some bread and cheese.

"The bomb's been found and dismantled, but Erlich's not talking," Alastair informed him. "I don't know if we'll get anything out of him. He'd rather die than be disloyal to the Company. Christ, what a piece of work. All these years he was right under our noses and we were too stupid to see it."

"I take it he was always above reproach?"

"Always." Alastair took another bite, chewed and swallowed. "If I could simply get inside his head I'd make him tell me. When I think of all the secrets he gave those bastards. . . ."

Luke lifted a tankard of ale to his lips and stopped. "Would you settle for his memories?"

His request was met with a very interested gaze. "Of course I would."

"Wait here." Luke went back to Arden's room and collected the helmet she'd made from where she'd left it in the armoire. She said she had wanted to look at her mother's memories before going back to the workshop for refinements. He took a box of punch cards as well. Dr. Stone watched him, but didn't say a word. When he returned to his room, he offered the items to Alastair.

"What the hell is that thing?" Alastair demanded.

"It's something Arden made. It records memories. You don't have to get Erlich to tell you anything. You only have to make him remember it."

Alastair lifted the helmet and held it in his two hands, regarding it with a lopsided smile. "She really is the most extraordinary woman."

Luke said, "I know."

And he had almost gotten her killed.

It was late the following afternoon when Arden woke up. She felt as though she'd been attacked by a labor automaton—one with hammers instead of hands. It even hurt to draw breath, but in that she had no choice.

She remembered being on the airship, Clivington and then Chiler—Erlich—with a gun . . . Luke. How could she have not seen the resemblance between Victor and his brother? How could she have let him get so close to her husband, who could very well be dead right now?

Desperation seized her as she struggled to sit up, but all that did was send a fresh wave of agony through her. She tried to bite back a cry of pain, but only succeeded in strangling it a bit.

"Arden?"

At the sound of his voice, she stilled. Ever so slowly, she lay back against the pillows and turned her head toward him. He sat in a chair but a few feet away. From the look of him that was where he had slept as well. He still wore his shirt and trousers from last night, despite them being utterly destroyed by bullets and blood. He was in need of a shave and his eyes were bloodshot.

He was, in short, the most beautiful thing she had ever seen. Alive, and beautiful.

She smiled. "Are we alive, or is this Heaven?"

His lips tilted. "I'd smell a lot better if this was Heaven."

Her gaze moved up to his forehead—his poor, battered brow. "I saw Chiler shoot you in the head."

"Turns out Dr. Stone augmented the bone 'door' the Company left in my skull with gregorite when she did her initial surgery. I asked her why, and she said she'd seen enough dead W.O.R. agents to know the Company always went for the head."

Arden was going to hug Evie the next time she saw her. She might even kiss her too. "Why would she remove one of the few ways to kill you when the W.O.R. didn't even know if they could trust you?"

Luke's eyes brightened. "Oh, the Wardens know a dozen ways to kill me, I'm sure. They'd never be so vulgar as to put a bullet in my brain—wouldn't be British."

She chuckled—then wished she hadn't. "Blast, that hurts. How badly was I injured?"

"Bruised ribs and a bullet to the chest." His face went gray as he spoke. "He thought he had killed you."

The bandages over her chest felt as thick as a pile of quilts and almost as heavy. She flexed the fingers of her left hand. They moved, and it wasn't too painful.

"Did we get them?" she asked around a yawn. Dear Jesus, that hurt too.

"The Wasp was found dead in his cell this morning. Turns out the other Company inmates didn't appreciate that he gave away secrets for his freedom. Erlich is in a private cell, drugged, tied to a chair with the helmet you made on his head."

Her brows drew together. "The one for storing memories?"

"Erlich wasn't going to talk. Now, he doesn't need to."

"Whose idea was it to use the helmet? Yours?"

He nodded, eyes glittering. "I'm smarter than I look."

Arden smiled and held out her hand. His intelligence wasn't something she had ever questioned, and she felt sorry that he had. Her mother had done the same thing often enough, when trying to understand some of the theories and ideas that came out of her father's mouth. They had been very happy together despite that.

"Any news on Dhanya?" she asked.

"She's doing well. Healing. She's coming back to work next week. Alastair's happy to be giving up the post. She came by to see you. Looked like hell, but strong."

"Good." To see something destroy Dhanya would be like watching Buckingham Palace crumble to dust. Chiler would wish for death before Dhanya was done with him. Proper thing.

"Come lie down with me."

"I don't want to hurt you."

"You won't." And even if he did, it would be worth it. She needed him near—as close as he could possibly get. She was cold inside, and only he could bring warmth back to her bones.

Luke left the chair and came around the bed to crawl in the other side. His every movement was carefully controlled so as not to disturb her, and she adored him for it. Still, the bed dipped under his weight. He was a few stones heavier than a man his size should be.

He propped himself up on his elbow. "I'm glad to see you awake."

"I can't guarantee I'll stay that way for long." She yawned again. Having him with her made everything better, made her realize just how exhausted she was.

"If you need to sleep, you sleep."

She stared at him. He stared back. There was nothing uncomfortable about it, yet there was a tension between them that hadn't been there before. She felt as though he was waiting for her to do or say something, and in a way, she was waiting for him to do the same. Had he heard her say that she loved him? Would it be good or bad if he had?

"I thought I'd lost you again," she murmured. In her mind she saw him lying there, bleeding from the shot to his head. The image brought hot tears to her eyes.

He wiped one away as it trickled down her temple. "I thought I'd lost you, too. I almost killed Erlich."

"What stopped you?" She was glad he hadn't killed the traitor—a quick death was too good. But every woman wanted to think her husband would retaliate against someone who hurt her, and she was secretly a little . . . disappointed not to hear that he had to be physically restrained from killing the bastard.

"Alastair reminded me that you were alive, and that you were my first priority."

"Did you need reminding?" She couldn't bring herself to add a smile. She was terribly afraid of the answer.

"No, but I really wanted to kill him for hurting you."

That certainly did away with any disappointment she might feel. His words filled her with a warmth that eased the terrible ache in her shoulder and chest. She smiled.

He kissed her then—softly, tenderly. So sweetly it caused an ache deeper than any bullet ever could. When he pulled back, he gazed down at her with eyes that made her want to stay in this bed forever. To hell with food and bathing.

"I would have gone mad if I lost you," he said softly. "You've become everything to me. I love you."

Arden swallowed hard. Her heart was pounding and her fingers tingled. "I love you, too." It had been so wonderful to hear those words from his mouth after so long.

"I know; I heard you on the ship." He wiped away another tear from her eye. "I don't think I ever stopped loving you. Even when my mind didn't know who you were, that you even existed, my heart did."

He was killing her, did he know that? "I never stopped loving you either."

"Not even when I was an arse?"

She shook her head. "Not even then, though it would have served you right."

They smiled at each other and he kissed her again—a lingering kiss this time that made her wish she wasn't an invalid, that she didn't hurt all over. There was something about almost dying that made one feel very much alive. It filled her with a desperate, anxious feeling. She wanted him naked. Hard. Inside her. But it was impossible, so she settled for simply having him near.

"Do you suppose the Wardens will give us commendations for this?" she asked with a grin. "I think we deserve them. It will certainly look good on our records of service."

Luke's smile faded. "Arden, there's something I need to tell you."

It sounded ominous. "What?"

He looked her straight in the eye. "You're no longer a Warden."

Chapter 22

"They dismissed me?"

Luke winced at the angry shock in her voice. This was not going to be an easy conversation. Perhaps he should have introduced it in a less abrupt manner. "No. You resigned."

Her cinnamon eyes narrowed. "I don't remember resigning."

"I did it for you when I turned in my own resignation." There, it was done. And there was no taking it back. He would not take it back, no matter how angry she was.

Her face went completely blank. "You resigned?"

He nodded. "Yes. As of tomorrow we will no longer have any obligation to the Crown save that of any citizen of the Empire."

She stared at him. The dark circles beneath her beautiful eyes were all the reassurance he needed that he had done the right thing. He was done with being a spy, with putting his life in jeopardy for a country and an agency that would just turn around and demand that he do it again. He refused to be separated from her again. Refused to keep secrets from her, or endanger her because of his actions.

"Why?"

Wasn't it obvious? "Because you almost died last night."

"You can't leave the Wardens just because of me." Her eyes were wide with astonishment.

"I can and I have. And it's not just because of you. It's because of us."

Her expression was incredulous at best—and a tad suspicious. He supposed he couldn't blame her. "But you always loved being a Warden."

"I don't anymore." How could he possibly make her understand? Last night he had faced the idea of life without her, and it nearly drove him mad. How could he have given so much of himself to the Wardens when he had her? Had he been completely selfish and vain? Had he been in such need of a pat on the damn head he risked his life to get it? Or had he simply labored under some misguided sense of honor? He didn't know, and he couldn't remember. It didn't matter anyway.

"This is not something we're going to discuss," he informed her, figuratively putting his foot down. "We're done with the Wardens, and if our marriage means anything to you at all, you'll accept that."

Color filled her cheeks. He didn't care that anger put it there, he was just glad to see it. "You don't speak for me, Lucas Grey."

"In this matter, I do. I don't give a damn if you think it's fair or not. I'm not spending another evening like I did last night, not ever."

"What of all the evenings I spent worrying about you?"

"I'm sorry for them. I'd take them back if I could, but

I can't. I can only do my best to make certain neither of us ever has to worry about the other again."

"Leaving the Wardens won't guarantee the Company won't come after us in the future." A hint of fear shone in her eyes.

"The Company has denied all involvement in Erlich's schemes. They say he acted alone out of a spirit of revenge, and send their apologies to both of us. They assure Her Majesty that nothing like this will ever happen again."

Arden's mouth fell open. "Do you believe them?"

"That he acted alone? No. I know for a fact he didn't, but I do believe you and I will be safe from now on. They've lost the Wasp, Erlich and me because of this operation, and the fact that Victoria has personally spoken out against them means all of Europe will be watching."

"When did the queen speak out?"

"In this morning's paper. Alastair received a telegram from the Company director at W.O.R. offices two hours ago. Basically they're crying for a truce."

"For now."

He nodded. "For now." Of course it would be temporary, but it would last long enough that the two of them wouldn't really matter to anyone once it was over. Erlich had been behind his abduction and the attempts on Arden's life. There was no one in the Company ranks to pick up the grudge. And if they did . . . Luke would kill them. He would die for Arden if necessary, and he would kill anyone who tried to harm her. It was that simple.

Her worried gaze locked with his. "It's over then?"

"Yes."

"And resigning is really what you want?"

He didn't have to think about it. "Yes."

She sighed. "All right. When the Season is over we'll

go to the country. You might change your mind after a few months with only my face for company."

Luke smiled at her. "I doubt it. I rather like your face." Then he kissed her and they didn't speak of it again. He was still smiling when she began to snore softly. A few moments later sleep claimed him as well.

It was the happiest he'd been in his life—he was certain of it.

Over the course of the next few weeks, Arden continued to heal, and at the end of the month she felt good enough to start being social again. There was no shortage of invitations, but two of the people she most wanted to see did not want to see her.

Alastair had left the country shortly after Luke informed him of their resignation from the W.O.R. They didn't speak of it, but Arden reckoned Alastair wasn't yet ready to see her and Luke work on their marriage—and their family. He was supposedly on an assignment in Saint Petersburg that had to do with the royal family there. Maybe one of those exotic Romanov ladies would make him happy for a time.

And Hannah still wouldn't receive her. In time she hoped her friend would forgive her, but for now Hannah blamed her for Clivington's death. She said Arden had no right going outside with them when she'd known there was an assassin after her. Hannah was correct, of course, and Arden was sorry for it, but she would never be sorry Clivington was dead. Since she wasn't about to apologize for that, she supposed it might be a very long time indeed before Hannah came round—if she ever did. So, she visited with Dhanya and Evie instead—Zoe too. It was so nice being able to be friends with them now without the Wardens hanging over them.

She had been right about the commendations. They were both given awards for their service. In fact, Luke was to be granted the Royal Victorian Order by Her Majesty in recognition of the sacrifices he'd made for his country. Arden was very proud of him. It was a nice way to end his career in espionage.

Of course, she and Luke would never truly leave the Wardens. They would indeed consult from time to time, but she looked forward to retiring to the country for a while, where it was peaceful and the most intrigue they ever suffered was a marital scandal on occasion—such as someone taking all the covers, or some other irritating behavior.

She didn't know how long it would last—how much time would pass before Luke began to crave excitement and chafe at the bonds of matrimony. It frightened her thinking he might leave her again one day. As more of his memory returned she began to fear that possibility more and more. She did not want him to feel like a prisoner. On most days, however, she didn't worry about it. She simply enjoyed getting to know him again—the new parts. There was still a lot of him that was the same as the man she married. She liked—loved—both.

He had his own social engagements as well. A few gentlemen from his past had come forward wishing to renew their old acquaintance, and since none of them were spies, or adulterers (that she knew of), she was glad he had the diversion.

They also had his brother, Henry. Once the younger Grey had learned of what had happened on the *Albion,* he'd come to call. There had been no falseness to his concern for Luke—or even Arden. He went so far as to admit that much of his foolishness stemmed from anger and remorse. He'd been angry at Luke for leaving them, angry at Arden for clinging to hope, and then felt terrible for not having more faith when Luke returned. He had tried to have his brother declared dead and everyone knew it. And now everyone knew he'd been wrong. He felt like an arse—to use his own word—and asked their forgiveness.

Well, of course Luke gave it. He was Henry's older brother, after all.

Now Luke was returning from a brief social call with one of his renewed friendships. They'd gone to one of the gentlemen's clubs on St. James's Street. He came home smelling of whiskey and cigar smoke, neither of which were unpleasant, though she had lost some of her taste for the former and had no interest in the latter. She had waited up because she couldn't put off talking to him any longer, and because she was rather hopeful he might come to bed with her after. He hadn't touched her *that way* since the shooting, and she was in desperate need of sexual validation.

She waited for him in his bedroom, wearing his favorite of her peignoir sets—the one with the Chinese embroidery on it.

"Still up?" His rich, melodic voice seemed to rumble down her spine as he removed his coat. "I'd thought you in bed by now."

"It's still early," she replied, twisting her hands in front of her. "I'm feeling almost one hundred percent healed."

"Excellent." His gaze held some of the amusement she'd come to find familiar. He wasn't laughing at her, he was just a little . . . giddy, if one could use such a word to describe a man, when he was around her. She supposed it was a compliment.

"Might we talk?" she asked.

He arched a brow at her tone and began unfastening his waistcoat. The scars on his forehead, she noticed, had begun to fade. He hadn't said any more about growing a fringe—thank the Lord. "Of course. About what?"

"About your decision to leave the Wardens."

He frowned. "Do you wish to continue working for them?" There was an edge to his voice that told her he would fight her on it if she did.

"No," she replied honestly. "Though I do think consulting on occasion was a good suggestion. My concern is for you. You've been a Warden for as long as I've known you. Every Earl of Huntley has been part of the organization as long as it's existed."

Luke shrugged and untied his cravat. "I don't care. It ends with me. We're going to the country."

"But are you certain that's what you want?"

He came toward her and cupped her shoulder with his hands—so gently her healing flesh didn't even pinch. "My duty is to you—as your husband. That's all I want to be. I want to get to know everything about the woman you are now. I want to read to you, rub your feet. I want to have children with you and live to see them grow up and start families of their own." He sighed. "Arden, *you* are my life. I don't want anything else."

"Oh." The word squeaked from her tight throat. Tears flooded her eyes and spilled over her cheeks and she didn't even bother trying to stop them. "Oh, Luke."

He took her into his arms and kissed her. Tenderness soon gave way to hunger, and when he picked her up in his incredibly strong arms her heart began to race. He carried her to his bed and stretched out beside her, his skillful hands caressing her until she writhed beneath his touch.

He undressed them both and joined her again, hard and ready. She accepted him eagerly. He braced himself above her—so careful not to hurt her—as they joined and rocked together, riding the spiral of tension upward until they came together in cries of pleasure.

Afterward they lay together, limbs entwined, simply enjoying the silence. Luke leaned over and kissed her, and Arden smiled happily against his lips. "I love you."

"I love you, too." And then they didn't speak again for a long time. After seven long years of living in the past, Arden knew she could finally look toward the future. Their future.

ACKNOWLEDGMENTS

My foray into steampunk happened quite by accident. In fact, I didn't know there was a name for what I wanted to do; I simply knew I wanted to combine my love of history and science fiction. Once I started doing this, and researching various subjects, I stumbled upon steampunk. And I wondered where it had been all my life. Turns out, steampunk has been around for a long time. I've watched it and read it—I've even worn it—without really knowing what it was. Since discovering there was a name for this wonderful genre I have met so many fabulous, giving people who only want to share their love of steampunk. These folks write books, make fantastic machines, wonderful films and beautiful music. It's not possible for me to list them all, but I need to make mention of these few: Dr. and Mrs. Grymm of Dr. Grymm Laboratories, who are simply the best; Miss Kitty, the Emperor, Bruce and Melanie Rosenbaum, who are so wonderful and sweet my teeth ache; Ay-leen and Lucretia, both of whom are so genuinely lovely and so supportive of the genre; Eli August, whose music could easily be a soundtrack for this book; and Mike Marchand of Ajar Communications, who is quite possibly the nicest person I have ever met.

I have some romance friends to thank as well—Sophie Jordan, Laura Lee Guhrke, Colleen Gleason, Julia Quinn and Caroline Linden, who are always there with a smile or a shoulder whenever I need it.

I also need to thank my agent, Miriam Kriss, for believing in this project, and Laura Cifelli and Claire Zion at Penguin for seeing its potential and buying it. Also, thanks must go to my editor, Danielle Perez, for her support and help in making this book something special, and for discussing TV shows with me. (*Supernatural* for the win!)

And finally, thanks to my amazing husband, who makes the world a better place simply for being the first face I see in the morning and the last one I see at night. I love you bunches.

Don't miss the next book in the
Clockwork Agents series by Kate Cross,

TOUCH OF STEEL

Coming in December 2012 from Signet Eclipse

The only sound louder than the breath panting from her lungs was that of blood dripping onto the toe of her boot.

Claire Danvers crouched behind the grimy chimney stack and pressed her hand to her side. Wet seeped through the boning of her corset and the thin wool of her coat, warming her chilled fingers.

Her lungs burned and her gun hand was cramped, but she refused to set down the pistol. Refused to give up the chase. It would take more than a bullet in her side to stop her now.

Across the roof, she heard Howard scurrying away like the rat he was. He could not escape, not when she had already chased him across five countries. Robert's death could not go unavenged.

Gritting her teeth against the ungodly burning in her side, she braced her shoulder against the sooty brick and leaned hard as she dug her bootheel into the rough stone. She pushed herself to her feet, biting her lip to keep from crying out.

She lifted her gun, blinked the sweat out of her eyes, took aim and fired. The dark figure running toward the edge of the roof ducked as the shot sent bits of brick scattering near his shoulder.

Damn it. A miss. If her vision weren't so blurry she would have gotten him.

Still clutching her side—blood poured over her fingers now—she ran after him, every strike of her heels a new lesson in pain.

You're not going to die just yet, she told herself. *Not until you know for certain you're going to take that bastard with you. He dies first.*

She thought of Robert, of how there hadn't been enough of him left for her to have a proper funeral for him, how he'd been betrayed by the organization to which he had pledged his life. The thought of seeing him again, whether in Heaven or Hell, wasn't what pushed her forward. What kept her running despite the sheer agony was that she had sworn to send Howard to his judgment first.

Moonlight cut through the clouds as Howard leaped from the edge of the roof to the next. Claire didn't hesitate, her stride easily bridging the narrow gap between buildings. A shot whizzed past her ear, and she pitched herself downward. She hit the roof hard, going down on her knees.

"Arrhh!" Lights danced before her eyes as agony ripped through her. Bile rose in her throat as darkness threatened to claim her. She swallowed and staggered to her feet. Howard was putting too much distance between them; he was already at the opposite side.

She raised her pistol and fired again. The sound cracked in the night like the lash of a whip. Howard made a guttural cry. She'd hit the bastard. A grim smile peeled back her lips as she forced herself to move faster.

Her battered knees protested, but her legs did as she willed. Howard had stumbled when she shot him and she was closing the gap between them.

This time, he hesitated at the edge of the roof. He clutched his shoulder as he turned his head to look back at her. His face was different from the last time she had seen him, but then his face was different every time. He was a master of disguise, and Claire doubted that even the higher-ups at the Company knew his true countenance. When she killed him she would peel back the layers of his disguise and see the real him.

He raised his hand—she had winged his gun arm—and waved before dropping over the ledge.

Claire froze, but only for a second. *What the hell?* She ran to the edge. Something closed around her ankle. She looked down.

Stanton Howard grinned up at her from where he hung on a crude rope ladder. She realized it was his hand wrapped around her leg just a split second before he yanked her off-balance. She raised her gun, but it was too late—she was already plummeting toward the alley below.

She twisted her body so that her back was to the ground, raised the gun at the man climbing back to the roof and fired. He staggered, and—

She hit with teeth-jarring force. Pain embraced her entire body, and everything went black.

She woke to the low murmur of nearby voices. Fog swam thick in her brain and her limbs were heavy—almost as heavy as her tongue felt in her mouth.

A dull, faint ache radiated across the back of her skull. Her back was sore and her side burned, but none of these complaints bothered her as much as the fact that she did not know the location of her gun.

Opium. They had given her opium—whoever they were. Drugged her and took her weapon. Her clothes, too. Damn it, that meant she was in a hospital.

Why wasn't she dead? Howard couldn't have allowed her to live out of the kindness of his traitorous heart.

Opening her eyelids took every ounce of strength she possessed. The room was a blur of motion and colors, and her lids felt as though they'd been lined with sand.

"She's waking up." The voice was female, the accent a strange, melodic mix of Irish and some exotic land.

Slowly, her eyes righted themselves and began to focus. Claire blinked. Standing before her was a dusky-skinned woman so strikingly beautiful, she probably had very few female friends, and a tall, stern-looking man with a very British nose. The two of them looked very official, but neither of them had the look of constabulary about them.

"How do you feel?" the woman inquired.

"Like I've been shot and fell off a roof," Claire replied, though her words were slurred—"thot," "rooth."

The woman actually smiled a little. "I imagine so." She came closer to the side of the bed. Claire watched warily as she poured a glass of water from a pitcher on the scarred bedside table. Then she bent at the waist and began turning a crank on the side of the bed. Slowly, as the mechanism ground into use, the upper part of the bed raised, until Claire was almost upright.

The cool lip of the cup pressed against Claire's parched lips. "Drink," the woman instructed.

Claire did not need to be told twice. She gulped the water greedily, closing her eyes in pleasure as the cold water ran over her tongue and down her thick, parched throat. She couldn't remember the last time she'd tasted anything so delicious.

When the cup ran dry the woman refilled it and gave

it back to her. Claire drank again, this time allowing her gaze to roam around the sterile ward.

There was one other patient in the room—a man several beds away. His face was a mask of bandages, and one of his legs was encased in a brass boot that extended above his knee. Rods and knobs attached to the boot kept the leg, and the broken bones within it, in the proper place.

He was obviously not the reason there was a heavily armed guard at the door. Damn. The weapon in his hands—a Baker Scatter rifle—was used to kill rather than simply injure or maim. It was very effective as well, the casings of the bullets designed to fragment and burrow once inside the body like little metal predators.

That gun was meant for her.

"Who are you?" she asked the woman.

"I'm Dr. Evelyn Stone." The doctor took the cup and set it on the table. "You are a very fortunate woman. If that carriage hadn't broken your fall, you might have ended up in far worse shape than you are now."

Yes, such as dead. "Where am I?" And where the hell was her gun?

It was the man who answered. "You're in Warden custody, Miss Danvers."

The Wardens. Hell. God, she wished Howard had killed her. Claire kept her face blank—it wasn't difficult given the heaviness of her muscles. Opiates were the very devil as far as she was concerned. She'd rather have pain than helpless oblivion. "Is that supposed to frighten me?"

The man stared down his imperious nose at her. "If you are not afraid you are clearly less intelligent than most Company agents. I wouldn't aspire to such a claim."

Arrogant British bastard. What did he know of fear? He probably spent his days behind a desk; the most worrisome thing he ever had to face was his undoubtedly bitter wife.

"If you wanted me dead, I'd be dead," she responded, words slurring around her lazy tongue. "That means you've actually deluded yourself into thinking you'll get information out of me. Which one of us is lacking in intelligence now, Mr. Idiot?"

A dull flush flooded his mutton-chopped cheeks. He looked as though he had scrub brushes bolted to the sides of his face, the things were so bushy. "Whether or not you cooperate is entirely up to you, Miss Danvers, just as whether or not you live or die is up to me."

Dr. Stone shot him a dark look, her striking features downright intimidating. "You mean it's up to the Director."

"Yes, well . . ." He sniffed. "She's not here right now, is she? And during her absence I am acting director."

Aw, hell. She had to go and piss on the boots of a man filled to the brim with his own importance. Being locked up or killed was not going to help her find Howard. Time was already against her. He was undoubtedly on his way north by now. Every moment put more distance between them. At least she knew where he was headed.

She had not come this far to lose him now. She could not let Robert's death go unanswered. He was all the family she'd had left, and now she was alone in the world. No one to lean on. No one to tell her when she was wrong or when she had gone too far—when she was too reckless for sense.

"What do you want from me?" she asked, lifting her gaze past that beak of a nose.

Cold eyes brightened with a malicious gleam. If she'd had full control of her limbs she would have stabbed him in the neck with his own cravat pin. "I want to know why you're in London. I want to know whatever Company secrets you have in that pretty little head of yours. I want the name of every enemy agent here on British soil."

And she wanted her brother back. "I can't give you all of that."

"You'll give me something or I'll see you hang."

Dr. Stone grabbed him by the arm. "I'll report you."

He shook her off. "What will it be, Miss Danvers?"

She had to get out of there and soon. This bastard wasn't about to let her go. She needed an ally—someone who knew her, who could provide a little protection until she could figure out how to escape.

"I want something in return."

He made a scoffing noise. "You're not in any position to bargain, girlie."

Claire clenched her jaw. "Then you may as well hang me, *laddie*." She affected a bad British accent on the word. "Then you can explain to your director how the Wardens missed out on capturing Stanton Howard."

What color the man had in his pasty cheeks drained. "Stanton Howard?"

She grinned. "Prepared to bargain now?"

He cleared his throat, glaring at her as though she were a bug he'd dearly like to grind beneath his heel. "What do you want?"

There was only one person she could trust in all of London. "Lucas Grey," she replied. "I want to talk to Lucas Grey."

"You look like shite."

Alastair Payne, Earl of Wolfred, wiped the dirt from his hands with the remains of an old shirt. Smears of oil and dirt stained the once pristine linen. He'd been working on the velocycle for a good three quarters of an hour before his oldest friend, Lucas Grey, showed up, and now the machine was in top condition.

"I've been back in the country for a fortnight and already you're trying to woo me with your considerable charm." A sardonic smile curved his lips. "Really, Luke. People will talk."

Many men would bristle at the affront to their masculinity, but Luke merely chuckled. "What I lack in tact I have in an abundance of sincerity. Arden's worried about you."

It was a cheap shot and they both knew it. Alastair no longer considered himself in love with Arden, but she was still a dear friend. In fact, she and Luke were possibly his only true friends.

"I'm fine."

"No pain?"

As though on cue, his left leg twinged—a bone-deep ache, though there was no longer any bone there to cause discomfort, just metal beneath the flesh. "None. Evie says I simply need to regain a stone or two and I'll be right as rain." He'd been putting his body through its paces in an attempt to regain the strength he'd lost after being left for dead in Spain. He would be strong again. Stronger.

"Good." Luke's pale gaze was sharp as it met his. "And mentally? Are you recovered there as well?"

Anyone else and Alastair would have told them to bugger off, but Luke was no stranger to the affects a life of intrigue and deceit could have on a man's mind. "Better than I ought to be, I'm told."

Luke frowned, dark brows pulling low over pale blue eyes. "According to whom?"

"Evie." He tossed the soiled rag onto a nearby workbench. "She seems to think I'm afraid to admit how deeply the attack affected me."

His friend regarded him for a moment, his sharp face as unreadable as a blank slate. "Are you?"

"No." Alastair settled his hands on his hips. "This concern for my welfare is appreciated, believe me, but I'm getting a little tired of everyone thinking I'm headed for a cell in Bedlam. I've had people try to kill me before."

Luke's expression didn't change. "This is the first time it was someone you fancied yourself in love with."

"I didn't love her," he scoffed.

"Fine. You cared for her, and believed she cared about you, right up until the moment she led you into a trap that resulted in you being stabbed, crushed beneath a carriage and left for dead. I don't understand how you can be all right with that either. I wouldn't be."

"You seemed fine enough when your former mistress tried to kill you," Alastair shot back. It had been little more than a year since Rani Ogitani had revealed herself as a traitor and had almost gotten Luke and his wife, Arden, killed. At the time, Alastair had been in love with Arden, and part of him wouldn't have minded comforting his friend's widow. After all, they'd believed Luke to be dead for seven years before Rani's confession.

Well, Alastair had believed him dead. Arden had never given up hope. Never stopped loving a man who really had no idea how lucky he was to have her. Luke knew now, though. The forced amnesia that had kept him from his wife hadn't completely gone away, but Luke hadn't needed his memories to fall in love with his wife once more.

"I never loved her, and she never pretended to love me."

"I guess that makes you a better judge of character than I am." He sounded like a peevish five-year-old.

Luke's scowl deepened. "This isn't about me. It's about you, you great ginger arse."

"I told you, I'm *fine*. Are you too thick-headed to understand that?"

"You're the one who's mentally impaired if you think

I believe that load of horse shite. You're not fine, Alastair. No one in your situation would be fine."

Alastair paused, on the verge of telling his oldest friend to go straight to hell with hopes of being buggered by the very devil. Luke was only concerned for his well-being, so why was he denying what the other man so clearly understood? What was he trying to prove by lying?

"You're right," he admitted. "I'm not fine, but I will be, and I don't want to talk about it. I don't want to discuss her or what she did—not until I can do so without blaming myself for being such a naive fool. That said, will you please leave it alone?"

Luke's mouth tilted. "Not another word. Show me what you've done to this great hulking beast." He gestured at Alastair's custom-built velocycle, which could travel at great speeds and was equipped with concealed weapons.

Grateful for the change of topic, Alastair showed him the modifications he'd made. "I put a new engine in her. She'll top fifty now."

"Miles?" At his nod, Luke whistled. "I'll have to get you to take a look at my machine. You've always been the more mechanically inclined of the two of us."

Yes, for all the good it had done him. "Bring it over some afternoon. I'll take a look." He pointed out the other improvements he'd made—mostly cosmetic. Tinkering on the velocycle had kept his mind occupied, giving him something to think about other than the fact that he'd been made an arse of by a woman he'd entertained a future with. Though, when he first met Sascha, she'd simply been a substitute for the woman he couldn't have—Arden. That only added salt to a raw wound—that he'd been completely taken in by a woman he'd seen only as a diversion.

A bell rang as Luke studied the velocycle. It was for the handset and mouthpiece that provided communication between the building that stored his engine-based vehicles and the main house. He grabbed the handset on the second bell.

His housekeeper's voice filled his ear. "Begging your pardon, my lord, but there's a young girl here who says she has a message for Lord Huntley's ears alone."

It had to be W.O.R. business. Only the Wardens of the Realm would send a verbal message. Notes were too easily found and read. Verbal messages could be turned into lies if the messenger was set-upon. Verbal messages could be taken to a person's grave.

"Send the girl out, Mrs. Grue."

"Of course, sir. Right away."

Alastair hung up and turned to Luke, who stood beside the velocycle, watching him. "Something wrong?"

"There's a messenger here for you."

Luke frowned. "Warden?"

"I assume so. Are you on assignment?"

His friend shook his dark head. "I haven't done any work for W.O.R. other than consulting on Company operative interrogations."

"It must be important for them to track you down here." They hadn't bothered with him for the last week and a half, but he had no desire to seem petty, so he kept that to himself.

"It had best be." Luke wore a dark expression that would make even Alastair think twice about engaging him.

A few moments later there came a knock upon the door. Alastair opened it to find a young girl of perhaps twelve standing at the threshold. "Lord Wolfred?" she inquired. "I'm Betsey Meekins. I've a message for Lord Huntley."

Her no-nonsense, very adult tone made him smile. "Come in, Miss Meekins." He stepped back so she might enter the building. She crossed the hold as regal as a queen and walked directly up to Luke, who was easily a full foot taller than she.

Betsey offered her hand, which Luke took, a vaguely amused expression replacing his scowl. "Pleased to make your acquaintance, Miss Meekins. What is the message?"

She glanced over her shoulder at Alastair. "They didn't say anything about having an audience, my lord."

"I assure you, Lord Wolfred is trustworthy, and can be privy to anything you wish to tell me."

She shrugged as she turned back to him. "So long as you'll take responsiblity for him. I'm to tell you that a Miss Danvers from America is in the infirmary and will speak only to you."

Color leeched from Luke's lean cheeks. "Danvers. Are you certain?"

The girl nodded. "I'm never uncertain, sir."

Alastair would have chuckled at her youthful arrogance were it not for the expression on his friend's face. He looked as though he'd seen a ghost.

"Tell the acting director I'll be there shortly." Luke took a coin from his pocket and handed it to the girl. "Run along now. There's a good girl."

Betsey curtsied to them both and quickly took her leave. Alastair waited until the door had shut and she would be out of earshot before saying, "Now it's my turn to ask whether you are fine."

Luke chuckled, but there was little humor in it. "I don't think so, my friend. Not at all. I'm off to the Wardens and you are coming with me."

"Good lord, man. What the devil for?" Alastair could not remember Luke ever having asked him to accompany him anywhere.

"So you can plead my case to Arden when my past bites me on the arse."

Understanding dawned. "So Miss Danvers . . . ?" He raised his brow suggestively.

His friend rubbed a hand over his brow. "Is a Company agent. And my former lover."

M883G1011